ANYTHING
FOR A DOLLAR

Visit us at www.boldstrokesbooks.com

Edited by Todd Gregory for Bold Strokes Books

Rough Trade

Blood Sacraments

Wings: Subversive Gay Angel Erotica

Sweat: Gay Jock Erotica

Anything for a Dollar

ANYTHING
FOR A DOLLAR

edited by
Todd Gregory

A Division of Bold Strokes Books

2013

ANYTHING FOR A DOLLAR

© 2013 By Bold Strokes Books. All Rights Reserved.

ISBN 13: 978-1-60282-955-8

This Trade Paperback Original Is Published By
Bold Strokes Books, Inc.
P.O. Box 249
Valley Falls, NY 12185

First Edition: October 2013

Credits
Editors: Todd Gregory, Stacia Seaman
Production Design: Stacia Seaman
Cover Design by Sheri (graphicartist2020@hotmail.com)

This is for every guy who ever danced on a bar in a bikini for dollars.

CONTENTS

INTRODUCTION: FLEX
TODD GREGORY

They are everywhere.
Wherever you look, you can't help but see them: young and beautiful, their well-oiled muscles glistening on magazine covers or in advertisements, in music videos and in movies and commercials. The demand for male beauty in our culture has never been higher; both the demand and the beauty were almost unthinkable thirty years ago. A film like *Magic Mike*, with its gorgeous male stars in thongs dancing onstage for the delectation of a crowd of screaming women, not only couldn't have been made in 1970, but would have never been thought up. The sexualization and objectification of men is definitely a late-twentieth-century phenomenon.

And while there is a price to pay for beauty, beauty can also command a price.

In 2006 I contracted to put together two anthologies as companion pieces. One was called *Rough Trade* and the other was *Anything for a Dollar*. While *Rough Trade* was primarily to be focused on hustlers or male prostitution, the other was to focus on other ways men could make money with their bodies: my brief description was simply "strippers, porn stars, and models." Yet *Rough Trade* developed into something far different than was originally intended: an exploration of dangerous sex rather than sex for hire. I was very pleased with it, and it was scheduled for publication in 2008. Around the same time *Rough Trade* was completed and turned in, another anthology I had put together for a different press was orphaned when that press shut down unexpectedly. I asked whether the publisher of *Anything for a Dollar*, which I hadn't even sent a call out for yet, would be okay with substituting the other anthology instead. I made a very strong case for the other anthology, and the contract was changed. *Anything for a Dollar* went onto my back burner. I was still interested in doing the anthology, but I had plenty of other projects to fill up my time.

Both of those anthologies were in the production pipeline when that particular publisher was sold, and the new owners jettisoned the fiction line. I was very fortunate to be able to move *Rough Trade* to Bold Strokes Books, and it was released in 2009. It sold well and was a Lambda Literary Award finalist for Men's Erotica that year.

And four years later, I finally put together *Anything for a Dollar.*

My editorial philosophy has always been to come up with a theme as a guide for my contributors to build their stories around. "Let your imagination run wild," I tell them, "and see what happens."

Inside these pages, you will find torrid tales of men making money from their bodies, whether through sex for hire, stripping, modeling, or doing porn. There are many tropes in our society about people who make money with their bodies—because in our Puritanical culture we are taught from earliest childhood that this sort of thing is bad, is demeaning, and only "bad" people could do such a thing.

But what really is bad, and *why* is this a bad thing?

As an adult exploring my own sexuality, I have been paid for sex. I've danced on bars and stages in G-strings. I've been filmed and photographed in the nude. Throughout this personal journey, I met a lot of people who were also making money with their bodies. I often found the stereotypes to be untrue—each of these men had his own reasons for doing what he was doing, and even the ones I didn't much care for had an interesting story to tell.

This anthology is an amalgamation of vastly different stories, of men with their own reasons and lives and foibles and ultimately, their humanity.

Editing this anthology reminded me of the days when I was one of them, and pulling it together was like taking that journey again.

So, read on, and enjoy these hot tales of lust and sex and muscle!

—Todd Gregory
New Orleans, 2013

In the Studio
Max Reynolds

He stood me in the corner the first time, facing the wall. He asked me to take my clothes off slowly. He told me not to turn around. He asked me to put my hands behind my back. He shot the photos on his digital camera with one hand, rubbing his dick through his trousers with the other. I heard the zipper go down, heard a slight rustling as he pulled his cock out of his pants. One sound vied with the other—the slow whirring of the camera, the faster and faster whacking of his cock in his hand.

I wondered which hand he used. I wondered how big it was. I wondered what he thought when he looked at my ass outlined by the black Diesel jock strap he had given me to wear, the thick band low on my waist, the thinner bands outlining each cheek, the mesh in front straining as my cock got hard, then harder, from the sound of him taking my picture, jerking off. I had asked him, the first day, if he wanted me to jerk him off, if he wanted *me* to jerk off. I told him I would do either. That I wanted to do both. That he could see how hard my cock was. That I could see how hard his was.

I'd said all this in a noncommittal way that I hoped was also sexy. The whole thing felt really staged, but then it was supposed to. But still, something about it was really hot. Creepy hot, slightly scary hot, but hot. I'd hoped that there would be real sex at the end of whatever it was this was, but I wasn't sure if there would be. I just knew I already had five hundred-dollar bills folded neatly in my wallet and I didn't want to screw this up by coming when I wasn't supposed to. I had the cost of supplies for the next senior project and half the rent; I was hoping for a repeat performance.

He had walked over to me when I asked about jerking him off and had slid his hand into the jock strap and curled his fingers around my already very stiff cock. I had tried not to make a sound, but there was no question his hand felt strong and good, and all I really wanted was to grab it and pump it until I came all over his hand and that crisp pale-blue French cuff of his sleeve. (I could get into fetish sex pretty easily, too.) The whole thing was very E.M. Forster circa my junior year of high school, except this was 2013, not 1913, and I was a senior at a prestigious art college, not somebody's rough-trade gardener.

Still…hot.

I wasn't sure if he wanted me to hold back or give in, so I went with holding back, deciding that since I was the one wearing only a jock strap that he'd provided and he was wearing what had been a suit and tie until he'd taken off his jacket and folded it neatly over the back of a chair, I really was in the role of rent boy. In the porn video, it would be CMNM and I was the naked male.

The fact is, staged or not, I was ready to give in. More than ready. I could feel my cock pulsing in his hand and automatically reached for his, without thinking. *Damn.* He stepped back so that I couldn't reach it without moving from where he had placed me in the corner, and I knew instinctively that he didn't want me to do that—move or touch his cock, even though it was right there, pressing against the front of his Armani—or whatever—trousers. I could see how hard it was, and I could tell he wanted me—it wasn't difficult. His breathing was a little sharp when he took my cock in his hand and clearly this was some fetish thing he had—he was just waiting to get off, like I was. And willing to pay for it. I fit the particulars and he wanted me. I just wasn't exactly sure for what. I hadn't actually done this before. It was all new and I was feeling my way—no pun intended—so I wasn't sure what the script was, since he hadn't given me one. *Yet.*

When he stepped back from me, his hand still on my cock, tightening involuntarily and making me want to come even more, I thought maybe I'd completely screwed up. But he gave my cock a squeeze that left it wet at the tip and slid his hand back out.

"Not now, no," he said. His voice was low and had that rough sex-edge to it and I liked the timbre of it and thought I could easily hear it in bed. "Thank you," he added. Then he told me to turn toward the corner again. He readjusted the jock strap the way he wanted it, his hand purposefully rubbing the front so that the wet tip of my dick pressed against the fabric, leaving a damp spot near the top.

He was standing incredibly close to me. He was older, probably in his forties, but handsome. His hair was a sandy blond and he had a light tan, which either meant travel or tanning bed, since it was February and we'd had way more snow than sun in recent weeks. He was as tall as I was—about six feet—and lean, but I could tell from the way his shirt fit that he worked out. I thought about what his body might look like out of clothes. It just made me hotter. If he didn't jerk me off when this was over, I would be doing it myself in the bathroom before I left. It would take me about five seconds to come.

"Imagine yourself in a play," he said to me when he'd gotten jock strap and me positioned exactly where he wanted. He looked right at me then—*he was so close*—and I had a perverse urge to kiss him and pull him up against me. But I didn't. I needed the money, and something told me that this would be a regular gig if I "performed" as requested.

❖

I had answered an ad I had seen at school for a model for a "theatrical short." In art colleges like mine the bulletin boards are full of ads for models, actors, stand-ins, grips, stagehands, all of it. Everyone was trying to jump-start a career before graduation—all and any kind of art—because we knew how many there were of us and how few jobs there were out there waiting.

Me, I was just trying to graduate, trying to make enough money to stay in the city and not go back to live with my aunt and uncle in the country. Tim, my best friend and roommate when I first came to the college, was always saying I'd do anything for a dollar, and it was pretty true. I used to joke that I drew the line at prostitution and murder, but that it was only a matter of time.

The time came that last day, standing in the corner.

For both.

❖

It had been a rough semester. My uncle kept e-mailing me—he never called, too expensive—telling me that he would need me to come home after graduation, that he didn't want to upset me, but my mother was back.

Back. That meant that the last guy she'd run off with a year ago had dumped her or she'd dumped him and she was looking for money and had run out of drugs. We'd lived in one of those small semirural towns outside a small New England city. My father worked for my uncle's electrician business and had died in a freak accident fixing some wiring when I was nine. That gave my mother, who had never been too stable, all the reason she needed to start acting out. She forgot she had other plans for her life and she especially forgot she had a kid. The first time she took off was two days after the six-month anniversary of my father's death. My uncle and aunt took me in and soon petitioned to adopt me. My mother didn't protest relinquishing her parental rights, but every time she came back to town she would swoop down on me and act like I was the most important thing in her life, ever.

For about a week, sometimes a month, until she and some new loser guy went meth nuts or got binge drunk and blew town.

So I didn't really care if she was back and didn't know what it had to do with me. If my uncle thought I was going to take care of his sister, even if she was my mother, now that I was about to graduate and head out into the world on my own, he was dead wrong. Whatever feelings I had had for her died soon after my father electrocuted himself. I barely cared about my uncle and aunt, but at least they had always taken care of me and without them, I wouldn't be here. It's not like artists ran in the family.

But knowing that he might be asking me for money instead of the other way around meant I had to look for more work than the crappy waitron job I had at a midlevel Tex-Mex and tequila place near campus. So I started checking out the bulletin boards I never really looked at except when the elevators were slower than usual.

There were tons of gigs, but most of them were unpaid quid pro quo deals like you paint my sets and I give you passes to my play and the credit for your résumé. I needed cash.

The ad was right in there with all the other crap, short and succinct:

Wanted: Young male actor/model. Must be over 18. Tall, lean, not overly muscular. Dark hair preferred. Waxed preferred.

Caucasian or Latino preferred. Role requires minimal dialogue, partial nudity. Possibly ongoing. Set fee.

The phone number had been at the bottom of the page in that sideways fashion where you just tear off the number. I looked around to see if anyone was watching and then I took the whole page, stuffing it into my knapsack pocket. This could work. This could be the money gig I was looking for. I went down the hall to the men's room, went into a stall, and called the number.

❖

I had stared at the wall at first. The paint was mauve, I think—purple with some gray in it. Too dark, I thought, for the room. It felt claustrophobic, but maybe that was the idea. The baseboards were white, there was a thin strip of white molding around the ceiling that I could barely see as I looked up without moving my head from the angle he had asked me to keep it. When we'd come in here I had seen a screen behind the love seat–style sofa on the other side of the room. I wondered if he showed movies on it and if he did, what kind. I wondered if I would end up on that screen in some kind of fetish montage. The idea didn't bother me like maybe it should have. It actually made me hot to think he'd be looking at me later and wanting to fuck me. I wanted to look around, examine the room, but we'd come in quickly. He was very businesslike, except for the part where you introduce each other. I'd started to tell him my name and he'd put a finger right to my lips and said, "Don't tell me. I will call you 'Jack.' That is the name of your character. My character is known only as 'Sir.'"

It was weird, really weird and part of me had that feeling you get when you're watching a horror movie and the girl runs upstairs instead of out the back door and you're yelling at her to get out of the house. I had that feeling. But just like the girl in the movie—whichever one, they always run upstairs—I walked with him down a long hallway with a couple of closed doors on either side and then he opened one on the right and it was this one. He had taken off his jacket and folded it neatly over one of the chairs. He'd gone to a cabinet and taken out a pretty high-end digital camera, I knew it right away from school, a Canon, the kind that takes photos as well as videos and adapts to light and space. I coveted that camera. It would take ten or more of these sessions for me to buy one, though.

The camera distracted me for a minute, then I snapped myself back to where I was—except, of course, I had no idea where I was. Some upscale town house fairly close to campus, but in a neighborhood I only ever walked through because I would never know anyone who could afford to live here.

Once my clothes were off, the jock strap on, and the camera out, the acting part started.

He wanted my hands behind my back, one wrist over the other. He had shown me the first time. Taken my wrists in his hands, placing them the way he wanted. His hands were large, but the fingers were slender and tapered. I wondered briefly if he got regular manicures. It was one of many things I would wonder about in these sessions. His hands on my wrists made me want to have them on my cock. "Please keep your wrists together like this," he had said in his theatrical sex voice. "I hope it's not too uncomfortable. It won't be for too long."

I had asked one more question in my fake noncommittal actor voice. "Would you prefer to tie them?"

I had heard the almost imperceptible intake of breath, then he'd said, "No. It will spoil the line."

I was an artist. I understood about line.

And then we had begun. Whatever it was we were doing. The camera with its low digital whir, his hand unzipping his trousers, his hand jerking off, slow at first, I could tell—it's not like I didn't know that sound—and then faster and faster until I heard the rhythm change and I knew he was squeezing the last bit of juice out of his dick. It was strange, but it was also one of the hottest things I'd ever done. I couldn't wait to come myself.

❖

That first time, I'd just left, afterward. There had been no sex. Between us, at least. Just an hour or so doing the "theatrical session," as he called it. And then he had handed me my clothes, asked me to dress, and I was out the door in the time it took to zip my pants. He'd given me a time and day for another one of these fetish scenes and told me the next one would be videotaped, would I mind? There might be "another actor." Would I mind? There would be an extra hundred dollars for that. I said sure, shrugging a little thuggishly, confident now that he was hot for my "look" and that he wanted some weird combo that was a refined, semi-deferential, rough-trade rent boy and I had managed the role well. I kept the noncommittal tone, absentmindedly (like hell) rubbing my hard dick through my jeans as he gave me the little card with the phone number and the date and time for the video session.

I still didn't know his name, but Mr. Armani Fetish Photog— "Sir"—didn't take his eyes off my dick and my hand on it until the door closed behind me. I knew he'd be looking at those pics and getting off again soon.

Problem was, despite the money, my dick was still throbbing and I'd never felt the need to get off quite as intensely as I was feeling it after this whole strange scene. Did I dare head over to the Tom Cat bookstore with the video back room? I had first been in there four years ago when I landed in the city. I hadn't had *that* kind of sex in a while—a long while.

I didn't care, suddenly. I needed it, I had some cash I could drop, it was less than a mile from where I was. If I was lucky, I'd make a little more money when some other guy in a suit decided sucking me off was going to be the best thing in his day.

The brisk, cold walk to the Tom Cat did nothing to make the need to get off go away. If anything, I started to feel I needed it more with each passing block. It was getting to be that gray pseudo dusk that starts in late afternoon in the winter and it was flurrying hard when I hit the bookstore, the snowflakes stinging my face, making my hair wet.

I knew they'd ask for ID the minute I walked in. I'd been twenty-one for a while, but I knew I looked younger. I was lucky that I had that kind of not-quite-adult, but-still-handsome, not-a-baby face that all the men in my mother's family had. It meant I never had to worry about getting laid. I was hoping that was going to happen in a few minutes. If it didn't, I'd watch a movie to a DIY session. I could still hear the sound of Mr. Armani unzipping his pants and whacking his dick. Just thinking about it made me so hot, I involuntarily "adjusted" my dick through my pants, hoping no one noticed—or the right person did.

I wasn't even sure why I was so hot. I'd just been sucked—so to speak—into the "role" I'd been given. I was still wearing the jock strap. He'd told me to keep it. It felt tight because my dick was so hard.

"Wear it, get some use out of it," he'd said, one of those long fingers running along the waistband, slipping just under it, but no further, as I was about to get dressed to go. "Just remember to wear it when you return." I was pretty sure he was thinking that I'd go out and fuck someone else with it on and he'd be imagining that. And he was right—that was exactly what I was going to do.

At the Tom Cat, the tatted-up guy with the shaved head and ear plugs behind the high counter gave me a nod and then signaled to the back when I walked in, pushing my hoodie off and holding my driver's license up simultaneously. *Is it that obvious I need a fuck?* Or was it just that everyone my age always wants it? Or was it that I now looked the part I'd been playing a little while ago? *Hustler.*

I wasn't even sure why I'd decided to come here. Just the night before I had ended up rolling around with my friend Sean from the film department. I'd gone over to his place to pick up these pieces of old film he was giving me to use in the mixed-media piece I was doing. He'd offered me a beer—a nice little microbrew. "My brother came down this weekend for a visit and brought me beer and cash. How great is that, right?" He'd clinked his bottle against mine.

We stood in the kitchen drinking and I was looking at the pieces of film—all spliced-out things he didn't want—and he'd just said, "Want a quick fuck?"

We had that friends-with-benefits thing that everyone likes to talk about like everyone's doing it when hardly anyone is. We'd always done it—for the three years we'd known each other. We'd gotten ripped at a party the first time I met him and we'd ended up half-drunk, jerking each other off in the backyard of this girl we both knew from sculpture. It was one of those impromptu, super-hot, who-gives-a-fuck things that happen only at parties and probably only at college parties. I sure didn't get anything like this when I was in high school, but then it was small-town New England, home of the original Puritans. More bears than queers where I was from. And I don't mean the hairy gay guys kind of bears. I think I spent my whole freshman and sophomore years at college making up for all the sex I *didn't* get in high school where it seemed like every night I was on my stomach fucking my pillow after watching some gay porn on my computer and making myself hot listening to the voices of guys jerking themselves or each other off. I understood the guy with the corner fetish, all right. I had my own fetishes—I almost couldn't come if the guy wasn't moaning and asking me for it.

I'd read somewhere that we develop our sexual preferences—and I don't mean guys or girls, I mean what we *do*—early on. I know I developed mine. I liked looking at blond guys with hard bodies jerking themselves off or fucking someone up the ass, slow, then faster, then faster, then pulling it out so you could see them come. Maybe it was because all the porn guys are Russian or Eastern European, but that's where my tastes had been developed—on Internet porn sites when I was in high school. It still amazes me how much you can see for free. And how many times you can roll over and fuck your pillow till it's the hot Russian ass you just saw. It's where I learned to fuck, too, and so far, it was working well because everyone I'd been with had liked it a lot. Porn really *was* educational, after all.

So when Sean asked, I said yes. I liked Sean. He had that sandy-blond hair and a kind of ruddy complexion that always made him look like he'd been running. He rode a bike everywhere and his legs were awesomely hard, as was his ass, which I really liked to fuck. He had these intense tattoos over his right hip—black flames that turned into barbed wire that ran across his stomach low, like where a bikini line would be on a girl. It went all the way across and then right below his other hip was a key with a Celtic knot at the top. He'd told me the first time we'd had sex not in a yard that he knew the barbed wire and the Celtic thing were "pretty predictable for an Irish guy, but you know, I went to the tattoo place with some friends and it just called to me."

I liked looking at the art as much as I liked looking at Sean's hard stomach and thighs. *I really have to start riding a bike…* We took the beers into his bedroom and did a quick strip. "Want to watch some porn?" he turned toward me as he asked, his pants halfway down his legs and his hard-on already pressing against his blue boxer briefs. I wanted to see that ink again. His cock twitched just a little in his briefs. *Oh yeah.*

I walked over and pulled the waistband and put my hand inside, just rough enough to make us both hot. "Don't need it and don't have time to watch other people fuck," I told him as I kissed the side of his neck and threw my arm around him, pulling him tight, sliding my hand right down to his hard ass. "Great ass," I told him and kissed him again, this time on that soft space between his neck and shoulder.

Sean liked to get fucked and he'd clearly prepped for this, knowing I was coming over, obviously hoping I'd have time to give it up. Everyone has their fetishes, I guess. And definitely their desires. Sean liked having a pristine ass when he got fucked. Knowing he wasn't like some of the other guys at school who've made grunge their real art form was nice and made me feel...closer to him. Like it all meant something. Like he really cared about me.

He rolled the condom onto my dick, pulled a tube of lube out of the drawer in the table by the bed, and I tried to think of things that would keep me from coming too fast, because Sean's tight ass was one of the hottest I'd had in my life and I liked to enjoy it, not rush.

One of the things Sean liked was having me jerk him almost completely off before we fucked. "It makes it hotter when you fuck me," he'd told me the first time.

So I'd started off like that, pushing him back onto his little day bed and pulling his legs up against me. I felt like licking his ass and balls first, so I did, and then I heard that sound come from him—I can't tell you how much I love that sound, how hot it gets me—and then it was over, I had to fuck him. I told him to go ahead and jerk off while I fucked him, that I wanted to see him do it. I was on my knees with his legs up against me, just watching him as I pumped him. It was cold in the room, but we both were sweating just a little and I ran my hand under his balls as I fucked him, then when I could tell he was going to come, when I asked him if he was going to come, to *tell me, tell me* he was going to come, that he had to come, that was when I slammed him hard and swore I saw stars when I came, it was that intense.

I'd hung around for a little, just lying there with him on that stupid small bed of his, half on him, half hanging off the bed. He felt good—smooth yet muscled—next to me. But I had to wake up and get home and get back to work. But it was nice. It was always nice with Sean.

I'd told him about the "theater" gig and he had laughed at me and shoved me a little, saying, "Dude—you know it's going to be some creepy old queen who wants to sniff your underwear and drool on your dick. You know that, right?"

I said at this point I didn't care—I was ready for whatever, I just needed the money and it was way better than robbing people in the subway, and I'd pointed at him like my hand was a gun and made a clicking trigger noise with one eye squinted shut. He'd laughed then and told me *good luck* and I'd said I hoped it wasn't too gross and then I'd gone home and worked until I couldn't stay awake any longer and had to crash.

And now, instead of going over to Sean's and fucking his nice, clean, tight ass, I was headed to the back room of the most traveled of the gay porn bookstores in the city. Looking for some stranger, preferably in a suit and tie, to either jerk me off or give me a blow job, which is what I'd wanted Mr. Armani to do. I quickly felt in my pocket for a condom, just in case. I knew they had them in a basket at the counter, but I didn't feel like going back for one and being even more obvious than I was when I came in. It already felt a little sleazier than I had remembered and I didn't want to get turned off, I wanted to have a little fantasy action.

The back room of the bookstore was painted totally black. I guess they're all like this. I stopped at the machine where you get the tokens for the videos, then I walked past the first two doors, which were closed, then slipped into the third booth, where the door was open. I could hear muffled sounds of men fucking each other, but I didn't know if it was video or real. It almost didn't matter. I left the door partially open—I'd learned the protocol right away the first couple of times I'd been here when I'd first gotten to the city. I liked the whole idea of the doors. I liked the blackness of the rooms, the little slab of bench along the wall across from the screen, the discreet black wire-mesh trash can in the corner and the box of tissues on a little shelf above it. I liked the whole sordid thing, and now that I was here, I decided if no one dropped in to visit me, I was just going to spend some time watching movies and thinking about those hot Russian guys with their thick uncut dicks and their slightly scary good looks that made me think of Viggo Mortensen in *Eastern Promises*. Something about that naked knife fight in the bathhouse had really turned me on. It might have been the full frontal nudity in a movie that wasn't porn. I know it wasn't the violence. But I did love his muscles and tattoos and seeing his dick. Somehow he seemed even more naked because of the setting. Like I had felt so naked earlier at Sir Armani's house.

Everything was starting to feel connected to that. I couldn't figure out why. But I was only here because of it. And I was going back in a couple of days for the video shoot. What was going to happen then? Would I officially be a porn star? Part of me thought that was really cool. And part was totally freaked out. *What the hell am I doing?*

Right now, it was just about finishing out the fantasy. I was thinking I might just stand up in the corner of the room with my pants unzipped and pushed just slightly down over my hips and see what happened. I felt like I was still in some kind of movie—as if because I was still wearing the jock strap, Mr. Armani was still rolling film, or whatever they say now that everything's digital. I'd have to ask Sean when I saw him.

I didn't have to wait long. I'd really only had time to put some tokens in and unzip my jacket and pants when the door opened slightly and a guy stood in the doorway, just kind of looking at me.

He was pretty much what I wanted. In a suit, somewhere in his early thirties, not blond, but hey. He was dark—probably Italian—and looked pretty built, like he might want to shove me around a little, wrestle me for my dick. I felt open to anything. Now that someone was in the room with me, I was throbbing again. Part of me hoped his dick wasn't cut, just so I could get that Russian mobster fantasy going. Viggo Mortensen he wasn't, but I knew he'd want to do some nice things with my dick. He looked like he wanted to get off as much as I did.

I sat on the bench with my legs apart. I looked at him and leaned back, spreading my legs wider so he could see how hard I was.

He came in and shut the door. He didn't say anything and I didn't either. I stayed where I was to see what was next. On the screen in front of me a Latino guy was kneeling on a bed with his hands—both of them—in his boxers, which was pretty hot. He was talking in a low voice about his dick and how hard and hot it was and how much he wanted to get off. He was talking into the camera, like there was someone watching him, taking the video, and I wondered if there would be a point in my new "acting" career where dialogue would be part of the scene and my hands would be in the jock strap instead of behind my back. I slid my hands into my jeans, exposing the jock strap. I wanted this new guy to see what I had to offer.

The guy in the suit came over to me and stood over me, looking at my dick. His watching me made my dick throb. I rubbed my dick for effect, but also because I just needed to touch it, I was that hot.

He loosened his tie, looked around for somewhere to put his really expensive suit jacket. I took off my crappy jean jacket and put it on the bench and nodded in that direction. He put his jacket over mine, then turned toward me. He was really close. I could hear him breathing over the sound of the video.

"Take it out," he said. I liked his voice. He was probably a lawyer. We were near that part of town. And now that he was standing closer to me, I could see how expensive his suit and tie were. Two Armanis in one day. I was moving up in the world.

The metal button at the top of my jeans was already unbuttoned, the zipper was down, the jeans were low on my hips, and the jock strap was exposed. I pulled the jock strap over the head of my cock and opened my pants wide. I ran one hand up under my shirt, pulling it up a little so he could see I worked out, even if those weights under my bed were crap, and so he could see the pierced nipple I'd gotten as my high school graduation present to myself.

Then I ran my other hand over my cock, the tip wet, the rest tight in the jock strap. Mr. Lawyer reached down and took my hand and pulled me up on my feet. "I want to see you rub it," he told me and he already had that voice happening—deeper, hotter, *ready.*

I pushed my jeans halfway past my hips, showing the jock strap to full effect. My cock was pulsing. I was glad I'd come to the Tom Cat. This was exactly what I wanted. Another theatrical scene. Totally weird, totally hot. *What the hell?*

I hadn't said a word since he'd entered the room and shut the door. Now I said, "I want you to do it for me." I was practicing the voice I'd used earlier. I liked the sound of it. It didn't sound like me.

And there it was: he let out a low moan I almost didn't hear over the sound of the guy talking to the camera in a heavy Spanish accent about his dick being ready to shoot as he started to come into the camera.

He had me up against the wall in seconds. I heard the zipper, then I could feel his cock hard against my ass as he ran his fingers along my cock in a totally teasing way, then slipped them under my balls, one moving almost to my ass, making my knees a little weak, making me feel like I needed to sit down. "I want you to turn around and put your hands against the wall, like I'm going to fuck you and I need to get my dick into your ass. I want my dick in your ass." I must have made some kind of sound—it was hot, but I wasn't up for being fucked.

"I'm not *going* to fuck you," he said, "but I want you to feel my dick against your ass until I come." He added, "Okay?" like he should have asked first, but I was definitely okay with it. This was what I had wanted earlier and this suit reminded me of the other one, although the fingers were different when they fingered the straps on the jock and fingered my ass.

He slapped my ass with his dick a couple of times, then I felt him jerking off against my ass. The Spanish guy was moaning now, he was definitely coming, and hard.

"Turn around," the lawyer told me, and when I did, he grabbed my dick in his other hand and started pumping it hard. I was flat against the wall, feeling his hand on me. I put my hand over the one he had around his own dick and just said, "Let me," and he gave it up to me. It was quick after that—we came almost at the same time, I had one hand on his shoulder, he had one on my hip, now some guys behind us were another soundtrack to our own heavy breathing and his moaning as I urged him to come, to tell me how much he wanted to come, telling him I wanted to feel him coming.

It was surprisingly hot, hotter than I expected, although not quite what I was pretty sure it would be like with Mr. Sir Armani Photog Fetish Freak. But at some point, I knew I'd find out. The next session was two days away. I would have my script memorized by then.

Mr. Lawyer Suit left as quietly as he'd come in. I had a feeling he was heading home to a wife and kids, but decided not to think about that. I'd gotten what I came for. I put my jacket back on, put the tissues and condom wrappers in the trash, and headed out, leaving the door open for whoever was next.

There were more theater sessions almost exactly like the first one with "Sir." While he did move to videotape, there never was a second actor. I wondered if it was because I'd taken down his ad and gone floor-to-floor searching for other copies, but it seemed he just had chosen the "actor" he wanted and my role was secure. No upstart understudy was going to intrude on my starring role.

Each time I went, however, there was something new or different in the studio. It was beginning to look more and more like an actual theater set and less and less like some rich guy's studio. I was beginning to think that soon there would be a porn movie and I would be the star. It gave me a strange thrill.

The third time I had decided that I might step outside the role and change things up a little. I didn't want "Sir" to get bored and start looking for a replacement. Several more e-mails from my uncle had made it clear that I was definitely going to have to turn over some cash, especially if I wanted to keep from going back "home," as my uncle kept calling it. That booth at the Tom Cat was more home than where I'd come from, I felt at this point.

I couldn't tell my uncle that, though. Even though my feelings for him were minimal, I had no need or desire to hurt him. He'd been good to me when my mother had abandoned me. If he needed help from me now, then I'd do what I could. So I wanted to keep the acting gig. Plus, I had to admit, it was weirdly hot and I was starting to build a whole scenario about it in my head. I'd started a new project that was partly about these late February afternoons in the claustrophobic studio where I stood in that strange punishment pose, listening to that dick and the camera over and over. The last time there had been another sound, but I couldn't place what it was and I couldn't turn around to look.

❖

I purposefully hadn't worn the jock strap this time. I had it—it was stuffed in my knapsack, fresh from the laundry. But I intended to try something new.

When we entered the studio room, I took off my jacket, boots, and socks like always. But this time, after I removed my sweater, I unbuttoned my pants and pulled down the zipper, but didn't take them off. I walked over to the chair where "Sir" usually sat and sat down myself. With my hands behind my back.

I knew how good it looked. I'd practiced it at home, taken a few pictures with my phone to make sure I had the angles right and that my hair fell right and that I looked hot and a little surly and James Dean–ish because everyone liked that look. I knew I looked like I might cause trouble or bend to his wishes—whichever he wanted.

"Please stand as you usually do," he said to me. I wasn't sure what I heard in his voice. *Frustration? Excitement? Anger?*

"I thought today we'd try a new scene," I said in my fake actor voice that I knew he'd started to like. "I thought for this scene, you should take my dick out and jerk *me* off until those French cuffs have my cum all over them. I thought you should take a video of it and then play it on that screen over there." I nodded in that direction, my hands still behind my back. My cock had stiffened as I relayed the scenario and he was looking at it, right there, commando, in my jeans.

"Sir," I added.

He walked over to where I sat. The camera was in his hand. His face, always lightly tanned and thus unreadable—no flushing—had an expression I couldn't read. For a moment, I felt afraid—like I had run up the stairs instead of out the back door. But whatever fleeting menace had scared me dissipated, and instead he began to photograph me.

The role change—if it was a true role change—had excited him. His dick was eye level from where I was sitting and he could have just taken it out and put it in my mouth if he'd wanted to. But he didn't. He just photographed me, there, in the chair. He never touched himself this time.

At first, I was afraid I'd screwed the whole deal, but he just took pictures and then handed me my clothes at the end—except this time the end had no climax—and gave me the little card with another time.

Something had happened, but I didn't know what. That day I'd headed to Sean's. I needed sex with someone who wasn't a stranger. Something about this scene made me feel like I needed to be held and kissed, even if it was just for a little while. I was moving faster than even I wanted with this scene and there was no one I could talk to about it. I just had to keep doing it. And hope it would all work out the way I wanted it to.

❖

The next time was different. Really different. I knew we'd changed it up last time—I'd left the jock strap off, I'd changed the tone, he hadn't jerked off. I felt a churning mix of excitement and trepidation when I got there, like I was on a little speed or meth high.

When I arrived, he handed me a single sheet of paper. It looked like a scene from a play or a film. He said, "Please look at this for a few minutes and see if you can memorize the lines. It isn't much. It shouldn't be difficult for you. I'll leave you alone to get into character."

Get into character? For a second I thought I might burst out laughing, but I didn't. I'd been paying attention these last couple of weeks. I knew stuff was changing in more dramatic ways than it seemed and that my taking charge of the script last time had been serious—like an infraction of the rules, but almost as if he had planned it, not me.

Plus, the last two times he'd come to the door, he'd been dressed differently. No suit. The first time he'd been wearing black pants and a white shirt. He had on a tie, but it was loose and just hanging. I had thought that he might be thinking he'd tie my wrists with it, but he didn't. And just like before, he was positioning me and touching my cock through the jock strap. That time, the time with the tie, he put his hand inside and touched me all the way down to my balls. I knew I was supposed to stay silent, but it wasn't easy. I'd started to have a real thing for this scenario. It wasn't just the money, although the money was great. I'd been looking at him more each time and more at the house as we walked down the long hall to the studio room.

I was starting to think he really was a photographer. The walls were lined with photos—all exterior shots, all black and white, and all, to my art-student eye, pretty fucking good. There was one just outside the door that was of a cobblestone street with the stack of an old factory chimney behind it. It had rained and the cobblestones were slick and water had ponded near a rough-hewn stone curb. The whole composition was a chiaroscuro of light and dark and it had this really ominous look to it. I really liked it a lot. The photo definitely was taken in some other country. Even in an American city as old as this one, I didn't think there was a combination of things that looked like this.

I was also starting to think that maybe "Sir" wasn't as old as I'd first thought—maybe closer to forty than fifty. He had lines in his face—he was always a little tanned—but he didn't have any of that sagging face and neck thing going on that I saw on some of the professors at school. He also didn't look like he'd had work done, though. I'd see *those* guys at the bars and wonder if they thought we didn't know. *Really?* I hoped I'd be able to keep from doing that kind of thing when I got to be that age. One night Tim and I had been hanging out with some other guys from school and I'd danced with one guy and when we went outside to get some air and I thought maybe something else, I nearly jumped out of my skin—his face was like this smooth, tight mask. *Whoa.* Too creepy. I'd rather see the wrinkles. These other dudes, their faces looked like they might crack and the lips always looked kind of weird. I liked kissing when I fucked and no way was I going to be kissing any of those Halloween-lipped guys.

There was nothing like that going on with "Sir." But something was definitely going on.

The last time I'd been there he was wearing black jeans and a black T-shirt and when I arrived, even though it was the time we had set, he took a while to get to the door and he seemed a little out of breath when he let me in. It was a little different that day. Everything seemed to move really quickly.

It had been snowing lightly when I got there and my hair was a little wet from the snow. He'd taken my jacket—that had never happened before—and had gone through another door with it. "To let it dry," was all he'd said. Then he had touched my hair. His touch was light—he kind of fluffed the top of it, put his hand briefly on the back of my head, my neck. His touch went through me, electric. *That was new.*

We had gone into the usual room and this time I noticed one more thing was different. The fire was lit in the fireplace. The room was warm, but not too hot, and the sound of the fire seemed loud when neither of us was speaking. I had wanted to walk over to it, but didn't.

This time when he placed me in the corner, he was closer than he'd ever been before. Like the last time, he touched me. But this time, he'd put his whole hand inside the jock strap and just kind of laid it over my dick. We stood there like that for a minute or so, my cock stiffening under his hand. Then he took his hand out and rearranged my dick the way he wanted it, although he wasn't ever looking at it, he was always looking at my ass. But he obviously wanted to know what it looked like, remember what it looked like. Now he knew what it felt like, too.

He positioned my hands the way he wanted them: palms up, wrists touching. He was close behind me—we were almost exactly the same height. I could feel the heat of him standing behind me. The roughness of his jeans brushed one of my thighs.

That was when he leaned into me. I wasn't sure what was going to happen next. I didn't want to move. I knew he didn't want me to. But his body—the heat through his clothes against my bare skin, the light spitting off the fire—it was a strange sensation. Kind of a sensory overload. It was exciting, but it was also something else and I wasn't sure what that something else was.

The camera was over on the chair. I knew that. So he wasn't thinking about photographing or filming me now. He was thinking about fucking me. Or at least I thought he was.

He leaned into me more. His cock was hard and it pressed against my ass and he put both hands on my waist and I could feel his face against my shoulder, but I kept still. He shifted and then his cock was pretty much against my folded hands. He pressed into me harder and I wasn't sure what he wanted. *Should I press my hands against it?* I couldn't really touch him, not the way he had me positioned.

Then he spoke. It almost startled me, I was so in the kind of trance-y mode he had lulled us both into, with the fire and all.

"Do you remember what you asked me the first time you came here?" He hadn't moved and his breath was hot on my neck as he talked. I could feel his lips almost imperceptibly against my skin. I tried to remember what I had said. I tried to recover my actor voice. *Noncommittal. Rough-tradish. A little thuggish.* Or at least that's what I was going for. That's what I knew he liked.

"Do you want me to jerk you off?" I heard my own voice. It was full of heat. It was full of readiness. It was full of the feelings I had had every time I had left here over the past few weeks. The first time I'd gone right to the Tom Cat. The second time I'd gone there again and gotten a blow job from another guy in a suit who was wearing a wedding ring, but acted like he'd been waiting to suck my dick his whole life.

The third time I did something even more out of character for me than the bookstore back room. I went to the leather bar I'd only been in one other time, went to the back room, and waited with my pants open and down a little ways with the jock strap clearly visible. That jock strap had a story to tell to "Sir" and this was going to be part of it.

The first guy to come into the back room was older, in his thirties. He was wearing ripped jeans and there was a worn spot where his dick was. He had on a leather vest and a leather jacket and no shirt. Both of his nipples were pierced and he had a lot of dense black body art.

It didn't take very long. I was still hot from my acting job and like the other times, just wanted to get off. He'd pushed me up against this black banquette that was against one of the walls and he'd rubbed his hands on the inside of my thighs over and over as he stood inside my spread legs.

He put my hands on his waist so I could feel his skin while he rubbed my thighs. Then he pushed up my shirt and was playing with my nipples, which was going straight to my cock. He leaned over and pulled on the ring in the pierced one with his teeth and then licked around it. He grabbed me by the back of my neck and kissed me hard, his tongue thrusting as he started to push between my legs. I could feel his cock against mine through my jeans and I wanted him to take it out, but I didn't want to say anything—not yet. But the tonguing of my nipple had sent waves through my dick, so I whispered in his ear that I wanted him to come, I wanted him to take my cock and rub it against his. I told him how hot I was, I told him I'd just spent an hour modeling the jock strap with my hands behind my back and I wanted to get off.

He was taking it all in. He stepped back a little and unzipped his pants like he was going to take a piss on me. I didn't want that, but figured I had already given up having choices when I'd come to this place. Maybe it would be hot. I was pretty much doing whatever these days, so…

But instead he just wrapped his hand sideways over his cock and started pulling on it. He stepped back and I could see the cock ring and the black leather inside his pants. My first thought was *cool*. I rubbed my cock through the jock strap, but didn't take it out. He leaned into me and put his cock between my legs so it was rubbing my balls through the fabric, he rubbed my thighs, then he took my dick out and started stroking hard and fast as he pumped between my thighs. I came really fast—maybe a little too fast—and then he did, holding on to my waist as he slammed against me.

When it was over, he asked me if I wanted a drink and I did. He bought me a beer and kind of pulled me into his lap on the bar stool and it felt nice, better than the Tom Cat, but not as nice as Sean. I didn't care, though. I felt like I was doing something else right now, I wasn't sure what, but I liked it. I was acting the role that "Sir" had pulled me into. I felt like I was an artist part of the time and an actor the rest of the time. But I wasn't really an actor, I was just acting like an actor. I had to laugh at the thought. It wasn't going to last long, I knew that, but while it did, I was going to be as far into it as I could go.

For a minute I flashed on my mother and wondered if this was what she was doing with all those random guys. It wasn't a good thought, so I let it go and pulled Mr. Leather Vest onto the dance floor. We danced for an hour, had another couple beers, and then I went home alone and crashed till morning.

❖

Do you want me to jerk you off? When "Sir" asked me what I'd said, and I told him, I hoped it meant sex. I hoped it meant that he was going to get us both off the way I wanted him to. I hoped all these staged photo sessions were going to end in the kind of heat I'd been experiencing when I left here, but that was never quite it—never what I was imagining with Sir. I didn't need to know his name or what he did or why he liked these scenes and why he liked them with someone like me. I just needed to have this finally play out. Because it was taking me places I wasn't sure I wanted to go.

But maybe that had been his plan all along.

❖

That day, the day he'd asked me to repeat myself, things had gotten incredibly intense. He'd turned me around to face him this time. It seemed impromptu—it clearly wasn't what he'd planned, but something had happened when I'd said those words and now he wanted something a little different. He'd told me to forget about the dialogue. "We're going to do something—else."

That strange feeling of excitement mixed with fear went over me in a wave. The hairs on my neck went up a little, but the intensity of my desire—that was exponentially more. Not for the first time I wondered what the fuck I was doing, but I didn't care. I wanted this. It was working its way into my art and it definitely was in the rest of my life, too.

"Turn toward me." I did as I was told. He walked to the light switch and turned the dimmer way down. The room faded into late-winter-afternoon gray lit by the fire and the lowest amber glow from the now-low lights. It changed the look of the room. I liked it. But it made me feel more exposed. I wasn't sure why.

"I want *you* to watch *me*," he said and sat down on the love seat. He was handsome in that older-guy way. I liked seeing him in black jeans and the T-shirt. He had that sexy Berliner look that some of the

European students had at the college. It was a look I liked a lot, but not one I could copy or even wanted to. He unzipped the jeans slowly, without looking at anything but me. His hand went inside and I felt a surge in my dick. I really wanted to touch him. I wanted to shove him down on that little sofa and fuck him. I wanted him to slam me against the wall and fuck me. I wanted us to roll around on the floor and kiss and bite and rub and sweat and fuck. *Does he feel the same things I'm feeling? The urge, the heat?*

I felt slightly awkward standing there looking at him. I wasn't sure what he wanted me to do next. I felt a rush of cold air—I think I just imagined it—but it made my nipples hard and he noticed.

"Maybe not today. Maybe today I still have to watch you. Maybe I need to just touch that little ring you have there in that perfect nipple. Maybe I need to see your cock out of the strap. Maybe I just need to keep filming you because you are so perfect as you are now and we all—" He turned away then.

I had noticed the last couple of times that he had the slightest accent—like his English was a little too perfect. But I couldn't place that underlying note. Dutch? German? South African? I tried to think of the accents I had heard. It was one of those. I was thinking Dutch, although the perversity of these afternoons was definitely more German.

He was still sitting on the love seat and he was rubbing his dick just a little inside the jeans. I was close enough that I could hear his breathing.

"Walk toward me," he said.

I thought about what I should do next. Speak? Stay silent? Keep the thuggish note to my walk and my manner?

"Do you want me to jerk you off? Like this?"

I'd gone off script, but I decided it was time. I walked over to where he sat and stood just out of reach of him. I pulled the jock strap down over my cock and held it there. With the other hand I rubbed my dick and balls, pulling up on the shaft of my cock. I jerked it off just a little. I wanted to stay as hot as I was, but I didn't want to come. Not yet. Not when I didn't know what was going to happen here. But I couldn't remember feeling anything like this before. It was like I was drugged, but we hadn't drunk anything or taken anything. The low music that he always had playing in the background was just a murmur. The sound of the fire was another distant sound. But I could hear his breathing and I could hear my own and I was close to deciding to screw the money, I needed to get to the final act here and see how the play ended.

"We're going to do it together," he told me. "I'm going to set up the camera and you are going to masturbate yourself for me while I do the same."

It was surreal. *Masturbate*. I hadn't really heard that word in years. I don't think I ever even thought that word. *Okay, that's what I'll do.*

He had already paid me when I'd come in. He always did. He'd fold the money—always new, always crisp—and put it in my hand and I'd put it in my wallet. Now he took out his wallet and took more cash out. I saw it. Another $500. *Really?* He laid it on my jeans, which were folded on a chair near the door. "It will be more time than usual," he said. "Please wait while I set up the camera."

I stood there, my dick out but still amazingly hard, and watched as he set up a tripod and the camera I coveted. I saw him do the settings like he'd been doing them his whole life. *Yeah, this is what he does, all right.*

Then he came over to me. "Did you look at the script for today?" I had. Very few lines, all of them pretty hot in the right context. But I thought he'd said we weren't doing that?

"I want you to think about those lines. You don't need to say them unless you want to. But I think some of them might be useful."

He was right, of course, and this was his play or film or performance piece, whatever it was. He was so close to me, I could smell whatever he used on his hair and his soap. There was no cologne and no sweat. But he still smelled like what I thought men should smell like. *Strong.*

"I want you to come," I said, my voice low and with that tone that made him hot. "I want you to come and tell me that you can't wait, you can't wait for me to shoot because you have to come right now, right away, your balls are tight, your dick is so hard you feel like it will explode and it's because of me, because you want me that much, you have to have me that much."

He was so close to me, I could feel his breath. My hand was on my cock now. I'd turned myself on, talking about it. "It's going to make me come, watching you. Look—look at my dick." I stepped back a little, but not out of the range of the camera. *Is he jerking off, or just watching me?* I had been standing too close to him to know for sure. And everything seemed hazy to me now. There was this aura in the room that I couldn't quite explain, but the edges had gone blurry.

I'd crossed that line, the one where I could just stop and decide I was not going to come, that I was just going to let my dick get soft again and go back to doing what I was doing. Sometimes I'd be working at home and I'd just get hard and feel like I wanted to jerk off, that I wouldn't be able to keep working if I didn't get off. But then I'd stop and go back to work. It was hot, kind of. I'd always finish later—lie in bed and think about those Russian porn masters and their big uncut dicks and tattoos and how strong they were when they were pumping their cocks or pumping them into someone.

But now—now I had to finish. I was working my dick hard and decided to make a little noise while I did. I was watching him pull on his cock. It was just like the ones in the porn videos—big and uncut and ready. *Did I dare try to touch it?* I wanted to shove him over that sofa and fuck him, or fuck with him—something. This was really hot, but I wanted to be touched, I wanted to touch. I wanted to step out of his movie and into mine.

"Let me touch it," I said, my voice rough with the heat I was feeling. I let go of my dick—I wasn't ready to come yet. "Let me touch it," I said again and stepped closer. He was doing it harder now. I could tell he was aching for it. I reached out and put my hand over his and then curled my fingers under. He let me slide my hand under his and around his cock, but he didn't take his hand away.

His cock was big and thick and it looked hot in my hand against the black of his jeans. I wanted to see him come and I whispered that close to his ear, because now we were standing like I had been with the guy at the Tom Cat that first day after I'd been here. He put his hand on my hip and gripped hard. "Faster," was all he said—more of a breath than anything—and he started to pump my hand, the head of his cock wet and dark. *Ready*. He put his other hand on my balls, stroking, making them tighter and tighter. I could feel the cum welling up in my balls, into my dick. He was going to have to touch it, suck it, *something*. I wanted him to tease me, to make it last, to make me explode.

"Finger the tip," I told him and he did, pulling on the head and spreading the wetness down over it. I wanted his mouth on my dick, but I knew it wasn't going to happen this time. But he *was* going to get me off. We'd both gone off his script and mine, but now we were headed part of the way to where I wanted to go. This was going to be hot, but not as much as I had wanted. I wanted more than I was going to get this time, but it would still be good, it would still take me closer to that final act of the play. I knew after today he'd need me to come back, need me to finish what we were starting now. This was the foreplay, even though we were both going to come and hard. But this, what we were doing now, this wasn't where either of us was going with this thing between us. I knew that, even though I had no idea what he was going to do with me or what he really wanted.

"Take my cock. *Take it.*" My voice was almost rough. I felt a little wetness at the tip of his cock. He was nearly there.

"Stop." His voice was a whisper, but a command. "Not yet." I took my hand off his dick and he reflexively rubbed it himself for a second. It was out of his jeans and hard and really great-looking. I hadn't realized how close Sir looked to my Russian porn guys.

He led me to the love seat, then moved the camera toward it. "Lie back," he told me, and I did. My cock was hard and pulsing. I was aching for it. He pulled off his shirt and I tried not to make a sound. He was ripped, like I'd thought he would be, and tanned. He had thin silver bolts in both nipples, and the left one had a woven symbol tattooed above it. I didn't recognize it. I didn't care.

What's next?

He rolled the jock strap down, pulled it off, and cupped my balls. One of those long, tapered fingers found its way to my ass, making my cock surge. He lowered himself next to me. I could smell him—that vague soap scent, something expensive. His chest was hot and smooth—hairless—against me. I wanted him to kiss me. I wanted to feel his tongue on my neck, in my mouth, on my dick. He took my face in his hand and looked at me. I stared back, exuding heat. Neither of us spoke.

When he kissed me it was hard and his tongue thrust deep in my mouth, making my cock pulse. He started to grind against me. I could feel his cock on my stomach, next to my own. I reached my hand down to touch it and he whispered in my ear, "Give me what I want, Jack." His tongue was on my neck, that space between my neck and shoulder. A *frisson* of heat went through me. *Right. I'm "Jack."*

I remembered the script. "I'm what you want, Sir. And this—" I had my hand around his dick, pumping it. Then I grabbed for his hand and put it on my cock. "Jerk me off," I whispered, "make me come. Do it. I need you to do it for me." I said those words over and over, I had my hand on his, rubbing my cock all the way down to the root and up to the head. "Faster," I told him. "Faster." I was going to come any second. I wanted to roll over onto him and come between his thighs but I knew that was way too far off script, even for where we'd gotten. I was in a kind of frenzy of heat and so was he. We were sweating now, our chests slick with sweat as we jerked each other off. I kept talking to him, but he said nothing, except the occasional "Jack" whispered and moaned in my ear.

Then it was pulsing up the shaft of my cock and I couldn't stop. I gripped his hand around my cock tight, like I was rocking his ass, and fucked his hand, coming into his hand, onto his hand, onto his stomach, I just kept shooting. *Fuck. Fuck. Fuck.* I was wrecked, it was so intense.

"Let me see you," I said to him, looking at him. "Let me watch you. Do it for me. Show me." I was trying to remember the script, trying to get us to that final act.

He was damp with sweat. He leaned into me and rubbed his dick hard and fast. "Hard, Jack, hard," he said as I slid my hand under his again. I didn't want to stop him, I wanted him to feel it harder than he'd ever felt it. He gripped my hand around his cock and leaned back and fucked my *hand, hard, hard, hard* and then I felt the spurts on my hand, my stomach. I milked every bit out of him and then he fell back. We were both just so wrecked.

Why do I need anything else after that? I stood out on the sidewalk in front of Sir's house, the snow falling lightly, and wondered how I could possibly want to do anything but go home and sleep. The intensity of the starting and stopping and finally coming was incredible. And yet I knew there was more, although I wasn't sure what that *more* was. But I also knew that next time would be it—that final act. We were almost there, but I had to know where we were going, what the end of the play was. I had to know what my role really was. And why it had to end.

Maybe it didn't have to, maybe it could just move to a different place, the place where I was Jack, instead of...myself.

Am I looking for danger now? Was that what was happening? Was he bringing out that side in me? That side I'd inherited from my parents, but had managed to avoid until now, until I'd gone off in Sir's jock strap and taken it on a tour of the most salacious parts of the city? How had I gotten so far from my friends at school and Tim and Sean and into all these guys whose names I didn't know and to whom I was always Jack?

Still, that was where I was heading—into that world, back to that world, further and further away from what I knew and what I did in the daytime and into what I did in the cold and dark, like I was some kind of sexual vampire now, living for the next hottest thing, because at some point, I was sure, Sir was going to ask me, he was going to ask me where I had been when I left his script and went to mine.

But was it even mine? Or was it still his? Because before I'd taken down that ad at school, my script was jerking off to Russian porn, fucking Sean's nice, tight, clean, sexy ass and sucking his really hot dick, tracing my fingers along his beautiful hard stomach and those fantastic muscled legs and kissing the back of his neck as I fucked him. It was working on my art and hanging out with my friends from school and drinking beer and talking about our projects. *That* was my life before Sir. And now...

Now, when I left Sir's house, all I could think about was getting off again, getting off in some really intense way that both knocked him out of my head and gave me something new to tell him—if that ever actually happened.

I headed to the one kind of place I'd never been before. I headed to Pump, the S/M bar that catered to men in that 1980s, pre-AIDS, poppers, meth, lube, and leather slings kind of way that I had only read about and never thought I would ever be into.

Except now I was into everything. Now I would try anything.

As I walked there, my jacket collar up against the cold, a few cars slowed as they approached me. A few windows rolled down, a low voice here and there asked me, *How much?* I just shook my head. I had a different plan in my head now, a new script. I didn't want to get into some random car and do whatever. I wanted to go to Pump.

I wanted a scene, I wanted theatrics, I wanted, if I was honest with myself, *danger.*

I *was* going to ask for money, though. Because I was going to the club specifically to hustle, I was going there with my own next act, which was starting to run like one of Sean's reels in my head. I was going there to fuck, to do the kind of fucking I had wanted to do with Sir, that I had sort of done at the Tom Cat. And I was going to get paid, *again.* When I saw Sir in two days, I was going to show him what I'd done and I was going to do whatever I felt like doing with him. We were going to have our own final act. And it was going to be more than a hand job or a blow job. He was going to tell me what this was all about. And I was going to do whatever he wanted. For the last time.

Pump was the right place for me that night—I'd made, or rather "Jack" had made, a surprising amount of money whispering *I just turned 18, but no one has to know that but you* to several different guys. And then I was fucking. Slapping ass. Fisting. All in that James Dean mode I'd pulled on "Sir" last week.

Before the night was out I'd pushed myself to yet another edge, past yet another limit I hadn't even known I'd had.

For money.

I'd lubed up my fist and pumped into the surprisingly open ass of a guy dressed only in a black leather jock strap and unlaced black boots.

I'd used a big, thick, black neoprene dildo on another ass, slow at first and then so hard and fast that I thought I might come from all the moaning the guy was giving me.

I'd slid six slender needles into the head and shaft of a dick and still more into the smooth inside of a thigh each with the same studied precision I had threaded Sean's film splices into my mixed media project.

I'd fake-pushed some guy dressed only in his massive tats and a cock ring with a chain that looped up to a ring in his nipple to his knees to suck my dick while someone else played with my balls and someone else rubbed the inside of my thighs as I leaned back against a black banquette. I came hard—harder than I would have thought—and as I was about to come I was remembering Sir's cock in my hand, gripping my hand, telling me *faster, Jack, faster*, and I held the guy's head further down on my dick and pumped until there was nothing left.

I was good with my hands, no question. Good enough to be paid, good enough to be let into the back of the back rooms without question. Jack had been accepted so easily at Pump. But then fresh meat *was fresh* and it had a spiciness to it that the usual fare did not. I'd be welcome again, that I knew. Maybe I'd even come back.

Unless, of course, I snapped myself back into my old pre-Sir life and stopped doing whatever this was. Because I was starting to go off the rails a little. I knew it, Sean had said something to me about it, so had Tim. I hadn't stopped working on my projects, though. If anything, my art had become a focal point for me and was getting better and stronger. A couple of my profs had even said they were really liking my new work. My portfolio was growing as the days ticked down toward graduation. But I couldn't help wondering if the turn my life had taken over the past few weeks wasn't important to my art—and I hadn't even known it. I'd even done a piece just titled *electrocution* that was, sort of, about my father. It was good, I liked it. It didn't make me feel connected to my family, but it *did* make me feel connected to danger.

So I wasn't entirely sure that I didn't want to keep going to see where the crash would take me. Pump was closer to driving head-on into a tree than I thought I wanted to go, but then again, there I was, fucking one guy after another, letting this one suck my dick and then, later, jerking off onto the face of another guy like in some bad Asian porn because he said he wanted to taste me, taste how young I was. It was hot, it was creepy, it was nuts. Near the end of the night I'd gone in to take a piss and another guy wanted to hold my dick while I did. I told him no. Soon after that, I left.

Money was the high at Pump. Like going to a casino where you played fuck roulette for money. That and the touch of meth I did with the first guy. That and being Jack, not me. *Jack, the hustler.* That and not really remembering who I was or what I was doing. Since I'm not actually *Jack.*

Not Jack. Not the guy who pressed Sir hard into the love seat as he whispered that name over and over in my ear as he kissed and bit and grabbed at me as I slammed my cock against him, the weeks of aching for it building and building despite all these other rendezvous and assignations and whatever else Sir might call them.

The rabbit hole was looming in front of me. I was pretty sure I could keep myself from falling in.

Pretty sure.

It wasn't snowing the next time I went back to Sir's house, but it was misting and damp, that through-and-through damp that comes at the end of winter. The wind was up and it felt as if it might get really stormy—the sky was that roiled gray that comes with storms, a very Ansel Adams kind of sky. Except this was a cityscape, not some Big Sky expanse of clouded horizon. The barometric pressure was dropping; you could feel it in the air and on your skin. The hairs were standing up on my neck. Spring was hovering around the edges of the days now, but it was still gray more than it was sunny, and this day—this day was holding on to winter hard.

It felt like a long time before Sir answered the door, but when he did, I was surprised by how glad I was to see him. I almost smiled, but caught myself at the last second. We weren't about smiles, Sir and I. We were about heat.

He took my jacket again, as he had the last time. But this time when he ruffled my damp hair, his hand lingered at the back of my neck as he said, "You look cold, Jack," and I felt his touch go through me. I wanted to pull him to me, to kiss him, to shove him against one of these walls covered in the gorgeous photographs. I wanted to rattle him the way he had rattled me. But I didn't. I just felt the pressure of his strong hand on me and then felt its absence. He'd be touching me again, soon. Of that I was sure.

We both pretended that the sex last time hadn't happened. Just like the time before that when we'd pretended that I hadn't tried to take over the scene, leaving him unsatisfied—or at least unsatisfied while we were together, since he'd taken plenty of photos of me that day.

I didn't know what he had planned. I wasn't sure what I had planned, either. Were we coming at this fresh? Was this the denouement or the do-over?

I didn't know. I couldn't know. It had never been my play—I realized that now. And I was about to discover just how much it wasn't my play as we entered our little studio together.

This time the stage was set. The lights were already dimmed to that amber glow. The tripod was up behind the love seat and the camera was safely ensconced there. On the little table to the side of the love seat were some green bottles of a foreign water, two glasses, and a bottle of something—I assumed wine, but it might have been something more E. M. Forster or Evelyn Waugh, like sherry or port, because we were definitely moving into a pattern of my youthful rough trade against his cultured upper-class man. After all, I was Jack and he was Sir. That had *manservant* written all over it, even if we were a century late in telling *that* particular story and totally in the wrong country for it.

Was I going to stay on script this time—this time that I knew, just *knew* was our last? I felt like going off it. I felt like smashing those glasses into the low fire he had going. I felt like cracking the wine bottle over his skull. I felt like taking the X-Acto blade out of my bag and slicing up that love seat till it was nothing but confetti. I felt like tossing the camera into the series of photographs that lined one part of the wall, framed photographs I hadn't ever noticed before.

I felt like doing damage.

But I didn't do any of that. Instead I walked over to the table and picked up a glass and turned to him, saying simply, "Sir?" as I held the glass out toward him.

He walked over and poured me a glass of a pretty fragrant red wine. I'm not big on wine, but it smelled good and tasted better. I felt the alcohol almost immediately—drinking in the day always does that to me, even though it was late afternoon. I took another small swig, then set the glass down. I didn't want to get high. I knew I shouldn't.

Sir took his glass and sat down on the love seat. His legs were open, the way some guys sit on the subway, taking up two seats, and you know it's just so they can show off their dicks in their pants. He was doing that now, showing me his dick, hard against the black jeans he wore. He took another sip of the wine, then he said, his voice low and so full of heat it took me by surprise, "Tell me, Jack, about your *cock*."

Of all the things I thought he might have said, this was not a line that I had imagined I would hear. I wasn't sure how I should answer.

And then I was.

I walked over to him and stood in front of him. I looked straight ahead for a moment, rather than down at him. I saw the light on the camera. Heard the slight digital buzzing over the music that played in the background—some techno lounge thing. I liked it.

This was my scene. He was waiting—he'd schooled me for weeks. I was suddenly getting it, what these last weeks had been about, who my character was, and what was expected of him. I was getting all of it. Whether I wanted realization or not. We were at that point in the play they call Chekov's gun—I'd somehow missed all the foreshadowing, but now I saw it like those films that happen in reverse like a Christopher Nolan movie—*Memento*, where the guy is backtracking to find out what happened to him. Or maybe I was the guy floating in the pool at the beginning of *Sunset Boulevard.* We'd seen that in one of my film classes last year or maybe the year before. Was that guy's name Jack? I think it was.

I started with my sweater. There's no hot or graceful way to take off a sweater. Better to just do the butch thing and tear it off and toss it aside, like it's keeping you from something. So I did that.

My boots and socks were already off and neatly behind the love seat. I came closer to him—just within reach, although I was pretty sure he wouldn't reach for me. That I would be doing the reaching. I undid my belt and the button above my zipper.

He took another sip of wine. I leaned forward and took his glass. I took a small sip and then flicked my tongue against the rim of the glass and handed it back to him.

I started to talk. I moved closer, so that I was standing in front of him, and then I said, "You forgot to pay me, Sir."

I knew it was the right thing to say even as I was afraid to say it. And I was right. I saw his dick twitch slightly in his pants and I heard just the slightest intake of breath, which he tried to mask with another sip of wine.

He stood up and walked to the back of the room, to the little secretary or whatever the French call that's a mostly useless but very pretty piece of furniture and opened a small drawer in the center. He walked back toward me, an envelope in his hands. He was looking straight at me and I had no fucking clue what the expression on his face was. *Lust? Excitement? Loathing?* A little of all three? I was pretty sure neither of us was supposed to have gotten to the point where we were— which was feeling something other than a really overheated desire to fuck and be fucked. But the intensity in the room was palpable and for a second I wasn't sure if I could breathe.

I took the envelope and was about to slip it into my pocket when he said, "You should count it."

Really? Count it? Are we playing that *game?*

The envelope was a pale blue, like the color of his shirt the first time I had come here. Inside were a lot of hundred-dollar bills. Way more than usual. *Too many.* For a second I had that *run run run* sensation that I had had a few times before, but it passed and I folded the envelope and put it in my pocket.

Now it was time. We were definitely in the final act. The only question was, *whose?*

The wind was strong when I left Sir's place. It was fully dark out and the mist had turned to a light rain. I walked quickly toward my place, my hood up to keep the rain off my head and neck. About three blocks into my walk, a car slowed beside me, following me to the corner. The window rolled down.

He was forty-ish, dark hair, deep-brown eyes, wearing a business suit. Good-looking for this kind of thing. He'd forgotten to take off his wedding ring as he fluttered his hand out the window for me to come closer. I jogged over.

"It's really raw out there. Can I drop you somewhere?"

He had pulled in at the end of the block. The sidewalk was deserted, even though it wasn't that late.

"Put your mouth on my cock right here, first," Jack told the married guy in the car, because Jack had begun to love danger.

I rubbed my dick just a little—it didn't need it, but he did. I saw his right hand go to his own dick as I pressed myself into the window and he pushed his lips against my jeans. I could see how much he wanted it. I could tell this was the most dangerous thing he'd ever done in his life. He was already making that sound I loved. Maybe I'd take him back to my place and do the whole thing with him. *Why not?*

"How much?" he said, as he pulled his head away from my dick.

"As much as you want it," Jack said. I stood there, in the light rain and wind. I slowly unzipped my jeans, pulling just the head of my swollen cock out from behind the jock strap. I was imagining him up against the wall in my apartment, hands against the wall, my cock slamming into him the way I'd done at Pump a few nights ago.

He reached up and touched my cock, looking around as he did, expecting someone to turn up and arrest him or something. The tip was wet and he leaned forward and took it in his mouth. It was awkward, how I was standing. No way he could really suck me off like that. I pulled back, slipping my dick back in my pants. I could hear the sigh from him over the sound of the wind.

"You still want it?" Jack's genteel thug asked him.

"Yes." His voice was eager, but trying not to be. I thought about what Jack was going to do with him and how it was going to be the best night of his life.

"Then we'll go to my place. You know it's going to cost you, right?" Jack said, cool, but edgy, like the hustler he was.

"I don't care," the married guy said as Jack got into the car. Jack reached over to massage the guy's cock as they drove.

"Tell me how much you want it," Jack said, in a low, practiced voice. "I want you to tell me."

The guy took Jack's hand and rubbed it against his dick, rock hard in his trousers. "I've wanted it for a long time," he said. "I just didn't know how much until now."

The stairs to Jack's apartment seemed endless, but once they were inside, Jack plugged in the set of twinkling lights Sean and I had strung up around the room at Christmas and had never taken down because I thought at night it made the room look like sky, like when I was a kid back in New England.

The guy stood inside the doorway to Jack's room, unsure what to do next. He said, "I've actually never done this before. Not since college. I…" His voice trailed off.

Jack went over to him and pulled him into the room and shut the door. Jack told him to undress, quickly. "I'm not interested in the stripping part," Jack said.

Jack/I, whichever one of us was doing this—I took off my jacket and hung it over my chair to dry. Off came my boots and socks and sweater. I unzipped my jeans and opened them wide, but didn't take them off. Yet.

He stood in front of me in just a pair of gray boxer briefs. His dick looked really big, which made me suddenly hot for some reason. I didn't usually care. I could tell he was Italian, which made me think he would be uncut, which I was starting to like. That old porn fantasy washed over me for a minute. He looked good out of the suit. Obviously his wife made him go to the gym. Or he went to look at the almost naked guys, all sweaty and then raw in the shower. I bet he wanted to have sex every time he went there. I bet he jerked off in one of the stalls while he listened to the sounds of men all around him.

I pulled him to me. "Pay me first," Jack told him.

He took his wallet out of his neatly folded pants and pulled out a small wad of cash. "I've got $500," he said. Jack took $400 and stuffed it in his pocket, next to the blue envelope with the $2,000 Sir had given him. He felt something as this money touched that, but he wasn't sure what it was. *Something.*

"Now," Jack's tone was commanding, "I want to see you touch your cock. Just a little. Do it," I told him. Jack told him.

I went over and lay down on my bed. I pulled my jeans down over my hips and tossed them to the floor, but kept the jock strap in place. I put my hand inside and started jerking off a little—slow, a tease for him, the kind of thing a hustler would do, the kind of thing you'd see in a porn film, the kind of thing Sir liked to see me do for the camera.

The Italian came over and knelt between my legs on the bed, his cock in his hand. I had no idea what I was doing now, but I didn't care. I wasn't even sure if I was Jack right now or myself. I'd been Jack for weeks. I was Jack earlier that night. Maybe I'd be Jack forever now.

I reached up and pulled him onto me, then I flipped him over onto his back, my hands pressing his arms into the bed. I could tell he liked it. His breathing got quicker and his cock was super-stiff against me.

Up close I could tell he was handsome in that Mafiosi kind of way, but I knew in another ten years he'd be fat and this part of his life would be over completely and he'd be a suburban husband and dad full-time. But he'd jerk off to memories of this night or others like it every time, or watch gay porn in the den when everyone was asleep. Because he was really gay, he just didn't know how to be.

But he knew he wanted gay sex, just like I'd known when I was watching those uncut Russian guys all through high school. "Tell me what you want," I whispered in his ear as I put his hand on the nipple with the ring in it and heard him moan just a little. "Tell me what you want," I repeated as I peeled back the jock strap. My dick was throbbing—or Jack's was. I wanted to get off, but I also wanted to drag this out, to tease him, to make him want it so much that he was ready to give up everything else just for this. *For Jack.*

I rubbed my dick against his, I rubbed my balls against his, I pulled on his nipples, I ran my tongue along the space between his ear and his shoulder and down his torso to his dick. I held him down by his shoulders and told him to put his hands on my hips and I fucked him a little between his thighs until I was afraid I might come, so I stopped, but I could tell it made him crazy with desire.

He was telling me how hot I was, how hot *this* was, how he'd never had this before, but knew he wanted it, had driven that same strip every night after work for the past three weeks and looked at guys, but hadn't done anything until tonight.

"Do you want me to fuck you or do you want me to jerk you off?" Jack spoke low and soft and right into his ear, because he knew that would go right to Married Guy's dick just like it went right to his own. "Tell me you want to come, tell me you want me to make you come, tell me how hot you are right now." He moaned softly against my ear and I felt his cock twitch next to mine. He put his hand inside the jock strap, rubbed my balls hard, wrapped his hand around my cock, and started to jerk me off. This time I wasn't going to stop him.

I thought about Sir. The jock strap was damp from my own cum as well as the Italian's. I put my mouth on his and kissed him hard. His hand squeezed tighter on my dick and I reached down and held it for a moment, stopping him, but not taking his hand away. We kissed. Hard, then harder. I pulled off the jock strap and slammed myself against him. His dick and mine were rubbing together. I put my cock between his thighs and pumped a little more. I liked the feel of it against his balls. I wanted to fuck him, but I could tell he wasn't ready. Maybe another time.

"I want you to tell me when you're coming," I whispered. "Tell me, tell me…" I was ready to come now. Part of me wanted to shove my dick in his mouth and have him suck me off, but I wanted to keep kissing him and slamming my dick into his hand until I came.

He was moaning now, telling me not to stop, *faster, oh God, faster*, and then he was spurting over my hand, jerking me off so hard I was dizzy from the intensity as he told me this was how he jerked himself off at home, *this hard, this hard, this hard*, and then I was wrecked as his finger went up my ass just as I came.

❖

I fell asleep after Married Guy—his name was Dante, as Italian as his thick, uncut dick—left to go home to the wife and kids. I woke up in the middle of the night, in the stillness and silence.

I thought of Sir.

I wasn't sure which of us was responsible for things going so far, but there was never a point where either of us tried to stop. The weeks of tension had built up to an impossible level. We were never going to hit in reality where our expectations were in fantasy, but we were both determined to get close.

"Tell me about your cock, Jack," was the story of the jock strap. The story of what he had wanted me to do outside his place rather than in it.

This time we stripped naked. He sat sprawled on his love seat, his cock in one hand, the other rubbing his thighs and his balls as I told him all the stories. I moved close until finally I was straddling him.

"After all this time, you should suck my cock," I told him and rubbed it against his lips. And he did. He grabbed my hips in his hands and sucked me, periodically stopping to lick my balls and suck at the base of my cock.

He pulled me down next to him and suddenly I knew that he was going to fuck me, not the other way around. He was much stronger than I had remembered from the last time, the time we weren't supposed to talk about, the time that was foreplay to this time, the time that allowed for one more time.

He pushed me back against the throw pillows. For a moment I thought how comfortable it felt—the warmth of the fire, how his body felt next to mine—smooth and hard and hot. I felt dazed with something I could only describe as longing—a word that went with that whole *Maurice, Brideshead Revisited* world that we weren't actually in. I was going down that rabbit hole, and fast. I should have gotten up to leave, to just run out of here like one of those girls in one of those movies, but I didn't. Instead I turned on my side just a little and took his right hand

and pulled it to my lips, then just laid it on my cock. Then I started to tell him the story of the past few weeks.

❖

When it happened, it wasn't like anything else. But I knew it wouldn't be. He'd taken the cushions off the love seat and put them in front of the fire and he'd fake-wrestled me on the floor a little bit as he asked me more questions about everything I had done when I left *here* and went *out there*. He wanted details—my fucking Sean, the guys at the Tom Cat, the guy at the leather bar, my night at Pump, a few other things in between. Each new detail pulled him closer to me.

It was hot, what we were doing. But it was also strange—at first it seemed more like two guys who had never had sex instead of two guys who had had a lot of sex and also seen a lot of sex and knew all the kinds of sex two guys could have and were talking about that sex with each other. It had this sexy sleepover quality to it that was enhanced by the wine and the heat of the fire and how much we both wanted the sex but didn't want things to end yet.

And then he began to tell me the story of Jack.

Midway between the story of Jack and when I left, he started fucking me. He began with kissing me—it was so tender that I felt tears prick at the back of my eyes. *I have to stop drinking the wine.* Then he went to my nipples and down my stomach before he had his mouth on my cock, my balls, my thighs, and back again. It was hot, but I felt removed from it somehow, because now I felt like I was Jack, not myself, and I was feeling Jack and Jack held himself back, just like at Pump or the Tom Cat. Jack didn't quite let go.

Which was what Sir loved about Jack—his distance, his refusal to give in.

I don't know when I realized what was happening, but I did know that I was pretty much past caring. He'd straddled me and rubbed his cock against my lips and I knew I wanted to suck it—I'd wanted to suck it since the first time. Every time I'd been here he'd reminded me more of those guys in my high school porn videos. Except he was Viggo Mortensen in *Eastern Promises*, wrestling me naked on the floor, with his strong, honed body and his thick, hard cock. So when he rubbed it against my lips, of course I took it.

It went on this way for what seemed like hours. We'd start, we'd stop. We'd have more wine, we'd talk. I'd tell him a story, he'd tell me more about Jack. He'd rub my cock, I'd rub his. I can't explain how it felt. By the time I realized where we were going, I didn't care. I was like those girls in those movies. Except I wasn't even going to bother to run.

❖

I loved Jack. He was actually very like you. A beautiful boy. Lean and tall. He had eyes like yours—not quite green, not quite amber. That hair— Here he stopped and fluffed my hair as he had when I came in, slipping his hand back behind my neck, pulling me forward and kissing me briefly.

And like you, he was an artist. We met—well, it doesn't matter where we met. We did. It was one of those things. A surprise, you know? His accent was suddenly much stronger. Definitely South African. Or Dutch. *Not love at first sight so much as we were obsessed with each other. Once we understood how much we both wanted it, we couldn't get enough of it. Just like you and I can't. I wanted him all the time. It was difficult to get anything done—I thought of him constantly, as he did me. It was like a bad nineteenth-century novel, you know? We were trying always to find ways to be together. We'd do a little drugs, we'd have some more sex, we barely did anything else. Obsession—you know. It leads to tragedy.*

He paused. We had been lying next to each other. He slid his leg between mine, spreading them open. He rolled over onto me. *Obsession—it leads to tragedy.*

This was the point where I knew I should get up, run, and be grateful I had escaped.

But I couldn't. I needed to know where this would end. I needed to get what I had come for: a final act.

Sir was whispering in my ear as he turned me over and pulled my ass to him. He was telling me that he wanted to fuck me, that he wanted his cock inside me, that he wanted to hold my ass on his dick, that he *wanted, wanted, wanted.* Then he told me what I needed to hear. Whispered it. *I know you're not Jack.* Heat coursed through me, overwhelming everything else. I wasn't sure if it was the wine or the languid way we had been lying around, playing with each other's dicks, rubbing each other's balls, licking and kissing each other, but suddenly everything revved up and where we had been just playing with each other, now we had to have it. He was grabbing at my ass and slapping it, reaching between my legs and stroking my balls. He turned me back over and lay on top of me, touching my cock with slow strokes. It was like he couldn't decide if he wanted to fuck me or just watch me touch my own dick—he kept telling me to stroke it and wrapped my hand over his, then slid his out. He was straddling me now, and whacking at his cock fast. I couldn't stop watching—it was like I had fallen into one of those porn movies that ran in my head at the slightest provocation. He had walked out of one of those films and given me the hottest sex I'd ever had in my life.

I pulled him to me—me, not Jack. I wrapped his hand around my cock, tight, and moved it fast. "Fuck me," I said, my voice barely audible. "Fuck me. I want you to fuck me. I want to come with you fucking me." I was moving underneath him, pumping his hand. I felt wild, out of control, like I wanted to spread my ass cheeks wider, suck him into me. I had a flash of the guy I had fisted at Pump and how he had just given up his ass to me. I wanted to do that now—I was ready.

When I tried to remember what happened, I couldn't really. Sir had body-slammed me onto the cushions. He'd kissed me hard, thrusting his tongue like it was his cock. I couldn't get enough of him. We were tearing at each other, rubbing our bodies together. We moved back a little from the fire, our bodies glistening with sweat. He had spread my ass open and slathered lube onto me and his dick, he'd leaned over and taken my cock in his mouth, I could feel the skin of my cock moving up and down as he sucked me, taking my whole cock in his mouth, his hands grabbing my balls and rubbing them, sliding a finger, then two up into my ass. I felt like I could come any second. He pulled back, jerking my cock up and down, but licking at the head, his lips hot over the head of my cock.

And then it was time, I told him I was ready to come, I wanted to come with him fucking me. And so he turned me over, for sure, for real this time and I could imagine him holding himself as he guided his dick into my ass, then he was on me, in me, holding my hips, slapping my ass, fucking, fucking, fucking me. It wasn't like anything else I ever felt.

I told him to tell me, tell me when he was coming. "You'll feel it," he said. "You'll feel it. Now, now, get ready to feel it." *He was pumping me so hard, the sound of his skin slapping mine sounded sexy and hot and I could feel him all through me.* "Try to wait," *he told me.* "I want to watch you. I need to watch you. I need—"

He came hard, slamming into my ass and moaning, grabbing my hair, my ass, my shoulders. He had finally lost control, finally given it to me. I needed him to get me off now, I needed to have him take my cock, make me come.

This wasn't our final act after all.

We had fallen asleep together in front of the fire. It was dark when I woke up. The fire was a low glow now, and Sir was on his side, facing away from me. His glass of wine had fallen over and a small dark stain had spread from the cushion to the hearth. I sat up. I felt dizzy, my mouth was dry. I stood slowly and walked over to the little table where the wine bottle had been. There were several small bottles of water on the table. I took one and drank the whole thing.

Sir still lay there, in front of the fire. I walked to the camera and turned it off. I wasn't sure why. Then I walked over to the little French desk.

I had no intention of taking anything. I wasn't even going to look at anything, really. I turned away from the desk and saw them, the bank of photographs that I had never noticed before.

They're all of me. Me in the corner, me on the chair with my arms behind my back, me with my cock in my hand, me pulling the jock strap down below the head of my cock, me in thirty-one framed poses that some would call erotic, others, pornographic. At the corner of each photograph was a date, and Sir's signature—he did have a name and I suddenly recognized it and he was German after all—and then the titles: *Jack, Jack, Jack.* Numbered and dated.

But he'd told me, he'd told me he knew I *wasn't* Jack. Just when I was starting to feel maybe I was Jack after all. Not just *Jack,* the Jack where obsession turned to tragedy. Not the he-hadn't-fully-explained-how Jack. But the Jack who was floating in the pool in *Sunset Boulevard*. Except I remembered his name wasn't Jack, it was Joe. *Close enough.* I was that Jack.

So this was how it was going to end for me and Sir. The play had closed, I had finished my role. No understudy had ever had to take the stage for me.

I looked at the framed photos. I could have taken them down and smashed them, but why? It was a role, I played it, it was over, and these photos were the playbill. It didn't matter. It really didn't. What made me think it did?

I'm not sure why I didn't hear him come up behind me, but I didn't. His arm was around me, around my shoulders. It was companionable, like my lover had come up to me in a museum to see what art I was looking at. We stood there for a moment, naked, him holding me, looking at the photos of me in various states of undress. He leaned over, kissed me, and said, "They are wonderful photos of you, aren't they? You look so handsome, so—" He paused. He kissed me again, both hands on my shoulders now. Then he said, "You should get dressed, don't you think? *Jack?*"

❖

I lay in my bed in the silence of my room, looking up at the starscape of twinkling lights on the ceiling. I turned, picked up my cell phone. It was nearly 4:30. I could get up and work, or go back to sleep for a few more hours before class. I reset my alarm for seven, deciding sleep was the best thing. I thought briefly about the Italian, wondering what he would tell his wife when he got home.

Then I thought about Sir one more time, remembering his hands on my hips, his mouth on my cock, before I fell asleep. *Sometimes obsession leads to tragedy*, I thought, and fell asleep beneath the twinkling stars.

THE ADVENTURE OF THE RAGGED YOUTH
AARON TRAVIS

(Transcribed from the secret diary of John H. Watson, M.D.)

The story I am about to narrate is the most secret and perhaps the most scandalous of all the adventures relating to my great friend and colleague, Mr. Sherlock Holmes. Readers familiar with my previous accounts will recall that, due to their sensitive nature, I have withheld the details of many adventures for months, years, and even decades before consigning them to print. The story I am about to write may never be published, and certainly not during my own lifetime or that of Holmes. Nevertheless, as it contains its own intrinsic interest, I feel compelled to record every detail of so strange and sordid an adventure.

The year was 1895, in that busy period to which belong so many of the published adventures, when Holmes was at the very peak of his energies. The month was October. The weather was brisk and chill. Along the tree-lined curbs of Baker Street leaves of ochre and gold shivered against a pearl-grey sky. It was a fine afternoon for a fire, and I set about reviving the smouldering embers in the fireplace as soon as Mrs. Hudson admitted me to Holmes's study. Holmes himself, the landlady informed me, had gone out shortly after noon, promising to return within two or three hours. As the clock on the mantel showed twenty minutes past three o'clock, I expected him to arrive at any moment. I took off my hat and gloves, lit a cigarette, and took a comfortable chair close by the window, which gave me a clear view of the tobacconist's shop across the street.

I had hardly inhaled the first draught of smoke when Holmes stepped into view. He walked briskly down the street, swinging his cane, then abruptly stopped before the tobacconist's window. He stared intently at the display of cigars and pipes for sale, then stepped inside. A moment later, emerging from the crowd of pedestrians, a ragged, hatless young man paused in front of the shop just as Holmes had done. He was of slightly less than middle height with a mop of jet-black curls, a bit too old to be described as an urchin, but not yet old enough to resemble those hopeless wreckages of manhood who litter the streets of London. His endlessly patched and tattered clothing bespoke his poverty, while at the same time his proud chin and upright carriage bespoke a poignant attempt at dignity. I found myself meditating on the melancholy of such a youth, poised at the cusp of manhood with no prospects for a decent future, staring into the window of a tobacconist's shop whose pleasures, simple and cheap enough, even so were beyond his means.

At that moment Holmes made his exit from the shop. He appeared to take no notice of the youth, stepping obliviously past him. Then, as I looked on in horror, Holmes abruptly turned on his heel and struck the side of the young man's head with his cane, swinging it like a cudgel. For all his slenderness and grace Holmes is a man of remarkable strength, and I was not surprised to see the object of his assault drop straight to the cobblestones. Holmes loomed over the dazed youth, brandishing his cane and barking some question in tones so sharp I could hear them even through the window. The young man clutched his hands to his face and tried to scramble away, but Holmes badgered him with his stick until he was cornered against a lamppost. The next instant Holmes had pulled the young man upright by his ear and was striding rapidly across the street with his captive in tow.

I felt a powerful compulsion to conceal myself. Even as I heard the door open and a confusion of footsteps ascend the stairs I rapidly extinguished my cigarette and gathered up my hat and gloves. The only sure place of concealment was the closet. Once inside I peered through the keyhole and discovered that it gave a clear view of the entire room. I took a deep breath just as the door swung open with a crash. The ragged youth tumbled headfirst into the room. Holmes immediately followed and slammed the door shut.

"You have been following me all afternoon, from the moment I stepped onto Baker Street," said Holmes. He stood with both hands on his hips, glowering down at his captive with a look of utter contempt. "There is no use denying it."

"Please, sir, I'm not denying nothing." The youth attempted to stand, but Holmes ruthlessly poked him down with his cane. I stared through the keyhole, appalled at the spectacle.

Holmes leaned against the mantel and appeared to relax somewhat, though his insistent tapping of the cane against his shoe betrayed his agitation. "Explain yourself, young man."

"Please, sir, can't I even stand up?"

"Does a cur stand after he's been justly beaten? Are you any better?"

My ears burned with shame at the unaccountable cruelty of my friend's behaviour.

The young man rose up, flinching pathetically when Holmes tapped the cane with renewed vigour against his heel. He stood biting his lips and clutching fistfuls of his loose, ragged clothing. The glow from the fire shone on his smooth, clear face, and in its light I saw a glistening tear tumble down his cheek.

Holmes saw it, too. "Save the weeping for your mother, boy. It will you do no good with me."

Again I was appalled.

"Please, Mr. Holmes, you needn't be so cruel."

"Holmes, you call me. Then you know my name?"

"Please, sir, I never denied it. Yes, I was following you. I admit it. But with never a bad intention, I swear."

"Then why?"

"Because..." The young man began to stutter and fumble his words. His face, already ruddy in the fire's glow, burned an even deeper shade of red. "Because..." Again he fumbled. Then he spat out the words: "Wiggins says you got a big one!"

Holmes drew his eyebrows together. His thin lips compressed into a smile. Wiggins was the captain of what Holmes called his Baker Street Irregulars, that ragtag group of street urchins whom he sometimes called upon to comb the city for bits of information, giving them small coins and certain other favours in compensation.

"Ha! Wiggins! Imagine that, betraying my deepest confidence. The whelp! I shall have to punish him for that."

The dark-haired youth shivered in the firelight. "Wiggins says— Wiggins says you pay pretty well."

"Indeed? And does that matter? There are some young men, like your friend Wiggins, who must be paid. There are others who would gladly pay me for the privilege. I deduce that you are one of those—following me like a dog through the streets, practically sniffing at me, hungry for something thick and warm in that pretty mouth of yours." Holmes stepped away from the fire and with the tip of his cane caressed the young man's cheek. "What is your name?"

"Jack, sir. Jack Martin."

"How old are you, Jack Martin?"

"Eighteen, sir, last month."

"So. What else did Wiggins tell you about me?"

Young Martin swallowed hard. "He says you like to do it rough sometimes. Says you sometimes like to knock your boys around."

Holmes pursed his lips. "And does that excite you, Jack Martin? A frail young thing like you?"

"I may be small, sir, but I'm stout. Believe me, anything you might care to give out I'm tough enough to handle." There was a strange tone of defiance in his voice, and a note of desperate desire.

"Really, Jack Martin?" Holmes continued to caress the youth's face with his cane. "And what experience could a lad like yourself have had in such matters?"

Martin opened his mouth, then twisted it shut with an expression of pain. He shut his eyes. "Me old man, sir. Not a bad man, but a drinker. He beats me, sir. And sometimes he makes me…"

I shook my head at the shame of it. Such tales are all too common among the wretched masses of London, where poverty and twisted passion go hand in hand. Certainly the youth had been corrupted against his will, but he would never redeem himself by seeking the favours of gentlemen for money.

"I understand," said Holmes. He lowered his cane and began to circle the youth like a cat traipsing around a canary. "Well then, let me see what you have to offer, Jack Martin. Take off your clothes. Warm yourself by the fire."

As the ragged clothes were thrown together in a pile on the rug, more than once I had to suppress a gasp of astonishment. Concealed beneath the layers of patched rags was a physique that might have modelled for Praxiteles. His arms were superbly shaped, his shoulders broad, his torso hard and sleek as if carved from marble. His legs were stout with muscle, surmounted by the sumptuous twin curves of buttocks that glimmered in the firelight like pale alabaster. I am no stranger to naked youth, having served in India with the cream of Her Majesty's manhood, but I had never seen the like of Jack Martin. His beauty was extraordinary.

If Holmes was impressed he concealed it well. Indeed, he seemed almost scornful as he slowly circled the young man, wearing a fixed expression of disdain. Jack Martin seemed to wither under his gaze, shifting nervously from foot to foot and shivering despite the hot breath of the fire on his naked flesh.

At length Holmes sat in a plush padded chair close by the fire and lit his pipe. He sat wreathed in smoke, his head thrown back, his narrow eyes focused on the nude youth. I did not notice when he laid his pipe aside, but all in an instant his trousers were open and springing up from his lap was what remains to this day the hardest, thickest, longest shaft of manhood I have ever gazed upon. I must confess I had seen it before, and was no stranger to its every sinuous curve and vein; but those experiences were already far in the past, and Holmes and I had not dallied with one another since the earliest days of our friendship. I, of course, had married, while Holmes had pursued his own satisfactions.

Holmes sat smugly in the chair, wafting the monstrous thing in the air like a bone to tempt a cur. With no further encouragement Jack Martin began to stumble toward him in a kind of daze.

"No," Holmes said sharply. "On your hands and knees, like the dog you are."

Without protest the young man obeyed, crawling between Holmes's legs. For the next quarter hour I watched as the youth rendered passionate, shameless adoration to the sturdy pole of flesh, licking it, kissing it, desperately attempting to swallow it whole and for the most part failing, gagging it up and spewing great masses of saliva into Holmes's lap, but never tiring or drawing away from the task. For his part, Holmes used his sex as both a cudgel and a reward, slapping the young man's cheeks with it, withholding it and forcing him to kiss the great drooping mass of his scrotum instead, finally offering it to the lad to suck and then cruelly jabbing it full-length into his convulsing throat.

I had never witnessed anything to match the young's man's devotion, except for a singular incident in India, when a dozen soldiers had crowded into a smoky den to enjoy the favours of a Bengali courtesan. The young woman had gorged herself on man after man, working herself into a frenzy of sexual self-abasement that was almost frightening. So Jack Martin abased his perfect body before Sherlock Holmes, worshipping the man's tremendous sex with a blasphemous communion.

At length Holmes stood, pushing Jack so roughly from his lap that the youth was sent tumbling against the floor. Instead of protesting he gazed up at Holmes with a doglike expression of hurt and an eagerness to please that was embarrassing. His mouth and cheeks were shiny with saliva, and great glossy masses of the stuff coated the upright sex of his tormentor. Young Jack rolled onto his hand and knees, narrowed his eyes, and opened his mouth preposterously wide, as if by providing a hole large enough he could induce the great shaft to jam itself into his throat.

But Holmes had finished with the lad's mouth. He stepped to a nearby escritoire and swept it clean, scattering pens and paper across the rug. Grabbing a fistful of hair he pulled young Martin to his feet and flung him over the flat table top, commanding him to spread his legs and grip the far edge with his fingertips. The position forced the youth onto tiptoes and constrained his own stout erection to poke uselessly against the underside of the table. But he seemed positively to revel in the discomfort, writhing against the hard wood and gyrating his buttocks in lewd invitation. His nude, sweat-covered flesh glistened in the firelight as Holmes stepped into position behind him. Holmes snapped his hips forward. Martin gave a gasp and a whimper. His body stiffened, forcing each supple muscle into stark relief. The tendons of his neck and throat were drawn taut as he helplessly thrashed his head against the table.

He moaned in a great extremity of agonized submission. Then, above his keening wail, I distinctly heard the voice of Holmes muttering my name! For a sweet instant I thought that he was invoking me in the throes of passion, recalling those halcyon days long ago when we had taken such a fancy to one another, imagining my presence even as he plunged himself to the hilt into young Jack Martin.

It was with some disappointment and even greater bafflement that I realized he was summoning me not in spirit but in the flesh. Even as he buggered the panting youth he gazed toward the closet door and called me forth. "For heaven's sake, Watson, come out of there! Join me!"

It was useless to continue hiding. I rose from the keyhole and stepped into the room, much to the shock of Jack Martin. The youth stared at me in dismay and struggled to rise from the table, but Holmes held him effortlessly in place, skewered on the thick pole of his sex.

"But, Holmes, how did you know?"

"My good Watson, there is a handsome mouth waiting for you to fuck it, and you ask a ludicrous question! Very well: while it is true that Mrs. Hudson might have stoked the fire in my absence, there is only one man I know, unless you have changed your tobacconist, whose cigarettes are marked Bradley, Oxford Street. There is a stub in clear sight in the ashtray, and its unmistakable odour hung fresh in the air when I entered the room."

"Then you knew I was here all along."

"Of course. Now hurry, please. If I recall, your fuse is short. If you plant yourself in this handsome lad's sweet mouth in the next half minute, I believe we can pull off the feat of filling him up at both ends simultaneously. Go on, he's a paid whore. There's no need to let one of his openings go to waste."

Whatever objections I might have made were lost in the tide of desire that welled up in my loins. I had never in my life looked upon the naked body of a more desirable youth, and certainly not a youth in such a desirable predicament, impaled on the hard-driving horn of Holmes's gargantuan sex. As I stepped toward Jack, taking down my pants, his face went slack with hunger and he opened his mouth wide. I daresay my own shaft is not as long as Holmes's, but it is very nearly as thick, and certainly large enough to stretch the lips of Jack Martin and reach deep into his throat.

I was already in a state of high excitement. Holmes, of course, had been ravishing the youth for over half an hour. In minutes we were both near to climax. When I saw Holmes reach under the table to grasp Martin's neglected cock, I knew the time had come. I planted myself deep in the lad's throat. Holmes drove into his bowels. Young Martin began to buck wildly on the table and gave a scream of ecstasy that tingled up and down the length of my throbbing shaft.

The act was completed. After a long, breathless moment Holmes and I pulled free at the same instant. I managed to pull up my trousers, then staggered to the nearest chair.

Jack Martin seemed in a great hurry to leave. Blushing bright red from head to toe, he sprang up from the table and almost fell from dizziness. His shaft, still erect, bounced in the air and dribbled a steady flow of semen onto the rug. Nude and ravished, he was the very picture of beauty laid waste. His hair hung in sweaty tendrils, and his face wore an expression of utter wretchedness, as if the taste I had left in his mouth disagreed with him. As he bent over to reach for his clothing a great mass of Holmes's semen erupted from his fundament and trickled down the insides of his legs. He groaned in shame.

To my dismay, Holmes reached for his cane and deftly pushed the pile of rags out of the young man's reach. Martin clenched his fists in frustration and began to weep.

"Holmes! Must you continue to torment the lad? Haven't you humiliated him enough? Pay him and let him go in peace."

"Pay him? My good Watson, I have no intention of paying him, for then he would collect his wages twice."

"Whatever do you mean?"

"I mean, Watson, that this young man was dispatched here by his employer, with the intention first of seducing me, and then of murdering me."

I opened my mouth in astonishment, but one glance at Martin assured me there was something to the accusation. The naked youth stood in a posture of abject guilt, with his eyes downcast and his shoulders hunched. He took a deep shuddering breath. "It's true, sir, every word. I told him you'd find me out. I told him I'd be no good, but he said I was the only one you wouldn't be able to resist. Oh please, sir, forgive me. Forgive me!"

Holmes scowled in disgust. I could see it gave him no pleasure to have deduced the truth.

"But, Holmes, how did you find the lad out? Who sent him on such a mission?"

"I have been expecting an attempt on my life for some days, Watson. Recent investigations have once again brought me dangerously near to the very heart of evil in this city. I have once more embarrassed the schemes of the Napoleon of crime, and he would have me pay for it."

"Moriarty!" I gasped.

"The very one. He knows of my weakness for young men. He shares it. When I noticed this especially alluring specimen following me today I was immediately suspicious, particularly as I have seen him before in the vicinity of one of Moriarty's many dens of vice. Oh, not dressed as a ragamuffin, but in a reputable suit and tie. The atrocious accent he has affected all afternoon is just as false as his poverty. Jack Martin is a professional and very well-paid whore, Watson, of the sort who prey on the rich and powerful. He pretends to be an innocent victim, but in fact he is a corrupt and very beautiful blackmailer. Am I not right, Jack Martin?"

"Please, sir, I'd never have fallen into such a life if it hadn't been for *him*."

"He refers, Watson, to his foul master. When he spoke of the 'old man' who violates and abuses him, he spoke the truth, but he did not mean his father. Look here, Watson, on the underside of his right foot."

Holmes seized the young man's ankle and twisted it toward me. Martin clung to the shelf of the mantel to keep from falling.

"What do you make of it, Watson?"

I looked upon a jagged, irregular discoloration on the sole of the lad's foot. "A strange birthmark," I suggested, "or a scar."

"No. A brand, placed there by Moriarty himself. Look closely: it is the letter *M*, disguised to appear as a natural aberration, yet unmistakably the initial of the master of crime. Thus does Moriarty brand those wretched young men and women whom he claims as his personal chattel."

Holmes released his grip. "I was able to get a glimpse of the mark by leaning forward in my chair while young Martin was so hungrily devouring me on his hands and knees. But I had already made up my mind about his duplicity when he claimed to have been recommended to me by Wiggins of the Baker Street Irregulars. Wiggins may be abysmally poor and untutored, but his integrity is beyond dispute. Never would he betray my confidence, not even to you, Watson."

At length the whole truth was extracted from the youth, who told us between hysterical sobbing that he had been instructed to stay with Holmes through the night and to murder him in his sleep. He was to do this by locating the hypodermic that Holmes used for his cocaine injections and then to administer an overdose, or else inject a syringe full of air. Either method would have sufficed to kill Holmes in an embarrassing manner that could have been ascribed to suicide or accident. Even if he had been found out, Martin could still have alleged that Holmes seduced him and thus threatened a scandal that would have eclipsed the murderous truth.

"But everything went wrong," he sobbed. "I was to ask for cocaine before you took me, so I'd know where it was. And when Dr. Watson appeared, I knew I hadn't a chance. But I couldn't have gone through with it. Please believe me, sir."

Holmes made no answer, but released a deep sigh as he gazed a final time upon the young man's naked perfection. He allowed Martin to dress and then to leave, giving him a sound blow across the buttocks with his cane before he slammed the door.

"Perhaps you should have called for the police," I suggested.

"In an affair such as this? Impossible, dear Watson. Have you not been following the case of the most unfortunate Mr. Wilde? To be threatened with murder is nothing in the public's eye as compared to exhibiting a taste for beautiful young men. No, Moriarty is quite clever. He sends an assassin I can prove nothing against, whose only weapon is his body and whom I could have had arrested only at the risk of my own reputation. My only defence is to be constantly on guard."

"It is a terrible world we live in, Holmes."

"It is, indeed." He flashed a grim smile. "But there is some satisfaction in having so thoroughly pillaged Moriarty's favourite plaything at no charge—and to have done the honours with you, dear Watson, as my witness and my colleague."

With that he bent down to give me a chaste kiss upon the lips, for old time's sake.

PRIVATE DANCE IN RIO
JAY STARRE

Joao hiked quickly up the steep stairway that served as a street in the chaotic jumble of buildings that was home to tens of thousands of Rio residents. This particular favela was not really all that far from the glitzy tourist district where he usually worked at a gay club that catered to wealthier gays and tourists. Not far, but definitely a different world.

It was late in the afternoon and the hottest part of the day, but fortunately the breeze off the ocean below mitigated the heat. Regardless, he was dripping sweat when he reached his destination. The building was on his left amongst a ramshackle group of other homes. The plaster walls were painted in lively murals, though, which were actually quite good. Amidst the squalor of the slum there were numerous bright spots like that where the residents took some pride in their surroundings.

Just outside the doorway a pair of very young gang members squatted on wooden crates. Joao thought they looked even younger than him, and he was only twenty. One of them displayed a handgun in a holster draped across his chest. The other no doubt had a similar weapon hidden somewhere on his body. They both wore skimpy tank tops and sweatpants and eyed Joao with a mixture of suspicion and interest.

"Are you Joao? The stripper?"

"Sim," he replied.

"Pietro is waiting. Go inside."

"Obrigado."

The one with the holster cupped his crotch and squeezed it, then winked at him as he passed by. The pair snickered behind his back and Joao wondered if they would have dared it if their boss was watching. After all, he was here at their leader's specific request.

He climbed another few stairs and pushed open the door. Inside, the main room was surprisingly spacious with two doorways on either side that led to other rooms. It was also surprisingly tidy, although the furniture was plain and well-used. Someone cleaned up for the gang, obviously, but no women were in sight, girlfriends or wives.

"Boa tarde, Joao. This is my friend Alexio. He will watch, and if he likes what he sees as much as I have told him he will, he will join in."

Pietro stood behind a rather large wooden table as he welcomed Joao to his den, a toothy smile on his dark face. Alexio, his friend, sat on one of the couches against the wall. Both men were huge. They boldly displayed packed muscle with skimpy tank tops, like the guards outside.

Joao hadn't been completely certain what would be required of him during the visit, until now. There could only be one meaning to the phrase "join in."

Before he could think of anything to say, Pietro pointed to two stacks of Brazilian reais on the otherwise bare table. "This one is yours. And this one will be yours if you especially please us." His big grin only got wider.

That smile did little to fool Joao; the gang leader's reputation was no different than those of any of the other gang bosses in the favela. Dangerous. Unforgiving of anyone who didn't agree with them. Even vicious. And the blond on the couch was just as bad. Joao recognized him as a rival gang leader he had seen around town. He did wonder what the two were doing together—conspiring about some kind of criminal activity, no doubt.

But the money on the table did look good.

And he was here. Nothing to do but go along now. He thanked the grinning leader with his usual politeness. *"Obrigado. Multi obrigado."* Then he looked around the room and asked where he should begin. *"Onde?"*

"Here. Now. Go ahead and give us a show like the one last night."

The blond on the couch leaned over and pressed Play on the small CD player on the stand beside him. Music blared out, a bright and energetic mix that the local capoeira martial artists danced and gyrated to on the streets and alleys of the South American metropolis.

It suited his purposes well enough and he began what he'd come for, right there in the center of the room with Pietro standing behind the table and his buddy lounging on the couch.

Even in that rather uncomfortable situation, Joao immediately became calm and collected as he began to dance. He loved to strip and believed it was the easiest money he ever made when he was actually paid to do it.

It was the something more that he wasn't always keen to provide.

He smiled at both men, genuinely enough since he was already enjoying what he was doing. He wore a deep purple T-shirt that fit his athletic torso well and showed off his toned arms. That would be the first item of clothing to go, and he began to slowly raise it to reveal his rippled abs, his smooth tanned skin, and finally the swell of his hairless chest. Off it came to be tossed aside on the threadbare carpet beneath his feet.

He swayed rhythmically to the beat of drums and the chorus of chanting singers in the background, moving around the room to gyrate in front of the seated guest and then toward the table and the standing gang boss.

His expressive hands began their work. He used them to stroke his own smooth torso and toned arms, as well as his hips and thighs. At first it was more sensual than sexual, but quickly descended into bolder actions as he dropped a hand to his crotch and squeezed, just like the young guard had done outside the door, then cupped his own round ass cheeks and squeezed them too.

He wore a pair of knee-length denim shorts that left little to the imagination, revealing the bulge in his crotch and swell of his ass cheeks. His fingers found the metal buttons and began to undo them with tantalizing slowness. One, two, three, four, and out popped his cock.

A substantial tube of some length, it was already swollen and beginning to rear upward. With a sudden swiftness, he shoved down his shorts and kicked them off. They landed in Alexio's lap.

The blond on the couch smiled for the first time. And to Joao's surprise, he lifted the shorts to his face and pressed the crotch to his nose.

Pietro let out a guffaw and even Joao giggled as he continued to sway and swagger to the beat of the music, now naked other than his electric-green sneakers. He had decided not to wear underwear for the assignation.

A broad window above the couch allowed in brilliant sunlight. And on the opposite wall, a pair of big mirrors reflected the light back at him. His every move was illuminated in a shimmering glow. He had a short haircut and the slightly curly cap was bleached platinum blond, contrasting sharply with his soft brown eyes and tanned complexion. His skin was naturally smooth, but he shaved off any hair around his crotch and pits so that he was totally hairless. He was fairly light-skinned due to his Portuguese-English ancestry, but he spent hours tanning at the beach to create a golden-brown hue all over—except for one area. He wore a skimpy swimsuit on the beach, and consequently his crotch and ass were starkly pale in contrast to the honey-brown of the rest of his body.

This was deliberate. His lush ivory-white bottom was outlined and accentuated by that tan. As he wriggled the sexy globes in a provocative grind, there was no missing the sweet plumpness of that ass. He was rather short at only five-eight and athletically slender, except for his muscular legs from soccer playing in his spare time, and that jutting ass.

It was certainly one of his best assets, and he used it now to offer up an increasingly provocative show for his clients. He pranced and paraded around the room, first halting in front of the seated Alexio to wriggle and wink. Then he danced his way over to Pietro, who leaned on the table with his large hands planted firmly and burly arms spread wide. Joao rocked and thrust with his bare crotch before turning around and offering a tempting view of his protruding ass.

His cock had grown stiffer and stiffer and now reared up from his crotch in bright-pink glory. He always got hard when he stripped and danced, which was one of his claims to fame. And all that naked gyrating in front of the gang leaders, close enough to touch and dangerous as hell, had turned him on even more than usual.

He knew what he was doing, and it was dangerous in itself. The teasing and testing sometimes had consequences. That was why he was there. It was only the previous night that Pietro had ventured down to the gay club where Joao had been dancing. The blond stripper spotted the hulk of a gang leader and purposely approached his table to offer up a similarly provocative dance.

A note had been passed to him. He was to attend Pietro in the favela the next day at three in the afternoon. Now here he was, strutting his stuff in private and unable to prevent himself from offering up his best show!

Facing Pietro again, Joao pumped the air with his stiff cock, teasing a dribble of pre-cum from the head, then he turned back around and humped the air with his round amber ass. He spread his cheeks with both hands to offer up his client a good view of his puckered pink asshole. Then he went all out and bent farther over to pout his hole, displaying a tempting treat for the burly black gang leader.

Pietro pounced.

It happened so swiftly, Joao emitted a little shriek as he found himself lifted in the air by a pair of gigantic arms and then plopped down roughly on the wooden table top. It was completely bare other than the two piles of reais and apparently very sturdy, as it didn't seem to budge when he landed on his hands and knees atop it.

He turned to look in the mirrors and saw Pietro behind him in the act of shoving down his fancy sweatpants and underwear to reveal a jutting monster of a cock. Dark purple, it reared up from his crotch in a wicked curve. The head was a bulbous knob.

Joao's eyes were huge as he contemplated the length and girth of the gigantic tool, but his eyes strayed as he spotted a completely naked Alexio in the mirror beside them. The rival gang leader had jumped up from the couch and kicked off his own baggy pants while discarding his tank top at the same time. Apparently he had found a bottle of lubricant because he was already in the act of squirting a big stream of the clear goo all over that big black cock.

In the mirror, the contrast between the three of them was quite striking. On his hands and knees on the table top, Joao was much smaller. His skin was golden-brown, except for the gleaming white of his ass and crotch, and his hair a brilliant platinum cap. The other two were both giants and powerfully built. Part of the favela gang culture revolved around growing as immense as possible with hours and hours spent lifting weights. It was a dominance thing, Joao had heard.

They certainly looked like they could dominate him! Yet the two of them were also very different from each other. Pietro's skin was midnight black. His hair was buzzed short around his skull. He had attractive features in a big and bold manner, and grinned often. In contrast, Alexio seemed quite somber. Unlike Joao he was a natural blond, and even though he was as Brazilian as the others his family was originally from Germany. His skin was even paler than Joao's and he didn't take to the beach as often. He had a lot of freckles and a lot of colorful tattoos. They swirled up his arms and across his broad chest. There was even one that splashed across the side of his neck.

Both men had one obvious similarity—really, really big cocks, which they were about to use on him!

Now that Pietro's hard-on was shimmering with a coating of slippery goo, he didn't waste any time thinking about what to do with it. His large black hands seized Joao's hips to hold him in place. The table was low enough so that Joao's ass crack was at the perfect height for the tall gang leader to thrust forward and impale him.

The blunt head rammed past Joao's puckered sphincter. He let out a tremendous squeal, more because it was what he believed they expected and wanted out of him rather than from any real pain. His asshole was far too talented to offer up a fight when it was tested.

There was incredible pressure and a sharp pain that was hardly distinguishable from intense pleasure, but that passed almost immediately as he arched his back and spread his knees on the smooth table top to offer up an even more tempting target. He willed his ass rim to relax and expand, and it obeyed.

That was very fortunate because Pietro was really worked up. He held Joao in place with a viselike grip and pummeled his ass with a series of deeper and deeper gut punches. Alexio stood beside him gawking at the furious assault and pumping his own stiff cock.

Pietro pulled out with a slurp and laughed. He let go of Joao's hip with one hand to point at his rearing black cock and the spread crack of the stripper's ass.

"Look at his hole. Look at how I make it big and sloppy with my monster cock. Look at how he takes it, even though he whimpers like a little slut."

Joao could see his own ass and hole in the mirror, and it was definitely gaping after that powerful invasion. And, as Pietro had claimed, after his initial shriek he'd been whimpering with a mixture of helpless pain and pleasure.

Alexio nodded, his big green eyes unable to move away from the lube-leaking hole. He continued to pump his own cock and obviously wanted a turn. Pietro laughed again and then rammed his cock back up Joao's ass.

"You will have your turn. Our little slut will not get tired too quickly, I believe. He really wants it, I am sure. Don't you, slut? Tell us you want it."

"Por favor! Ohhhhhh! Obrigado! Ohhhhh! Multi obrigado," he shouted out. Please and thank you and thank you very much, which was certainly what they wished to hear.

Pietro pumped his monster cock in and out with ball-slapping ferocity while pointing at Joao's round ass as it jiggled and commenting on how much Alexio would like it when he got a chance.

Sooner than Joao expected, the gang leader decided he would give his pal a turn at his hole. He yanked the curved black tool out and stepped back. "Get in there, Alexio, before he comes to his senses and runs for it!"

He laughed loudly and winked at Joao in the mirror as he pulled his friend in to step up in line with his spread ass. Equally tall, he had no trouble aiming at the dripping hole with his massive meat. If anything the pink weapon was even bigger than the black one that had just gutted him. The head was tapered rather than blunt, but the shaft was thick and lined with veins. It seemed to pulse and quiver with a desperate need. Joao quailed inside as he imagined how hard the eager gang leader was going to fuck him!

Pietro squirted a stream of lube over the pink tool and over Joao's ass. Then, with another loud laugh, he shoved a pair of thick black fingers up the stripper's ass and twisted them around.

"Sweet and sloppy. Just what you need, Alexio. Fuck him now. Fuck him hard."

There was to be no question of who was in charge. He placed one big black hand on Alexio's beefy white ass and shoved him forward. The blond grabbed hold of Joao's ass cheeks and held them apart as he took aim and drove forward.

Already stretched open by Pietro's massive cock, Joao managed to take half in one slippery gulp. Alexio let out a big groan and then pulled back out.

"Deeper! He needs it so bad. Don't you?"

"Sim! Por favor!"

Alexio took aim again with his pink rammer and thrust with his big hips. This time Joao pushed backward at the same time and the giant meat was buried right to the balls.

Joao squeezed his anal muscles around the buried pole and wriggled. "*Sim! Sim. Aye, aye, ohhhhhh. Por favor!* More!"

In the mirror the stripper could see that the blond gang leader had turned beet red and he was panting so hard he looked and sounded like he might faint. Joao almost laughed, while Pietro did.

"Fuck his sweet ass! Fuck it good," he egged on his pal.

Alexio pulled out, took a deep breath, and slammed back in. In and out in a series of slow but gut-deep strokes, he fed the stripper all he had. Joao wriggled and heaved his round ass while Pietro encouraged them with nasty words and some slaps to both their naked asses.

The gang leader, though, was soon eager to get more hole himself. "Let me up on the table. Time to dance on my big black cock, Joao. Show us how talented you are."

The black stud crawled under Joao and lay on his back with the stripper straddling his lap. He grinned up into Joao's face and winked. "Sit on it," he ordered.

The blond stripper got up to squat on his feet over Pietro's lap and aimed the gang leader's huge cock between his spread thighs. From behind, Alexio added more lube to both cock and hole, stabbing into the gaping slot with two fingers before they were replaced with the bulbous head of Pietro's dark tool.

By this time, Joao's hole was wide open and he easily swallowed that giant head. Next he slowly dropped down to engulf the rest. Pietro's grin got wider and his eyes actually closed as he felt that steamy slot surround his entire cock.

The blond stripper proved himself now. As a dancer, he was agile and capable of great endurance. He rose and fell over that giant black bone with writhing glee, pounding his round white ass down over the prone gang leader's husky lap.

"Fuck him when he pulls off, Alexio," Pietro commanded with a nasty laugh.

Both Joao and Alexio understood. The blond gang leader had been standing between Pietro's legs at the foot of the table all the while and watching the stripper ride that giant cock, feeling his ass with his massive hands at the same time. Joao fucked himself deep, then when he lifted up his ass and Pietro's cock slid out, Alexio seized the opportunity presented by the suddenly empty hole. He rammed in with his own pink cock. When he pulled out, Joao sat back on Pietro's cock. They worked together in perfect rhythm, Joao rising off black cock, presenting his gooey hole, Alexio then slamming deep and pulling out, then Joao once more squatting down over Pietro's monster meat.

Joao's hole felt like it was on fire, and so stretched it seemed capable of practically anything. The test of that notion came suddenly. Alexio abruptly lost patience and thrust forward to stuff his cock inside Joao while Pietro's cock was still inside the hapless stripper. Joao squealed for the third time that night and toppled forward into Pietro's powerful arms. Laughing heartily, the black gang leader held the stripper in an implacable embrace as he and his pal fucked his hole simultaneously.

Nothing like that had ever happened to him. It was incredible. On his belly in the arms of the giant black gang leader, his knees spread wide, his asshole gaping and stuffed with two thrusting monster cocks, he could do nothing but groan and whimper and accept his lot. The stretching of his sphincter and the massaging of his prostate created an unbelievably intense pleasure. The searing heat of it seemed to emanate outward to envelop his entire body.

He almost believed he should be paying them for such an unbelievable fuck! Almost.

The sensation of another cock in that churning, snapping hole besides their own must have been as exciting for them as it was for Joao. He proved his powers of endurance by taking it all without a word of protest as they fucked themselves to orgasm in a shouting, pumping frenzy.

"*Sim!* Ohhhhh! I am coming!"

"*Sim!* Me too!"

Both laughing now between their exhausted pants, they lazily disengaged. Joao wondered if it was over. He hadn't shot his own load, but he guessed they wouldn't really care about that. He was wrong.

The grinning gang leader ordered Alexio to stand on the opposite side of the table while Joao was placed back on his hands and knees on top of it between them.

"You have earned your money. Here it is."

He shoved the twin piles of reais together under Joao's chest, then he placed his giant paw on the back of the blond stripper's neck and forced his face downward into the piled bills.

On his hands and knees and helpless between them, Pietro made him grovel in the combined pile of reais, forcing him to sniff them and lick them. At the same time he had Alexio reach between his spread thighs and start pumping his stiff cock. To top it off, the black gang leader forced three big fingers up Joao's stretched hole to pump and gore the tenderized aperture.

He was also ordered to shout out his appreciation for all that money.

"*Obrigado! Multi obrigado. Multi, multi obrigado.* Ohhhhh! I'm shooting!"

With one giant paw pumping his cock and another rough hand rooting around in his aching ass, his face buried in a pile of reais he'd just earned, he blew a geyser of cum all over the gang leader's table.

They let him go after that. As he limped away the sun set behind him while the ocean spread out below. He had earned quite a wad of cash for only a few hours' work. But what a workout it had been.

He couldn't complain. Anything for a real.

THE LAST GOOD-BYE
JEFFREY RICKER

Whenever I tell someone I'm a licensed clinical psychic sexual surrogate, there's no telling which part of my title they're going to fixate on. More often than not, it's the word "sexual" that gets their attention.

Then they think I'm a whore.

Getting righteously offended is exhausting after a while. Everyone seems to think all I do is give people the business, and nine times out of ten, it doesn't even come close to that. But they'll always latch on to that tenth time.

Nelson doesn't like that I freelance—that's his word for it, for the clients I take under care without his consultation. There are risks, he says, but for some clients the traditional counseling route is impossible. Either they don't have insurance or they can only afford sliding scale. Some are just plain embarrassed that they haven't been able to move on. Some need to apologize. That's where I can help.

It's not as if traditional counseling clients who come to me through the normal channels, with full insurance coverage, aren't without their risks either.

James, for example.

Sure, Nelson's been working with him for a month already and has given me all the particulars—relationship of ten years, boyfriend killed in a car accident, no warning. Does that mean he's completely without danger? Of course not.

His file says thirty-five, but this afternoon he looks more like mid-forties. Grief does that; no big secret there. I already know he's not sleeping even before I ask the question.

"Not very well lately," he says, his eyes aimed at the floor somewhere near my feet. He laces his fingers together in his lap. It's late afternoon on a Tuesday. It's my first consult with him, and the last session of the day. Usually, the first consult is low-pressure, minor contact, definitely no intimacy. James is a couple inches shorter than me, his reddish hair so light it's more blond, especially where it curls on his forearms. Freckles there too, and on his face. He looks like the sort of person who's used to having someone take care of him…or who's used to having someone to take care of.

So the first wave of empathy off him is not much of a surprise, but it's stronger than I was expecting. I try not to grip the arms of my chair, concentrating just on what he's saying, how his performance at work has been suffering, how he keeps having these thoughts of Mick—that was his boyfriend's name—and he can't seem to shut them out.

"Whenever I close my eyes or find my mind wandering, it wanders to him," James says. He shivers, almost imperceptibly, but then he rubs his hands along his arms as if there's a draft. "It's not just that I can't stop thinking about him, it's like he's actually *there*." He shakes his head. "I'm not explaining it right."

"Take your time," I say, even though we only have an hour scheduled for this session. Nelson wants me to work up to contacting Mick to see if that will help James achieve some resolution to these feelings and overcome his anxiety about those memories.

James stops rubbing his arms and sits instead with his hands pressed between his knees, hunched forward a little, still staring at the carpet. It's a bright afternoon, especially for early March, and when James leans back a little, the sunlight through the window splashes the side of his face with gold and he squints.

He's thinking, I can tell, looking for words, and that wave of empathy is still battering against me. James isn't looking at me now, so I do grip the armrests. He's getting lost in his thoughts as more time passes in silence.

"It's been six months since he died, is that right?" I ask. I already know it's correct. I'm just trying to get him to talk. "It's natural to think about a loved one frequently after they've died." He flinches—again, it's almost too small to be noticed—each time I say the word "died."

James shakes his head. "It's not like that. Even when I'm not thinking about him, he'll come to mind at the weirdest moments that have nothing to do with him. I won't even be thinking about him, and then suddenly it's like he's right there next to me." He gestures with his hands as if there's someone sitting next to him on the sofa. "And then I can't stop thinking about him, even if I try to distract myself. That's why work has been such a nightmare for me lately."

He gets out his phone and holds it up so I can see the screen. It's a picture of him and another man who must be Mick: tall, dark hair cropped short, an arm around James's shoulders. It's one of those self-photos, the kind you take with the phone held out in front of yourself. Mick is the one taking the picture, his arm extending forward and away into the corner of the frame. He looks like he's reaching out to someone who can't be seen.

"That's us," James says. "We were on vacation last year when we took this. Hawaii. I'd never been and he said he wanted to take me someplace special." For a moment a smile flits across James's face, and it's possible to see a bit of what he must be like when he's not depressed.

I hand the phone back. He keeps talking, and I try to nod at the right points and be ready to ask a question if he trails off again. The longer he speaks, though, the harder it is to concentrate on his words. The wave of empathy has become a pulsing behind my eyes, tempting me to rub the bridge of my nose, as if I have a sinus headache. For the moment, I'm able to resist the urge. The light from the window travels across his face slowly, shadows from the tree outside cutting diagonally across his features. I'm not accustomed to seeing auras—it's not part of my skill set—but there's a white halo building up around James now, making him hazy. I close my eyes for a second, but the aura persists.

He's stopped talking now. When I open my eyes, he's leaning forward, brow furrowed. "Are you okay?" he asks.

I nod—even that makes my head throb. "I'm really sorry about this, but I seem to have come down with a terrible headache all of a sudden." I glance at my watch, the hands on the dial blurring. "I realize we haven't gone the full hour, but do you think we could pick up again on Thursday? I'll block off extra time so we can talk a bit longer."

James nods and gets up, brushing his hands along the thighs of his khaki trousers. He leaves dark streaks on them; his hands have been sweating. "You sure you're going to be okay?"

Definitely used to having someone to take care of. I smile and nod. "I'm sure it's nothing. In the meantime, though, I'd like you to consider that maybe you haven't been able to stop thinking about Mick because you're still surrounded by reminders of him. So I'd like you to do a few things to reduce his presence around you."

James frowns. "Like what?"

"Well, for starters, change your phone's wallpaper image. I'm not saying delete it, but every time you look at it, you're seeing him. It's no wonder he's on your mind a lot. Look for other examples like this in your everyday life, and see how you feel when you encounter them. We'll talk more about that on Thursday."

"If you think it'll help," he says. Honestly, I'm not sure it will, but I don't want to leave him with nothing to do between now and our next meeting.

After he's gone, I close all the blinds and lie down on the sofa, pulling a cushion over my face and pressing hard. It helps a little, but when I move the cushion away, my vision's grayed out and my ears feel like they're stuffed with wax. This has *never* happened to me before. I lie there for half an hour before it finally begins to subside. When I sit up, I glance toward the door.

What the hell just happened?

❖

I mention it to Nelson when I follow up with him on Wednesday. After I explain what happened, it's like I can hear him frowning on the other end of the phone when he speaks.

"How long after the session did the headache subside?"

"Maybe half an hour, but I still felt off-kilter the rest of the evening." I'm sitting at my kitchen table while we talk. It's late morning, and I don't have any clients until after noon, so I can take my time. Honestly, I still feel a little wiped out, like I went for a long run uphill yesterday. My shoulders are sore, my legs aching.

Nelson's gone quiet. If I have to guess, he's stroking his beard. It's what he does when he's thinking about saying something I may not want to hear, which I can also guess because it's the only time I've ever noticed him at a loss for words.

"Spit it out, Nelson. What do I not want to hear?"

A sigh comes through the line. "I had a similar reaction during my first counseling session with James. Roberta"—that's his receptionist—

"said it sounded like migraine symptoms. Which I've never had before. Have you tried contacting the deceased?"

"Not yet. Honestly, I couldn't even see straight by the time James left. What makes you think contacting him will make a difference anyway?" Communicating with Mick could increase James's feelings of attachment.

"James has unresolved issues where this relationship is concerned—"

"You don't say."

"Hear me out," Nelson says, a little testily. I keep quiet. "It seems fairly straightforward. Mick died very suddenly and James was not able to say good-bye to him in any meaningful way. If you're able to contact the deceased, I think you may be able to mediate a resolution to these feelings of loss."

Any psychic worth his or her salt could have done that in an afternoon. Why do I need to be brought in? Not that I'm ungrateful for the referral, but it doesn't exactly fit my area of specialty.

"And?" I ask.

"The fact that Mick was James's first relationship with a man complicates matters."

"Really? At thirty-five?"

I hear a smile in his voice. "By which I mean long-term relationship. They *were* together for ten years. Unlike you, some people *do* commit."

"Hey."

"I'm sorry. Too far?" Even Nelson is not above giving me grief. I've met his wife on a couple occasions and cannot understand what she sees in him. I can only assume he must be spectacular in bed—though the idea strains credibility.

"Just tell me what you know about the headaches."

"Sadly, I haven't a clue." I can almost see him shaking his head as he says it. We're rarely in the same room anymore, but I've known him long enough that reading his moods is like second nature. I think that would be the case even without the psychic abilities, which only seem to work on the dead anyway. Nelson and I, we're like this sexless, bickering old married couple sometimes.

"Should I be worried?" I ask. "Did they happen to you every time you counseled him?"

He's silent a moment. "Yes, though the first was by far the worst."

"I wonder if anyone else around him gets these."

"That'll give you something else to ask him during your next session," he says. "And when is that, again?"

"Thursday."

❖

It turns out I don't have to wait that long. Late Wednesday afternoon, in the parking lot at the grocery store, someone calls my name when I'm headed to the car. I'm pushing a cart with two bags in it—the bags aren't that heavy, but for some reason I don't feel up to even that minor exertion.

I turn toward the voice. James is standing over by the entrance. He crosses the parking lot toward me and now I'm glad to have the cart, which I turn around and manage to keep in between us, though I try to position it without looking like that's what I'm doing.

If anything, James looks even worse than he did yesterday. Seeing him outside of the office is completely inappropriate, but I can't stop myself from asking, "Have you slept at all since yesterday?"

His laugh's hollow. "What gave it away?"

I don't smile. "James, this is serious. If you're sleep deprived—"

"I haven't slept a full night for six months," he says, his voice rising just enough that another shopper one row over slows down as she pushes her cart past. I catch her eye and she looks away. That first wave of empathy rolls over me, and there's a tug to it, as if it might pull me under. Already there's pressure building up behind my eyes.

"Six months?" I say, just to do something to fill the silence.

"Ever since he…" James trails off. He can't even utter the word.

"You need to say it sometime, James," I tell him, trying to be gentle, but still keeping the cart angled between us. He's starting to look hazy around the edges again. What Nelson experienced must not have been anything like this. He would have warned me.

James is easily three inches shorter than me, but still I feel—not threatened by him, but endangered, as if I need to keep my distance. I rub my temple.

"Say it," I repeat.

James sighs. "Ever since he died." I wouldn't be surprised if he bursts into tears, but he holds it together. I, on the other hand, want to curl into a ball and start rocking until this feeling goes away.

"You didn't follow me here, did you?" I ask.

He shakes his head, vigorously. Just watching him do that makes my own head start throbbing. "No, not at all. But..."

For a moment he doesn't say a word. "But?"

"I don't know *why* I came here. I just had this sudden compulsion to go to the store."

For a moment, I feel clarity. I pick up my bags and push the cart toward him. "Do me a favor. Put that away and then meet me at my office. I think it's time we contact your boyfriend."

❖

My office is in a small professional building off South Hampton, a place on the western edge of St. Louis with a few other businesses but mostly restaurants and houses. There's a park across the street to the west, and the windows in my office face that and the setting sun. I get in a few minutes before James arrives and angle the blinds so the sun's not shining right on me. My head's cleared, but I still don't feel quite all there.

I turn the lights on low and sit in my chair. It's an old leather recliner that I've had ever since I opened my practice. It creaks and squeaks and reminds me when I'm fidgeting. I've become remarkably adept at maintaining stillness over the years because of it.

Almost as soon as I close my eyes, there's a knock on the door.

"Come in."

I don't have to open my eyes to know that it's James. After the door opens, the wave surges into the room. It really *is* like a wave now, this cold tingling climbing up my legs. When I open my eyes, I expect to see water and seaweed around my feet.

"Are you okay?" he asks, frowning in concern. I must look awful if he's surfacing enough from his own grief to take notice of my condition. I shake my head.

"To be honest, I've been having headaches ever since our first consult. Has anyone else around you had this experience since Mick died?"

James settles onto the sofa. His eyebrows dip in concentration. "Not that I can think of. Is it bad?"

"They're making it fairly difficult to concentrate," I say. I indicate the corner of the sofa closest to me. "I'll need you to sit over here while I try to contact Mick."

He slides over. "Do you need anything?" he asks. "A glass of water?"

I smile. "Don't worry about me. I'm here to help you, not the other way around. Trust me, I'll be fine."

Even as I say that, I'm not sure it's true. Still, I need to believe it. "Did you bring something of his?"

James reaches into his jacket and pulls out a red Cardinals baseball cap. "He loved the Cards. We had season tickets even though he knew I wasn't a fan. I just liked going and sitting in the sun. It was enough to know that he was having fun."

Definitely a nurturer. Chalk one up to my intuition.

I place the hat in my lap, settling my hands over it. We leave a trace on things, a sort of background hum that grows stronger the more of an attachment to the object in question. Mick wore the ball cap a lot. It emits not so much a hum as a note, like hitting a tuning fork. It travels up my arms and tingles along the back of my neck, spreading into my scalp, and I'm sure my hair must be standing on end by now. Also, my headache is going away. It's like the vibration from Mick's hat is canceling out the pain.

I send the note out wider, so that the hum is not just in me or the hat in my lap, but extends beyond the room and out into the street, into the sky. I'm never sure how far I can amplify it, but it's almost always enough, like a homing signal. Sure enough, I can feel the same note coming toward me until it's in the building, in the room, and finally in me, the two notes merging in harmony.

When I open my eyes, it's me seeing, and yet not me. It takes Mick a few moments to settle into my body, to remember how to move physically. I look down at the hat in my lap, pick it up, and put it on. It's a little tight. I adjust it and try it on again. Better. When I look up, James is staring at me, his mouth hanging open a little. The white halo that's been enveloping him has faded. Does he see the change already, that I'm not the person I was a few moments earlier?

"Hey, Sparky," I say. It's always a shock for the client when the voice comes out of my mouth, and James is no different. He leans forward.

"Mick?" He's almost whispering. "You're really in there?"

I nod, or rather, Mick nods. "Yeah," he says, uncertain. He's staring down at my hands, and for a moment there's that disconcerting feeling of seeing myself through my own eyes and from someone else's perspective at the same time. It gets easier after a while. It always does. I allow myself to recede a little into the background of my own mind.

More confidently, Mick says, "Yeah, I guess I really am."

A lot of what happens after the initial contact usually doesn't require guidance from me. I never know if this is real or simply my own projection, but I visualize myself in a white room. Well, not a room exactly. There are no walls, hardly a floor even, just a flat space for my feet to stand on, everything featureless and blank beyond that. Somewhere in front of me, typically, are my client and the departed, talking, working out whatever it is they need to resolve. For them, of course, they're still in my office. If things move into more intimate directions, I turn away and let them have their privacy. I'm always aware of what's going on, that it's happening with my own body, keeping just enough of a connection to intervene if things go in an uncertain or unsafe direction.

Something's different this time. I'm still in the white room, and I can see Mick, but James is not there. I can still hear him talking, telling Mick how much he's missed him, but it's as if I'm hearing him from another room. I'm still responding—or rather, Mick is responding through me—but the avatar of Mick standing in front of me is not parroting the words, like they usually do.

Instead, he's staring right at me.

"So who are you?" he asks. In the office, I can hear him still keeping up his side of the conversation with James, who is crying now.

The more comfortable Mick gets, the more clearly I can see him. The photo on James's phone hardly does him justice. He was handsome, a little older than James, a little taller than me. In my office he flexes my legs, getting used to their shorter length, getting used to having legs at all. He mimics the gesture here in the white room as well.

"I'm James's psychic surrogate," I say. I leave out the sex part. I'm not about to have that argument with someone in my own head.

"Don't worry, I won't argue," Mick says. That's another first.

They've rarely acknowledged my presence, and then only obliquely, asking their loved one whose body they're in for the time being. But this one's not just talking to me; he's reading my mind.

Which makes me shiver—not in my real body. Mick's made himself at home there, but in the white room I find myself suddenly cold. What if he decides not to leave?

"Whoa, who said anything about setting up permanent residence?"

Mick holds up his hands, and something clicks for me.

"You're psychic too, aren't you?" I ask.

"Ding ding ding! It's like you read my mind." Mick smiles, and I can really see what James found attractive in this guy, cheesy jokes notwithstanding. "Actually, I'm—uh, I *was*—more telepathic than psychic. I couldn't predict the future or communicate with the spirit world, but I could tell what a lot of people were thinking." His grin gets a little wicked. "Like that you think I'm attractive."

In the best professional tone I can muster, I say, "Let's stay on the matter at hand. Namely, that your partner is having issues with moving on after your death."

"I know." Mick's smile fades and he looks off to the side, away from me. I can hear James more clearly now, and if I concentrate I can draw my attention back to my office. James is sobbing now, his hands lying uselessly in his lap.

"Babe," Mick says gently, "why are you doing this?"

"I just miss you so much," James says. "I never got to say good-bye."

In the white room, Mick says to me, "I don't know if I can do this."

"But you have to." It hits me then; that he really *does* have to. "He's tethering you to the world, isn't he?"

Mick nods. "I know there's someplace I have to go, but he's missing me so hard, it's like—it's like I'm a balloon that can't rise any higher until he lets go of the string."

James is going on; I should be listening to him, but instead I remain focused inward. Mick won't look at me now.

"Is this doing him *any* good?" he asks.

"Dr. Sampson felt direct contact was necessary before James could reach closure on your relationship."

"Yeah, and what about you?"

I frown. "What do I think, you mean?"

"No. Why do you do this?"

"It's my job. I help people."

"Who helps you?"

I shake my head. "I don't need help."

"Of course you don't."

"Hon, I know you miss me," Mick's saying to James, "but you've got to move on."

I narrow my eyes, scrutinizing Mick even as I hear James still weeping and Mick trying to soothe him.

"James never knew you were telepathic, did he?"

He shakes his head. "He never realized. I knew every one of his moods, his fears. The things he liked. The things he wanted."

"From you."

"From me, for me." Mick laughs a little, remembering a moment. An image flashes through my head, Christmas in front of a tree, Mick opening a gift and James looking on intently, as if the gift for Mick is just an excuse for James to see the look of surprise on Mick's face when he opens it. I know—Mick knows—it's the baseball cap and the envelope with the Cardinals season tickets. He also knows there's a Cards jersey still under the tree.

It was a perfect gift, and Mick had known it even before Christmas Day arrived.

"You *did* love him, didn't you?" I ask.

His expression changes like clouds blown by the wind. "He was my life," he says. "But I can't be his life anymore, not like this."

"He knows that, though," I say. "That's why he's come here."

Mick's face goes blank, and about the same time, I notice he's gone quiet. I've gone quiet. Something about the blankness of his face is more chilling than his reading my mind earlier.

"James," Mick says, "let me see what's in your pocket."

Before James reaches into his pocket, Mick lets me glimpse a fragment of an image: a box in James's hand, small and velvet. From days earlier, when James had taken it from a drawer in his bedroom. Their bedroom.

Nelson's going to have a field day with this.

"I know it's silly," James says, trying to laugh a little, but the laugh catches in his throat and he chokes a bit. Mick leans over and pats James on the back. James leans into him, sobbing as hard as before.

"I know I can't really give it to you," James says when he finally regains a little control of himself. "I just wanted you to know it's how I felt—feel. Still, I mean."

"You think I didn't always know that? But, Sparky, this is not good for you," Mick says. "You're scaring me."

James nods. "I know. I'm sorry."

In the white room, Mick stares at me, arms crossed. "So tell me about what *you* haven't moved on from."

I shake my head. "This isn't about me."

"I get the feeling it's never about you, is it? At least, not about how you are now. What about how you were then?"

The image surfaces almost at once: me, twelve years old, in the basement of my best friend Alex's house. His parents are away for the weekend. His older sister, who's supposed to be looking after him, has snuck out with her boyfriend—well, not really snuck out so much as walked out after warning us not to burn down the place while she's gone. We're playing video games on the Atari hooked up to the TV in the rec room. Even though the basement's been finished, the house is old and it smells of damp and dirt down there.

I don't remember who started the fight—one of us must have accused the other of cheating, or at least playing dirty—but pretty soon we drop the joysticks and are wrestling on the floor. This has happened before, and each time it stops when one of us holds the other down until he says uncle. This time he wins. I'm practically hyperventilating and he's got his knees pinning down my arms, and that's when he leans forward and kisses me. My little twelve-year-old, hormone-riddled mind practically short-circuits while at the same time I realize that this is what I've wanted all along.

And that's when I see Alex's grandmother, storming down the basement stairs with a broom in her hands as she screams at me to get my perverted hands off her grandson. Alex's grandmother has been dead for two years by that point.

I scream, flip him off me, and scramble into the corner as far away from her as possible. She follows and swings the broom at me, though it passes through me and all I feel is a faint chilly breeze.

By the time she vanishes, I've wet my pants and Alex is standing over me, afraid that I've gone crazy. He lends me clean clothes to wear, I go home early, and we never speak of what's happened.

We never touch each other like that again, either.

But I start to see more and more ghosts, and it's not long before I realize that I can let them enter me, live through me, even just for a short while.

I shake my head, dispelling the memory, and glare at Mick in the white room.

"There's more to it than that," I say. "And none of that changes the fact that I *do* like my job."

Mick frowns. "I never said you didn't."

"And I don't need your pity either."

To cut off any further discussion, I look away and focus my attention on the office. Mick has me sitting next to James on the sofa. James has stopped crying and wipes the back of his hand across his eyes.

"I feel like an idiot," James says.

"There's nothing to feel bad about here, Sparky," Mick says, and kisses him.

Sometime during that kiss I can feel something shift, and whatever's been holding Mick here loosens and comes unraveled. James puts a hand on Mick's chest—well, my chest, really—and pushes just enough that their lips part.

"This isn't really you, though," he says.

Mick smiles. "Close your eyes and tell me that again."

Mick kisses him again, and this time James reacts as I would have expected someone in his position to do: he latches on to Mick, on to me, like a drowning man. I can hear his heartbeat quickening. His hands are in my hair and it doesn't even matter to him at this point that it's sandy and curly and not Mick's straight, brown crew cut. As far as he's concerned, I'm his dearly departed.

This is the point where departing is what I normally do. I step back to give them a respectful distance. Apart from making sure that adequate safety precautions are taken and that no boundaries are crossed beyond those already agreed to, I'm not in this.

Except that I can't seem to get out of it. In the white room, I look down and see my hand in Mick's. I give a tug, but he's got a firm grip.

"You can let me go," I say.

A surprising thing happens then: Mick—the Mick in my head, the one I'm standing next to in the white room—pulls me forward and kisses me.

Normally I don't have to concentrate, but it takes a considerable effort to not break contact—with Mick or with James, who now has one hand on my ass and is tugging at my belt with the other.

"You don't have to do this," I say to Mick when he lets me come up for air. He's got his hand down my pants, James has his hand down my pants in my office, and my grasp on events is rapidly slipping away.

"Then just let go," Mick whispers in my ear before he tugs my pants down and kneels in front of me. At the same time, in my office he's pushed James onto his back on the sofa and has tugged James's trousers off over his shoes. He makes quick work of the rest of James's clothes before peeling off mine and pressing himself full against James, grinding our hard-on into his.

This is not the way things are supposed to go at all.

It's just after James comes that Mick slips away. I'm not sure if I came twice or just once. The white room is gone; it faded when I closed my eyes while I was straddling Mick. When I open my eyes again, it's just me and James in my office. He's halfway off the sofa, bent forward over the cushions. I'm on my knees behind him. I take my T-shirt and wipe off his back. He rolls over and sits on the floor with his back against the sofa. I sit back on my haunches, feeling suddenly more naked than I have in a long time.

"He's gone, isn't he?" James asks, his voice low. He's searching my face for any sign of Mick's presence. I nod.

"I feel like I have to apologize," I say, gathering up my clothes. "This is so far outside of accepted protocol, you have no idea."

"Somehow I think that has more to do with Mick than either of us. He liked giving 'acceptable' a swift kick whenever he could."

James smiles, but for the moment he doesn't move to get up or pick up his own clothes. There's no denying how handsome he is, the dusting of red hair on his chest and belly catching the fading sunlight. More than that, though, he looks relaxed, more relaxed than I've seen him up to that point.

Eventually he does get up and start putting on his clothes. We say nothing as we dress—me, quickly; him, casually, as if he's in no great hurry. He seems to wait as long as possible to put his underwear and jeans back on.

"Thank you," he says at the door. He takes my hand and shakes it, then thinks better of it, apparently, and pulls me in for a kiss.

"I suppose that's outside of protocol too, huh?"

To my surprise, I feel heat spread across my face. It must be a pretty obvious blush because he smiles right away.

"You could say that, yeah," I reply.

"How far out of bounds is it to go on a date with a former patient?"

"I prefer the term 'client,' and it's so far out of bounds it's in the next state."

He rests a hand on my arm. "How about if I give you a call a month from now, then?"

I frown. "You realize my work involves potential intimacy with a number of people over the course of treatment, right?"

He grins again. "I think I have a pretty good idea of that, yeah. Does that prevent you from going out to dinner and maybe a movie?" I shake my head. "Okay then. I'll call you."

I stand staring at the office door long after it's closed and he's gone. If nothing else, I have something new to discuss with Nelson tomorrow.

PENTHOUSE
JEFF MANN

It takes three milky-green absinthe frappés to lend Jamie Doolan sufficient courage to enter the Hotel Royale. Flushed, he makes his way across the vast lobby, past bouquets of stargazer lilies arranged atop marble tables. He's doing his best to look confident, as if he belongs here. Beneath his backpack, his black T-shirt sticks to his skin.

Inhaling deep breaths of the air-conditioned cool—more than welcome after Bourbon Street's humidity—Jamie fidgets in the short queue before the check-in desk. While he waits, he checks his phone—no message from Björn yet—and studies his reflection in a gilt-edged mirror.

Jamie's six feet tall, lean and muscled. His face is strikingly handsome: sculpted cheekbones, sensual lips, thick eyebrows, and a neat auburn beard. Over the last five years, his looks have landed him several modeling jobs, as well as time as an erotic dancer, a male escort, and a porn actor. Though he aspires to sophistication and more legitimate acting jobs, he's given up any hope of trying to eradicate his mountain accent. Right now, in these fancy surroundings, the country boy's regretting his defiantly redneck wardrobe—along with the tight T-shirt emblazoned with ALMOST HEAVEN WEST VIRGINIA, he's wearing tattered Carhartt jeans, a chunky-buckled belt, a camo baseball cap, and cowboy boots. *Hell, I look like what I am. A hustler. Poor white trash reared in a Kanawha County trailer park. I shoulda worn a dress shirt. I shoulda trimmed my beard. At the very least, I shoulda polished my fucking boots. Man, I am outta my element.*

It's Jamie's twenty-fifth birthday, and his first time in New Orleans. This afternoon he's spent several hours exploring the French Quarter: ranging around the cathedral, loping along the Mississippi, and peering into antique shops along Royal Street. With the money perpetually generous Björn sent him, he's treated himself to Dixie beers and a hot muffuletta at the Napoleon House, then a batch of beignets at Café du Monde, then a hurricane in Pat O'Brien's leafy courtyard bar, and finally those bravado-building frappés at the Old Absinthe House.

Jamie's thought about massively muscled Björn all day—his ivory skin, close-cropped beard and golden-furred thighs, his bubble butt and sad sapphire eyes—surprised at the eagerness he feels to see the Stockholm-born businessman again after so many months apart. Now, as he recalls certain details of their past assignations, his cock thickens in his jeans, a prominent lump he rubs through the thin cloth lining his pocket.

Their erotic relationship used to be pure business, but somehow, after three years of infrequent but much-anticipated rendezvous, it's become a lot more, though Jamie's hesitant to admit it. *Hell, every man I ever fell for, in DC or back home in the hills, has either beaten or dumped me. Ain't so sure letting Björn know how I feel's a good thing. It might fuck everything up.* Without Björn's "patronage," as they both call it, Jamie might have to return to infrequent hustling. His salary as a part-time graphic artist is never enough to pay the bills, and he certainly could never spend a night in a hotel as grand as this without Björn's credit cards.

"May I help you, sir?" the lady behind the desk asks, jarring Jamie from his anxious pondering. She's as refined as her surroundings, dressed in a cream-colored suit. Her face is a gleaming brown, like polished walnut. "Portia" is inscribed on her name tag. Instead of regarding him with the contempt and suspicion his class-conscious insecurity leads him to expect, she gives him a warm smile.

"Uh, yes, ma'am. Please." Jamie whips off his cap and runs a hand through his mess of chestnut hair. "M-my name is Jamie Doolan. I have a room here? Mr. Gunnarson should have…Björn Gunnarson, he, uh, should've reserved it."

"Mr. Gunnarson?" Portia touches her computer screen, clicks a red fingernail on the desktop while the data comes up, then smiles more broadly. "Yes! You have the penthouse. You'll love it, Mr. Doolan. It has its own balcony-patio and a Jacuzzi. You'll also have access to the concierge floor. Complimentary breakfast from seven till ten a.m., and complimentary cocktails starting at five p.m."

The boy's green eyes widen. "Free booze? Lord, ma'am. Really?"

Portia gives a soft laugh. "Yes, sir. Free booze. Do you like rye whiskey?"

"I like Jack Daniel's real well." Jamie's grin is sheepish. "Is rye like that?"

"Yes. Though not as sweet. Be sure to ask for a Sazerac. They're a specialty of our city." Portia hands Jamie a laminated card. "Here's your key, Mr. Doolan. The elevator you need is just around the corner. If you put your key card in the slot marked 'Penthouse,' it'll take you right up."

❖

"Holy shit," Jamie mutters. For half a minute, all he can do is gape. He drops his backpack on the parquet floor, tosses his cap onto the coffee table, strips off his sweat-wet T-shirt, tugs off his boots and travel-smelly socks, and begins his exploration.

Huge couch, huge television. Deep armchairs. Fireplace. Roomy kitchenette. Refrigerator stocked with bottles of Abita beer, one of which Jamie pops open and swigs as he continues his tour. Small office with carved wooden desk. Bathroom as big as Jamie's tiny apartment back in DC. The promised Jacuzzi, all marble, mirrors, and chrome. Out there, the promised patio. Jamie unlocks the French doors and steps outside.

The patio's broad, canopied, with a wrought-iron table and chairs and a cushioned couch. This high above the Quarter's bustle, it's breezy and quiet, far from prying eyes. Jamie leans against the chest-high parapet in a slant of hot sun, looking out over the rooftops of the Quarter. There are the twin bridges crossing the great brown river, there the spires of the cathedral, there white ships moving upriver.

Somewhere a calliope is playing. Somewhere a blooming magnolia is wafting lemony scent. Jamie sighs. *Not bad for a hill-hick from Cabin Creek. Thank God Björn came to the strip club that night and saw me dance, otherwise we never woulda met. Wonder when he'll show up? He said he was gonna take me someplace fancy to eat tonight.*

Already, thanks to the sun and humidity, Jamie's torso is slick with sweat, beads of it gathering in his armpits and trickling down his sides.

He scratches his fur-dusted chest and thick treasure trail, then lifts the bottle in a silent toast, to the city, to his good fortune. Gulping another mouthful, he steps inside. Here are stairs, leading to a dim loft. He lopes up them, ready for a nap.

At the top of the stairs, he freezes, mouth again agape, staring at the king-sized bed in the room's far end. A naked man is sprawled on his side on the bedspread, his broad back turned toward Jamie.

Jamie pads forward, heart speeding up and cock hardening fast. He knows well that massive build and blond ponytail, those plump, blizzard-pale ass curves. Björn's wrists, wrapped in hemp rope, are crossed together in the small of his back. His ankles are likewise roped together. The base of a black plug is just visible between his buttocks.

"Ohhhhh, daahh-yum," Jamie growls, excitement thickening his accent. Leaving the beer on the bedside table, he gently rolls the trussed-up giant over. Two long lengths of black fabric are wrapped around Björn's head. One covers his eyes, blindfolding him; another's threaded between his red lips and white teeth, gagging him. Everlast boxing handwraps, Jamie notes, leftovers from Björn's amateur boxing days. Björn's genitals are swollen and glossy, bound tightly with a thin leather cord. His cock, thick with arousal, oozes pre-cum across one hairy thigh.

"Holy hell. Hot, hot, hot!" Jamie says, grinning as he squeezes his own crotch. No need to ask if Björn's fallen prey to a ruthless robber. Jamie's found him this way several times before, the last occasion on a hotel bed in snowy Minneapolis, where Björn's business has its U.S. base.

"Mmm!" golden-bearded Björn grunts, nodding toward his right. On the low dresser there, Jamie sees a big collection of BDSM gear. There's also an envelope, which Jamie rips open. Inside is a note, written in Björn's clumsy scrawl.

Dear Jamie,

Happy birthday! Welcome to New Orleans! I thought I'd greet you in a memorable manner. My self-made knots are loose, so you should probably bind me more securely, else I might get free and turn the tables on you. You're welcome to use me in any way you please.

Your Viking Captive,
Björn

Chuckling, Jamie studies the bound man with horny admiration before continuing on to the postscripts.

PS. I have an alarm set for six p.m. since we have dinner reservations at Galatoire's at seven. It's a formal place, but I have a handsome outfit for you in the closet. You'll love their oysters en brochette.
PSS. No one can hear us here. Be as rough as you like. I need to hurt.
PSSS. You're welcome to leave marks. As many as you want.

This last statement causes Jamie's dark eyebrows to rise. *Marks? What's changed? He's always telling me not to leave marks his wife might see. Well, great! I've always wanted to bruise him up.*

Excitedly, Jamie sorts through the leather stash. Hanks of rope, a ball gag, a bit gag, camo bandanas, dildos, lube, a hunting knife, a thin bamboo cane, a bag of clothespins, bondage tape and scissors, nipple clamps with leaden weights, a chain-and-padlock slave collar… everything Jamie needs to punish the big man and keep him powerless. And vice versa, since, every once in a while, Björn insists on topping Jamie. As much money as Björn pays him, the boy can hardly refuse, and besides, he likes to be tied up and forced to take Björn's thick dick up his ass. Even sweeter than those mock rapes is how tenderly Björn treats him after such scenes.

"All right, bud. Sit on the edge of the bed," Jamie commands, shucking off his jeans and bikini briefs before picking up the slave collar and bondage tape. "You're about to get your money's worth."

Björn obeys. Constrained as his limbs are, it takes him a good bit of awkward struggle to heft his frame into the required position. Once he's in place, Jamie wastes no time in locking the collar around his neck and layering several feet of tape around his roped wrists.

"God, what a chest," Jamie murmurs, running a finger along the deep cleft between Björn's pale, hairless pectorals. "What a set of arms," he sighs, squeezing the gym-dense biceps. For Jamie, part of the excitement in topping Björn has always been the differences in their ages and sizes: the Swede's thirteen years older, sixty pounds heavier, and four inches taller. Dominating him is like taking the god Thor captive.

"Built like a brick shithouse. You're fucking magnificent. Let's truss you up a little more to make sure you behave."

Grinning with sadistic delight, Jamie applies more tape, several yards encircling Björn's torso and biceps just above his big nipples, several yards more just beneath his pec mounds, securing his elbows to his sides.

"Going nowhere now, huh?" Jamie wraps an arm around Björn. The burly Swede shakes his head, heaves a deep sigh, and leans against him. Björn's fat cock has responded to the intensified bondage by growing even harder. Pre-cum pools in his piss slit and strings off his cockhead.

"Fuck, I love it. A man as big and butch as you a bottom." Jamie kisses Björn's bewhiskered cheek. "Don't want you to summon help, right? I think you need a more substantial gag." Pulling off several strips of tape, Jamie plasters them over Björn's mouth and bearded cheeks.

"That'll keep you quiet. Feel good?" Jamie strokes the silenced man's chin, then the tape-covered furrow of Björn's lips.

"Ummp!" Björn nods, bowing his head in surrender.

"I've sure missed you, big guy," Jamie says, pulling loose the cord of Björn's ponytail and letting his long hair fall free. "Have you missed me?"

Björn mumbles and nods. Jamie can discern the curve of a smile beneath the mouth tape.

"Good to know." Gripping the shaft of his captive's cock, he starts a slow stroking. Fervently the Swede humps his hand.

"You need it bad, don't you? This is one damned fine birthday." Already Jamie's fist is moist with Björn's welling juice. Bending, he takes Björn's prominent right nipple into his mouth. He licks and nips. Björn trembles, pressing his huge chest against Jamie's lips.

"You said you wanted hurt. You want me to hurt these?" Jamie gently grips the tit point between his teeth and tugs.

"Mmm-mmm," muffled Björn rumbles. "Mmm-hmm."

"That's all I needed to know."

Jamie gives Björn a sudden shove. Huffing, the blond giant falls backward onto the bed. Jamie climbs on top of him, straddling his waist. "Time for the torture you pay me for. I want you sore as hell by the time we sit down to those oysters tonight."

The torso torment goes on for a good half hour. Jamie's fingernails dig into the tender pink areolas, twisting and tugging; his teeth worry the nipple tips, sink into the hard mounds of the pectorals; Japanese clover clamps stretch the tit flesh into protuberant cones. Björn thrashes and moans, his cock never flagging. Jamie forces him down again and again, increasing the cruelty by slow degrees till Björn's chest is covered with teeth marks and his nipples are red-raw.

"Enougha that," Jamie says, lapping Björn's wounded tits a few more times before rolling his burly captive onto his belly. He unbinds Björn's feet and spreads his thighs. When he nudges the butt plug's base, Björn's response is a bass groan, followed by a jerky bucking of his hips.

"Feel good, huh? Yeah, yeah, I know what you want next. After tit torture, you're always aching to get fucked. But first I'm gonna beat your butt. I been wanting to mark you up since the first time I topped you. Get on your knees. Here, right on the edge of the bed. Good boy. Now, ass in the air. Face down. Good. Now stay that way."

Jamie runs a palm over Björn's propped buttocks. The Swede trembles, lifting his ass higher.

"Nice. Nice. You really want a beating bad, don't you? Okay, buddy, I'm gonna spank that yummy rear end of yours till it's red. And then I'm gonna fuck you till you're raw."

Jamie brings his open hand down hard, slapping the right buttock. Björn yelps, tensing his gluts. A red handprint materializes, then fades. Jamie does the same to the left buttock, then the right again, admiring the way the curved white flesh blushes beneath his blows. Left, then right. Left, then right. Left, then right. Beneath his layered gag, Björn gasps and grunts.

Jamie pauses. When he grasps his captive's cord-tied cock, he finds it harder than ever, still drooling pre-cum. When he runs his fingers over the reddened butt cheeks, Björn whimpers and sighs.

"More? Harder?" Jamie asks, kneading the dense mounds.

Face veiled by his shaggy hair, Björn nods.

"Say 'please.'"

A muffled mumble. Another. Another.

"Good boy." From the floor, Jamie fetches his jeans, tugging off the thick leather belt. He doubles it over and snaps it, making a loud crack that causes blinded Björn to start.

"Belt now, okay? You can take that?"

Björn's head bounces up and down. He cocks his ass in tacit invitation.

After fifteen minutes of Jamie's belt wielding and Björn's muted yelps and moans, the captor's forearm is sore and the captive's ass bright red. Dropping the belt, Jamie presses his cheek against the big man's rear. He grins with satisfaction, feeling heat radiating from the abused flesh. Already, faint bruises are beginning to show.

"I'll save the caning for another day," Jamie says, fetching lube and a condom from the gear-strewn dresser. "Right now, you need plowed hard." Jamie helps Björn shuffle forward into the middle of the mattress, then again positions him on his knees and roughly shoves his face into the blanket. He wastes no time in working the thick plug out, adding lube, then replacing the black rubber with two of his fingers.

"Nice! All opened up for me." Jamie works in a third finger. "Fuck yourself."

Björn spreads his thighs wider and pushes backward; Jamie's fingers sink deeper. For a few minutes, Björn rocks back and forth on the inserted digits. Then Jamie pulls on a condom, greases himself up, rubs his cockhead over Björn's wet asshole, and with a slow steady movement pushes into him.

Björn lifts his head and heaves a rapturous groan. When Jamie's fully embedded, he grips his captive's hips and begins a slow in-and-out.

"Oh, *God*, it feels so good to get up your ass again," he sighs, gazing down at Björn's tape-wrapped back, the great muscles flexing and bunching there, Björn's bound hands clenching and relaxing.

Impatient, balls aching, oh-so-ready to come, Jamie speeds up, delighting in the way the Swede's ass ring expertly clenches his shaft. "Oh, God, yeah. Milk me, man, milk me," Jamie hisses between gritted teeth. He pulls out only long enough to shove Björn forward onto his belly and pry his thighs farther apart. Cock-ramming back into him, Jamie begins a steady pounding.

For a time Björn submits. Face pressed into the bedspread, he rocks beneath the thrusting boy, breathing hard through his nose. But soon he begins to struggle, straining against his bonds and tossing his head, long blond hair flying. Finally, with a muted shout, he begins to twist and kick, as if he were frightened, hurting, unwilling.

Jamie's come to expect such mock resistance. Indeed, he relishes it. "Shut up, bud," he snarls, clamping a hand over Björn's bellowed protest. "You know I love it when you fight me, but there ain't no use in it, big guy. I got you. You're all mine. I fuckin' *own* you." He pulls halfway out, then jabs into him again. "Right? Right?"

"Uh-huh! Uh-huh!"

"You want loose? Want me to stop?"

In answer, Björn's asshole squeezes Jamie's cock. "Huh-uh! Naaaah!"

"That feels great. Want me to fuck you harder?"

Nodding wildly, the Swede shoves his plump butt back against Jamie's groin.

"That's what I thought." Digging his fingernails into a wound-moist nipple, the boy plows him savagely, Jamie's hairy groin slapping noisily against Björn's smooth rump, Björn's bronco bucks keeping perfect time with Jamie's thrusts.

"Yeah, that's it! Uhhh. God, you're tight! Here I go!" Jamie grits his teeth, tenses his thighs, and comes, spurting into the condom. He keeps thrusting, his speed slowing, his spent cock dwindling inside his captive's taut tunnel. At last he pulls out, wraps his arms around Björn's chest, and pulls him close.

For a long time, they cuddle contentedly, Björn snuggling back against Jamie, Jamie stroking Björn's tousled hair. Both have fallen into sweaty sleep when the alarm by the bed beeps. With a curse, Jamie turns it off. Björn rolls over, facing Jamie, nuzzling his chin. Jamie covers the Swede with soft kisses: his high forehead, his bearded cheeks, his tape-plastered mouth, his great breast and strength-swollen shoulders.

"Time to get ready for those oysters you promised," Jamie says. Pulling Björn up by his elbow, he helps him stagger into the shower. There, in the warm rush, he soaps Björn up, running his fingers over the Swede's splendid physique. When they're both rinsed clean, Jamie falls to his knees, cups Björn's bound-up balls in his hand, and takes his fat dick into his mouth. As expert a cocksucker as Jamie is, it takes well-fucked and horned-up Björn only forty seconds to flood his lover's mouth with a huge load of cum.

❖

"Goddamn, these oysters are good!" Jamie finishes his second Sazerac in between bites of the rich appetizer. "What're they called again?"

"Oysters en brochette. A specialty here. I'm glad you like them."

A striking contrast to the way they appeared a little over an hour ago, Jamie and Björn are neatly dressed in linen suits and ties, Jamie in dove gray, Björn in pale blue. Jamie's muss of chestnut hair is combed; Björn's blond locks are once more bound back in a ponytail. About them are the gleam and bustle of the elegant dining room: mirrors, chandeliers, silverware, china, expensively dressed patrons and dignified waitstaff in black and white.

"Best birthday ever, man. Thanks." *God, what a smile. And those sad blue eyes. Jesus, he's the best-looking man I've ever seen. Why the hell's he hanging with a redneck like me?* "The drink's tasty too. And strong. I've already got a serious buzz on. The lady at the hotel told me I should try 'em. What's this place again?"

"Galatoire's. It has a long history. Supposedly married men met their mistresses here, in this very room."

"Mistresses, huh? Ah, okay. Appropriate, I guess. I figured I wasn't the only whore who'd ever been in a place this highfalutin."

Björn frowns. "Don't say that. You're not a whore."

Jamie rolls his eyes, knocks back what's left of his drink, and smiles tightly. "Not a whore. As if I could afford to be here if—"

"Here you go, sir." The waiter appears at Björn's elbow. "Crawfish etouffée for you," he says, lowering a plate, "and seafood-stuffed eggplant for you," he adds, as his compatriot places Jamie's meal before him, then uncorks and pours champagne.

Björn lifts his glass as soon as the waiters depart. "It's so good to see you, my friend! You look very handsome tonight. Happy birthday!"

"Damn good to see you again too, man," Jamie says, gazing

into his companion's beautiful eyes. "You look pretty fine yourself." Smiling, they clink glasses. For a few minutes the men tuck into their meals, both emitting soft sounds of gastronomic appreciation.

"Hell, this is *super*-fine eating," says Jamie, licking his lips. "So how long's it been?" He sits back, stretches, and takes a casual sip of champagne. "Since we got together?" *As if I don't know. I miss you all the damn time.*

"Five months. Sorry I couldn't arrange a weekend like this sooner. Things lately have…been complicated. You know I—"

"I know. Your family. How's things with them? Something's changed, hasn't it?"

Björn lays his fork down and bows his head. When he looks up, the expression of grief in his face is so profound that Jamie gasps.

"Changed. Yes. How do you know that, Jamie?"

"The note you left me. You said I could mark you. Before, you always said… My God, Björn, what's wrong?"

"I don't want to talk about my family right now. Later, please. Let's talk about you. How's the job these days? And are you still feuding with—"

Jamie takes his cue, rolling green eyes. "Grandma, yep. She had her whole damn church pray for me. She wants me to join an ex-gay program, can you believe it? Hell, all she knows is I'm queer. If she knew about my dancing at Secrets, or the porn I made…or about you, she'd probably shoot me. Hell, I don't wanna talk about her. Or the job. It's boring. I wouldn't be able to live in DC if it weren't for the money you send me."

"So what do we talk about?" Björn shrugs his huge shoulders. Tearing off a chunk of French bread, he butters it. "How about we talk about how wonderful it is to see you? And what a wonderful scene we just shared? And how hot it is to sit here with a plug up my ass and a slave collar locked around my neck and know that no one here would ever suspect? And how, every time we meet, you make my dreams come true?"

Jamie pulls a slice of souffléed potato from the pile, dips it in Béarnaise sauce, and bites off the end with a lewd grin. "You just like me 'cause I have a nine-inch dick."

"A dick so long and thick that the only way I can take it is to be plugged for a while first? A dick that really fills me up, a dick that makes me feel like a man, a dick that makes me feel cherished. No wonder they cast you in that porn."

"God, man, cut it out!" Blushing, Jamie shakes his head.

"I care about a lot more than your dick, Jamie. Surely you know that."

"Yeah, you like my ass too. You gonna top me this go-round?"

"Yes. I hope to. But that's not what I meant."

"So I'm not your whore?" Jamie says, forking up a chunk of crabmeat. "Then what am I? You pay me to tie you up and fuck you, right?"

Björn empties his champagne before topping off their glasses. "Do you still sell yourself to other men?"

"You know the answer to that. No. I gave all that up six months after we met."

"And are you dating anyone? Since Dirk?"

"Naw. Your looks and your money…they've sorta spoiled me. There's a guy at work who's interested, but he ain't half the man you are. Naw. Right now, you're the only guy I sleep with. Otherwise, I'm just in my apartment, jacking off to online bondage porn."

Björn chuckles. "I do a good bit of that myself. Then we're lovers. I have greater financial standing, so I…keep you. It's well worth what you give me in return."

Jamie lifts his flute and swigs it. "Man, I'm drunk. Drunk feels good." He sits back, scratches his bearded chin, and squints at his emptied plate. "Lovers? So you love me?"

"Yes. Yes, I do. That's one of several things I wanted to tell you this weekend."

Jamie stares at him, open-mouthed.

"Gentlemen," says the waiter, "do you need anything?"

"Dessert menus, please," says Björn, his voice deep and calm. "I think we're going to have crème caramels and café brulot."

"Uh, okay." Jamie swallows hard. "But first I think I'm gonna need me one more Sazerac."

❖

After hours of dancing and drinking at Oz, Jamie and Björn, flushed and happy, return to the penthouse of the Hotel Royale. Naked, they relax on the dark patio, sipping mineral water and relishing the river breezes. They say little, as if, after Björn's admission at Galatoire's, further speech were unneeded. They hold hands, looking out over the Quarter's lights. Near midnight, they go to bed, curling up beneath the covers in the air-conditioned cool, each cherishing the other's closeness. Once during the night, Jamie nudges the tossing Swede from a nightmare. Pulling him into his arms, the boy strokes his hair and soothes him back to sleep.

Early the next morning, Jamie wakes to find Björn grinding his still-plugged butt against Jamie's hefty hard-on.

"Please?" Björn begs. "Please?"

"You got it, bud. After you help me take a leak."

Deftly, Jamie ropes acquiescent Björn's wrists together behind him, then does the same to his elbows. Dragging his colossal captive into the bathroom, he forces him to his knees, crams his dick into his mouth, and pisses. Björn, gazing up at Jamie, wide blue eyes full of unspoken adoration, clamps his lips tight, gulping mouthful after mouthful of the pungent fluid.

Finished, Jamie helps Björn rise, buckles a bit gag between his teeth, fetches a condom and lube, and leads his willing slave down the stairs and out onto the patio. There, in the slanting morning sun, high above the city streets and any likelihood of witnesses, Jamie pushes Björn down onto his knees, bending the big man forward till his chest is resting upon the couch cushion. Then Jamie works out the plug, lubes them both up, and, kneeling, takes Björn up the ass from behind.

This morning's lovemaking is as tender as last night's was brutal. Björn rocks back onto the cock impaling him, whimpering with gratitude, drooling copiously around his rubber bit. Thrusting steadily, Jamie wraps his arms around the Swede's chest, plucking his sore and sensitive nipples. They take their time, a deep, lengthy butt-fucking of mingled sighs and hoarse moans. Jamie comes up Björn's ass with a repressed roar.

"Damn, oh damn, that was sweet." Jamie catches his breath, pulls out, and wipes off. He trails a fond finger down the Swede's sticky butt crack. *God, I'm addicted to your ass, Björn. Why cain't we do this more often? Damn your wife and damn your daughter.* He caresses a yellow-furred thigh, kisses those wide white shoulders, fondles the fingers of Björn's bound hands. *Don't you know I'm crazy about you?*

"Up now." Jamie heaves Björn to his feet, then helps him sit back onto the couch. "Hungry?"

Björn leans forward, great arms straining against the rope restraining them, then leans back with a sigh of satisfaction and palpably relaxes. His white teeth grit the black rubber bit; he smiles faintly, long hair falling over his face. "Yah."

Jamie brushes back Björn's mussed locks and stares into his blue eyes. Björn stares back, unblinking. The silence that presages statements of significance gathers and lengthens.

"Last night you said you loved me," Jamie says, running a finger over his captive's gag-parted lips. "Did you really mean it?"

Björn bows his head and takes a deep breath. Clear drool strings off his chin and drips onto his sculpted chest. He lifts his head, meets Jamie's eyes again, and nods. "Yah."

You love me but you look so damn sad? Why? Are you about to leave me? About to tell me we cain't meet again? Jamie forces a cocky grin, wipes saliva from Björn's golden-bearded chin, and drawls, "You're making a mess, Mr. Gunnarson. You're so fucking hot when you drool around a gag. How about I fetch us some breakfast?"

Without waiting for an answer, Jamie rises, leaving Björn slumped in a pool of sunlight. Inside, he tugs on underwear, cargo shorts, and a tank top. In the concierge lounge one level down, he fetches breakfast, bearing it back to the penthouse on a platter.

Jamie places one fragrant plate on the glass-topped table, another on the floor, then strips down to his black bikini briefs. "Okay, bud, time to take your gag out." He ties Björn's hair back before unbuckling the straps behind his head and pulling the spit-shiny rubber rod from his mouth.

"Thanks," Björn rasps, licking his lips. "That smells great. What do you have there?"

"Grits. And grillades, they called it. I cut the meat up for you. And beignets dusted in sugar. It all looks great. On your knees, big man," Jamie orders, pointing to the plate on the floor. "Eat up."

Jamie eats at the table, Björn from the plate at Jamie's feet. Every now and then, Jamie pats Björn's rump and emits an approving "Oh, yum" or "Good boy" as they savor their breakfast. When they're done, Jamie makes Björn lick the plates clean before fetching a wet washcloth and wiping the big man's food-smeared lips, cheeks, and chin.

"How was that?" Jamie asks, removing the ropes that bind Björn's wrists and elbows. "You look pretty happy."

"Fantastic! God, I love your cock up my ass. I can't get enough of it." Björn flashes a shining smile, kneading the rope-grooved flesh of his wrists.

"Feeling's mutual, stud. My cock cain't get enough of your asshole. Just wish we could do it more often." Jamie's tone is carefully casual.

"I feel the same. That eating-from-the-floor scene, I've always wanted to try that. That was as exciting as being forced to drink your piss. I don't know why humiliation arouses me so, but it does." He kisses Jamie on the brow, then stretches out on the couch, resting his head in the smaller man's lap. "But I guess you knew that already, yes? After all the imagined scenes I've e-mailed you?"

"Yep. That's what you pay me for, ain't it, bud? To fulfill your fantasies, one by one?" Jamie caresses Björn's six-pack, his navel, his golden pubic hair. *God, I cain't keep my hands off you. I just cain't.*

"Yes. And speaking of fantasies, what would you like to do today? You told me you'd always wanted to see the city. Did you read those guidebooks I sent you?"

"Oh, yeah! I wanna ride the St. Charles Avenue streetcar, and see the zoo, and the Garden District, and those graveyards Anne Rice wrote about, and the Confederate Monument, and the Voodoo Museum…and, well, all sorts of stuff!"

Björn gives a deep laugh. "You're like a little kid." Reaching up, he strokes Jamie's auburn beard. "That boyishness is one of the reasons…I've come to cherish you, my handsome friend. We have all day tomorrow. No need to rush today."

"Naw, I don't wanna tour around tomorrow. Tomorrow I just wanna spend the whole day here with you. Okay?" Jamie clasps the big man's hand in his. "This penthouse is so great, and I never get enough time alone with you, and there are the canes I still gotta use, plus I wanna sketch you again. Can we stay here tomorrow? I think you need to be kept roped up most of the day. And marked up pretty bad. How's that sound?"

Björn's smile is one of pure bliss. "Yes, sweet Jamie, we can do that. It sounds superb. I do want to take you to breakfast at Brennan's tomorrow morning, but after that, I'm all yours. And you're all mine." He lifts Jamie's hand to his mouth and kisses it. "I'm so grateful that we met."

"Me too. Hell, yes. So let's get dressed and get going. Lots to see! The sooner we leave, the sooner we get back and snuggle."

❖

The lovers return to the hotel in early evening, exhausted from a full day of touring the Crescent City. Once more dressed in their expensive suits, they share another Creole feast, this time in the city's oldest restaurant, Antoine's: Sazeracs, champagne, oysters Rockefeller, soft-shell crabs, Brabant potatoes, and broccoli with hollandaise. Afterward, they enjoy the penthouse Jacuzzi, then cuddle on the couch and watch *The Avengers* on the big-screen TV. They go to bed early, Jamie wrapped in Björn's thick arms.

Jamie wakes abruptly in the middle of the night, to a flash of lightning illuminating the room. He pads to the toilet to piss, then stands by the bedroom window, watching the storm. Thunder rumbles; a violent rain slashes the panes. He's about to return to bed when a big arm encircles his neck and another pins his arms behind him.

"Time you took your turn on bottom," Björn growls, nuzzling Jamie's ear. "I need to come inside you."

"Oh, yeah?" Grinning, Jamie resists, writhing in Björn's arms. "I don't think so."

"I'm three times your strength, my adorable little man." Björn drags Jamie over to the bed and shoves him down onto the mattress. They wrestle for a while, Björn chuckling, Jamie giggling, both of their dicks stiff with arousal, before Björn flips Jamie onto his belly and wrenches his arms behind him. Within a minute, the big Swede has taped Jamie's wrists together.

"Let me loose, you bastard!" Jamie pants, feigning outrage. He knows exactly what to say to goad Björn further. "Or I'll scream for help."

"Good luck with that." Björn stuffs Jamie's mouth full with his own bikini briefs, then seals them in with several layers of tape. Restrained, silenced, Jamie musters a few minutes of halfhearted squirming and stifled shouting before giving up.

"That's my good lad." Björn lifts Jamie onto his lap and cradles him in his arms, kissing his taped mouth and the tip of his nose. For several minutes, Björn rocks him like an infant while they catch their breath and gaze into each other's eyes.

Björn stands, effortlessly hoisting Jamie over one shoulder. "Let's get some air, shall we? It's a theatric night."

Down the stairs Björn strides. Unlocking the door, he carries the bound boy out onto the patio. The storm resounds, wind whipping the canopy, rain so wild they're both drenched in seconds. Björn lowers Jamie to his feet and bends him forward over the back of a chair. Kneeling behind him, Björn licks and nibbles Jamie's furry ass cheeks and rims his fuzzy hole till the boy's trembling, moaning with delight.

"Ready?" says Björn, fingertip lubing up Jamie's entrance.

Jamie takes a deep breath and nods. He tries to relax, but when Björn eases into him, he grunts with deep discomfort. The Swede's condom-clad cock isn't as long as Jamie's but it's very thick.

"Easy, my boy. Easy, easy. Open for me, yes? Please?" Björn murmurs, stroking and soothing him, his prick thrusts shallow and gentle. Soon Jamie's rarely ridden asshole has adjusted to the thick flesh transfixing him and they're both groaning with pleasure. They rock together for a long time, storm-doused bodies illuminated by forks of lightning and the city's gleam, before Björn grips his lean prisoner's cock in his palm and begins a tight fisting.

Soon they're done. Björn carries limp and drowsy Jamie back to bed. Freed, toweled dry, wrapped in the big Swede's arms, Jamie drifts off, feeling safer, more loved and protected than he's ever felt in his young life.

❖

Jamie wakes to sunshine and the weight of Björn's head on his shoulder. *Our last full day together*, he thinks, watching the brawny man sleep. *Shit, time moves too damn fast. When will we get to meet again?*

The lovers have brunch at Brennan's. For Jamie, brandy milk punch, turtle soup, and eggs Benedict. For Björn, a Bloody Mary,

Creole onion soup, and eggs Bayou Lafourche. They split an order of flaming bananas Foster, then head back to the penthouse, ready for a day devoted to power play and rough sex.

In the early afternoon, Jamie ropes ass-plugged Björn to a chair in a patch of bright sunlight. Saliva drips from Björn's tightly ball-gagged mouth; weighted clamps hang from his aching nipples. Jamie keeps him that way for hours, alternately jacking him, sketching him in an artist's pad, and torturing him. With the hunting knife, Jamie rakes the Swede's cock, balls, pecs, and quaking thighs, scratching Viking runes into the skin of his biceps and belly, "Property of Jamie Doolan" across his chest's curved muscle mounds. He removes the tit clamps, only to beat his slave's white torso pink with a riding crop. Björn drools and whines, writhing in his bonds, begging "More," begging "Harder."

In the late afternoon, Jamie hogties Björn on his side, ropes a piss-soaked bandana in his mouth, covers his wincing chest, genitals, and thighs with clothespins, and wedges a big dildo up his ass. Once more, Jamie sketches him and jacks him for hours, relishing the way the Swede's massive muscles flex and bulge as he suffers the affixed pins and fights futilely to free himself.

At six, they take a break: mint juleps, fried oyster po' boys, and bread pudding in the hotel's bistro. Again Jamie asks about Björn's home life. Again Björn changes the subject.

Back at the penthouse, they split a bottle of Pinot Grigio on the patio, reminiscing about their past rendezvous and watching the Louisiana light fade. When night falls, Jamie leads Björn upstairs. He ties the Scandinavian giant down to the bed, spread-eagle, on his belly, and gags him with yards of rope and taut tape. With the bamboo cane, he beats his lover steadily, lengthily, till Björn is sobbing softly and his back and buttocks are covered with red welts.

Jamie sits back, sucks down a beer, and makes another sketch of his prisoner. Björn thrashes, fighting his bonds till the bed rattles. Jamie climbs on top of him and ass-fucks him so violently the headboard bangs the wall.

After hours of edging, Björn comes in the sheets. The orgasmic pulsing of his asshole finishes Jamie off immediately thereafter.

Jamie keeps his lover bound down for another hour, holding him close, stroking his hair, reluctant to let him go.

❖

"Okay, big man. Your flight's in five hours. Talk. You cain't put it off any longer."

Jamie and Björn sit naked on the patio couch. Dirty breakfast plates and empty coffee cups scatter the table. The river calliope is playing again. Chimney swifts dart across the cloud-free sky.

"I've wanted to tell you. But it's hard." Björn kneads his temples, rises, paces, then sits back down.

"Look, man. Just tell me. I know something's going on. Like I said at Galatoire's, all those times meeting, and you never once let me mark you." Jamie runs a palm over his lover's chest. "Now you're covered with bruises. You're black and blue all over. Was I too rough?"

"Too rough?" Björn chuckles, rubbing his butt. "Not at all. It hurts to sit, between the belting, caning, and fucking, but you gave me exactly what I needed. Don't doubt that. You're such a treasure, Jamie. Such a blessing in my life. I need blessings now. I need the strength that you give me. Very badly. I'm just afraid to…I'm afraid what's going on might be too much for you to handle. I'm afraid you'll run away."

"Why, Björn? You can count on me. I ain't a little boy. I'm a man."

Björn squeezes Jamie's hand, then releases it. "I know. It's just that this…what I'm dealing with is the most…"

Björn bows his head. Leaning forward, he rests his elbows on his knees and cups his forehead in his hands.

Jamie swallows hard, suddenly frightened. He watches warm wind off the river ruffle Björn's lush hair.

Beneath Björn's face, a drop of liquid spatters the floor, then another, then another. *Rain? No, not rain.* Jamie watches, stunned, as tears evaporate in the intense Southern sun.

Björn lifts his face to Jamie's. His eyes are rimmed with wet. His bearded cheeks gleam.

"Oh, Jesus," Jamie sighs, gripping Björn's bare shoulder. "What? What, dammit?"

"My daughter Emma is very ill. She may die."

"Oh, no." Stunned, Jamie wraps an arm around his lover. "Hell. Hell, hell, hell! I'm so sorry."

Trembling, Björn leans against him. "That's not all, sweet man. Marie's left me. She's been suspicious for months, and lately, she's been half-crazed, worrying over Emma, flying into rages. She found some of our e-mails, some of, uh, the scenes I requested. She threw me out."

"Oh, Christ, Björn. If we'd never met, if we'd never—"

"Fuck that, friend." Björn rises. "Fuck 'never met.'" He walks over to the parapet, looking out over the Quarter and the river beyond. "Marie's insisted that they move to Boston for Emma's treatment. I'm getting a place there, to be nearby. I want to ask you something now."

"Go for it." Jamie stands. "Anything."

"I told you at Galatoire's that I love you."

"Yep. You did. And it was honey to hear."

"Good. But do you love me?"

Jamie emits a curt laugh. "Are you retarded? Love you? I fucking *adore* you. I think I have since the first night we met, when I cuffed you, stuffed a sock in your mouth, and ass-fucked you in that hotel shower. I'd do anything for you, Björn. Money or not."

Björn's tearstained face lights up, a weak smile.

"Good. Because I have something for you." Björn leaves the patio long enough to retrieve an envelope, which he hands to Jamie. Inside, Jamie finds his usual weekend payment, plus a plane ticket and a key.

"The ticket's for a flight from DC to Boston. The key's for my new town house in the Back Bay."

"You're saying…"

"Yes, my little hillbilly friend. I don't know how…"

With clenched fists, Björn rubs tears from his eyes. "Damn it, I hate to cry. I don't know how Emma's treatments will go, and…I need you badly. I want you to move to Boston. I don't care what Marie thinks. I don't care who knows we're together. What do you say? Or do you need some time to—"

"Time? Fuck, I don't need time." Jamie rolls his green eyes. "I been waiting for you to ask me this. I say, 'Hell, yes, you glorious asshole! Hell, yes!' I'm sick of having to say good-bye to you. Don't you know I been wanting more from you, with you, for years?"

"Thank God," Björn whispers, grabbing Jamie's hand. The two men embrace, Jamie's face resting against Björn's crop-bruised chest.

"C'mon, bud," Jamie says, breaking the silence. "Lemme buy you lunch before your flight. I'm hankering for some boiled shrimp and fried green tomatoes. They're on the bistro menu downstairs."

"You're always hungry, aren't you? Well, good. Your outrageous appetites might save us both."

"They might at that," replies Jamie, patting Björn's plump ass, nudging him toward the door.

PARIS EUROS GILES
DAVEM VERNE

From where he stood, Giles suspected he was out of the running. The two men ahead of him said they had been waiting for over three hours and still the line hadn't moved. The sidewalk outside the Foundry was bursting with too many faces, too many restless men. No one was getting ahead, no one was getting in, and no one was getting paid.

By four o'clock that afternoon a tall, penguin-like man stepped outside. He wore a thin mustache and smoked a thin cigar and announced in a thin masculine voice, "There will be no more calls today. The Foundry, she is closed."

He apologized with a shrug and added with a puff, "You come back next season? And maybe bring your portfolios with you?"

All the men in line moaned. The man with the cigar retreated inside and closed the Foundry doors, leaving one hundred male models standing out in the cold.

"Will January be another month without work?" someone asked.

"It's unnatural," lamented a second, untying his scarf.

"It's indecent to make us wait this long!" complained a third.

It's only business, Giles thought. The lucky ones were inside. They got up early and arrived before dawn and brokered their way in. They were upstairs now, getting their waists measured, their stomachs squeezed, their groins tucked. The studio lights would soon shine on their creamy faces and the cameras would be too kind. Everyone else who arrived past noon—the ones still standing on the street—would have to wait another year.

Giles felt relieved in a way. He was glad not to face another room of contemptuous *couturiers*. The Paris designers usually sat in a row with crimped noses as they inspected hundreds—maybe thousands—

of enthusiastic young men, hopeful male models who bobbed up and down the stairs, filed into the hall, and waited their turn. All morning they examined teeth and torsos, tummies and thighs, asses and crotches, searching for that rarest prospect among them, the one who would grace their spring catalogue—and maybe win a modeling contract worth €50,000!

Giles bit his glossy lip. That's what he wanted. That was his dream. On the day he left fashion school, he knew what he wanted to be. A male model, a Male Superstar! But competition was cutthroat. Models were known to sabotage with interest. They might trip you on the runway or shred a guy's wardrobe or cut off a heel. He even heard that some *couturiers* carried a palette knife to see if a cheek was naturally rouge.

"*C'est criminel!*" everyone cried.

Giles glanced around.

He wasn't the only one who added a little blush that day. Behind him stood the evidence: a sidewalk lined with peacocked young men. They had poured out of the Paris *arrondissements* carrying purses filled with makeup in the desperate hope of landing their first modeling job. The sidewalk overflowed with painted cheeks, matted chins, and contoured jaws. As the models dispersed, Giles watched them linger, hard-pressed to find the least artificial among them.

"Well," he sighed, wiping his lips. "I bet those *grands couturiers* are just as happy not to see me as I am not to see them."

Giles picked up his portfolio and began to walk. He blamed himself for not waking up early. What was he doing all night? Reading? He flipped open the pages of his modeling portfolio, where his fashion double stood frozen in time.

Look who's going home now. The photo grinned shrewdly. *Are you ready for the truth, mon cheri? You're too short. Oui! You're idle all day and unchaste all night. You can't even come on time, let alone be a Male Superstar. As for moi?* The photo turned a clever cheek. *I don't care. You're the one who cries all day, "Put money in my purse!" Okay then. Be a prostitute—you petite amateur!*

"Shut up!"

Giles slammed the book tight. He clenched his fist and stormed down the street.

"What am I going to do?" he cried out loud.

He dug into his pockets to see if he had any money. His hand met with cold empty cloth. No euros there.

"What will Odette say? I'm returning home a faceless nobody, an out-of-work model who lives off his sister!"

Giles stomped an impetuous heel.

When he was a boy, maybe twelve or thirteen, he oftentimes sulked if he didn't get what he wanted. Like a coat made of cashmere or an Armani silk tie. Even then, the amateur understood what moved society: fine clothes and great looks. Now that he was a full-grown man, a fashion-obsessed Parisian standing five foot three—decidedly petite for a professional male model—nevertheless he had boyish charm and a compact physique and was capable of finding his own stylish way.

"That's right!" Giles said. "Remember Milan? Remember Gino?"

Giles blushed. How could anyone forget the Italian Rhino?

Last winter, he swore on his teeth that he'd walk the runways of Milan for the January collections. He escaped his sister's glare and hitchhiked all the way to Milan, where he haunted the top model agencies, pleading with anyone to let him fill a vacant spot.

"I want to earn my first euro as a professional male model!" he declared boldly. "I'll work all day! I'll work all night! I'll forgo all the perks, like free makeup and one-of-a-kind clothes. Only let me model. Let me earn my first euro!"

That's when he met Gino, sweeping the top floor.

"I'm here for the winter collections! I'll do anything to model!"

Gino paused from his broom. "I take you where you can model."

At the bottom of a stairwell, in the basement hovel where he lived, Gino threw down his broom and grabbed his crotch.

"Now you collect this—you collect sperm! Now you suck!"

Gino grabbed Giles's hair and swarmed him with his manhood. A dark, grimy dick sprang out of his uniform. It slammed into Giles's face. The amateur model choked—he hadn't blown a guy in weeks! The dick arched up in the air like a rhino's thick horn and was practically made of bone. Gino thrust it at Giles, lifting his mouth higher, sending the horn deeper and roaring loud. The spit of Naples rocked inside his balls and a thick wad spat out, catching in Giles's throat.

"Ahhgg!" Giles cried. "It burns and stinks!"

He gagged some more, this time in French. That enraged the Italian beast.

"Now you bend, *fenucca*! You bend over knees!"

Gino threw Giles down on the broken concrete floor and trampled over him, tossing him across the boiler room like a piece of savanna meat. Gino stalked and charged, blaring the darkest sounds out of his rhino-sized dick, while Giles chased around the mattress, hopelessly trapped. At the last charge, Gino seized Giles's ankles, dragged the youth over, and stabbed his prick between Giles's tender hips.

"You model now! You model for free!"

The young man protested.

"I'm a working model! I'm a hanger, not a hole!"

Gino tore Giles's pants off and glared at the tight rectum.

"You model now." Gino breathed deeply.

Of course, none of that would have happened if he had dressed better.

Back in Paris, the thrift shops—called consignment shops or *les dépôt-ventes*—overflow with designer goodies. One need only walk inside with an eye for fashion in order to walk outside with secondhand chic.

As he loitered down the street in his thrift-shop specials—an Yves Saint Laurent navy-blue blazer with a Helmut Lang cable knit scarf, a Dolce & Gabbana V-neck T-shirt topped with a Kangol wool twill cap, a pair of Gianni Versace slim-leg jeans hoisted by a Christian Lacroix unisex belt, a Jean Paul Gaultier man purse with matching Louis Vuitton coin purse, plus Prada ankle boots, Hermès golf gloves, a Gucci wristwatch, and Karl Lagerfeld sunglasses—Giles felt certain he was dressed for success! May Charles Hix be proud.

In spite of the Foundry doors closing, the day was still sunny and his pants were still tight. Giles had an hour left before Odette would make dinner. He could take a stroll through the park and hang around the stables, or find a newsstand on the corner and engage some working stiff. He could cruise down a boulevard and hustle some aristocrat, or make love with a concierge in some *découpage* backroom. There were plenty of things to do in Paris; no need to sweat over a lost opportunity. In fact, no need to sweat at all!

And if he was really daring, if he was quick on his feet and didn't take *non* for an answer, there might be time left before—

Giles turned around.

The long stream of male models poured down the sidewalk. Their arms were folded over their portfolios like Calvin prayer books. They nodded solemnly and forgave the old Foundry and its iron-willed *couturiers*. Many agreed to meet up later and mourn this afternoon like it was a darkest day in the modeling calendar. They would drink wine and share stories and remember those who got in. And by midnight, a few would find themselves snared between the legs of another model, entertaining shadow pleasures. Lips and loins, faces or feces, to some it was all the same, the endless search for beauty. Inevitably, some would go home dissatisfied, realizing that their careers—and their physiques—were not as pretty as they once thought.

Giles looked ahead.

The Paris Métro stood one block away. Its art nouveau entrance beckoned him. The rod iron vines pulled at the cement under him and his little Prada boots felt the fateful tow.

In their nostalgic dejection, none of the models realized what had suddenly crossed Giles's mind. The e-mail that morning indicated there was another modeling call in nearby Montmartre, just a few stops away. Of course, it wasn't for a premier fashion house like the Foundry. Its doors were modest in proportion, which was why Giles stood in line for the better catalogue.

But now Giles must be shrewd, like his portfolio double. He must think on his feet and shake off the herd in order to salvage his career. If there was still a spot left at the other fashion house, it was possible— just possible—he could make a spring catalogue after all.

Giles picked up his pace.

"Be cool, *mon cheri*," he warned. "Act sulky, as if you were modeling."

Giles strummed his portfolio with a downcast thumb. He hunched his shoulders in a pitiable pose. He even peered glumly at his friend, the luminous sun.

"But just think, Giles, to be working for once! In a modern studio with sunlight pouring in and a photographer's assistant making everything look lovely: straightening your cravat, styling your hair, painting your face, fluffing your cock!" Giles blushed. "And adjusting the camera a little to the left in order to capture the best shot—"

A model cut past him. He walked faster than Giles. His long legs pulled up from the rear and he passed with a grunt before heading for the Métro.

"What's this?" Giles asked.

A second model stepped forward too. He hit Giles with his knee and both ran in front of him. They looked like a pair of racehorses, picking up speed and turning their heads to catch anyone on their tail. Their salon manes flowed in the January breeze. Their veneered breath frosted like white silk. And their eyes—no one but Giles could see the glycerin in them! They locked portfolios and began a controlled sprint for the Métro.

"Pardonnez-moi!"

A third model brushed past Giles. He was taller than the others— six foot five, a real skyscraper! He wore faded jeans atop prodigious thighs. He tore ahead of Giles, his breath burning a nervous course, and he carried a massive portfolio under his muscle-piped arm. In five easy paces he gained ground beside the others and passed them too.

Giles watched the model run. He looked like an athlete, too gymy to be pretty, but his buttocks bounced behind him, perfectly shaped. They were like the hind on a bull! They expanded inside his jeans, each 'tock mannish and round and magnifying power.

"Is he for real?" Giles asked. "Is he all natural? No runway model, with cotton-rump padding, would be safe with his awesome ass around. I'll bet my first euro he's a Bruno Gmünder centerfold!"

Giles stared at the model, so quickly had he fallen in love, when suddenly another rival sideswiped Giles—then three—then four.

Immediately, the race began.

The sidewalk awoke with the flight of one hundred sexy men. They surrounded Giles, crisscrossing his steps. His little Prada boots scampered every way to avoid them. Several edged forward, thrusting their powdered faces and snapping their bleached fangs, but Giles reined them in by a whip of his scarf. The rest galloped behind in a feverish herd, sensing an opportunity, some photo on the make, a few euros to be crowned.

Giles leapt over a crate. He ducked under a cart. He stole a croissant for maximum nourishment. Though Giles was short, he was also quick. In a minute he was racing up front, leading the race.

"I thought models don't sweat?"

He patted his dewy forehead. He abandoned his scarf and unbuttoned his blazer. The jeans he wore were far too tight. "Damn you, Versace!" He tugged at the pockets for a little billiard room. He debated whether or not to let in some air. "Who cares if anyone sees my pretty *pipi*? Look at these overstuffed groins! No one will notice!"

With every step he took, Giles loosened his belt and unzipped his fly—when suddenly someone called his name.

"*Giles, un moment! Giles, c'est moi!*"

He paused. "Bruno?"

Giles spun around.

"My beloved Gmünder?"

"You model now!" the Rhino's voice commanded.

Giles screamed at the thought. He tore open his jeans and unzipped his briefs and hurried down the street with his fly wide open. His balls bounced out, soaking up sun; and his penis flopped around, begat with freckles. But the air felt good; he felt more natural; he could outrun them all, even a rhino!

The Parisian street yawned wide. It stretched out its cobblestone tongue for the stampede of models. A curb lay ahead as the sidewalk protracted, but there were too many of them. The iron railing snapped like the barricades on Rue Gay-Lussac and the street flooded with men, heels clapping, portfolios slapping, and accents waving in the breeze.

Giles ripped off his belt and waved his prick around. "*Regardez-moi!*"

And the models went wild, charging through the crowd and trampling over civilians. Around a deadly turn, one model slipped. He was a comely blond, part Norwegian and part French—but now partly chafed. The model behind him didn't stop either. He snarled and kicked and took a nosedive himself, falling on his wrist—fantastically mauled! And another cut in front but ran into a woman, an elderly *grand-mère* with a plastic shopping cart. He knocked the granny down—and her groceries went flying!

Giles managed to stay ahead of the pack. He tied his belt into a sailor's knot and threw it down an alley. The flash of cherry exploded before them. The models went berserk, turning in every direction and fleeing down the street. Meanwhile Giles cupped his crotch and ducked his legs and ran down the Métro.

But they were savage, these beauties. They changed direction in the alley. They gorged each other with their heels and raced toward the Métro. Like the bulls in Pamplona, the herd bottlenecked at the entrance and expelled a loud cry, "The Métro, she is blocked!" No one could move and no one was getting in!

Their contoured chests heaved and huffed. Their phony groins screwed forward. And their padded thighs conjoined together. In this way, they pushed and pulled, back and forth, driving each other senseless, like a massive beast fucking itself to be free, until one of them lost consciousness and fell to his knees.

"Mon Dieu, sauve-moi!" He collapsed on the steps.

"No one cares about you!" A model kicked the man down.

"You are a sacrifice, nothing more!" A second ripped his false buns.

"You fall, we win!" A third plowed the man's hole.

More models jumped in until the man was covered with luxury condoms.

Those who didn't get in, who forgot to bring a *préservatif*, popped out onto the platform like perfect cum shots. They seized the train for their own and hurried the doors shut, locking out fifty or more of their closest companions.

"C'est dommage, Pierre! Au revoir, Jacques! Ha—ha—ha!"

It was perfectly fair and probably predictable. There were only a few modeling spots left, so why waste time? Why waste a trip on these half beauties? The spring catalogues were destined to go to print, their glossy spreads filled with the finest male faces. So you run for your life. You slam the doors shut. You chase that elusive, erotic euro! You stay lean, you trim your abs, and you cut your V-lines! You do anything it takes to be stave off imperfection and subdue the old feeling that one day you may be back in that *hôtel* or *café* or *cinémathèque*, back to ushering and waiting tables and tediously nodding *oui, madame* and *non, monsieur* while one of your peers, the manliest in the stock, goes to the magazine racks a Male Superstar!

Giles grabbed on to the handrail with all his might. The train jolted out of the station. It sped down the tracks, away from the Foundry and

toward an unknown future. His body swayed with the force of gravity.
The models leaned in unison. Their synthetic groins pinned Giles down
and their designer *derrières* locked him into place. But Giles wasn't
afraid. He was overjoyed! He tried to find that third model—his dearest
friend Bruno—but he couldn't spot that spectacular rump anywhere.

The croissant he had pilfered broke into pieces and crumbled into
the void between his feet. He loosened his crotch, which he'd been
choking as tight as his Versace jeans, and he wagged his dick out.

"Just hang loose." Giles turned meekly. "Breathe in, breathe out.
Twist your body this way, ignore your bladder that way. And keep on
the heels, you have to run!"

It is a popular myth that models like Giles are desperately
conscious of their own physiques. But the greater truth is they are
routinely *unconscious* of their own limbs. So often is the strobe light
poised on one feature, their face for example, and the camera focused
on a single lock of hair that they forget about their other extremities,
ignoring any part of their body not in the camera's eye. Scrutinized,
paralyzed, and routinely starved, these limbs grow accustomed to
professional indifference and quietly seek a little amusement, a sudden
frolic from under the shadow of neglect.

So it was at that moment as Giles dangled from the handrail,
afraid to let go and with one hand twirling his dick about, that a male
commuter found himself face-to-face with Giles's hips. He lowered
his newspaper. Giles's waist rocked to and fro in a burlesque manner.
He curled his lip. Giles's crotch thrust at him. The lifelong Parisian
swallowed. Could this be for me? he thought. The dick danced in and
out of Giles's little fist. He could not resist the temptation any longer.
The commuter reached out and caught the young man's hand.

Giles did not flinch. In his mind, the camera was elsewhere.

The commuter peered around.

Hips and portfolios, purses and scarves swayed in the car like
the veiled partitions in a medina, too many to reveal his folly. Thus
the commuter, while maintaining his silence, gently unfolded Giles's
knuckles and beheld the cock.

It was clean and white and slightly buffed—it had been self-abused
the night before. With a punitive frown, the commuter peeled back the
foreskin. He extended his tongue and licked the still-puffy head. He
even squeezed the recovering nuts to see if they were fully loaded. He

leaned in closer and with his lips produced ten, maybe twenty, feisty tugs, encouraging Giles to swell like a sausage coming up to boil. The commuter's mouth was wide (it routinely accommodated footballers), but he tightened his cheeks and pursed his lips until the cavern grew narrow and just right.

Giles's freckled cock filled the commuter's mouth. The tender head nuzzled to the back where a pool of spit washed over it. Sensing a good scrub, Giles inched in some more. The commuter reciprocated. He began to gulp. His throat caught the lazy head and started sucking.

Immediately, a pop! A shot of semen escaped Giles!

The commuter leaned back. "I'm not *fini!*"

None of the models noticed as a second shot sprang through the air, setting others loose. An unwarranted stream splashed out of Giles's cock, hitting the man's newspaper. More doused his lap, then sprinkled on the croissant lying between their feet.

The commuter grinned. *"Je comprende."*

He licked the tip of Giles's bashful head. The taste was delicious and more concentrated than before. It was a promise, that was all; some boyish pre-ejaculate, the sweet surface above a growing spring. There was more to be mined, if only he took the time.

He buried his face in Giles's groin. The curly pubes ruffled against him. The sweat filled his nose as he massaged the skin backward. The sausage began to boil. It was more auspicious now. He swallowed the penis deeper and swept his tongue over it, exciting the head to nestle as it did before. With his chin between Giles's thighs, his jaw clamped tighter. Every ounce of spit immersed the young dick until the saliva began to steam. The prick began to bake. The cream began to churn, bubbling and frothing until—

"Bruno," Giles mimed. He added, "Odette!"

Giles felt he was going to explode, so hot were his loins. Often he liked to tease himself in Odette's shower, holding his dick in a fevered grip, then covering the shower with fresh morning piss. Wait—wait—wait! He tried to hold it longer. But his dick was getting sore and his balls were turning hard and his bladder was filling up. He had to hold on—just another minute—until Odette walked in with one of her lovers, that laborer from Provence who didn't like boys—and they saw her little brother strap his penis and choke his balls and douse the tiles with fresh boyish—

The warm center burst and liquid swarmed the commuter's mouth. He gulped it down savagely. It was white and greasy with a base of vinegar flooding his throat. It dumped into his gut, more concentrated than before and far more puerile. He moaned out loud, drinking down the mix—the glorious confection of idle youth! Suddenly he recalled a military academy and a dorm room in Saint-Cyr where two wealthy brothers did nasty things and he was the one they practiced on—so happy was he to lie between their beds!

The amateur came more, adding to the mouthful. Then Giles's prick began to melt. But the commuter held on, self-consciously waiting, wanting to teethe it until he stole the last drop. His belly splashed with semen and his tongue tasted of piss.

When it all settled down, he wiped the spittle off and combed his mustache down. Then he tucked the penis away. He even shoved a fresh euro into Giles's pocket.

"There," he stammered, "go buy yourself some peanuts."

The commuter blew his nose and returned to his paper, casually reading the financial section.

"Montmartre! Next stop, Abbesses!"

Giles woke up. He saw the platform coming. What a relief!

He squirmed his way to the opposite end nearer the door. His knees felt a little shaky, but he supposed that was due to the ventilation with so many faces sucking in air. A few commuters were brave enough to risk the mayhem too and battle their way to the door so that everyone, including Giles, began pushing to get off.

The train turned a corner. The station lights broadened.

"Abbesses! Watch your step! Disembark!"

All eyes turned as the platform came to view.

Glistening tiles flashed before Giles like the tiles in Odette's shower, and the bright ceiling lamps illuminated his gaze. One by one, the billboards flickered before him. There was GAP, Benetton, and J.Crew, his childhood favorites. Their fresh-faced models beamed like professionals, smiling where they were placed—and getting well paid. Toward the center of the platform hung the more upscale, Calvin Klein, Tommy Hilfiger, and Ralph Lauren. Giles whined as they fluttered in a cinematic dream.

"Is that really Polo?"

Indeed, an exquisite chap rode a spring pony and was dressed in a blue blazer, just like Giles, though the crest on his lapel was not secondhand Yves Saint Laurent.

Giles squirmed to get a closer look when someone yelled out.

"*Regardez-vous!* Donna Karan!"

Egos froze. Eyeballs stared.

The ads for Donna Karan shuttered before them. A bourgeoisie boy relaxed on a velveteen sofa. He wore steel-gray slacks and a white cotton top with large brass buttons. Giles counted the buttons and his blood began to boil.

"Why is *he* up there? Why is *he* lying on that beautiful sofa in that beautiful loft with some girl in the background ironing his shirts? I can do that! I have the buttons! I can look pretty doing nothing at all!"

Giles was about to shout—well, he was already shouting—when a voice called to him above the roaring train.

"*Giles, où êtes-vous? Giles, c'est moi!*"

Giles snaked his way forward, ignoring the searching voice. His hands clung to his portfolio while his eyes teared up. Why was he so pitiful and so unprofessional? He dug into his pocket to remind himself how poor an amateur will always be.

"What's this?"

Giles pulled out the euro. It was shiny and crispy and warm too.

"A gift?" he asked.

Giles glanced around.

"From the fashion gods? Is this a sign?"

"*Oui, Giles.*"

He looked down at the euro. Was it talking to him?

"*Je suis ici, Giles,*" the voice said, so near as if to touch him.

Giles forgot he was on the Métro. He forgot about the race or the Foundry doors closing or his foundering career. Giles focused on the euro and was about to caress it—when the waist of his jeans steadily rolled down.

"*Giles, maintenant?*" the voice asked politely.

His freckled butt was gripped by a hand so large that it wrapped around both cheeks and pinched them together.

"*Maintenant, Giles?*" the voice asked again.

His briefs were edged down a few inches more and the hand found his hole. A fatherly finger rubbed the closed hatch and a large fingernail pried the flesh open.

"Maintenant, Giles?"

A long penis found its way to the opening. It circled outside, extending its length, then slowly slipped in. It spread his cheeks, inched up the butt, scooped up some batter, and dug in hard.

"Oui, Giles, maintenant!"

With each rock of the train, the man stuffed his prick deeper. Giles held on to the euro, oblivious to the pain. He kept folding it in his hands, then unfolding it clockwise. And it called his name, "Yes, Giles, now!" He dropped his portfolio and listened more.

"Giles, avec moi!"

In quick fits the man fucked the youth harder until his breath escaped him. Their slapping could be heard, but no louder than the train. Giles sensed something awry, but the euro kept talking: "Giles, with me!" It soothed his fears and stirred sensations that only his mind could endure, like being fucked by the Rhino, being fucked by the euro, being fucked by the model as tall as a skyscraper!

The model made milky fun of him, holding Giles's hips and encouraging Giles to come, to squirt into his jeans and feel it run down his legs. He lifted Giles once, twice, three times in the air as his dick arched higher.

"I come now!" Gino fucked louder.

The voice cried, *"Giles, permettez-moi!"*

The man swallowed Giles's ear, drenching it with spit as he came inside him, spanking the hole faster with his undressed head. Cum heaped into the amateur where only spit had gone before. It rose like a wave and soaked the hidden flesh. Then it sank into his balls and mixed with Giles's cum, producing a crude concoction of boy and man.

"Giles, mon cheri!"

The man tightened his thighs and skewered Giles higher. Giles held on to the handrail, refusing to let go. The long penis got stuck, but only for a while. Soon it slipped out and dangled beside them. Giles groped behind. He felt the swollen creature. He rubbed it against his thigh and wiped the mud off. Then he reached back farther and found what propelled it: a great, solid, uncompromising ass.

As the train slowed down, the man retrieved his catch. He zipped himself up. He also yanked Giles's briefs back into place. Tenderly, he kissed the neck of the amateur and followed the line of freckles that zigzagged around to Giles's little mouth. He was about to kiss Giles too and take the euro (after all, he won the Gmünder bet), when he looked out the window—

"Abercrombie et Fitch!" Bruno pointed, hysterical.

Giles gasped, "The American gold standard!"

Abercrombie & Fitch were the super male models, the American athletes who never wore clothes. Witnessing the ad, something freed inside Giles. His Versace jeans loosened and his briefs began to stretch. He felt Gino rip them. Bruno too. And his sister's lover Georges. In fact, all the men in Paris—the ones who were natural, who earned their own euros and didn't wear makeup. They all surrounded Giles, tearing off his jeans, ripping off his briefs, stroking his cock, feeding his hunger, encouraging him to bone up and be a man.

"Métro 12, Abbesses!" The doors swung wide.

The commuters ran out first, escaping the male models and all their debauchery.

Abbesses is the deepest station in all of Paris, and it takes forever climbing up the spiraling stairs. But not for Giles. His little legs scaled the steps three at a time and burst out onto Rue des Abbesses.

"But where is the fashion house?"

Giles spun around. Bruno stepped beside him and looked around too, his granite face and chiseled ass briefly confused. Giles looked up at the model.

"You were in the Métro too?"

"Oui, Giles, avec vous."

"There!" Giles pointed.

Quickly, Giles ran up the street toward the fashion house. Its corrugated walls and faux-wood doors were still open for business. Giles fought his fatigue, the perspiration in his blazer and the wet sensation clinging to his jeans.

As they neared the entrance, Giles did something strange. He kicked off his boots and unbuttoned his jeans. He tore off his cap and tossed his clothes aside. In that crazy moment of immodest inspiration, when the decadence of clothes no longer mattered, he anticipated success and the greatest reward and welcomed it with bold, naked arms.

"Oui, Giles, oui!" Bruno sang triumphantly. *"Comme Abercrombie et Fitch!"*

Bruno held Giles's hand as they ran together, an athletic man with a naked boy.

And if they ran faster, if they added speed to the equation which they hadn't all morning, their feet might carry them beyond the common herd and through the open doors, up the long stairs and past the casting curtain, into the wardrobe and before the *couturier*, who took one look at Giles and the model standing beside him: that manly face, that rippling chest, those healthy thighs, and that godly ass! And he'd speak in a voice filled with glory.

"*C'est vous!* You're the one! You're our new model! Congratulations!"

He kissed Bruno's cheek, once, maybe twice.

"You're our Male Superstar! Sign this contract here!"

Bruno signed the contract worth €50,000.

"And this little one beside you. Why is he naked? *Quel est votre nom?*"

"Giles," said the boy.

"Ah—okay—you may go home."

REVENGE OF THE 97-POUND WEAKLING
ROB ROSEN

Ironically, I spotted the ad in the back of a *Hulk* comic book. Not that anyone had kicked sand in my face or stolen my girl—mainly because there was no girl—but the tough guy, the bully, well now, he really sprouted a *boing* in my shorts. Charles Atlas had it all wrong, you see; it was that muscle-drenched asshole that was the hot one, the one I wanted to fuck silly, not that pissed-off dude with the fickle girlfriend.

Still, I was that proverbial 97-pound weakling, give or take a few ounces, and if I ever wanted to land the beefcake, I'd have to do something about it. And quickly. In other words, I sent away for Mr. Atlas's program.

Well, that, and I ate right and exercised, sucked down hundreds of raw eggs for protein, whey shakes for lunch, jogged, and lifted, pushed up, sat up, and crunched until every friggin' joint in my body ached. And still my physique stayed the same. Years down the line, leaner, perhaps, more defined, yep, but scrawny just the same, I was now a nutrition expert. I couldn't build myself up, so I taught others how to do so. Bitter irony.

Still, when I went to the gym, I ogled them, those big men, the dudes who were rife with muscle, sweat dripping down over thick limbs and ripped torsos, ultra-tan and mega-veined, shorts so snug it seemed like they could tear at any moment, tank tops bulging at the seams. No sand in my face here, just snubs; no time of day for the likes of me, teacher or not.

In other words, I was screwed. Close, but no cigar. Still, there had to be another way, something they'd want from me, need from me besides my knowledge of what not to eat.

My salvation came, not surprisingly, in the locker room, that sacred place where they sauntered by, naked Adonises, Herculean men with muscle on top of muscle, dicks swaying, balls hanging, my mouth, naturally, watering.

I tore the poster down and stuffed it in my pocket, reading it in bed, cock in hand, pumping away while I formulated my plan. Such a beautiful means to an end, having my cake and eating it too, my credentials at last proving beneficial.

"They need an extra judge for the regional body building competition," I panted, balls rising, sweat trickling down my face, "well now, they just found their man." The come spewed, ropes and ropes of it, splattering across my taut belly, hot and aromatic, dripping over the side and onto the sheets, a luminescent smile plastered across my face.

❖

I arrived the next day and was hired on the spot. They were desperate; that made two of us. It would be one-on-one interviews first, twelve guys, any questions I wanted to ask. Lucky fucking me. They entered the room individually, Speedos only, oiled up and ready to go, my first look in order to get a feel for the contestants, to better judge their strengths and weaknesses. It was the latter I was looking for, counting on, my cock rigid inside my jeans beneath the table, hand in lap, pushing and prodding.

In and out they paraded by, striking their poses, exposing their assets while I lobbied questions at them. "How long have you been competing? What titles have you won, lost? What would you do to win?" The last question was innocuous enough, though asked with an edge, a lilt to the voice as I watched for the telltale signs, their desperation to compete with my own.

Two of them picked up on it. Two with a keen desire to win at any cost. After all, the grand prize wasn't just a nice trophy; two grand went to the winner as well. And building all that muscle of theirs didn't come cheap, a fact I knew only too well.

"Do?" the first one asked. "Anything," he readily replied. *"Anything."* The edge was volleyed back. Bing-fucking-o. "Haven't won a title all year. Need the cash."

I smiled, a quiver to my lip, my cock now pulsing with blood. "Lucky for you, I'm not immune to a little, um, *persuasion*," I cooed.

His grin mirrored my own, his mitt of a hand suddenly gripping his crotch. "How about a *big* persuasion?" It was followed by a leer, a come-hither wink.

Naturally, I came hither, standing up and walking over to him, a foot apart, half that, my eyes roaming him like a map, veiny trails leading to giant peaks, etched valleys, a hidden world beneath a tiny swatch of Lycra. "Try me," I moaned.

His hands moved down, thumbs within the material, pecs flexed, nipples rigid, glinting under the fluorescent light. A mirage or an oasis? I gulped, watching, waiting, the suit sliding down, a trimmed bush revealed, the base of his cock, then the length of his shaft, thick and getting thicker, arcing up as it sprang out, seven meaty inches, a bulbous head already leaking copious amounts of glistening jizz, balls the size of lemons swaying as he removed what little he had on to begin with.

"How's this?" he asked, his voice reedy, cock as thick and posed as the rest of him.

I gazed, nearly voiceless, the dream suddenly a reality. "You ever kick sand in anyone's face?" I managed.

He tilted his head, smirked. "Not on purpose."

"Close enough." I narrowed the gap, my hands on his massive chest, dense mounds of muscle, smooth as granite, eraser-tipped nipples twisting between my fingers. His eyelids fluttered, a moan escaping from between his lips, his cock bobbing, hands behind his back now, sensing what I wanted, craved.

I punched and slapped at his oversized torso, playing his chest like a bongo, his belly like a drum. He flinched, grinned, but otherwise remained in place. I spanked the underside of his cock, sending it springing, up, down, pre-come gliding loops around the wide, mushroomed head. I yanked on his heavy balls while he groaned, his legs crouching, thighs thick as tree trunks growing even thicker with the exertion, calves like mounds of stone sprouting out from bone and sinew.

I backed away, my button-down unbuttoned, flung to the floor, penny loafers, black socks kicked and rolled off, khakis slid out of, boxers quick to follow, until I was just as naked, just as hard. Though beyond that, nothing else was *just as*. David and Goliath. Like the former, I swung the power, circling him, looking for my way inside, a chance to dominate, apart from pulling the purse strings.

"On the floor," I barked, amending it with, "On all fours."

He did as I said, head up, eyes staring into mine. I bent over, cupping his smooth chin in my palm, brushing my lips against his, soft like down, my tongue gliding out, snaking and coiling its way inside, lashing around its partner, mouths colliding in a burst of cool adrenaline, his moan smothering my groan.

I pulled an inch away, a light smack across his cheek, my hand moving up and over his shaved head, down his back, so broad it could almost be two, tanned to Tahitian perfection, a spank on his ass, my hand throbbing, like striking a boulder, the movement repeated, again and again, the red barely working its way through all that fake bronze.

I crouched down behind him, sitting cross-legged, my way inside clearly marked, pink and crinkled, tight as a drum. I leaned in for a deep whiff, the smell of musk and sweat and baby oil wafting languidly up my nostrils, intoxicating as ambrosia. I licked and sucked on his hole while tickling his dangling balls, his body rocking as he stroked his billy club of a prick.

I spat on his ring, the saliva dripping down. I cleaned it up with my finger, then slid it on in, quickly joining it with its neighbor, both of them pushing and prodding their way up his ass. He inhaled, sharply, clenching around the intruders before giving way, allowing a third into the mix, his smooth, muscled interior sucking me in like a Hoover, until I was entrenched up his rump, my hand jacking my prick, matching him stroke for stroke, sweat pouring down both our backs, our moans and groans and grunts swirling around the room.

When I started ramming up against steel, I knew he was close. Thankfully, so was I. *"Fuuuck,"* he sighed as I piston-fucked him, popping my digits out and then shoving them back in, out and in, all the way inside, his massive body quaking as he shot, his heavy load hitting the floor, one *splat* after the next.

I stood up between his parted legs, head tilted back, a deep groan erupting forth from my lungs as I gave a final tug on my prick, the come flying out, thick bands of it that landed on his ass and lower back, vivid white against orange tan, a kaleidoscope of spunk that soon dripped over and down. It was a beautiful picture, forever burned into my memory.

Though another one was soon to follow, framed in burnished gold.

We cleaned off in silence. He winked and nodded on his way out, strutting his way past the remaining competitors. So sure of himself, so sure of all that do-re-mi-dough.

"Lunch break," I grumbled. "Come back in an hour."

I shut the door behind me, my back against the wood, a smile big and bright and wide, the scene unfolding again and again inside my head, all that muscle at my disposal, a gargantuan mound of flesh to do with as I pleased. My cock stirred, the beast reawakened. Six more to go, a half dozen possibilities. Like Cindy Lauper sang, *money changes everything*.

Too excited to eat, I imagined what the rest of my afternoon would look like, filled with mostly naked behemoths posing and flexing for me, acres of muscle, a landscape of perfection, mine to do with as I pleased, to pose in any stance that I saw fit. And that is, more or less, how it went down.

With eleven completed, he sauntered in, the last of the bunch, a mean smirk on his handsome face, eyes that lit up like the night sky, sparkling sapphires made all the more brilliant by the layers of bronzer beneath them. Shorter and leaner than the others, strangely he stood out all the more. Still, he knew the odds were stacked against him, which landed squarely in my favor. What's more, he meant to level the playing field right quick.

He stood before me, arms akimbo, blue orbs roaming my body as much as my brown ones roamed his. Then he upped the ante, reaching into his tiny trunks, removing a small tube of lube and a rubber. "What's it gonna be?" he asked. "I'm selling if you're buying."

Heart pounding out a mad samba in my chest, I managed a "I'm sure I don't know what you mean." Though clearly I did, evidenced by the tenting in my khakis. Not only did I mean to buy, but also to clean out the entire store.

He snickered, moved a few inches in, his mouth against my ear, hot breath, teeth on a tender lobe. "I'm sure you know what I mean."

I saw his snicker and raised him a chuckle. "Then I suppose your ass is mine, big man."

"And so is that trophy and all that nice *cash*," he whispered, the last word a purr as he moved away, laying himself out on the floor for me like a veritable buffet, mounds of muscle to chow down on, to gorge upon. Little did he know how much of a glutton I could be.

I quickly got undressed for the second time that day and sat between his legs, taking him in, head to toe, amazed at how the two men that offered themselves to me had the same parts, the same ridiculous number of hours at the gym, but looked so completely different. This one had bigger pecs, wider lats, a thicker neck, narrower waist, much weaker in the legs, stronger up top. It was no wonder they both needed me, both hedging their bets. Funny enough, they were still perfect specimens in my eyes. Go figure.

I craned my neck down and sucked on one of his hairless and leathery nuts, yanking on it with my mouth, his back suddenly arching, a moan tinged in both pleasure and pain. The other got its fair shake, then both together, pulled to their limit, his cock now at extreme vertical. Thickly veined and dripping, it towered above me, my mouth eager to climb its summit, my tongue making the trek up, one lick at a time.

He moaned, loudly, as my mouth made its way from top to bottom, a happy gagging tear flowing down my cheek as he pumped my face, his hands behind his thick neck as he watched my steady progress. "Hope you fuck as good as you suck," he said.

I released his prick from my oral grip and replied, "Only one way to find out."

His mighty legs rose up and out, surprisingly limber for such a hulking giant. I slid on the rubber and slicked it up, then zoomed the lube around his twitching hole before greasing up his tool, all while he watched, eyes big and bright, bluer than the sky on a cloudless day. I rested his heels on my shoulders and spanked my cock against his hole, glancing at the mirror to our side, his mammoth browned body engulfing my slight pale one.

I pushed in gently, easy as pie, my dickhead disappearing, a sigh from him, a moan from me, a million volts of electricity burning like wildfire up and down my back, exploding in my belly. Another inch inside, two, slow and steady winning the race, his ass eager to meet my crotch, his muscles flexing with each thrust, hole gripping me like a vise.

"Easy, big fella," I rasped, halfway there, three-quarters, his eyes disappearing for the briefest of moments behind his head. Then I was all the way in, balls lapping up against his fleshy shores, my body melding into his, his neck craning up, our lips at last pressed together, firm, insistent, hungry, while my cock glided in and out, in and out, warm eddies of pleasure swirling around my belly.

His knees went farther back, edging toward his shoulders, my prick pumping inside him, his huge fist stroking madly away, his breath pushing its way inside my mouth and down into my lungs. I pulled my dick out, then shoved it back in, all the way out, all the way in, both of us grunting with each thrust. He reached around with his free hand and grabbed my ass, palming it like a basketball, pushing me all the way and keeping me there, panting for air as he did so.

"Fucking close," he grunted.

"Let 'er rip," I told him, also gasping now, drenched in sweat, my cock ready to explode.

We came together, my whole body spasming as I came in buckets, that rubber getting stretched to its limits with my heavy load, his own load just as massive, spurting out in one long, steady stream, a blanket of white against his bronzed torso, hot enough to melt butter. I collapsed on top of him, his arms suddenly around me, giant limbs and hands surprisingly soft and tender. Two contented sighs from two sticky messes got released.

"You fuck even better than you suck," he eventually said, once he'd caught his breath.

"Big things, little packages, and all that."

He laughed and lifted me off him as if I was nothing more than a rag doll. "Oh, hell no. Big *package* too." He cupped my shrinking cock and gave me a long, final kiss. Then he slipped back into his barely there outfit and was gone in a flash, leaving me naked and exhausted, not to mention way ahead of the game.

I scratched my head and smiled. "Tomorrow should prove interesting."

Which, of course, was a gross understatement.

❖

Crowded into a nearby auditorium, packed with family and friends, interested onlookers, the five of us judges with ringside seats sat a mere ten feet away. All twelve of them came out together, pumped and well-oiled, a sea of muscle and naked flesh, ready for the challenge, one of my men to the far left, the other to the far right, both of them lingering when they caught my eye.

They were all introduced, posed for the appreciative audience, then left the stage before returning one by one, each pumped to the gills, flexing every muscle for us, exposing their biggest assets while hiding their flaws, of which there were noticeably few. I graded them as they finished, snatching glances at the other judges' score cards. Of the twelve, three would go on to the state semifinals, one winner and two runners-up, on to a prize of a cool, even ten grand, enough to keep them well-tanned for years to come.

The dozen were called back on stage for a final pose-off, my heart beating a mile a minute at the sight of them, knowing something that none of them knew, at least not yet.

The announcer dwindled the pack down to six, my two still standing, bookends to the other four, the middle man picked off next, then the one next to him, leaving my two and two others. They both stared down at the judges, giving me a slight nod and a wink. I sat there, straight-faced, giving nothing away.

The final three were announced, a cheer going up from behind us, the contestants still posing, biceps, triceps, quads, and abs, all tight and popping, smiles wide on their faces, eyes on the prize. My two stood on either side of the man in the middle.

The announcer turned and thanked the judges, introducing us one by one, then talked briefly about the semis. There'd be seven judges that night, bigger arena, like I said, more cash for the winners. I'd be there too, which I found out just before the evening got under way. Seems like another replacement was needed. Guess I'd done a bang-up job, so to speak.

The second runner-up was my first fuck, surprise quickly replaced by fake good cheer, a nasty frown down at me. Two to go. I already knew the outcome, the results largely my doing, revenge of the 97-pound weakling. In other words, fuck number two came in second. In truth, the better man did in fact win. Still, I could tell that neither one of my recent paramours saw it that way; they'd traded their bulk for my pull and had gotten shafted, literally.

Too bad, right? Then again, I'd be judging the next competition, one they'd both be entered in. With more to lose, they'd need my supposed pull yet again. As would two dozen others, even bigger men this go around. More muscle, mine for the taking. Or trading. See, in real life, the bully almost always wins out, Charles Atlas or no Charles Atlas. Lucky for me, I finally realized which side of the fence I was on, brains beating out bulk almost every fucking time.

HAVEN'S REST
NATHAN SIMS

A shadow separated itself from the series of shadows creeping across the veranda stretched tight along the old mansion's front. The shadowy figure made its way among the columns groping their way up two stories of the house's façade, their capitals clutched tight to the roof. Floorboards creaked as he passed, like old gossips revealing long-buried secrets. An abandoned rocking chair moved slightly, as if enjoyed by some specter taking in the late-night breeze, as if there were any breeze to take in.

An afternoon storm had passed through earlier, leaving air so thick it was a chore to breathe. Now, past midnight, another storm threatened to take its place, some bastard cousin intent on impressing Mother Nature. Distant flashes of lightning crossed the vast Virginia sky. Rolls of thunder echoed through the woods encroaching on the house.

The figure stepped down from the porch, circled the house silently, and skirted the woods. An ancient barn came into view, its presence visible only by the snatches of light squeezed through its seams.

Another flash of lightning reflected off the long blade of a hunting knife in his grip. Studying his surroundings, he absently rolled the knife's handle over and over in his palm. A grumble of thunder applauded his skill.

The figure drew close to the barn and peeked inside. A stretch of sockets hanging from the rafters housed naked light bulbs that dropped splatters of light down the length of the barn. They revealed a ramshackle maze of cluttered storage and debris: discarded and broken furniture; boxes stacked one on another, their sides caving in under the mingled pressures of weight and time; a bicycle turned on its seat and handlebars, its rubber tires rotted away. The only thing of use seemed to be the lawnmowers and weed whackers meant for upkeep of the estate's few manicured lawns. Overhead was the loft. It appeared dark and empty.

Near the center of the barn was a man bent over the engine of a worn-out Chevy Citation pockmarked with rust. Once, it might have been gray or silver with a red pinstripe stretched down its side. Thirty years ago in its prime, it had been no looker; now age and wear made it less so.

Music crumbled from a clock radio sitting on a nearby worktable. It sounded more like static than music. Somehow, the man discerned a melody from the crackle and sang along merrily, lost in the engine's innards.

The figure in the shadows slid the serrated edge of the knife into a guard hidden beneath his shirttail. He assembled a smile onto his face and opened the door. The hinges squealed and drew the attention of the mechanic.

"Well, hi there," he said. "Can't sleep?"

The figure maintained his vantage in the doorway. "Not so much, no."

"First night in a new place," the man said, hunkered over the engine. "I get that. Sleep's the last thing on your mind."

"Especially in this place."

"Oh, we're not as bad as all that." The man offered an inviting smile. "Give us a chance, Wayne, you might find you like us a whole lot."

"Dyson," the figure corrected.

"Sorry?" The mechanic offered his full attention.

"Most people just call me Dyson." He stepped into the barn's light revealing broad shoulders, a thick chest (a football player's body, really), and a short crop of brown hair on his head.

"Dyson." The other man tested the name, then grinned. "It suits you." A flash of conspiracy crossed his face and he scratched at his nose, leaving a grease mark in his wake. "Can I be honest with you?"

"Sure," Dyson answered, intrigued by that swipe of grease. He wanted to take a rag and wipe it away, or perhaps his thumb would do. A gentle swipe of his thumb down the length of the other man's nose.

"When you were introduced in group, I didn't think Wayne fit you all that well. No offense."

"None taken. It's actually Gawain."

A doubtful look mingled with the dirt on the mechanic's face.

In spite of himself Dyson blushed. "Yeah, Ma had a thing for Camelot."

"So, just when I stop looking, a knight in shining armor finally shows up?" the other man teased, then caught himself and groaned. "Sorry, you've probably gotten that like a million times before."

"Actually, you're the first," Dyson lied. He smiled, his dark, beady eyes lost in the expression.

"I'm Tony." The man offered his hand. Unlike Dyson, his name suited him. Italian blood ran fresh and undiluted through his veins. He was tall and broad with wavy black hair and warm brown eyes. He wore a smudged wifebeater stretched tight across his hairy chest, a dirty rag draped over his shoulder. Dyson wouldn't have minded just standing there all night, staring into those innocent brown eyes of his. How big were they, anyway? Instead, he shook the man's outstretched hand.

"Tony, right. Sorry, I should have remembered that."

"Please, I know what it's like to be new here. A dozen of us, only one of you." The handshake lingered a moment but neither man seemed interested in letting go. Finally, Tony broke away. "I'm sorry, I wasn't thinking. My hands are a mess."

Dyson looked at his now-dirty palm and shook his head. "No worries."

"Here." Tony tossed him the stained rag from his shoulder. "Though I can't promise that won't just make it worse."

Dyson caught the rag and wiped his hands. He nodded toward the Citation. "So does that thing run?"

"It will when I get done with it."

"How long will that take?" From the look of it, Dyson guessed a lifetime.

Tony shrugged and smiled. "It takes time to repair what's broken."

For a moment it looked like he might say more. Instead, he smiled and crossed to the worktable and popped a socket out of the wrench in his hand and began hunting for the next largest size. The discarded socket rattled across the table before rolling to a stop.

"So, what do they need this place for?" Dyson asked, glancing around the cluttered barn. "I mean, there's no farm here, is there?"

"Used to be," Tony replied. "Back in the day this was one of the biggest plantations in Virginia. It was owned by Mrs. Whittier's husband's family. They called it Haven's Rest. Once her husband died and her son ran off, Mrs. Whittier kept the house and the land surrounding it, but sold the rest. That's how she started the ministry."

Dyson handed back the rag. It hadn't done much good, but he didn't mind. He was used to his hands being dirty.

"Not much point in a barn with no farm to go with it," he observed.

"Well, there's still Talulah and Blackie," Tony replied. "They're at the other end."

Dyson glanced down the length of the barn. From around the corner of their stalls he was delighted to see two horses return his stare. "You ride?" he asked.

"Not much chance to ride back home in Baltimore. You?"

"In Illinois, I did. But not for a long time now, no." It had been years since Dyson had smelled the musk of farm animals mixed with the scent of earth and sweat—too many years, in fact. He hadn't thought of home in so long, it was a surprise when he realized he still missed it.

In the dim light, he found the other man's eyes still on him. Despite himself, despite the reporter and the potential relationship waiting for him back home, he liked the feel of Tony's eyes on him. After all, what harm was there in looking, especially in this place?

Soon enough, Tony caught himself and returned to the engine, saying, "So, from the cornfields of Illinois to DC, how'd that happen?"

"How'd you know I live in DC?"

"Please! You're the new kid at school. We knew everything about you before you ever stepped on the grounds."

"Well, that's not fair."

"How so?"

"'Cause I don't know anything about you other than your name, I'm guessing a Ravens fan, and you don't ride horses—"

"And I like working on cars."

"And you like working on cars."

"You know something else, too."

"What's that?"

"I'm here, at the ministry." Tony winked. "That tells you something."

"I suppose it does at that," Dyson agreed. "I've figured out another something about you, too."

Tony raised an eyebrow. "Now, no one mentioned you were a detective."

Dyson grinned. A single dimple appeared in his left cheek. Tony was not going to make his job easy. "No, no detective."

"Okay, so what did you figure out, Sherlock?"

"You don't frighten easily."

"How so?"

"Way I hear it, you got yourself a spirit running around here."

"Oh," Tony sighed, rolling his eyes, "that. I guess you've been talking to the others."

"You don't believe it, then?"

Tony crossed his arms over his chest. The socket wrench was still in his hand. Dyson couldn't help but notice how its tip poked out from under his biceps, pressing the muscle into prominence. "You've seen the house. It's ripe for that sort of thing. Add in a bunch of guys with too much time on their hands and who knows what they'll come up with?"

"But isn't that part of why you're here, belief in a higher power and all that?"

"Believing in a higher power isn't the same as believing in spirits or demons. Faith is one thing; paranoia is something else—"

As if to prove him wrong, a scream erupted from the mansion.

Tony sighed and said, "Here we go again."

The two raced back across the lawn toward the house. Another swash of lightning cut the sky in half, illuminating their passage. It was followed soon after by a matching rumble of thunder. The storm edged closer.

In the upstairs hallway, they found a small group made up of nearly a dozen young men. In their midst were an elderly woman of sizable girth and a willowy, white-haired gentleman who struggled to tie his bathrobe closed.

"It was right there!" one of the young men in the center of the group shrieked frantically. His thin frame was covered by a T-shirt and a pair of shorts. The large, elderly woman stood beside him, her arm draped over his shoulder comfortingly. He pointed a shaking finger back toward what Dyson guessed was his bedroom. "I rolled over and there it was! In the corner of the room! Coming for me!"

"Was it naked?" Dyson asked. All eyes turned toward him.

"Where have you been?" the woman demanded, her Southern drawl clipped and thick with accusation.

"He was in the barn with me, Mrs. Whittier," Tony volunteered as he mounted the last of the stairs. "He couldn't sleep."

"I was walking the grounds," Dyson clarified, meeting Mrs. Whittier's glare unwaveringly.

"Wain." Mrs. Whittier said his name with two syllables and an extremely tight smile. "Please join me in the study."

"I should really talk to—"

"Now, please." Mrs. Whittier squeezed the frightened young man's shoulder a final time and said to the elderly gentleman, "Gerard, please see to Raymond here and then join Wain and me down in the study, won't you?"

Gerard nodded. His bed-tousled hair waved with the gesture, and he moved to take Mrs. Whittier's place next to the frightened young man.

"Back to bed, boys," Mrs. Whittier announced, "all the excitement's over." She brushed past Dyson and took the stairs at a clip. It was a mystery to Dyson how she managed to move so quickly with her girth. "Wain, with me, please," she instructed in a singsong tone.

Dyson followed her down the steps and across the house's once-grand foyer to the study's open double doors. Stepping into the room, Dyson took in the room's former elegance.

A bank of windows crept up the exterior wall toward the room's ceiling, their transoms hidden in dark recesses behind faded curtains and yellowed sheers. Crown molding framed a painted ceiling covered in a spider's web of cracks. Hand-carved bookcases lined the interior walls, their shelves filled with tattered books whose spines were frayed and worn. Threadbare furniture was scattered across worn rugs.

At the far end of the room was a great marble fireplace yellowed with age, its shadowy innards blackened by years of use. The portrait above it was of a frail, elderly gentleman. Despite his advanced years, the portrait's subject held an air of dignity and confidence. Dyson didn't care for the portrait, though. No matter where he moved in the room, its eyes seemed to be on him.

He was brought out of his observations by a flash of lightning and a clap of thunder. The patter of rain on the windows followed immediately after, announcing the arrival of the storm.

Mrs. Whittier switched on the floor lamp beside a large wingback chair. She squeezed into the seat, causing the chair to squeal in protest.

"Please, shut the doors behind you," she said.

"Mrs. Whittier, you hired me to solve this problem for you. To do that I need to talk to that kid."

"You may speak with Raymond once I have spoken with you."

"Yeah, but—"

"I am not in the habit, young man, of repeating myself to the help." She raised a large, beefy hand and gestured to the couch opposite her.

Another flash of lighting illuminated the storm beyond the windows. Dyson wondered if the downpour outside might not be preferable to what was about to be unleashed in the study. Resigned, he shut the double doors and crossed to the couch.

Once he was seated, Mrs. Whittier attempted a smile. It was a weak effort. Her round, broad features creased at the edges of her mouth, pushing pounds of fleshy cheek toward her eyes. She folded her hands across her expansive stomach, the palm of one hand tapping out an odd rhythm against the back of the other. "Pray tell," she began, "what exactly were you doing out in the barn with Tony?"

"Like I said, I was walking the grounds. I saw a light on in the barn and went to investigate."

"I don't recall mentioning that there had been any activity in the barn."

"I needed some fresh air."

Without even acknowledging he'd spoken, Mrs. Whittier went on, "In fact, as I recollect, you were informed that all of the activity had happened here, inside the house. Is that not correct?"

"Yes, but—"

"Then why were you out in the barn luring one of this ministry's most faithful members—"

"I wasn't 'luring' anybody," Dyson interrupted. "Nothing happened."

She sized him up before continuing. "Yes, well, your 'nothing' and this ministry's 'nothing' are two very disparate things, I'm sure." She leaned forward, her face threatening to take up his entire field of vision. "I'm paying you well, Mr. Dyson, quite well, as a point of fact. In return I expect very little of you other than to do the job I hired you to do. And stay away from my boys."

"And pretend to be one of them," Dyson added.

Mrs. Whittier eased back in her chair. It groaned so loudly Dyson worried it might break. Well, he wondered at least.

"My boys have been disturbed enough. They don't need to know you're here to roust this…entity from our midst."

"And once I get rid of it? Won't they be suspicious when I just up and leave?"

A titter of laughter gurgled up from her broad throat. It sounded odd to hear a delicate schoolgirl's laugh emanate from such a large body. She shook her head as if enjoying the naïveté of a child. "Oh, Mr. Dyson, my boys have seen their fair share of cowards come and go from this house. I'm sure watching one more won't come as much of a surprise."

Dyson squelched the first thought that came to mind. He went with the second instead. "Mrs. Whittier, it's obvious you've done your research on me, otherwise you wouldn't be making such a big deal about what didn't happen in the barn. But why contact me at all? I mean, there are others out there that could handle this job."

"Well, don't think I didn't consider just that thought," Mrs. Whittier said, that strained smile back on her face. "You, however, have developed quite a reputation in a short period of time and were just a stone's throw away in Washington DC. You see, I want this demon out of my house as quickly as possible."

"Mrs. Whittier, if it is a demon, that's a job for a priest, not me. I don't do exorcisms."

"We tried that. It didn't work," a voice said from across the room. Gerard stood in the doorway. His bathrobe was finally tied shut and his bed-twisted hair had been pressed down into some semblance of normalcy.

"How is Raymond?" Mrs. Whittier asked.

"Still upset." Though his white hair spoke to his age, the thin man still struck Dyson as hale and fit and surprisingly energetic. His accent was as thick as Mrs. Whittier's and spoke to a lineage deeper in the South than Virginia. "I left him in the kitchen with Terrence, nursing a cup of tea. Everyone else is back in their rooms, though I imagine we'll have a nest of weary birds in the morning."

"So you tried an exorcism?" Dyson asked.

"Yes, we did," the old man answered, shutting the doors behind him.

"What happened?"

Before Gerard could reply, Mrs. Whittier interjected. "It was less than successful."

"And no one has been able to give a description of what this thing looks like?"

Gerard shrugged his shoulders. "They're too traumatized by the experience to remember."

"And neither of you have seen it?"

"No," Mrs. Whittier replied. "I'm wondering, Mr. Dyson, if this sounds like anything you've encountered before."

"Well," Dyson hedged, "I like to be sure of what I'm dealing with before I rush to judgment."

Mrs. Whittier impatiently tapped the palm of her hand off the back of its twin again. Dyson wondered if she wasn't practicing some form of personal Morse code. "Mr. Dyson, I will remind you that you are in my employ." She leaned in close again. Her eyes looked like she might swallow him whole. "For the time being, I own you—body and soul. So if you have any suspicions—any suspicions whatsoever—I expect you to illuminate me. Please."

In the dimly lit room, a spark of lightning shone clearly through the window. It was followed instantly by an explosion of thunder. Dyson crossed to the windows and watched as the rain slapped against the thin panes of glass.

He cursed himself for taking this job. When he'd gotten the call, a sinking in his gut warned him to steer clear of the house and its ministry. But times were hard and he needed the money. After all, his last attempt to make money by saving a band of dwarves from a cannibalistic witch had been less than profitable. And Mrs. Whittier had offered him a lot, enough to maintain his Spartan lifestyle for quite some time. Now he questioned if any amount of money was worth a pact with the devil seated across the room.

Resigning himself, he turned back to face the pair. "I believe you have a succubus in the house."

"A succubus?" The word sounded strange and alien in Mrs. Whittier's Southern dialect.

"A spirit," Dyson said. "It sucks…the life force from men. It tends to thrive in environments where there's a lot of…sexual frustration," he explained. "This spirit will come to the men, usually while they're sleeping. It will get them…excited, so excited that they—"

"I believe that's enough, Mr. Dyson," Gerard interrupted, flushing red. He took the seat next to Mrs. Whittier and said, "Poppy, perhaps you should—"

"Don't be ridiculous, Gerard. We're hardly children in the schoolyard anymore," Mrs. Whittier replied without taking her eyes off Dyson. "Am I to understand that you believe a spirit has been drawn to this house because of the vow of abstinence taken by the young men of this ministry? And that this spirit's intent is to prey on their sexual energy?"

Dyson shrugged. "You gotta admit, twelve gay guys in one house, abstaining the way they are, they're bound to have a lot of pent-up… well, like you said, energy."

"And this being wishes to steal their seed?"

A bit embarrassed by the woman's candor, Dyson stumbled over his response. "Not just their seed. It wants their energy, their life force. It's draining them. Sucking them dry."

Mrs. Whittier's face went pale. "Are you saying this thing could kill my sweet boys?"

"With enough time, yes. Once it's strong enough, its nature changes. It becomes what's called an incubus. Once it does, it turns on them. It torments them. It attacks them. And eventually it will kill them."

"I see." Mrs. Whittier nodded, studying the floor, lost in thought. Finally, she looked back at him. "And what do you suggest we do to rid ourselves of this creature?"

"There's only one way to stop it. When it makes contact with its victims it has to take on corporeal form. That's the only way it can absorb their energy. When it does you have to cut off its source of power." Dyson slid the knife from the guard on his back and displayed it for the pair. Its serrated edge snatched light from the lamp beside Mrs. Whittier and shone proudly. Dyson continued, "You have to chop off its penis."

Gerard shuddered. Mrs. Whittier smiled. It was the first real smile he'd seen the woman give.

When she spoke again, her voice had returned to the light singsong air it had contained earlier. "Thank you, Mr. Dyson. I appreciate your time. You are free to go."

Dyson looked at her, shocked. She wasn't really going to accept all of this so easily, was she?

"Is there something else?" she asked, catching his stare.

"No. It's just you're taking this much better than I expected."

She smiled as if explaining something to a child. "Mr. Dyson, I already accepted the fact that my house was inhabited by some preternatural force. It's hardly a leap to give that force a name and intent."

Dumbfounded, Dyson slid the knife back into its guard and headed to the door.

"Mr. Dyson." Mrs. Whittier stopped him. "Remember, they're not to know the reason you're here."

Dyson nodded and left the room.

Once they were alone, Gerard turned to his childhood friend. "Poppy, are you certain you want—"

"What would you have me do," she asked, "allow this succubus to continue attacking my boys?"

He glanced nervously about the study. "Still..."

"Gerard." The single word was enough to still him. Mrs. Whittier placed her hands on the arms of the chair and hauled herself out of its depths. She crossed and stood before him saying, "Do I need to remind you that you gave me your word? Years ago. You promised you would stand by me no matter what."

Gerard wilted in his seat. A wisp of hair waved as he shook his head. He had not forgotten his promise.

"Then I hold you to your word." She headed toward the door. Before leaving she looked back at him and said, "It's a small price to pay, after what you did."

The old man sat alone in the dimly lit study. He gazed at the faded carpet, the storm just beyond the windows, the threadbare pillow crushed into the seat of Mrs. Whittier's vacated chair, anywhere but at the pair of eyes still watching him across the empty room.

It waited until the lights were out and everyone had fallen back to sleep. It left the first floor and took the stairs to the second. The only proof of its presence was the chill in the air. Fresh-cut flowers displayed in an alcove on the landing took on a sheen of frost as it passed by. Stopping at the head of the stairs, it studied the length of the darkened hallway. Someone new was here, in the house tonight. Someone strong. It passed down the hallway to investigate.

Avery snuggled close against Dyson's broad back. Dyson felt the reporter's arm slip around his naked body, pulling him tight. The sweat and heat brought on by their proximity was a fair trade for the pleasure of having him so close.

The reporter kissed his back and he felt the scruff of the man's auburn beard tickle his neck and shoulders. Dyson sighed and pressed into the embrace. He felt the other man's need, firm and resolute, tight against the cheeks of his ass. He ground against it and Avery moaned. A tongue joined the kisses and glided across Dyson's neck. A gentle hand caressed the firm muscles of his stomach before sliding lower.

He quivered as the man's tongue went to work against the flesh of his ear. He turned in the embrace to find the reporter's waiting lips. Tongues explored. Dyson reached down between Avery's legs and fondled the hot swelling he found there. Avery matched his rhythm stroke for stroke as the two men luxuriated in their kiss.

When their lips finally parted, Dyson sighed and chuckled. "This is nice."

"Yes, it is," a voice replied. Only it wasn't Avery's voice. It was quieter, more reserved. A voice Dyson hadn't heard in some time.

He opened his eyes. A face stared back at him, one without tousled auburn hair or a roman nose taking up the center of his face. A dark-haired boy, one used to wearing brown robes and spectacles, had taken

Avery's place. Only the boy was dead—a few years now. The proof was there, before Dyson's eyes. The boy's skin was pale and his flesh flaking away. His eyes were glassy and dull. The young man smiled that quiet smile of his, exposing rotted teeth. He leaned in for another kiss.

Dyson jerked awake. His breath came in gasps. He struggled to remember where he was. He glanced about the darkened room.

The sun was showing its first hint of rising. A dull, gray light peeked around the corners of the pulled blind. The matching twin bed opposite his was empty and still held his bags, not yet fully unpacked. His dream receded. He remembered where he was and the job that had brought him here.

Something caught his eye. There. In the corner. A fluttering between the closet door and the window. Something was there in the shadows.

He drew the knife from under his pillow, easing it from its guard. Swinging his feet off the mattress, he sat on its edge, ready to pounce at the first sign of trouble. He slowed his breathing, calming the pounding of his heart. He sat silently studying the darkened corner, waiting for a sign, ready for attack.

The curtain shifted. A slight breath of air funneled through the cracked window. Nothing more.

Dyson sighed, releasing taut muscles. He sheathed the knife and returned it to its hiding place beneath his pillow. He lay back on the bed. He grew achingly aware of the dream-induced throbbing between his legs. He thought about taking matters in hand and reached down to do so but stopped.

Had he just been victimized by the succubus? Had his brain attempted to fill in the blanks while a spirit manipulated his flesh?

Or had it only been a dream, a reshuffling of the cards of his subconscious?

His former lover and his new—exactly what was Avery was becoming? Dyson couldn't quite say—they had never shared equal billing in his dreams before. So if it wasn't the succubus, what had caused his brain to stir such an odd concoction? Dyson rolled onto his side.

The ministry's dress code required he wear a T-shirt to bed, and the fabric twisted on his shoulders and chest. He shifted, freeing the fabric, but felt no less constricted. He felt hot and cramped in the stifling room.

Rising, he stripped off his shorts and slid into a pair of jeans and sneakers before heading from the room. He took the stairs and left the house still troubled by his dream.

Though it hadn't been real, he couldn't get the feel of Avery's body out of his mind—the touch of his flesh, the taste of his lips. So far, the two men had shared a single kiss, and that had been after Dyson had saved the reporter from the witch with a soft spot for human flesh—not exactly the most romantic of settings.

Then again, most places Dyson found himself these days weren't exactly romance-inducing. Alleys fighting trolls. A Georgetown brothel filled with elves no taller than children. The homes of victims devoured by goblins. Hell, even his sparse apartment above his landlady's garage was hardly fit for guests, much less a potential boyfriend to impress.

Dyson sighed. Maybe that was what his dream was about. Maybe his life was such a mess it just wasn't fit to share with anyone special. The cold touch of his dead lover's skin, the sweet scent of his rotting corpse came to mind.

He pushed the thought away and stepped off the back porch onto a lawn of swirling vapor. The rains had passed during the night, leaving humidity mixed with the early-morning chill. Slight wisps of fog clutched at his legs like ravenous phantoms as he crossed the lawn to the darkened barn.

He stopped at the Citation with its open hood and thought of the man who he'd met working on it the night before. Fortunately, Tony had chosen not to make a guest appearance in his dream. Dyson snorted. That's all he would have needed.

His thoughts lingered on the man, though—but not in that sense. It seemed odd to Dyson that someone so confident, so assured would be in a place like this, a place that made him question the very core of who he was. He couldn't imagine what Tony had possibly experienced to make this place seem like the best option.

A snort from the far end drew his attention. He walked through the shadows to where the horses were housed. Blackie eyed him cautiously but Talulah accepted his gentle pat without question, whickering her approval.

"Hey, girl," he said, the thick hair of her mane coarse between his fingers. "How are you? Huh? How are you?" He patted the dense muscles of her neck reassuringly as he caught a whiff of the stalls. "Damn!" he exclaimed. "How long's it been since anyone cleaned these out?"

He opened the double doors at the end of the barn and found a small paddock on the other side. The mist cast a thick veil over the enclosure, blurring the woods just beyond the fence. Releasing the horses, he guided them to the corral to graze while he went to work mucking out their stalls.

Normally, Dyson would have found the effort invigorating. Life in DC gave him little opportunity for manual labor like this. And any time he had the chance to put his back to a task he welcomed it. It gave his reflections a chance to float free, like the early-morning fog easing its way through the open barn doors. His thoughts would tumble over one another, carrying him further and further till he found himself down a path with no idea how he'd gotten there. Not this morning, though.

His dream stirred up memories that preyed on him in an avalanche of accusation and guilt. He relived every choice, every action that had led to the corruption of his first and only relationship. Not just that relationship, though. His thoughts went to all those who had suffered because of his choices and to those who had died because of his failures. There'd been so many over the last six years he'd lost count. And what about Avery?

How many times had he put the reporter in danger just by being close to him? Could he continue to risk the man's life? Was he really that selfish?

He threw the shovel with all his might. It clanged into the wall and tumbled to the ground with a thunk.

"I must remember never to upset you." Dyson whirled to find Gerard standing nearby. Dressed in a gray cardigan against the morning chill, the man asked, "Are you all right?"

"Yeah, sorry," Dyson said, startled. He picked up the shovel. "Just slipped out of my hands is all."

"I'd hate to see it when you intended to throw it."

Dyson glanced at the elderly gentleman. There was a gleam in his eye. "What are you doing up so early?"

"When you reach my age, young man, one finds one's aches and pains are best remedied out of bed, not in." Gerard crossed his arms and studied Dyson. "And what about you? Why are you the early bird?"

Dyson offered no explanation but bent back to his task.

"Wondering if you made the right decision taking this job?" Gerard volunteered.

"I'm not one of your boys, old man. Don't try getting in my head."

Rebuffed, Gerard turned to leave. "I wouldn't dream of it," he said.

Dyson could have let it go at that, but he didn't. He needed to vent frustration, and the old man was an easy target. "You know, you got a hell of a nerve," he said, "trying to brainwash these guys into believing they're something other than what they are."

Gerard smiled. His eyes were shadowy holes in the barn's early-morning light. "Mr. Dyson, being gay isn't the end-all and be-all of their identity. It is only a part of them, a part that has caused them great pain and suffering."

"You can't say that," Dyson argued.

"Indeed I can. That pain has touched this household more profoundly than you can imagine." Gerard pondered whether to continue. After a moment's reflection, he made his decision and went on, "You may not be aware, but the Whittiers had a son—Jerry. My namesake and godson, as luck would have it."

"Yeah," Dyson said. "I heard he ran away."

"That's one version of the story. The version Poppy has chosen to propagate. The truth is that his mother banished him from this house."

Reflecting on his godson, the old man smiled. "Oh, he was a bright boy. Intelligent. Athletic. Charming. He was all that a mother could hope for in a son. Except in one way."

"He was gay," Dyson offered.

Gerard turned back to Dyson, startled—as if he'd forgotten someone else was present. "Yes, he was. Poppy learned the truth in a most unfortunate manner. It was all quite plebian, actually. There were, of course, tears and accusations. The hired hand was fired. And ultimately Jerry was driven from this house. Poppy never attempted to find the boy. She said as long as he lived in depravity, she wanted nothing to do with him."

The old man's alacrity vanished. "In less than a year word came that Jerry was dead. He'd overdosed on drugs. We never knew whether it was intentional or an accident."

"Couldn't Mr. Whittier have done something?"

"Claymore, Poppy's husband, had already passed by then."

"What about you? I mean, you were his godfather."

"Me?" Gerard chuckled. "No. Despite a friendship that has spanned millennia, I was in no position to make any claims on this household or Poppy, not at that particular time. No one could stop the inevitable, dark path this family took."

Gerard's mood lightened as he went on, "Out of his death, though, this ministry was born. Poppy came to me with her plan to dedicate her husband's home, her resources, her life to saving boys like Jerry before they made the same terrible choice."

He smiled. "So, yes, Mr. Dyson, I'd say we have one hell of a nerve to do what we're doing. It's a nerve born of personal pain and loss and the desire that no one else need go through what we've experienced."

"And that gives you the right to manipulate them? Prey on their doubts, on their fears, to convince them that they're bound for hell unless they live a lie?"

"We want them to be happy."

"They're gay. Nothing else is going to make them happy."

"Oh really?" Gerard asked. An eyebrow raised high on his forehead. "And are you?"

"What?" Dyson asked, struck.

"Are you happy, Mr. Dyson? In your gay life? Do you feel complete and fulfilled?"

His nightmare and all the doubts it had caused resurfaced. He looked away from those delving ancient eyes to the soiled hay at his feet.

Gerard let their silence linger a moment longer. Finally, he said, "Breakfast will be ready shortly, if you wish to join us." The old man turned and walked away from Dyson.

❖

In the loft above, the presence lingered. Waves of rage poured from it, chilling the space around it. Rats scurried away. The thing listened to the old man's lies and observed the young man's pain. The air surrounding it grew colder still.

❖

The house was silent. Dyson stood guard before a curtained window on the second floor. The corridor running the length of the house was dark and endless. An eternity of blackness crept out before him, much like the day behind him had.

He'd done his best to keep up appearances, sharing in the ministry's daily activities: meals, work on the grounds, games, quiet time—even group.

He'd sat in a circle listening to one young man after another explain how hollow and empty his life had been before the ministry, and all the while Dyson found himself considering Gerard's questions. Are you happy? Do you feel complete and fulfilled? The questions swirled around nipping at his soul.

In truth, he didn't know. He couldn't say when the last time was that he'd been truly happy or felt complete. And the longer he mulled it over, the more miserable he became. The only respite he had was the few minutes when Tony spoke.

Head bowed, the man picked nervously at the engine grease under his fingernails and began, "My life before, it was like…it was like watching a glass jar tumble from a shelf, you know? I mean, you see the jar hit the counter, right? And then it bounces off into the air. Your mind knows you should react. It knows you should grab the jar and stop it from falling, but you can't. You watch, mesmerized, as the jar hits the floor and shatters, splattering all over the place." He glanced up. His brown eyes found Dyson's small beady ones across the circle. "That's the way my life was. I could see what was happening. I knew I was spiraling out of control. I knew I was going to shatter, but I couldn't stop myself."

Dyson understood what Tony meant. It seemed like he'd been falling forever—ever since he'd started on this path, fighting the goblins and the elves and every other damned creature imaginable. And what about his sexuality? The two had happened simultaneously, his coming out and his learning that the dark actually was filled with monsters. After so long, they were knotted so closely together, the body count left from both so high, that he couldn't tell where one ended and the other began. Maybe Tony was right. Maybe he'd shattered years ago but was just too dense to realize it. And, oh my God, did he really want to bring Avery into the middle of all of that mess?

"Still can't sleep, Sherlock?" Tony stood beside him in the darkened hallway.

Dyson cursed himself. He needed to get his head in the game. If this guy could sneak up on him so easily, he didn't stand a chance against something as dangerous as a succubus.

"Where'd you come from?" he asked.

Tony nodded toward the backyard. The grease stains on his shirt were all the answer necessary. He turned his large brown eyes on Dyson and asked, "What's wrong?"

"Can't sleep," Dyson replied.

"You want to talk about it?"

Dyson didn't want to talk. He had no idea where to begin or how to put words to the questions hounding him. Finally, though, he did what came naturally and just dove in. "Are you happy? With the way you are now?"

"Sure I am," Tony answered instantly. "My old life is nothing compared to what I have now." Tony's answers, just like the rest of ministry's platitudes, all smelled like so much bullshit when held up to the reality of his life. None of it answered the questions churning in his head.

Tony studied him a moment. It was clear there was something else he wanted to say but didn't know how to give voice to it. He sighed and took a stab. "But sometimes I lie in bed at night and remember what it was like, back before. I remember Saturday nights out with friends. Sunday-morning brunches. Movie nights. Boys. Lots and lots of boys." He chuckled, embarrassed, and looked away. How long had it been since he'd revealed any of this to another person?

"What do you miss most?" Dyson pressed. He knew he was walking a fine line here. It would be so easy to frighten Tony back into hiding, back behind the ministry and everything he'd come to believe while at Haven's Rest. But Dyson needed him. He needed the truth. He needed to know if there was another option than the pain and loss that seemed to be the only thing holding his life together anymore. Because if it was all there was—really, what was the point?

Tony looked at him and then back at the floor. He glanced a second time and snickered, shaking his head. After a moment he eased himself back against the wall. His face was hidden by the shadows from the curtains framing the window. Even so, Dyson could feel his eyes on him.

"I miss the feel of a man's body next to mine."

Dyson chuckled, surprised by his honesty. "Well, sure."

"Feeling another human being's touch. Feeling alive in the way that only being close to another person can make you feel." Then the damn broke. Words came pouring out. Tony couldn't seem to stop himself.

"I miss watching a guy jack off, lying there beside him. Just watching him, his secret stroke, that one he knows better than anyone, that one that drives him crazy. Its nuance. Its variation. And then trying it out on yourself just because you're curious, just because you have to know. The rhythm of it as he finds his stride, his head tilted back, his eyes closed. The breather he takes so he won't come too soon, so he can enjoy it as long as he can. That glistening strand dripping onto his stomach, taunting you with what's in store. The single jerk as his dick lays there resting before he goes back at it, before he finds his stride again, and his knees lock, and his ass clenches, and it carries him all the way over into oblivion."

The hallway went silent. Dyson's heart pounded in his throat. His mouth was dry. His hands quivered.

From the shadow of the curtains, a smudged hand reached out toward Dyson's face. He watched it cross the distance between them and stop short of his lips. The tang of engine oil filled his nostrils.

"And in that moment," Tony whispered, "you see a little bit of his soul."

Dyson wondered what it would feel like if Tony touched him with that stained hand, that hand still black and rough with grease from the Citation's motor. Before he had a chance to find out, though, it withdrew, back into the shadows, lost from view.

From the darkness Tony said quietly, "That's what I miss."

Dyson's head spun. He'd hoped for something to pull him back, away from the questions tormenting him. He'd hoped for an answer that might guide him in a different direction, not new questions causing more doubt and confusion. Sure, he'd felt the attraction between them, but he hadn't expected anything to come of it. What was he supposed to do now? Damnit!

"Tony, I—"

A scream from one of the rooms interrupted him. Years of training took over as the knife appeared in his hand before the scream had even died.

Tony jumped away from the knife. "Dyson, what…?"

Without answering Dyson raced down the hall. Cracks of light appeared under bedroom doors as he passed by. He reached the room where the shout had originated and threw open the door. Switching on the light, Dyson saw two wide-eyed men lying in their matching twin beds staring across the room in horror. He turned to see what had terrified them. It wasn't what he'd expected.

In the corner beside the chest of drawers, the figure of a young man glowed. Through its translucent form the flower print paper covering the wall could be seen. It bobbed slowly and silently near the ceiling. It was dressed in a suit and tie from a bygone era (not the naked succubus Dyson had expected). His hair was parted down the center and combed tight against his head.

There was something to the face that Dyson recognized. The eyes looking down on him seemed somehow familiar. Where had he seen them before?

"Let me through!" Mrs. Whittier's voice could be heard on the other side of the door. "Boys, out of my way!" The men parted as she wedged herself through the door's frame. The apparition turned his gaze on her, and her face went pale. "No," she said weakly. "No, it can't be."

"Who?" Dyson asked, "Who is it?" The eyes? What was it about the eyes? "Mrs. Whittier, who is it?"

"Claymore!" Gerard exclaimed from the doorway. "Clay, is it you?"

Mrs. Whittier crumbled to the floor. A whimper in her throat bubbled up past her lips.

The old man's slippers whispered across the carpet as he crossed to the hovering spirit. Heads stretched around the bedroom's door frame as every member of the household tried to see the ghost. The apparition appeared expressionless as the elderly gentleman approached, his hand outstretched to its face.

"Clay, is it really…" The words caught in his throat. Gerard's fingers reached out to gently touch those glowing lips. It was a gesture Dyson recognized. He'd seen it in the shadows of the hallway just moments before. He wondered if Clay yearned for Gerard's touch the way he'd craved Tony's in that moment. His answer came quickly enough.

Claymore's eyes flared wide with rage. Gerard flew across the room and tumbled to the floor with a cry. The men in the doorway gasped. Mrs. Whittier shrieked and covered her head. Her whimpering grew to keening as she rocked back and forth on the floor.

"Clay!" Gerard said, struggling back to his feet. "Clay, what is it? What's wrong, my love?"

A dozen pairs of eyes turned to the old man in shock, coming to the same conclusion Dyson had reached a moment before.

"Shut up, Gerard!" Mrs. Whittier screamed. "You promised!"

But the old man ignored her. "What did I do, Clay?"

"Shut up!" Mrs. Whittier howled, her hands covering her ears.

"Please tell me, what did I do?"

"Shut up, you faggot!" the woman screeched.

The ghost turned on her, his eyes aflame. His widow cowered.

"What is it, Clay?" Gerard said, drawing the specter's attention. "Why are you here?"

In response, the ghost looked at the young men in the room. His rage dissipated instantly, replaced by compassion.

"No, no. You don't understand," Gerard said, limping back toward the spirit. "We don't want to hurt them. We're trying to help them. We want to keep them from ending up like Jerry."

Reminding the specter of the first life they had ruined, of the way his wife had rejected his son, of his lover standing by letting it happen, this was not the thing to do.

The room grew cold. Dyson guessed the temperature dropped fifteen degrees in an instant. The ghost swelled in size as he rose to the ceiling before diving down, encircling his widow and his lover. Gerard and Mrs. Whittier screamed in terror as the ghost tossed them about, an empty-sounding howl of anger escaping its lips. Gerard ran from the room followed by a gaggle of screeching men. Mrs. Whittier lay facedown on the carpet sobbing, blabbering gibberish. And as quickly as the ghost of Claymore Whittier had attacked, he returned to his spot in the corner, glowering down at his widow.

Dyson realized he still had the knife in his hand and returned it to the guard on his back. He turned to leave the room. Before he could, a hand clutched his ankle.

"Please, Mr. Dyson. Please," Mrs. Whittier said, grasping desperately at his leg. Tears oozed down the pounds of flesh making up her cheeks. "Please, you have to help me get rid of him. You promised."

Dyson glanced at the specter near the ceiling. It returned his gaze, silently awaiting his response.

"Can't help you there, Mrs. Whittier," Dyson said. "Everyone has to make peace with their own ghosts." He turned back to the woman and asked, "Why should you be any different?"

He left her alone with her husband.

❖

By the time Dyson woke the next morning, the heat had returned. It clung to anything it could find. This included the small group of men sitting outside with bags packed, waiting on their rides. Gerard was nowhere to be found. Mrs. Whittier stood in the window of her second-floor bedroom, still in her robe, muttering to herself as she watched her boys abandon her.

Dyson walked through the near-empty house. The presence of Claymore Whittier was still as prevalent as it had been the night before. Whether visible or not, he could be felt in every room and down every hallway. Dyson was sure the ghost would never again let Mrs. Whittier use his ancestral home to destroy a young man's life.

His inspection of the house didn't turn up the one person he'd hoped to see most, though. Several of the men had left before sunrise, calling on whomever they could to take them as far away from the haunted mansion as possible. Dyson hoped Tony hadn't been one of them. He had too much to say to him before he headed back to DC.

It had been a long, sleepless night for Dyson. The image of Gerard reaching up to touch his dead lover's face haunted him still. He thought of his own lover, gone now, and tried to imagine himself one day like

Gerard, old and alone, guilt-ridden, pretending to be something he wasn't. But Dyson could never do that.

His life might not have been perfect, but it was a hell of a lot better than living the lie Gerard had for so many years. No amount of pain or guilt, no amount of loss could ever make him deny who he was or the chance to love again.

And who was to say that he might not do just that—find love again someday? Maybe even with an auburn-haired reporter with a knack for getting himself into trouble? Hell, it was possible. It was as possible as making an old Chevy Citation run again.

He opened the barn door, praying Tony would be there. Sure enough, the familiar figure was bent over the engine, humming to the indiscernible tune crackling from the clock radio.

Tony peeked over the motor, the soot and grime from the engine staining his face. "Hi," he said. Dyson tried to decipher his tone. It was less casual than the last time they'd stood here, yet still open and inviting. At least, Dyson hoped it was.

"Hey," he ventured. He stepped inside the barn and let the door shut behind him. It was roasting inside. The smell of hay and rotting cardboard mingled thickly in the air. Sunlight filtered down through the gaps between the barn's clapboards, a dazzling display dancing across the floor. From her stall at the back of the barn Talulah whickered at him.

"So, your bags packed?" Tony asked, his attention once again on the engine.

"Not yet. It shouldn't take long, though. I didn't really have time to unpack."

"Right, 'cause you weren't expecting to be here that long anyway."

Dyson let the comment ride and asked, "What about you? When are you leaving?"

"I might stay a while," Tony replied.

Dyson stared at him dumbfounded. "What?"

"Mrs. Whittier's going to need some help around here once everyone's gone."

"But they lied to you—all of you."

"And you'd know all about lying, wouldn't you, Sherlock?" Tony glanced at him to see how the comment landed. He could be proud of his aim.

"Tony, I'm—"

"Look, I get it. This is your life. In some weird whacked-out reality where ghosts and spirits exist, this makes sense."

"I know it's confusing, but if you—"

"Well, this is my life," he said, gesturing to the barn and the estate beyond. "This makes sense to me."

"How? How can you feel that way?"

"I spent a year here," Tony replied. "I believe in what this place is about. Just because the messenger was a fraud doesn't mean the message was. I have to stand by what I believe is right."

Dyson's head swam. This was not how he'd imagined this conversation going. Sure, he'd guessed Tony would be angry with him for lying about his reasons for being there. Still, he'd hoped, with time, there might be a chance to rescue their friendship, once they were both away from this horrible place and back to their lives. Looking into Tony's eyes now, though, he didn't see much hope of that happening.

Still, the fighter in him wouldn't go down without one last jab. "Are you standing by what you believe? Or hiding from whatever it was that brought you here?" Struck by the comment, Tony looked away. Dyson reached for Tony's shoulder. "We may be damaged, but we're not broken. We're not shattered on the floor. We just need time to work it out."

Tony looked back at Dyson. It was there in his eyes. He wanted to burst out of whatever jail held him captive, whatever past threatened to ruin his future. But as quickly as it appeared, the yearning in his eyes faded, and he turned back to the car, burying his head in its innards.

Dyson let his hand fall back to his side. There were no more words to be said. The barn door squealed as he opened it but then slammed back in its frame as he let go. He turned back to Tony.

No words to be said, maybe, but one last thing to be done.

He crossed and took the other man by the arm.

"Dyson, what—"

"Sit down," he said, pushing Tony backward into a pile of broken-down boxes. They collapsed further under his weight.

"What are you doing?" Tony demanded.

"Something for you," Dyson replied as he lowered the car's hood. "I'm leaving you with something." He slid up onto the hood and leaned back against the windshield. "A present."

A look of confusion crossed Tony's face. As Dyson unzipped his pants, the confusion vanished and he shook his head. "Dyson, I—"

"Nothing's gonna happen," Dyson reassured him. He lifted his hips to lower his pants down around his ankles. "From me to you."

Tony stood and headed to the door. "I can't."

"You can if you want to," Dyson said. "If you want me to."

Tony stood frozen, ready to retreat. The sound of a car horn announced the exodus of another of the ministry's former members, another wounded soul taken in by Mrs. Whittier and Gerard's promises. Another soul now disillusioned with their lies.

After a moment's hesitation, Tony turned back. His eyes scanned the cluttered floor of the barn before turning to Dyson, naked on the hood of the car. "You don't have to," he said. All the confidence that had drawn Dyson to him originally was gone. In its place was an uncertain young man. Dyson wondered again what ghost tormented him.

He shrugged and said, "I was hired to roust a spirit. I couldn't do much for Mrs. Whittier's, but maybe I can do something for yours."

Tony shook his head and smiled. He returned to his seat on the boxes.

With eyes on him now, Dyson's heart began to pound. The barn's stifling heat made him sweat. His hands shook nervously. His embarrassed chuckle filled the silence.

"What?" asked his audience of one.

"I've never done this before," he confessed.

"You've never jacked off before?" That wicked smile was back, the one that made it so easy for Dyson to smile in return.

"Not for someone to watch, no." He chuckled. "I'm not sure if I'll do it right."

"Just give it your best shot, Sherlock."

So he did. And when all was said and done, Dyson did just fine.

GIGOLO LESSONS
JAY STARRE

They first met for lunch at the top of the Space Needle. As the restaurant slowly revolved, Reynold and Paolo were treated to a sweeping view of Seattle in the springtime.

"The job I'm offering you will require two months of your time. You will be my traveling companion on a trip that will take us around the world."

Reynold's brother was a software executive and a friend of Paolo's. He had already explained this part of the deal to his younger sibling. Much had been left unsaid, and Reynold was silent as he waited for the suave Italian to reveal the real requirements for the job.

Paolo smiled, apparently pleased with Reynold's patience. "After lunch, we will retire to my hotel room where the real interview will take place, which should tell me what I want to know about you. As well, how you feel about what takes place should help you decide whether you want the job or not."

The blond grad would be paid $500 for the afternoon, regardless of the outcome of the interview. The hotel Paolo chose was world-class and the room fabulous. Afterward, Reynold believed it was the easiest $500 he had ever made—and he had enjoyed it thoroughly. But could he keep it up for two months? Hell yeah!

Once inside the fancy suite Paolo immediately began the interview. He was direct. The tall Italian also began to undress Reynold as he grilled him. They stood facing each other in front of a the big bed in the room as the Italian unbuttoned Reynold's dress shirt, button by button. He gazed into the blond's lovely hazel eyes with his own golden-brown ones while asking the most intimate of questions.

The mirror beside the bed reflected their bodies as Paolo stripped the college grad. Equal in height, they were otherwise quite different.

Reynold kept his strawberry-blond hair in a short, slightly curly mop and merely pushed it back from his forehead after showering. Once a month he had it trimmed down with the sides cut close. Round silver-framed and intellectual-looking glasses offered a contrast to his casual hairstyle. His eyes were a spectacular hazel with hints of green, blue, and gold. He shaved only once a week or so, but his beard was very light and hardly noticeable. His lips were full and pink and his smile, though slow to come, was genuine. He had a spray of freckles across the bridge of his nose and upper cheeks, which added emphasis to the casual chaos of his natural looks. Those freckles dotted his arms and shoulders too, but the rest of his body was ivory pale where it hadn't been exposed to the sun. A down of reddish blond coated his arms and legs, but his chest and ass were mostly hairless.

Reynold hit the gym for weight training on a regular basis, but it was more of a mindless pumping and pushing just to get his muscles in shape for what he really loved, which was hiking and cycling. Correspondingly, his body was more athletic than bulky.

He wore no jewelry, not even a watch, but had a woven leather bracelet around his left wrist and a similar one around his right ankle. He was without any tattoos or pierced body parts.

Paolo was just as handsome, certainly, but in an understated, almost bland way. He was clean-shaven and his olive complexion was flawless. His dark-brown hair was coiffed in a trendy short mop around his broad face. He had a small nose with a downward curve that pointed at his wide mouth and dimpled chin. His eyes were golden brown and wide-set. His smile was brilliant with teeth that were undoubtedly whitened regularly. His body was smooth and muscular, and Reynold was certain he paid a trainer on a regular basis to help him achieve that effect.

In that way they were physical opposites, with Paolo's looks calculated to flawless perfection while Reynold's were relaxed and natural. Later, Paolo would tell Reynold that this relaxed beauty was exactly what he had been looking for.

The last thing Paolo did was remove Reynold's glasses before he kissed him. Reynold himself loved kissing and found it highly underrated by many. Paolo apparently sensed this and they kissed with slow yet deep thoroughness. Still completely dressed himself, he ran his hands all over the younger man's naked body, which was both sensual and titillating.

Feeling those exploratory hands all over his naked body, Reynold was struck by a strange sensation.

It seemed as if the Italian was feeling him out—as if Reynold were a wrestler and the older man was contemplating buying his contract. Or more crudely, as if he were a racehorse Paolo was thinking of purchasing. In truth, those first few minutes of kissing and fondling with Reynold totally naked and Paolo still dressed and in command defined their future relationship.

Then Paolo smiled. The smile displayed white teeth between lush lips, engaging enough, but it was the way the rest of his face followed that made all the difference for Reynold. His golden eyes seemed to light up, while his nostrils flared slightly and his dark brows rose like wings above his eyes, not quite a wink but definitely a sign of fun to come rather than predicting a test of his abilities.

At the same time, his hands lingered particularly on Reynold's ass, which was high and round but very compact. He jogged, hiked, swam, and cycled, and the solidness of his butt cheeks reflected that energetic lifestyle. It was smooth, with just a down of faint hair on the marble-hard cheeks. It was particularly satiny in the deep crack, especially around the snug entrance to his hole.

Not shy about what he intended, Paolo slid fingers into that crack and stroked the bare hole. "Come, shall we retire to the bed?"

"Absolutely. I'm all yours for the afternoon. Lead the way, and I'll follow."

And he meant it. This was a lark, and he hadn't yet made up his mind about any future decisions. He felt no pressure and had no agenda. Of course he understood this was only how he felt now. Later, he would have to step up to the plate if he took the job. Whatever that required.

Once Paolo had stripped too, they started out by lying head-to-toe on the bed and sucking each other's cocks. Paolo's was plump and dark brown with a slippery hood. Reynold's was long and rigid, cut and bright pink with a flared knob at the head.

There was a lazy feeling to the slow slurping and swallowing that the college grad relished. There seemed no need to rush, and when Paolo finally rose to straddle his chest and grin down at him, he was completely ready for anything he might suggest.

The Italian produced a condom and lube and continued to smile down at him as he instructed him to wrap his stiff cock and apply a slippery coating that had it gleaming dark amber in the afternoon light.

They switched positions and it was the blond who now straddled the Italian. He reached back and fed himself that stiff cock. He rocked back and forth on it while gazing into Paolo's eyes and returning his smile. Paolo settled his fine hands on his solid ass cheeks and squeezed as he humped his lap. In return, Reynold ran his hands all over the Italian's smooth torso. He rubbed and tweaked his brown nipples and massaged his biceps and shoulders. He stroked his face, using his fingertips to caress his lips and chin. He cupped his face and bent down to kiss him deeply as he swallowed up the Italian's rigid cock with his warm asshole and clamped down over it.

Paolo grunted at the pressure and thrust upward. Now they fucked, neither capable of stemming the tide of need that gripped them. Cock rammed upward while ass slammed downward. Faster and harder, they fucked each other while they kissed and moaned and writhed atop the plush bed.

Reynold came first. Without even touching his rearing hard-on, he spewed onto Paolo's smooth belly. In the throes of his orgasm, his asshole convulsed around the pummeling cock inside it. Paolo couldn't resist the squeezing spasms and let loose himself deep inside the college grad's warm ass channel.

In the aftermath, lying naked on that soft bed in that fancy hotel room, they forged their agreement. Ten days later, they were in Valencia, Spain.

Reynold immediately found himself enthralled with the city. With a busy port that was the second largest on the Mediterranean, Valencia boasted a slew of historic buildings dating back to its Moorish past. The warm subtropical climate encouraged a local culture that revolved around agriculture and food.

In his spare time, which he had a lot of while Paolo attended to his business, Reynold rented a bicycle and rode along the old riverbed, which had been drained and transformed into a lengthy park. At one end of the park was the City of Arts and Sciences, with modern architecture and sweeping white buildings in lush green surroundings.

In his meandering rides he discovered the city was surrounded on the land side by garden agriculture of all types, from rice paddies to fruits and vegetables—oranges, lemons, onions, and wine. He rode his bike through some of the older districts where the buildings were either in a state of disrepair or reconstruction. Ceramic tiles, iron railings, wood, and stucco abounded. Grandmothers sat in chairs on the sidewalks and kids played all around them. The colorful buildings seemed to obey no housing codes like he was used to in a much more controlled Seattle. It was called the city of one hundred bell towers and they were literally all over the city, ringing out their clanging at regular intervals to echo in the narrow alleys and lanes.

Reynold discovered the Central Market, which was abundant with a myriad of cheeses, hams, fresh fish, vegetables, and fruit. Paolo joined him there and proved he was a food epicurean in his own right. The Italian not only liked fine restaurants but liked to cook as well. The men began to cook together more often instead of going out. The young American learned a lot about cooking, which had never been very important to him other than a means to get the right nutrition. Paolo taught him how to make an especially delicious local paella with rabbit and chicken. They also went out strolling at 8:30 p.m. and sampled the many tapas bars. The locals and tourists alike sat outside in the balmy air with fountains splashing nearly everywhere. The Valencians seemed to all dress well.

"Don't bring many clothes. Just the things you really like to wear and you find comfortable. We will buy you some clothes as we travel," Paolo had instructed him before they left.

And so they did. He felt a little like a dress-up doll as Paolo picked out what he should buy and paid for it. He then wore whatever his employer chose of those new clothes when they went out.

"I want you to look good. How you look reflects on me and my business."

It didn't take long to figure out what Paolo's business was. Although the Italian didn't discuss any business with him directly and during most of the day he was off on his own tending to clients, Reynold was asked to join Paolo for a number of business lunches and dinners.

Reynold's major in university was European history and languages.

He spoke fluent Spanish, Italian, French, German, and Greek. He had no problem listening and conversing with the businessmen Paolo introduced him to.

He learned that Paolo was a type of business agent, closing real estate deals for the most part, but also arranging for clients to come together for all kinds of other arrangements. Some of those "other arrangements" were about to involve Reynold himself.

Amidst the palm-lined streets and along the sandy beaches under clear blue skies, Reynold allowed the time to pass almost mindlessly. Until reality reared its head and he was asked to meet with one of Paolo's clients.

Paolo was direct about it, just as he was about everything. "The sheik has asked for your company tomorrow afternoon and evening at his house in the Carmen. If you are willing, you will earn a substantial amount for your time."

Reynold was silent for some moments as he thought over the ramifications.

"Are you a pimp?" he had to ask Paolo.

"In a way, I suppose. As you have seen, my profession involves making deals. If you are willing, I will provide you to my friends and they will provide me with a return favor. The sheik intends to purchase some expensive property another friend of mine is desperate to sell in Valencia. In Venice, where we will next go, we will meet with a soccer star whom we hope to sign with a lucrative endorsement after he has his fun with you. Again, if you are willing."

"So you must believe I can provide the service your friends require," he replied with a grin. "Have you been testing me over the past two weeks?"

"Of course, while enjoying myself at the same time. There is only one hard-and-fast rule. You must be prepared to play the hard-boned top or the ripe bottom, and at least pretend to enjoy both roles."

They both laughed out loud at that, proof of their growing ease with each other. It was clear that Paolo trusted him, bringing him along on his business meetings and now lending him out to important clients. It was easy enough to return that trust.

"Sounds like fun, then. I've never even met a sheik before."

The city was once a kingdom of its own under the Moors, and the

Carmen was the historic Moorish district of Valencia. That was where he met with the Arab sheik.

There was no doubt about what Reynold was there for. Some eye candy for the sheik's guests, certainly, but it was sex Abdul Azim was paying for. Big stucco walls surrounded the sheik's home on the narrow street, but once inside it opened up to a broad inner courtyard with Moorish ceramics decorating the flowerpots, the walls, and the splashing fountain. They had sex in the courtyard in the late afternoon, which was siesta time, then the Arab prince had friends over and entertained them, then he required sex again in the evening under the stars in that same courtyard.

Azim was older, probably in his early forties, with a black-and-gray goatee, a sharp nose, and brooding black eyes. He was extremely handsome even though he was intimidating. He spoke very politely and was genuinely courteous, until it was time for sex.

Then he practically barked at Reynold, "Get on your back and show me your pink hole, boy."

The young blond didn't mind the rough tone and merely nodded and obeyed. He had no idea what to expect, and perhaps he was naïve to think so, but he trusted Paolo's judgment. This sheik was probably domineering and nasty, but he wasn't dangerous.

Once Reynold had sprawled back on a tiled bench with his legs in the air and his ass bare and presented for the sheik's inspection, Azim got down on his knees and buried his face between Reynold's raised thighs. He ate ass like it was the best thing he'd ever tasted. He slobbered and spat and moaned, repeating over and over how beautiful the blond's hole was. He devoured that hole, then his balls and then his cock, and then his hole again.

After savoring crotch and ass for some time with his tongue and lips, he got up and stripped naked. Condoms and lube had been placed discreetly at hand by an attentive servant. The sheik's dark eyes gazed intently at Reynold's spit-gobbed pink asshole as he wrapped his curved dark cock and coated it with slippery goo. With a feral grin, he stepped up to drive his rigid pole balls-deep into the blond's wet slot. Amidst the potted orange and lemon trees and towering palms, they fucked right there in the afternoon sunlight with the splashing fountain behind them.

Later, in the moonlight, the sheik reversed their roles. He got up on the bench and raised his slim hairy thighs, pulled open his round ass cheeks, and presented his puckered brown asshole. There was little hair on the cheeks and nothing around the hole. Reynold licked it gently at first as the sheik groaned and wriggled, then he pulled the lips open with his fingers and stabbed deep into it. He ate that ass with as much uninhibited enthusiasm as the sheik had exhibited earlier when munching on his ass. Spit dribbled down the crack over the dangling balls, pooled in the amber-flushed hole, and oozed out of it when the pucker convulsed.

He repeated the sheik's earlier actions by getting up and plowing the spit-gobbed and lubed hole deep and hard. He drilled the grunting Arab so hard that when he shot, his cum rocketed out of his cock so far it hit his smirking face.

When they were done and Reynold was about to leave, Azim nodded to a nearby servant, who came forward to hand the blond an envelope. He had been forewarned by Paolo that he was to be paid discreetly and not make a fuss about it or thank the sheik.

Outside, he couldn't help opening it up and counting the euros. Two thousand in cash! He stifled a shout of joy, but couldn't help performing a little dance of glee before he hopped on his bike and headed back to their hotel.

A week later they were in Venice. It was a magical place. Even though the city bustled with tourists everywhere, the presence of water on every side created an atmosphere of lapping tranquility that was truly hypnotic. And with the ancient buildings all around, there was a feeling of timelessness that added to the dreamy reality.

After only a few days of enjoying the sights, it was time for work.

Paolo delivered him to their client in a water taxi. Not quite as romantic as a gondola, but then again the assignation was hardly romantic. As Reynold stepped off the boat and onto the steps above the water line, he looked up. The three-story building was typical, an umber stucco ornately decorated with wrought-iron railings on balconies above. He peered at the balconies and windows, hoping for a glimpse of the German soccer star he was to meet. He wondered if he would recognize him. He had only been told his name was Helmut, and discretion was a huge part of the game as far as this assignation went.

Everything he'd experienced so far had been a thrill, and he was more excited than nervous. His cock actually stirred in his fancy designer shorts and he had to smile to himself. He was definitely more excited than nervous!

As usual, Paolo had dressed him. This was to be a casual look, seeing as the client was an athlete. Reynold wore baggy shorts that fell to his knees. Pale gray and striped with blue, they were of the latest fashionable color. His expensive leather sandals were purchased right there in Venice the day before. A blue tank top matched his shorts and revealed his athletically muscular arms.

It turned out that what he wore hardly mattered. The moment he entered the Venetian apartment, the husky soccer star ordered him to strip. Apparently he had been informed that Reynold spoke fluent German.

Barking out his command in a deep-throated and harsh German, Helmut sprawled on a gleaming navy-blue leather couch, completely naked and sporting a tremendous boner.

"I want you naked and hard. Come here and I will prepare you for the fuck."

"*Ja*, of course."

Reynold offered his slow, unassuming smile as he came forward. He was rewarded by a nod and a smirk from his client. The man was quite a hunk! Very hefty, considering he was a soccer player, and very hairy, he had light-brown hair cut short and a light beard on wide cheeks. His mouth was round and the upper lip curled as he grinned. His nose was big and blunt and so was his chin, while his brows hung over the most amazing pale-blue eyes.

His body was powerful and his legs enormous. Of course he ran back and forth over a soccer field for a living and he would have the thighs to show for it. Reynold took in the length and girth of the man's giant dick with interest, but also noted a thick silver ring separated his ball sack from his cock. Stretched downward by the gleaming ring, his balls seemed gigantic.

The burly soccer player produced an identical silver ring from a stand beside the couch. Once Reynold was naked and standing in front of him, Helmut pulled him forward by the balls and fastened it around his nut sack.

There was no forgetting it was there! His balls dangled down between his thighs, the heavy weight of the silver ring stretching them with every move. Helmut increased the pressure by tugging on Reynold's balls as he reached between his thighs to slide his fingers into his crack. Coated with lube, those fingers found his hole and dug inward.

It turned out the German loved fingering his hole. While he stood between the big athlete's furry thighs, the soccer star smirked and growled as he tugged on the blond's nuts and twisted his fingers around in his quivering asshole. His gut was churning and his balls aching by the time the German pulled him down onto his lap.

He straddled the powerful thighs and arched his back as the German's giant dick pushed up between his legs along the crack of his ass. Helmut pumped the fat meat up and down along the smooth crack as he continued to finger the hole with his fingers.

"Now, you must fuck yourself on my big German dick! Sit on it!"

The blond rose up off the soccer star's lap as Helmut's fingers finally slid from his asshole and the head of his twitching hard-on replaced them at the entrance to his well-stretched slot.

As Reynold slowly sat down on Helmut's pipe-thick dick, the soccer player added a pair of slippery fingers to the mix, pushing his plump knob past the blond's straining sphincter with them, then ever deeper into his steamy innards. Reynold grunted at the extreme pressure, which only made Helmut laugh out loud. He landed a resounding slap on his pale ass cheek with one hand while he shoved his cock and fingers even deeper.

"Oh God, *ja*," Reynold moaned.

"*Ja!* You like this big dick and these big fingers up your hungry American butt, don't you? *Ja?* Tell me what you like. I want to hear how much you like this hot dick stretching your American hole!"

That's when Reynold found his acting abilities. Not that he had to pretend to like what was going on. Not at all. The extreme ache and pressure felt amazing. It was the other thing Helmut so clearly desired—demonstrative, nasty expressions of his feelings, which he had to dredge up from hidden depths in his psyche. The blond was quiet by nature, and this was totally unlike him.

He arched his back and pushed downward to meet that fat dick and those thick fingers, swallowing up most of them. He shouted out loud.

"Hell *ja*! Give me that big German dick! Fuck me with those big fat German fingers! I fucking love it!"

When Helmut did just that, heaving upward with his hips and impaling the ivory butt, he chortled happily and slapped Reynold's ass again. The blond let out a mighty grunt, then a squeal as more dick and fingers invaded him.

It was liberating. The shouting, the squealing and grunting, the nasty talk, it was as if he were someone else. It was an important lesson; he would have to become a good actor if he was to pursue the role Paolo was offering him.

Meanwhile, Helmut proved insatiable. After fucking the young blond ferociously for half an hour, until both were drenched in sweat and gasping for breath, he finally shot his steamy load. Not through with Reynold yet, he then pumped a load out of a flopping and groaning Reynold while digging deep in his well-fucked ass with a trio of big fingers.

They took a break while sharing a few beers, naked on the couch and chatting easily about soccer, then Helmut grinned and winked as he flipped Reynold onto his belly. With the blond facedown on the smooth leather sofa, the German chortled happily as he once more crammed fingers up the American's ass before shoving his huge dick back inside for a second round of intense fucking.

There was one more wild bout just as it got dark, this time with the hefty soccer player on his back. With his furry thighs up and his feet in the air, he offered up his own hole. Reynold laughed as he returned the favor and dug deep with his fingers in the snug soccer ass pit before ramming home with his lengthy pink pole.

It turned out Helmut was so insatiable he had to have Reynold back the next day, and the next. For ten days in a row, Paolo delivered his young protégé to the beefy soccer player to get the daylights fucked out of him. By the time they said good-bye, Reynold had made a small fortune.

He also had a new watch.

In passing, he had merely commented on how much he liked it. It was made of gleaming silver with a big face that included an interesting detail, a globe with times around the world. The smiling German had taken it off and handed it to him. "It is yours."

He could tell it was very expensive, and he didn't even like wearing a watch. But he didn't know how to refuse it, and afterward asked Paolo how he should have handled the situation.

"Always accept gifts from clients even if you don't want or need them. It is an insult to refuse, and you can always sell anything later."

Paolo then offered up more advice he apparently deemed necessary at that point in their journey. He must be uninhibited but also throw himself into the sex, which was beyond merely shedding inhibitions. He must please his partner—which in turn would please himself. Financially, he must learn to save whatever he could. His career as a gigolo might end at any time and he would want to avoid the fate of many others who had descended into the dreary life of a low-paid whore.

"Learn not to flirt with other men when with a client, yet also be charming and friendly so he is proud to have you at his side. Learn to lie along with your client when he claims you are his personal assistant he is training, or something along that line. Remember always that a client wants you because they don't want to have to work at a relationship. They want someone who is available, looks good—and I mean what they think of as looking good—and speaks only when spoken to. Can you do all this, my young friend?"

"So far, it's been easy."

It was true that the sex with clients was not the same as the sex he enjoyed with Paolo. The Italian was an attentive and rather easygoing lover. Reynold's two experiences thus far, with the sheik and the soccer star, had been more like workouts, sometimes verging on the marathon. Not that he disliked that aspect; in fact, he enjoyed the challenge. It really had been easy so far.

Paolo was more experienced and realistic. "We will see. The next one might not be so simple. Or the next."

Reynold understood what Paolo meant when they met Hiroshi in Hong Kong.

Before that were two more stops, in Delhi and Jakarta. In the Indian city, Paolo lent him out to a wealthy Brazilian who owned sugar plantations. In the Indonesian capital he was introduced to a Dutch entrepreneur who specialized in the cell phone market. Both proved interesting lovers, but not particularly unusual in their demands.

He did notice that so far on every occasion his clients had not been from the city they were currently in. "The world is like that," Paolo replied with a smile when he asked about it. "Everyone is always from somewhere else."

Finally they landed in Hong Kong, the gateway to China, which was their final stop before heading back to the good old USA. It was a city so totally different from any other he had been to that he was at first completely at a loss. The sheer density of the metropolis with the crowds and the skyscrapers was daunting enough. The fast-paced and rampant commercialism had him reeling.

Then Paolo took him to a Buddhist temple in the middle of the chaos. The tranquil garden and reverence for a religion ages old soothed his nerves. That was the afternoon before he was sent for his final gigolo lesson of their summer journey.

Paolo had a warning for him. "Hiroshi is a very generous businessman. In fact, his name means 'generous' in Japanese. But he does enjoy unique pleasures. Treat this liaison with an open mind and it will go well."

Reynold took an elevator that soared upward to the seventy-fifth floor in mere moments. Inside the ultra-modern suite, he was greeted by a stocky and unassuming young Japanese businessman. Hiroshi.

"Welcome, Reynold. I am Hiroshi. Is the view not splendid?"

His English was impeccable, as was his dress. A tailored suit fit his broad frame perfectly. His short dark hair was coiffed neatly to frame a broad face with delicate features. His smile was sweet, and his small hands were gentle as they took his and led him past the floor-to-ceiling windows that offered a stunning panorama of the city and the harbor. They entered the bedroom, which boasted the same amazingly huge windows, and went directly to a mattress on the floor beside the windows that were actually the wall.

It was a futon they settled down on, a mat that served as a bed for many Japanese. The businessman's soft and supple hands stripped Reynold as he continued to smile sweetly. Once the blond was naked, Hiroshi abandoned him on the bed momentarily to go to his closet and fetch some implements for the games ahead.

And it was to be games of an unusual type, Reynold understood as soon as the smiling businessman returned to deposit his gear on the bed in front of him. Dildos. Leather harnesses. Padded handcuffs. A leather paddle. Yikes!

In the brilliant light flooding in from the large windows, there was to be no hiding from the raunchy proceedings that followed. As Reynold silently contemplated the toys on the bed, Hiroshi stripped off his suit and then knelt before him naked.

"I will instruct. Please allow yourself to experience pleasure from my pleasure."

Reynold nodded. His cock rose pink and stiff between his legs as he knelt on the bed and looked over his naked partner. Hiroshi had a beautiful body. It was utterly smooth and hairless, even at the crotch, and although on the plump side, he was muscular as well.

His instructions were precise. First Reynold was ordered to secure him with the padded cuffs, his wrists to his ankles. The businessman was on his back, legs pulled back and in the air. His round ass was exposed. He looked downright voluptuous.

Next, the blond was told to paddle him.

It proved an exhilarating experience. Raising the leather paddle, he drove it downward to slap against that smooth amber butt. He slammed down the paddle over and over as Hiroshi whimpered and his lush ass grew bright pink. The puckered hole in the center of his ass crack pouted and clenched with every blow while the plump cheeks quivered.

"Thank you, Reynold. Now you must use the dildo. The large one."

There was lube, clear and slippery, which he applied to the fire-engine-red dildo, then to the flushed ass cheeks and crack. He took the heavy toy in hand and placed it on target. It looked far too big to fit into the snug sphincter, but he assumed Hiroshi knew what he wanted.

The toy was shaped like a giant cock, with a large head, then two larger heads farther down the shaft. Even if he got that first giant head inside Hiroshi, the next two were bigger!

He was amazed to see that enormous toy disappear up Hiroshi's tender brown hole, one huge head after the other. The cuffed businessman squirmed and grunted while he heaved upward off the bed, but he gave no indication he didn't want what he was getting. It took a few minutes, but eventually only the broad red base was left protruding from that stuffed hole.

It was awe-inspiring to imagine all that rubber up the squirming businessman's ass!

"Now it is your turn, my friend."

Reynold was fairly certain he could never take that giant dildo up his ass, but he was determined to let Hiroshi give it a try if that was what he wanted. Fortunately for the blond, that wasn't what he had in mind.

After he had been uncuffed, with that giant red toy still planted deep in his gut, he showed the young American what he did want. Hiroshi used his delicate hands to fasten a leather ass harness around Reynold's waist. A long strap was connected to the base of the harness under his balls to dangle from it. Before it was attached to the back of the harness the American was bent over on his knees with his face in the pillows. Hiroshi lubed up his smooth white crack, then slowly inserted a dildo from the pile he'd tossed on the bed earlier.

This one was big, no question about it, but no bigger than a rather large human cock. The Japanese businessman eased it up Reynold's quivering hole slowly but steadily until only the pale white base was left showing.

Then he pulled the strap back dangling down between Reynold's legs up under his spread thighs and secured it to the leather strap around his waist. Now the dildo was tightly secured deep in his ass by the leather harness around his crotch and waist.

"Now you will fuck me."

The harness surrounded his cock and balls but left them exposed, and with his hard-on bobbing in front of him, he mounted the sprawled businessman and fucked his ass crack, both of them with dildos plugging their asses.

After a few exciting minutes of that, he was told to remove the red plug from Hiroshi's hole. Once the big thing popped free, he slammed his cock deep in the gaping slot left behind. It was totally unreal to be fucking that stretched hole while his own hole was stuffed full of dildo, the harness holding it tight inside him.

Hiroshi whimpered and moaned nonstop while Reynold savaged

him from above until finally he cried out and shot his load all over the futon beneath him.

Not yet completely satisfied, the smiling businessman had the blond American kneel facedown with his beautiful ivory-white ass in the air, the dark leather harness outlining the round cheeks and the dark strap between them holding in the dildo. He ordered Reynold to jerk off while he used the paddle to punish his wriggling white can.

The sharp sting of the paddle and the deep ache of the dildo combined into waves of hot pleasure that flowed over his pink-flushed butt and into his cock and balls. When he blew, it was so intense he almost passed out.

Hiroshi was definitely generous in the aftermath of their tryst. The envelope he offered the blond was stuffed with American fifties.

On the flight home, Reynold contemplated the events of the summer. Paolo had already asked him to travel with him again in the autumn, and the following spring and summer. He would have to decide if that was what he wanted.

His past life had been totally unlike that amazing two months. He had never traveled farther than Vancouver, Canada, or Portland, Oregon. He camped and skied and swam and boated but otherwise had remained a homebody in Washington state. As a third child of a single mother he had grown up accustomed to working hard and scraping by. He had worked his way through college and had little time or money for travel.

The travel itself had definitely expanded his horizons. And he had learned from his Italian mentor what it would take to be a first-class gigolo, which he figured could be a good job for a few years.

He would be careful and save his money when he got it. He wouldn't spend any money on anything if his client offered to pay. He wouldn't require a lot of personal possessions because he would always get more from whoever was his latest client. He could not have an opinion. He must not have any sexual needs and must learn not to fake it in bed, but to enjoy whatever his client required of him.

None of that really conflicted with his innately compliant personality.

He turned to Paolo in the business-class seat next to him. "Sure, Paolo. I'd love to continue working for you. As long as you like."

The Italian smiled as he leaned over and kissed his cheek. "*Perfecto*. We will have much fun."

He knew what he had done. He had just agreed to a life as a high-class whore. No matter, he was young, and you only live once.

But what about love? What the hell, he would think about that later.

MARKED
HALEY WALSH

He moved sinuously, flexing the muscles in his arms and thighs. He wore only black thong underwear, but he still seemed to be fully dressed because of all the tattoos, covering him from the top of his bald head, down his nose, to the tops of his feet. I began to wonder what designs could be found beneath that thong, beyond what the public was allowed to see.

His eyes scanned the crowd as he turned his body this way and that. That's what we'd paid for, after all. To see the freaks. The Tattooed Man.

His gaze fell on mine. But unlike the others, unlike those who only saw the interlocking images sliding over the mounds and valleys of his skin, I was transfixed by his eyes. They were unremarkable except for their intensity. And he never moved his gaze from me. I edged closer to the platform.

The barker explained how this unnamed man tried to lose himself in the art on his body, becoming invisible except for the images. He turned slowly, showing off the leopards and jungle flora stretched across his back. Yes, if you looked at the images long enough, you could easily see how the man could disappear behind them. Until I looked up again as those eyes locked on mine.

The crowd moved on to the next exhibit and the Tattooed Man slipped behind a curtain. I didn't much care for the Blockhead, the man who could drive a nail up his nose. I couldn't watch that without my knees feeling weak. I dropped back to the edge of the crowd and got out of the tent.

The carnival seemed to awaken at night. Strings of colored lights hung over the aisles and the sounds of the games seemed louder, cheerier after dark. The faces of the people were shadowed but they always seemed to raise smiles toward the artificial light, cheeks gleaming.

I'd been following this carnival for a while. I'd never been anywhere before. Never anywhere but my hometown, where even my dad was gone before the bedsheets had gone cold. My mom was always working late or bringing home men who called her foul names when they drank too much. I never saw them hit her, but the next day she'd be wearing sunglasses to hide her eyes, or long sleeves in the summer to cover her arms.

"Let's get out of here," I told her. The small clapboard house at the dead end of the street had been our home for as long as I could remember. Two rooms, a faded kitchen with torn-up linoleum, walls dim from cigarette smoke, a chain-link fence around a tiny yard full of weeds.

She'd shake her head at me, her dirty-blond hair falling listlessly around her sunken cheeks. "Where we gonna go, Ray?"

I left for school one morning but never got there. I kept walking, past the old high school, past the liquor store on the corner, past the hay and feed store, past the edge of town, and kept going. My backpack was full of bags of chips, not books. I had ransacked the pantry and got nothing more than cereal, chips, and cans of beans and succotash. Three pairs of underwear, two pairs of socks, a toothbrush, and some comic books weighed down the backpack, too. And the contents of the sugar bowl full of five-dollar bills.

Hitchhiking here, hopping on freight cars there, I was going. It didn't matter where. I was seeing things, seeing places. Not great places. Because I encountered towns that looked just like the one I'd left. Too much like it. Same dead-end streets, same shabby grocery stores, same dusty cars, same dirty-blondes wearing sunglasses in the house.

But at least I was going. At least it wasn't the same town I'd been in all my life.

I saw a flyer for FunWorld Carnival on the window of a 7-Eleven and decided to check it out. This was the fourth town in as many weeks that I caught the carnival. I was now familiar with the midway rides, the games with their brightly colored stuffed animals hanging from their booths. I knew all the patter by now, how the carnies would entice their marks to play. I couldn't tell if any of the games were rigged, so maybe that made me a prime mark, but I didn't have the money to play anyway, even if I had wanted to.

A lot of the carnies recognized me, glancing at me curiously. Maybe they thought I worked there. Maybe I should. My money was running low. And I was tired of sleeping in doorways and under overpasses. I might be suited to the life of a carny. I was drifting anyway. Disappearing little by little like the Tattooed Man.

The buttery smell of popcorn and the oily-sweet smell of funnel cakes hung in the air, making me hungry. There was litter everywhere, from dented soda cans, to crumpled snow-cone cups, to half-eaten hamburgers. I'd grabbed a few of those to slack my hunger, either hot dogs and turkey legs people had abandoned at the makeshift tables, or snatching them fresh when the people turned away to get mustard or an extra straw. No one ever caught me. And the carnies, if they *had* seen me do it, didn't tell.

A man with day-old gray stubble on his chin and a cigarette dangling from his lips pushed a broom lazily through the debris. I touched his sleeve and he slid heavy-lidded eyes toward me, looking me up and down under the lights of the funhouse. So maybe I didn't look my best. I *had* shaved just yesterday in a gas station bathroom with a cheap disposable razor that I still had in my backpack, along with five bucks, a pack of Big Red gum, and some beef jerky. All I had left in the world. My hoodie was tied around my waist. And my dark T-shirt was getting kind of ripe from wearing it day after day. My jeans weren't the cleanest, either, but they hugged me tight in all the right places. Though I could tell that this was the last thing on his mind. And the last thing on mine, too, since he was definitely too old and worn out for me.

"Hey, mister," I said. "Who do I talk to about a job?"

He ran a finger under his nose. "Looking to join the glamorous life of the carnival?"

"Yeah. Something like that."

He shrugged, gesturing with his head toward the trailers. "Sign says manager. Try there."

"Okay. Thanks."

I didn't bother looking back. The idea passed through my mind that this could be me someday, but then I dismissed it. Not me. If I tired of something, I'd just move on.

As I trudged over the squashed grass and mud with my high-tops getting damper, I kept thinking about the Tattooed Man. Every time the carnival came to a new town, I'd be there and I'd sneak into the tent with the Tattooed Man. It wasn't just the tattoos. The dude was hot. And I couldn't get those intense eyes out of my mind. And those images. I'd seen a lot of tattooed men. In the gay community, it's an inevitability that you'd run into tattoos. Not that I was part of any gay community in my town. Like I'd let anyone I knew know I was gay. But I'd seen plenty of guys in roadside bathrooms, guys that gave me the eye for some action, and they had tattoos.

I even got one. It took almost a half a bottle of tequila to get me to sit for the tattoo artist, but I did. Hated it the next day. My mom hated it, too, and I got a lot of yelling about it. But I got used to the tat after about two weeks, mostly because my mom still hated it so much.

I wound my way around the midway games and spied some trailers tucked behind a rope barrier. I lifted the rope and made my way over the dirty sawdust and peered at the campers and RVs. Most were old, with paint flaking off their aluminum sides. Torn curtains hung in the smudged windows, and rusty steps swung precariously from the bottom of dented doors.

There was a small sign. "Manager" it said, in sloppy hand-painted letters. I moved up to the trailer and knocked. Waited. My palms sweated. I was losing the courage to knock a second time, but I did anyway. Guy was probably in the john. I mean, where else could he be in that can? I stood looking at the dented and dirty door for a moment more. The window was duct-taped with cardboard. I stood for only one second longer and turned.

The door opened. I spun and he stood in the doorway, looking down at me with those same intense eyes. "Didn't you get your fill?" he said.

"What?" I breathed.

It was him. He was wearing a T-shirt that covered his chest but left his colorful arms exposed. He leaned one of those arms against the doorway. "Haven't you seen enough of me?"

I swallowed and took in a shaky breath. "No. I mean…you're the manager?"

A smile cracked his face and his tattooed cheeks dimpled. He nodded, opened the door wider, and stepped back into the shadows of the trailer.

I hesitated only a moment before I leapt up onto the wobbly step and came through.

"Close the door," he said over his shoulder. He settled onto the wide bed and its rumpled sheets that took up the entire back half of the shabby trailer.

Peeling paneling, musty smells, dripping faucet. I took it all in for only a moment before I let it go. After all, the Tattooed Man was wearing shorts, revealing muscled thighs covered in colorful drawings of solar systems and streaking comets. He saw me looking but didn't seem to mind.

"What's your name?" he said.

My gaze settled on his eyes again. "Raymond." I cleared my throat. "Ray."

"Well, Raymond Ray. What can I do for you?"

"Just Ray," I muttered. "I…I just wondered…" What did I wonder? Oh yeah. Job. "I was looking for a…um…job."

But that's not what I wanted to say. I wondered what the tattoos we couldn't see looked like. I wanted to feel that illustrated skin against my own. Would it feel different?

I said nothing, reddening under his scrutiny. I was beginning to think this was a bad idea. Maybe he didn't…maybe he wasn't…

"Got any tattoos, Ray?"

I blinked. "Um…yeah." I dropped my backpack to the floor and pushed back my sleeve, showing him the Celtic knot on my bicep. Not only had I gotten used to it, I decided I liked it.

I yelped when his hand closed over my skin and he roughly turned my arm to look at it. Abruptly he let me go.

"Nice."

"Took me a long time to decide on that." I shrugged. "It hurt."

He smiled all the way to his eyes and leaned back on his hands. "Yeah. It does."

I shook my head, feeling like the biggest idiot. "I mean…you… I've got nothing on you."

"Relax, kid. I'm not judging. Some people like it, some don't."

"You must really like it."

"What makes you think so?"

I gestured feebly. "Well…it's just…you…"

He laughed. "I'm messing with you. God, you're easy."

I felt my cheeks flush and I turned toward the door. "Sorry," I said sullenly. "I didn't mean to waste your time."

"Whoa. Who said anything about you wasting my time? Sit down, Ray. Want a beer?"

I sat in the bench seat and nodded.

He didn't get up but reached over toward the rusty fridge and opened it. All that was in there was beer and a carton of milk. He hoisted a bottle of Coors from a twelve-pack and tossed it to me. I barely caught it.

I twisted off the lid and drank greedily. Wiping my mouth, I rested the cool bottle on my jeans-clad thigh. I guess he didn't care that I was eighteen. Or maybe he couldn't tell. I felt grown-up and encouraged. "So...do you mind if I ask a personal question?"

He hadn't lost his smile that he had aimed steadily at me from the moment he opened the door. "Let me guess."

"Actually, I was wondering why...why the carnival?"

The smile faded. He lowered his head. "Oh. I could say I spent all my money on the tats and had to sell myself to make it back." He looked up then to gauge my reaction. I'm not good at hiding my feelings and the corner of his mouth twitched. "Or I could say that I lost a bet. Or that I followed someone here and fell in unrequited love and got stuck."

I hadn't realized I was frowning, but his playful smile took the edge off it.

He sighed. "Or the truth. That I own this carnival."

"Y-you do?"

"That's the one you believe?"

"You said it was the truth."

"And you believe it when someone tells you that, kid?"

"I'm not a kid."

"Neither am I. Can you tell how old I am?"

I scanned his face. It was difficult because of the tats. They covered everything but his cheeks and lips. Finally I gave up. "No."

"I'm forty. I'd say you are about twenty-something."

"Eighteen. Almost nineteen," I added. It was a lie, but he didn't need to know that.

I hadn't noticed earlier that he had a bottle of beer sitting beside him on a ledge. He grasped it, pressed it to his lips, and knocked it back. Some of it dribbled down the side of his mouth he chased it with his tongue. Giving up on that, he wiped it with the back of his hand. "There's no great mystery about me, ki—I mean, Ray."

"Yes, there is." Emboldened by God-knew-what, I stood. "I wondered…how far down the tattoos go."

He raised his brows. "Oh, you did?"

"Y-yeah." I fidgeted and then slipped my hands in my pockets to keep them from shaking.

He showed his teeth for a moment before he sat up and peeled off his shirt. I had seen it before across his pecs and abs. An African savannah stretched across his skin, with a green-eyed lion, snakes winding around the trunks of trees, jackals, birds of prey. They fascinated, but so did the body beneath the art.

He shucked his shorts, revealing that black thong underwear he was wearing in the tent. He turned so that I could see the butterflies and insects curving over his round ass cheeks. The art was breathtaking, but more so were the mounds of flesh.

He watched me as he stuck his thumbs in the waistband and slowly eased down the thong. It glided over his thighs until it reached his knees and just fell away.

He was half-hard with a meaty dick. And I couldn't believe that it, too, was covered with art. A dragon. A red dragon wound round his cock breathing fire at the end of the cut crown. Even his shaved balls were covered in illustrated red scales with a dragon eye on each one. I didn't realize I gasped but he chuckled and they jiggled a bit. His dragon dick bounced.

"Like what you see?"

My jeans couldn't hide my erection, forcing itself against my fly.

He smiled. "Yeah, you do." And he reached over and cupped my dick, squeezing. I moaned and looked up at him and his tattooed face. Up over his forehead and to his bald scalp ran an Asian scene on a lake with tall mountains and a fisherman. The fisherman slid down his nose astride his nostrils. Strange that only his cheeks were free of ink. And his lips, lips ripe and ready. He ran his tongue over them, and with his hand still clutching my crotch, he slowly pulled me forward and touched those lips hungrily over mine.

The little bit of kissing I'd done didn't compare to this. He opened his mouth wide, devouring. His tongue lashed inside, slapping mine, probing the roof of my mouth, lips sliding, sucking. He let go of my cock and grabbed my biceps, yanking me against him. I slid my hands up as far as I could and wrapped around his waist, holding on with my fingertips. But it wasn't just my mouth he was mashing against mine. His hips worked in gyrating circles, rutting his naked dick against my jeans.

"Shit," I gasped when he let my mouth go. "I..."

His breath puffed harshly against my cheek. "You're not a virgin, are you?"

"No." Barely no. The few fumblings I'd had in gas station bathrooms didn't quite constitute experience. Nor the one time in that park. But I had a feeling it didn't need to be explained to him.

I could tell by his smirk that he had me figured out. But he wasn't kicking me to the curb. In fact, he was pushing up my shirt. "Eighteen, almost nineteen, huh?" I nodded, bobbing my head furiously. He smiled. "Let's see some of this pale white skin."

He helped me pull my shirt over my head and I felt a little embarrassed at the comparison. He was broadly built, wide chest, toned abdomen. Yet he ran his hands over my thin chest as if I was something he'd never seen before. "Smooth," he rasped.

His hands felt calloused, running over my taut nipples. He pinched them, eyes hooded as he watched them peak. "Pink boy," he murmured appreciatively. God, he was so hot. His fat dick was fully erect now, standing up against his belly, that dragon flicking its tongue, breathing fire. It was a bit intimidating, but it didn't make my hole stop clenching, thinking about him pushing that thick meat in there.

"Is...is this the job interview?" I squeaked.

He paused. Shit. What the hell was I doing? Why did I have to open my big mouth?

That smile again. "We'll see," he breathed and leaned down, sucking on my mouth again. I vowed to shut up. I didn't want him to stop. I didn't want him to take his hands off me for even a second.

And he didn't. His hands roamed freely down my back and slid over the cheeks of my ass over my jeans where he squeezed. Maybe a little too roughly, but I really didn't mind.

"You want to take these off?" he rumbled in my ear.

I dropped my hands to the button, flicked it open, and then with a trembling hand, pulled down the zipper. It was barely open before he yanked them down and my white underwear with it. "Hey!"

I was stripped, my pants hanging around my knees. He toyed with one of my nipples as he sat back. "Take them off. And finish your beer. Want something stronger?"

I scrambled, trying to get my legs out of my pants. But I'd forgotten about my shoes. I fell over my backpack and onto the bench on my bare butt, desperately trying to untie my high-tops, making a very unmanly whine when I knotted them instead. Finally, I pushed them off, still tied, and wrestled off my damned jeans.

When I looked up at him he was handing me my beer. He wanted me to drink, so I did. I knocked it back, thinking the alcohol might relax me. It was cold in my mouth that had been so hot when his tongue was in there. I drank it down, belched loudly.

"Nice." He chuckled.

"Sorry." I set the bottle aside. He laughed, a deep rumbling sound that made my dick even harder. I squeezed it, wondering what he was going to do, feeling kind of free about it all. Here I was, standing naked in my stocking feet in front of this gorgeous naked Tattooed Man. He could do anything to me. I wanted anything he could do.

"I like your tat, Ray," he said, drinking down his beer. He reached above the fridge and grabbed a bottle of liquor. Looked like tequila. He unscrewed the cap and drank a long dose before he pulled it away from his lips. He thrust it toward me and I took a swig, choking a bit, but put it to my lips again to prove I could do it. It was like all the other cheap tequila I'd had before. It burned on the way down and left a medicinal taste in my mouth. I tried to hand it back, but he motioned for me to continue while he slowly stroked himself. He lay back on the bed and watched me. "I like all of you, Pink Boy. Beautiful white skin."

I stood naked and drinking maybe too much for too long. I started to flush, feeling a little light-headed but also a little less self-conscious. I took another gulp, choked on it, and ran a hand over my mouth to cover my coughing. "So…uh…what…"

"Why don't you come here, Pink Boy. Ray." He patted the bed beside him.

I put the bottle aside before I climbed onto the surprisingly soft mattress. He scooted over, making room for me. He smelled of some sort of musky cologne that combined with his sweat. I breathed it in. He leaned in and stroked down my hair, over my neck, my shoulder, and down my left side. I knew he could feel my ribs. I was too skinny, too gangly. Elbows and knees too much in the way. He didn't seem to mind, though. He took my arm, the one with the tattoo, stretched it out, and licked it, licked where the tattoo started and down to the crook of my arm, down to my wrist where he opened his lips over it and sucked. How could sucking an arm be sexy? But the feel of his warm lips, his wet tongue, made me breathe hard, made my heart slam against my chest.

I wanted to touch him and so I reached up and fanned my hand over his chest. He had shaved his whole body so it wouldn't interfere with the tats. His muscles were firm under my touch, and his skin didn't feel any different for all the illustrations covering it. I nipped his chest, his pecs, and got a rumbling sound of pleasure for my trouble.

His heavy-lidded eyes looked down at me. "Pink Boy," he growled. He dropped his gaze to my dick, now red with need, aching. My balls felt swollen. He did what I was hoping he'd do. He leaned over and took my dick in his mouth, that hot mouth and slithering tongue. He swallowed me down, lips clamping on the root of it, nose in my pubes. I felt him breathe it in. God, I wanted to watch, but I couldn't. My head fell back, my hips bucked off the bed. He covered the bones of my pelvis with his big hands and gently pushed me back, held me there as his mouth worked over my cock, sucked it and laved it, and twirled his tongue around the head.

"Oh fuck!"

He chuckled, his throat vibrating on my meat as he did. I was sucked once before but not by an expert, not by someone like this. I wasn't going to last. I grabbed the covers.

He cupped my balls, rolling them over his fingers. His knuckle pushed behind my sac, massaging me deep. I clenched all over. I twisted my fingers in the blankets and cried out too soon, pumping my jizz down his throat. He sucked hard, his hot tongue squeezing the underside of my dick as he drank me.

Arched off the bed, I was slow to calm down. His hand guided me and I sank into the mattress. I looked up at him, licking his lips and smirking. "What's the matter, kid? Never been sucked off before?"

"Not like that," I managed to say. I was feeling lazy but still hyperaware. I glanced down at his dick. He hadn't come yet, and that dragon looked hungry. I gestured toward it. "Should I...?"

"What's the rush?" He reached over me and grabbed the tequila, pressing the bottle to his mouth and drinking. I watched his throat roll with it, imagining that was what he had looked like sucking me.

I was half-hard again.

The Tattooed Man reached above me to place the bottle on the windowsill and leaned down to suck my neck before licking in long strokes down my chest. I lay back with a moan as the man's busy mouth teased my pebbled nipples, licking on one lightly before he covered it with his mouth and sucked hard.

"Fuck!" I gasped.

I felt his deep chuckle through my chest as he moved to the other nipple and gave it the same treatment, pushing me down gently as I reared up.

He continued to kiss my chest and moved slowly down my torso. While his lips worked my too-pale skin, his hands were busy massaging my thighs, gently spreading them apart. I helped. I couldn't not spread them, feeling as if my dick and balls were huge throbbing masses.

His tongue dipped into my navel and his sweet breath blasted onto my belly from his illustrated nostrils. His chin was inches from my cock and my whole body stiffened in anticipation. Would he take me into his mouth again? I wasn't all the way hard yet, but I was getting there. But then he dragged his soft lips down past the nest of curly dark hairs and kissed the hollow of my thigh and hip. His lips teased, moving carefully toward the skin on the innermost part.

I touched him wherever I could. I ran my hands over the curve of his back, down to his firm ass, feeling the muscles flex under my touch. I reached around to his abs, down his flat stomach to his shaved pubes, and grabbed his cock.

He laughed outright, eyes sparkling at me.

"You like that?"

I nodded. "Yeah."

"You like dragons?" he purred. "My dragon likes you."

I didn't think I could drag my gaze from his dick, but I did, looking at his face. He had me sort of cradled so I reached up with my other hand and touched his face, running my fingers over the unmarked skin of his cheekbones. "Why here?" I whispered. "Why aren't you tattooed here?"

He closed his hand over mine and took it from his cheek. He looked at me a long time before he answered. "Because I needed something of my old self reflected back into my eyes. Can you understand that?"

"I guess," I said, not really sure what he meant.

Those eyes scanned mine before he lowered his head. I felt his breath on my dick and strained forward, hoping to touch the weeping head to his wonderful lips. His gaze dropped once to my stiffening cock and then back up to my eyes.

He pushed my legs up, told me to hold my thighs. I did, and he lowered his head and swathed his tongue across the bottom of my balls and I reared up, certain my head would explode right then and there. He took each testicle carefully into his mouth and sucked on it, balancing it on his tongue. Licking his way over the sac to touch his tongue to the root of my cock, he lapped the underside of it all the way up to the head. His tongue swirled around the crown, dipping the tip into the slit now weeping with pre-cum before he enveloped all of it in his mouth and moved his lips downward over the shaft. He brought his mouth up again, danced his teeth around the head, then swallowed it again. His mouth slipped up to the tip once more and sucked hard.

He pulled back abruptly and was suddenly lying on top of me, arms surrounding me, and when his lips covered mine, I tasted myself on his tongue.

"Pink Boy," he said softly, his hand stroking my outturned thigh. "I'm gonna come inside you." He gave a curt smile. The untattooed skin of his cheeks was flushed, and when he got up on his knees his cock seemed huge, standing tall and red with arousal. I found myself licking my lips.

I expected he would position himself over me right away, but he didn't. Instead, he dropped down between my thighs and nudged them even farther apart. He held me by the backs of my knees and raised my thighs so my legs were dangling in midair, coming to rest over his shoulders. I felt his warm hand parting my ass cheeks, felt his breath below my sac, and then I started when a tongue licked my hole. He paused, waiting for me to ease down again, and began anew. His tongue glided over the puckered skin, dabbed into the tight hole, and stretched past the firm ring of muscle.

He lapped at me and sucked my entrance while I squirmed, gasping, enjoying every moment of it until he suddenly drew away and I whimpered. *Don't stop now*, I wanted to shout, but he only leaned toward a shelf over the head of the bed and retrieved something. The crinkle of a torn plastic wrapper, then a plastic lid popped open, and soon I felt oily fingers probing my butthole. A finger slipped in and pumped. I hadn't gone this far before. I'd only sucked dick and had mine sucked.

"You need to relax, Ray," he said. He was definitely positioning himself to fuck me properly, and I could do anything but relax. But the Tattooed Man's finger had not left its warm place and he pushed it in farther. His knuckle nudged my open ass cheeks as he thrust. "Relax, Ray," he admonished.

He swathed his own condom-encased erection in the lube and removed his finger. Feeling loosened for only a second, I tried not to tense up again even as that fat meat dove in and split me wide.

He made cooing and shushing sounds above me. "Relax, Pink Boy," he purred. "Relax. It will be uncomfortable for only a second. You're beautiful."

It burned. Stretched. He pushed more in and stopped again. It still hurt but the sensation of fullness made up for it. And the tequila was sort of numbing me, too. He pushed in some more and I took a deep breath to open myself.

He smiled and then he pushed in all the way and stayed motionless again. He looked down at me and I was hyperaware that he had his cock in my ass up to the hilt. He pulled back almost all the way out again only to slam deeply into me.

"Shit!" I grunted.

But he'd been patient enough. He glided out once more, changed angles, and slammed in again, touching a spot inside me that I'd only found with my own fingers. It curled my toes and arched my body. My cock responded by springing upward.

The Tattooed Man thrust at that same spot several more times before he wrapped his fingers around my erection. He pumped it in rhythm with his thrusts and I didn't think I'd hold out much longer.

I watched his face, his eyes. Those intense eyes, now more focused than I had ever seen them before. I slapped my hands to his pecs, dug into his nipples with my nails, and squeezed.

His eyes narrowed and suddenly he threw back his head, ramming his dick into me. I felt it pulse. He was coming in me. So hot. My balls tensed and I came in spurts all over his hand.

He dropped his face, his bald head nearly brushing my sweaty and cum-covered torso. He slowly drew out of me. Breathing raggedly, he simply fell to the side onto his back and gasped a long sigh.

I tried to get my breathing to normal, too, but it wasn't easy. I stared at the dark curved ceiling. "That was awesome," I managed to say after a while.

He laughed and wiped his face. "That *was* pretty awesome there, Ray."

Coming twice in a row with half a bottle of tequila in me made my eyes heavy. I was heavy all over and I couldn't have moved even if I was given sacks of gold to do it. I closed my eyes.

Groggy. A little dizzy and confused, I woke slowly in stages. First it was the light behind my eyelids, then the buzzing in my ears, and then it was the needle prickles on my arm. I jerked up, tried to.

"What the fuck!"

I was on my stomach with a heavy weight on my ass. The Tattooed Man was sitting on my butt, holding down my arm and tattooing me!

I struggled under him. "What the *hell*, dude?"

"Calm down, Ray." His illustrated thighs held me captive, the muscles taut and strong on either side of my flanks. In his hand he had a tattoo machine. I stretched my neck to look at my arm. Seemingly growing out of my simple Celtic knot were the sinuous lines of a Celtic dragon.

How long had I been out? Sunshine flaring from behind the faded curtains answered that question.

I stopped struggling and looked at my arm again. My skin was an angry red where he'd been drawing. The dragon wound down my arm, covering most of it. My mom would have had kittens.

"Are you okay, Ray?"

"You're tattooing me!" My mouth tasted like it was full of sawdust. Must have been the tequila 'cause my head didn't feel much better.

"Yeah," he said.

"You…you didn't ask me."

"No."

I turned my head as best I could to look up at his face. His expression blank, he just looked at me expectantly.

"Why are you doing this?"

"You want me to stop?"

"I want you to tell me why the hell you're doing this." I pulled one hand free where it was trapped under my body and wiped my face. My stomach churned. The tequila hadn't done me any favors.

He sighed and lowered the machine to his thigh. "I can stop, but it's not finished."

"Dude, are you hearing me? Let me up!"

For a moment I didn't think he would. Damp heat filled my chest. I'd been bullied at school. Part of the reason I didn't stick around. And I'd experienced fear there. But not quite like this.

Finally he moved, lifted his ass off mine, and I scrambled out from under him. He was still naked, and his dick lay heavy between his legs, the tip caressing the mattress.

I was naked, too, and feeling like I'd been wrung out. My ass was kind of sore from him pounding me. I found my jeans and drew out the underwear and started pulling it on.

"You going somewhere, Ray?"

I yanked my jeans from the floor, backed up a little, and thrust a leg in. "Look, this was…um…it was good. Last night."

"I thought you were looking for a job."

"This is bullshit, dude. You don't just start tattooing someone without asking."

"Are you looking for a job or not, Pink Boy?"

I wasn't sure if I liked that nickname anymore. I wrestled my pants all the way up but I left the fly hanging open. "A job?" I ran my hand over my messed-up hair. My head felt pretty messed up, too. "Doing what?"

He sat back on his feet. His thighs were still wide open, his cock with its dragon still on display. It was hard not to look at it, hard not to look at *him*.

"Ray, what is it you think I do here?"

I scrubbed my face. My beard-stubble scratched my palms. I shrugged. "You…you know…you display yourself. People pay to see it."

He cocked his head. Along his jaw crouched one of those Foo dogs that sit in front of Chinese restaurants, but all stretched out, like it was flying. "Is that what you think I do, Ray?"

I shrugged again. "Isn't it?"

He lowered his face and shook his head. "Ray, Ray, Ray. Nothing so simple. Come here. Sit beside me."

I hesitated.

He smiled, showing his teeth. They were stark white against the colors on his face. "I promise not to touch you, if you don't want. Look." He raised his hand with the machine and slowly put it down on the sill. "Okay?"

I shuffled over and sat gingerly on the edge of the bed. He leaned in, took my chin in his hand, and turned my face to him. He planted his lips noisily on mine just for a moment before he drew back and dropped his hand away. "Sorry," he said. "I couldn't resist just one kiss. You were some sweet hotness last night."

My face seared red and I lowered my eyes, though through my embarrassment, there shot a spike of pride at his words.

"Look at me, Ray."

My head jerked up automatically.

"What do you see?"

I paused, shook my head, trying to get the wool out of it. "Colors. Shapes. Motion. Layers. Stuff like that."

He bit his unmarked lower lip and nodded. "Yes. You see it. I knew you did. Tell me something. Why did you follow my carnival?"

I started to rub my tattooed arm but he made an "uh!" sound that stopped me. My arm tingled and prickled where his needle had marked me. Permanently marked. "I don't know," I muttered, not looking at him. "I was fascinated by it. By the people who came. By the carnies. By…you."

"And…what was it about me?"

My face couldn't get any hotter. I rubbed the back of my neck, feeling the heat on my hand. "Dunno. The tats. But mostly…your eyes."

I jerked back as he sprang up, grabbed the back of my head, and kissed me soundly, using his tongue this time. My breath must have reeked but he didn't seem to care.

As quickly as he had jumped up, he bounced back to his place on the bed, breathing hard and smiling like an idiot. He pointed his finger at me. "You are a rare human being, Ray. And a beautiful Pink Boy. Do you want a job?"

I was touching my lips where he'd kissed me. They tingled like my illustrated arm. "What kind of job?"

"Not an ordinary one. That's not why you're here, far from home, is it, Ray? For an ordinary job?"

I shook my head. I didn't even know anymore.

"Good. So why don't you come back to the bed? I'm not finished with your arm."

"Why…why…"

"I'm giving you a gift, Ray. I'm giving you depth. Motion. Color." He patted the bed, where, still naked, he waited for me up on his knees with those strong thigh muscles tensed. "Come on."

I felt dreamy, suddenly. Like I was looking at everything through a veil. Like smoke. "Are you going to make me just like you?" I asked breathlessly. "Cover me with tattoos? Make me invisible?"

"Come here," he said softly.

I scooted closer until he reached out and drew me against him. He threw a strong arm around my shoulders. "Not invisible, Ray. Never that. I couldn't stand to cover *all* this skin, my Pink Boy. But some of it. More of it. You'll be my—what? Robin to my Batman?"

"Some kind of assistant?"

"Maybe more. How far can you dream?"

I looked up at him, at his face full of faraway places, places I'll never see. Except I *was* seeing them. On him. In his eyes.

What did I imagine for myself? I don't know. I never got that far. When I hitched, I just hoped for somewhere else. To *go*. When I followed the carnival, I hoped for different towns, different scenery, getting lost there.

His eyes were deep. Deeper than the dark oceans depicted on his backside. Deeper than the midnight of stars and comets on his thigh.

I breathed. With his eyes on me, I slowly turned over, lay carefully on my stomach, and stuck out my arm.

THE CONDUCTOR
LUKE OLIVER

I was in a cave. The air was chilled, I guessed by the sound of rushing water, by a not-too-distant waterfall, and created a map of goose bumps on my naked skin. It was too dark to see much of anything, but the light coming from the computer and the phosphorescent rocks embedded into the cave's walls were enough to discern everything but the most minute details. I was in the middle of a four-way. Well, a five-way, I guess, if I counted myself, but I wasn't sure if one counted oneself in these sorts of situations. Regardless of the math, this would, under any circumstance, be an unusual position in which to find myself, especially on a Wednesday, and especially when my TiVo was so filled I needed to be home watching *American Idol* in real time. But what really made this encounter particularly odd was the fact that I was being gangbanged by multimillionaire Bruce Wayne. *Batman*. Well, Bat*men*. Four Batmen. I was being Bat-banged.

I was on my knees, leaning on a pile of bank bags—the kind Scrooge McDuck had lying around everywhere—the ones with big dollar signs printed all over them. Christian Bale was behind me, pounding his dick into my ass so hard it pushed my face onto George Clooney's cock, which I was trying not to choke on as I simultaneously gave hand jobs to Michael Keaton and Adam West. A steady stream of hundred-dollar bills flew out of the money bags and floated down like happy green snowflakes. And as unusual as this already was—and it was—I was further astonished at how coordinated I was. I couldn't do a jumping jack without falling down, so jacking off two Batmen while being spit-roasted by two more at the same time was nothing short of a personal victory. But as I took in the scene, the cave, the money bags, the Batmen of varying degrees of celebrity, I felt like something was missing. I politely popped George's cock out of my mouth and asked, to nobody in particular, where Val Kilmer was. Though I'd half expected the Bat-computer to answer, suddenly, from out of the shadows emerged a tuxedoed Michael Caine. "Mr. Kilmer sends his regrets, sir. Sadly, his body image issues keep him from most appearances. Also, the Wayne Foundation determined that his minimum was too high for a mid-C-lister."

All of the present Batmen nodded, knowing how the camera adds five pounds but Burger King can add a lot more. "Thank. You. Alfred," they said, spitting out each word with a thrust of their hips. I took this as a Bat-signal that they were close. A few pumps more and I milked Adam onto my left cheek. That pushed Michael over the edge, and he shot his load onto the left side of my face. Christian growled as he slipped out of my ass and unloaded the contents of his utility belt all over my lower back. George, ever the gentleman, asked if it was okay to come in my mouth. It seemed rude to say no to a man who devotes so much for so many African orphans, so I gave him the sticky-thumbs-up. "Holy Cum Shot!" he yelled, and my mouth was suddenly filled with a thick liquid that tasted like a melted Frappuccino and sunshine. Soaked, exhausted, and suddenly in the mood for a Starbucks run, I rolled onto my back, propping myself on the half-empty money bags. Michael Caine emerged from the shadows again, his gloved hand holding a silver tray with a perfectly folded towel. "Would you like the cum rag now, sir, or would you rather just wake up?"

Wake up?

Awake and…in my office. *Holywetdreamsandholyshitwhat thehellwasthat?* I remember feeling tired, I remember thinking I'd stay at work for just another hour, I remember deciding to just close my eyes for a moment. And now here I was, the Excel spreadsheet detailing the Henderson account still on my computer screen, my beard wet from drooling, pants wet from dripping, and a paper clip pressed into my forehead. A surge of panic grip my throat. What time was it? 11:50. The train schedule tacked to my wall listed the next train at 12:02, followed by the 5:32. I had exactly twelve minutes to get to Penn Station to get the train out of New York or else be stuck in the city all night. It takes twenty minutes to make the up-and-across-town trek to and from my office. Twelve minutes to make a twenty-minute trip.

My brain went from zero to sixty before my body could get out of neutral. It was too late for the main entrance to be open, so I would have to run though the Kubrickian maze of cubicles of my office to get to the back stairs and run down six flights. Even if Jack Nicholson were chasing me, it was a minimum two-minute run, meaning there was no time for me to go two minutes in the opposite direction to retrieve my jacket from the closet by the front elevators. I reached beneath my desk for my backpack, stuffed it with the sweater I keep on the back of my chair, and sprinted to the back stairs. I took the stairs two by two and threw myself out of the service doors into the night. Manhattan at midnight isn't all that different than Manhattan at noon. It's darker, but I still had to dodge an obstacle course of clueless tourists, locals in various stages of drunkenness, buses careening down streets, sidewalk-spanning scaffolding blocking pedestrians from falling into enormous construction sites, and Naked Cowboys. I was glad to hit a Don't Walk sign on the corner of Thirty-Third and Eighth. It gave me a chance to catch my breath and try to get rid of the cramp in my calf. The kicky Steve Madden shoes I'd thought looked so good this morning were made for sitting, not sprinting. I cursed his sweatshop cobblers for not adding better arch supports. The digital clock on the Madison Square Garden marquee read 11:59. Three minutes. As I watched the streetlight change from red stop hand to white walking man, I realized that there was never a better analogy to the Indians selling Manhattan to Europeans and made a mental note to submit an essay about it to NPR's website. Snapping out of my White Guilt–fueled reverie, I ran across the street, into Penn Station, and over to the escalators leading down to the New Jersey Transit terminal. I ran passed the Track Indicator screens, saw I had one minute to get on the train on Track Two, and made a sharp left onto yet another escalator, silently thanking the sweatshop workers for affixing anti-slip pads to the bottoms of my Steve Madden shoes and stopping me from hurtling across the slippery waiting room tiles. Didn't make up for the lack of arch support, but I like to give credit where it's due.

I practically threw myself down the moving escalator and, seconds later, I reached the platform. Two men in New Jersey Transit uniforms were standing halfway down the platform beside the one set of open doors. For some reason known only to social engineers who majored in crowd control, at certain times of day, passengers can only board trains leaving New York by doors in the middle two or three cars. Running down the platform, I saw them look at their watches and head inside. I began to wave wildly, hoping they would see me coming and not leave before I could get on board. The shorter, stockier man waved me on. I hopped onto the train and he turned the key and closed the door. "Th-thanks," I said, or at least tried to say, as I caught my breath.

"You made it just in time," he answered, hooking the key to his belt loop. I noticed this for three reasons. First of all, I was slightly hunched over, wincing at the cramp that was now working its way up from my calf to my thigh so his waist was at more or less eye level; second, his keychain was bright green, so it really stuck out against his navy-blue pants; and third, as he clipped the keys on, they bumped against the bulge straining against the crotch of his pants. I was suddenly very worried about what I looked like. The run had made me all sweaty—did I soak through my shirt? The dream had made me all wet, too—did it soak through my chinos? Was I still bent over? I should stand up.

He went in one direction I went in the other. Every person who commutes in and around New York knows exactly where they need to be on a train. Whether it's situating yourself in the front car so you're positioned closest to the stairs that take you to the northeast corner, the middle so you're closer to the ramp that takes you straight to the parking lot, or the back so you can enjoy the silence of the cell phone–free Quiet Car, proper train placement is the key to any successful commute. I needed to be in the front car, which meant I had to walk through four train cars to get there. The train jolted as it started moving, and I noticed that the car I was walking through was completely empty. So was the next, but as I got halfway through it, the train slowed to a crawl and then stopped. I eventually got to my preferred seat: the first four-seater on the left in the very first car. With two sets of seats facing each other, it offered plenty of room to spread out when the train wasn't crowded. And when the train was empty, like this one was going to be, I could stretch my legs out onto the opposite seat and, maybe, get some sleep.

"Attention, ladies and gentlemen." I recognized the voice as belonging to the man who'd held the doors open for me. Low, with just the right amount of gravel, he made the announcement sound like the prelude to a Barry White song. "We're experiencing a slight delay due to earlier track work. We're going to be sitting here in the tunnel for a little while. Sorry for the inconvenience." *Nothing like hurry up and wait*, I thought, plopping down into the four-seater. I pinched my shirt away from my sweaty chest and tried, once again, to slow my breathing. I closed my eyes and tried to remember the calming mantra I'd learned during that one mediation class I attended with Julie. I couldn't remember anything from the class except for the great Groupon deal we got, so I dropped finding the mantra and focused on that instead.

"Ticket, please."

My eyes shot open. The Conductor stood beside me, his crotch even more eye level than it had been earlier. "Oh, yeah, sorry," I said, fishing through my backpack for my monthly train pass. I was embarrassed. I always have my pass in my hand and ready to show. Commuters know that a train conductor's tolerance for waiting for a ticket is anywhere between two and seven seconds. Less if you're traveling during rush hour. Train personnel have to check hundreds of people every day. They do not like waiting and are not necessarily above sighing loudly and/or otherwise shaming you to your fellow commuters. But this guy just stood there and smiled patiently, leaning against the wall and crossing his thick arms across his barrel chest. I couldn't help but notice the hair on his arms started beneath his short sleeves and extended all the way down to the backs of his hands.

I shifted my attention away from his arms and my embarrassment and back to the task at hand. I felt around in my bag for the pass. Nothing. I blushed and stammered out another half apology and emptied my bag onto the seat. First out was the sweater, then ten comic books and a graphic novel. Finally, stuck beneath my reusable lunch container, was the train pass. "Whew!" I said, proudly presenting the pass. "Thought I'd lost it."

"Sorry, man. That's not good anymore."

"But it's a monthly."

"Right," he said, removing his cap and rubbing the top of his shaved head, "but today's the first. Of a new month. Well, technically it's after midnight, so it's the second. That pass is expired."

It took a moment to process what he'd said. I couldn't take my eyes off the blue eyes that stood out from bluish-black five o'clock shadow highlighting his face and head, and I couldn't believe it was actually the first of the month. "Oh—oh gosh, I'm sorry. Um, okay. I guess I'll pay for a one-way ticket?"

"Okay. That's seventeen dollars."

"Really? I just need a one-way."

"Yeah," he said, scratching his neck, "but there's a five-dollar surcharge on tickets bought on the train."

"Crap."

"Yeah," he said, placing his cap back on his head. I started rooting through my bag again, this time for my wallet. "You want me to come back while you, um, get yourself together?"

"Yes, please. That'd be great." He turned and walked away. I leaned over into the aisle and watched him head back into the other car. His thick thighs and perfectly round ass strained the seams of his pants as much as his bulge did. At least he gave his arms a chance to breathe. Okay, $17. Highway robbery on the train tracks, but what other choice did I have? And then I remembered. Yeah, it's the first of the month. It's also a Wednesday—new comic book day. I had run out during lunch and bought my weekly stash. I remembered putting the comics into my bag and my wallet in my pocket. The inside pocket of my jacket. The inside pocket of the jacket that was hanging in the front closet of my office, that I left because I didn't have time.

Conductor returned. "So?"

"Um…I'm super embarrassed, but I only have an empty sandwich container and some gum. I think."

"You think?"

"Well, I'm pretty sure I have gum."

"Oh."

"Would you like some gum? It's Wintermint."

"No."

"Oh."

"Yeah."

"Yeah, well, it's the first of the month but it's, well, it's…well, it's new comic book day." I pointed to the books spread across the seat to prove my point. "So I, well, I put my wallet in my jacket and…"

"You like comics?" he interrupted.

"Yeah. I mean I'm not one of those guys who lives in his mother's basement or anything, but…"

"I think I have a solution," he said, moving everything aside to sit. He spread his legs just enough to give his package some room. "You're gay, right?"

"Um, well, yes. But…?" *Oh no*, I thought, beginning to panic a little. Was I going to get gay-bashed?

"Easy. You ran down the platform like a ten-year-old girl, and half of these books have Wonder Woman on the cover." He chuckled and smiled sweetly. Okay, no gay-bashing tonight.

I blushed. "I guess I'm a bit of a cliché."

He laughed a little more and then leaned over, putting his elbows on his knees and his face a less than foot from mine. "Yeah. So, here's my solution. You keep your gum, if you actually have any, but you still pay for your trip...another way." He placed his hairy hand on my knee.

"What makes you think I'd be open to that?" I tried to sound indignant.

"Well, I think I can show you something you'll like. A lot." I sat up a little straighter and looked around. "Don't worry. We're going to be stopped in the tunnel for at least fifteen minutes, and the only other people on the train are some drunk Wall Street guys. They're busy trying not to throw up."

"But what about the guy driving the train?"

"Billy's cool. He's got one eye on the stop signal and the other on the porn app on his iPhone. He won't bother us." The Conductor leaned back and, with his thick fingers, slowly loosened his tie. I could see a wispy hedge of hair emerge from beneath his collar, and as he opened the top two buttons, a patch of dark fur spilled out.

This was going to happen. I was going to pay for my ride home by getting laid. Talk about getting your ticket punched. I smiled at my own joke, but tried to cover. "You're right," I said, "I do like it." I did.

"Oh no," he answered, "there's more."

He continued to unbutton his shirt, stopping when he got to the last one, which was tucked into his pants. He grabbed both sides of his shirt and, with a smile, opened it to reveal a Superman "S" symbol shaved into the pelt covering his chest. I couldn't believe it. I'd been spending hundreds of dollars a month on books with illustrations of men who I'd imagine looked like this in real life, and here he was—in the flesh.

"Are you kidding me?"

"No joke, man. I've been a fan since I was a kid. So," he said as he rubbed his chest, fluffing out the hair a little, "ready for a little Action Comics action?"

I rolled my eyes at the terrible pun, but the truth was I *was* ready for it. I knelt between his legs and rubbed my cheek against his chest, hoping I'd be able to feel his fur through my own beard. I could, and the friction shot from my face right down to my cock. I stuck out my tongue and traced the shaved "S" over and over. While my tongue focused on the bare trail through his fur, my hands went to work rooting through the hair to find his nipples. After a few moments, my fingers found the hardened, quarter-size treasures, and I alternated between slathering the "S" and nibbling, pinching, licking, and sucking on the two red disks barely visible beneath his fur. The Conductor's deep moans vibrated down my body. He raised his arms and put his hands above his head, holding on to the luggage rack secured above the seats. His shirt opened just enough to expose his hairy armpits. Their musky scent was too much for me to ignore, so I abandoned the shaved "S" and buried my face beneath his arm. He giggled and I pulled away.

"Don't stop," he said, placing his meaty paw behind my head and gently pushing me back in. "Fuuuuck, man. Your tongue is my Kryptonite." I stopped again, backed up, and stared at him. Did he really just make another comic-book joke? A smile crept across his face, and we both laughed at the tops of our lungs. After a few seconds, I pulled a long curly hair from between my teeth.

"So are we going to make bad super-jokes the whole time?"

"Nah. Your mouth's going to be too busy to talk from now on." The Conductor slid down to the edge of the seat, propping his feet up against the seat behind me. I leaned into him and went back to feasting on his underarm. I could feel the Conductor's dick throb beneath me, so I left his armpit once more and knelt back against the seats. Reaching forward to give his nips one last tweak, I rubbed my hands down his torso toward his belt, unbuckled the hard leather strap, and slowly drew it out from around his waist. Throwing it to the ground, I unbuttoned his pants and slowly…slowly…unzipped his pants. I loved this part. The reveal is always exciting. What was it going to be? Uncut? Monster? Pencil-thin? I didn't care. I never do. I just wanted to get to it.

He was wearing red briefs. Just like Superman. "Part of the uniform?" I asked.

"Kinda."

I lowered my face and gnawed on the outline of his dick. Working my way up toward his stomach, I found the head of his dick peeking over the top. I hooked my fingers onto the waistband and pulled the front of his shorts down. His dick jutted forward, hitting my nose and splashing a bit of pre-cum onto my forehead. My head reflexively went back, but as I secured the waistband beneath his hairy, heavy balls, I just as reflexively put my face back to within inches of his crotch. There's nothing in the world quite like the smell of a package held captive for too long. The mix of sweat, semen, and piss intoxicated me. If I didn't get him into my mouth immediately, the world would end.

I stuck my nose underneath his balls and inhaled as much musk as I could before slathering them with my tongue. I took each one into my mouth. His cock pulsated against my face with every lick. I paused for a moment, wanting a good look at what he had for me. About six inches long, cut, and veiny. I circled my fingers around the top of his sac and gently pulled it down, lowering his dick so I was able to look at it straight on. I started licking around the head of his cock. Slowly, at first, to get as much flavor out of it as possible, I flicked my tongue over his hole and coaxed out a bead of pre-cum. I gently gripped the base of his shaft and pumped up and back down, coating his dick with the sweet-and-salty mixture of my spit and his lube. The Conductor threw his head back. He was pinching his tits and tracing his finger along the "S" pattern. I assumed that meant I was doing a good job, but I am a perfectionist and I wanted to do a *great* job. I opened my mouth as wide as I could and took him deep into my mouth until I could feel him hit the back of my throat. Relaxing my gag reflex, I tugged his balls further past his underslung briefs until they hit the seat beneath him. The cool plastic made his sac retreat a little, but his cock stiffened even more in my mouth. Taking the cue, I started sucking up and down. The Conductor spread his legs farther apart. His breathing became more rapid as I kept bobbing up and down. He was getting close, and his meaty hands started pushing my head up and down. The train started moving, and the gentle vibrations and back-and-forth of the train car were clearly working for him. Up and down, up and down, I took him as deep as I could, occasionally tickling his hairy taint and asshole. The Conductor's moans were getting louder.

"I'm gonna...gonna..." He pulled my head away from his cock and grabbed himself, angling his dick to the window and stroking it just once more. His cum slashed across the window just as the train exited the dark tunnel into the moonlit landscape of the New Jersey swamplands.

"Helluva Bat signal!" I said, grinning as his cum, backlit by a full moon, slid its way down the window.

The Conductor laughed. He cradled my face in his meaty hands and brought me to his mouth. We kissed, tentatively at first. Our tongues grew bold as they played against one another. I wondered if he liked tasting himself in my mouth. Still holding my face, he guided me away and up, until I was standing in front of him. I was just short enough to miss banging my head against the luggage rack. He skimmed the sides of my body with his hands and rested them on my belt, then pulled my shirt out, unzipped my fly, and reached inside. It wasn't hard for him to find what he was looking for. I bent over a little, giving him better access to my cock. He could feel how much pre-cum had been flowing, and he used my own lube with his thumb around my mushroom head. I sighed as he angled me up and out of my pants. Catching a drip of pre-cum on his finger, the Conductor brought it to his mouth and licked it off. "Waste not, want not, right?"

"Right," I replied, as I leaned my head back and held on to the luggage rack. His heavy hand slowly worked its way up and down my dick, squeezing lightly at the base, drawing it up, swirling around the head, then back down. Again and again. I took a breath every time his hand reached the root. Again and again. I began to shudder a little, and the Conductor stopped.

"You ready?"

"A few more and I will be," I whispered. He reached up and pinched a nipple through my shirt. I thought about him, half-dressed, and me, fully clothed with my dick out. When I opened my eyes and looked at him, I was reminded of the sexiest part of all, the "S" symbol, shaved into his fur and shining in the light. I was a man getting jerked off by another man. By a Superman. By the Conductor. I mumbled… something unintelligible, but he knew what I was getting at. He quickened his pace and I shot my load onto the headrest behind him.

A few pumps more and my legs turned to jelly. I collapsed backward onto the seat, and we sat there for a few moments, each of us smiling, tired, dicks out, and drained. The Conductor's radio crackled. "Minute to station" came a voice. The Conductor shoved his still-leaking dick back into his pants and zipped up. I watched him get dressed, and helped straighten his tie. "Back in a bit," he said, leaving for the control panel located in the other car.

We continued on our journey for another thirty minutes. The Conductor would come back to me after each stop. Sometimes he'd kiss me. Sometimes we'd just look at each other. Once he told me about the time his mother gave away the comic books he'd kept in her attic. We figured out that she'd effectively donated thousands of dollars. Then we talked about how much I'd spent on comics that day and tried to figure out how many round-trip tickets that amounted to. We were too tired to do math, so we just estimated that it was "a lot." Then he came back and handed me $12, so I had enough cash to buy a one-way ticket back to work in the morning. I took the money with one hand and rubbed his crotch with the other to thank him. And then, after his gravelly voice came from the speakers to announce that my station would be next, he came back one last time. We stood and hugged in the vestibule. The gentle swaying of the train rocked us into one another until, for the last time, the train began to slow.

The Conductor turned his key and the doors opened. As planned, I was perfectly positioned directly in front of the stairs to the parking lot. I flung my backpack onto my shoulder and stepped onto the platform. I turned back to look at the Conductor. "You know, I don't even know your name."

He smiled, leaned toward my ear and whispered, "Can't tell you. Secret identity and all." He smiled, stepped back, and closed the doors between us. And then, faster than a speeding bullet, but just as powerful as a locomotive, the train, and the Conductor, sped down the tracks into the night.

DEBTORS' PRISON
WILLIAM HOLDEN

"Please, I beg of you, a shilling is all I ask," I pleaded from my ground-level window. "My lady, how about you. Can you spare a shilling?" The woman grimaced, but stopped and dropped a shilling into my cup. "You, my lady, are an angel from heaven."

"Sod off, you miserable prat," the woman hissed.

"Good day to you as well," I called out after her. "Hateful bitch," I muttered as I looked into my collection cup with growing despair. "Fuck, I shall never make enough to pay off my debts." I shook my head, looked back out the window, and witnessed my wife coming down the street. "Prudence, I am down here," I shouted as I waved my hand with excitement.

"I do not need for you to tell me such foolish things; where else would my louse of a husband be except in prison? Besides, anyone on the street can see and hear your pathetic pleas for assistance." She leaned against the building and lifted her shoes. "Look at this filth. My shoes are ruined." She shook her head in disgust.

"Why did you not come by carriage?" I reached out and grabbed at the hem of her petticoat. She pulled away from me.

"How was I to pay for such a luxury with my adoring husband up to his chin in debt and locked away in Fleet debtors' prison?"

"Pru—"

"Oh, that reminds me. Mr. Baker came by the house yesterday asking about you. Since you were arrested a fortnight ago with no ability to pay off your debt anytime soon, he has ended your employment. He paid me your final week's wage, which I have used to send the children off to live with my parents until things can be sorted out."

"I cannot believe that after thirteen years of faithful service, he would do that to me."

"What did you expect him to do? He needed you and you let him down. You let everyone down. If he does not fill your position, he could lose his business." She squatted in front of my window.

"Pru, my love. That is not a very attractive way for a lady to sit. It looks as if you are taking a shit."

"You are a vile little man, Reece Bristol. Would you prefer me to sit my ass down on this filth and waste, soiling my dress? It would cost a fortune to have it cleaned. That is another one of life's luxuries that I can no longer afford."

"Prudence, please. This is a temporary setback and nothing more. I am doing what I can to pay off my debts. Look, I have earned four shillings today," I replied with fake pride, hoping she would not disapprove of the pittance.

"Four shillings?" She snatched the cup from me and emptied the contents into her hand.

"Why have you stayed away, my love? I have missed you." I played ignorant, a role I had become quite good at over the course of our marriage.

"The only thing you have missed is your gambling, my dear." She looked out across the street. "Excuse me, madam. How much are your pies?" She stood as the woman approached.

"One shilling, two pies," the older woman responded with a toothy grin.

"I shall take two." Prudence handed the woman a shilling and took the pies from her cart.

"It appears that you have your hands full." The old woman snickered as she looked at me. "I let my old man rot in that place."

"Well, my wife is not going to let that happen, are you, darling?"

"Shut up, Reece," she snapped. "I take it that you did not feel obliged to help pay off his debts?"

"Certainly not, and neither should you. Make the man suffer for his deeds, that is my motto."

"And your husband?" I asked, curious as to his fate, since my loving wife seemed inspired by the woman's story.

"He is back home, but not before a good five years in that place.

I found my way, and you, sweetie, shall find yours. We ladies always do." She laughed and patted Prudence's shoulder before turning and pushing her cart down the street, shouting about her fresh-baked meat pies.

"Well, that was informative." Prudence looked down at me. The smile on her face coupled with the sparkle in her eye told me that I was not going to be as fortunate as the old woman's husband. "Shall we get down to business? I believe three shillings is what is required for admittance, is it not?"

"Prudence, I earned that money to go toward paying down my debt."

"Earned?" She guffawed. "You did not earn this. It was handed to you out of pity. Are you telling me that time with your wife is not worth three shillings?"

"No, my dear—"

"Then it is settled. I shall find a turnkey and pay my entrance fee. I shall see you in a few moments." She smiled and then stomped down the street toward the entrance of the prison.

"I am fucked," I muttered as I pulled myself from the prison window. I sat down on the bed of straw and contemplated what possible means she could have for paying off my debt. Knowing my wife, I was not going to like it.

As I waited for her to pay her admittance fee and be escorted through the prison, I tried to reassure myself that she was a reasonable person and that she would not ask any more of me than she would be willing to do herself. I was the husband, after all—the man of the house—the wage earner; that had to count for something. "Yes, I shall demand that she go to her family for money to pay off my debt." I stood and chattered to myself. "Or perhaps convince her that, as my wife, it is her responsibility to find a job so as to help with expediting my release." I looked about the filthy conditions of my cell and felt deflated. "She will not listen to me in here. I have no air of authority. I am fucked." I leaned against the cell wall as I heard footsteps descending the stairs.

"Back here, my lady." A gruff voice echoed through the stone hallways. "Mr. Bristol is one lucky man to have such a fine, caring wife as you." He pulled out the keys and unlocked the cell door. They both entered the cell.

"It is so good to see you, my dear." I wrapped my arms about her waist and gave her a kiss before taking the pies from her. "You, sir, may leave."

"Please, sir, if you do not mind, I would like you to stay for a moment." Prudence reached out and touched his arm. "I may need to ask for your assistance." She smiled and nodded at him with a sparkle in her eyes.

"My lady, how can I help?"

"I hope that we can help each other." She smiled.

"Prudence, you cannot be serious about this?" I came to her and held her hand. "Please, my love, we shall find another way." I could not believe that she was willing to give her body to this brute of a man, out of love for me. Tears of pride and love filled my eyes. My heart warmed with the love that she was showing. I felt as if it were melting through my body.

"Reece, sit down and eat your pie." She turned back toward the gaoler. "I have heard from a few of my lady friends about a gaoler here who has on occasion been willing to help wives out with their husbands' debt. Would you know who that might be?"

"That would be me, my lady."

"Oh, how fortunate. I would hate to speak of such things to someone who is not aware of these arrangements." She gripped his upper arm and then patted his chest. "Yes, you will do just fine."

"Pru, my love, I beg of you not to do this. I could not bear to know that another man is pleasuring you."

"Me, oh no, my dear, you have it all wrong." She leaned over and kissed my cheek before returning her attention to the gaoler.

"May I inquire as to your name, sir?"

"If you do not mind, my lady, I prefer to leave my identity out of this."

"But I must insist. If I am to let you use my husband's ass for your own pleasure, then I believe I have a right to know who is fucking him."

"Prudence, have you lost your mind?" The warmth and affection I had felt for my wife drained from my body. I felt weak at the thought of what my wife was insinuating. I dropped the pies on the floor.

"Culpepper, my lady. Virgil Culpepper." He smiled at her and then looked at me and winked.

"Then I take it that we have a deal?"

"We most certainly do not!" I spat as I tried to wrap my weary mind about the details of what my wife was contemplating. "I will not let this man, or any man for that matter, shove his prick up my ass. No, I forbid it!"

"Shut up, Reece, and stop your pathetic whining. You got us into this mess, and it shall be your ass that gets us out of it."

"You cannot be serious. I will not be sodomized for the sake of money, not to mention that sodomy is an illegal act that could send me to the gallows."

"That is a risk, my dear, that I am willing to take. You shall give your body to Virgil in any way or fashion that he wishes. You shall do this or I shall make sure that you rot in this godforsaken place without any hope of release. Do I make myself clear?"

Mr. Culpepper interrupted us. "My lady, a small detail of my arrangements might have been left out of your conversations with your lady friends."

"What is that?" Prudence questioned without taking her satisfied gaze from my desperate one.

"You must watch," he said as a grin crossed his face. We both looked at him in the same instance.

"What?" we said in unison.

"You, my lady, must watch your husband and me in the act of fucking, or any other activity that I so choose. At least for the first fuck. After that you do not need to be present. That is how this works." Virgil grabbed his affairs and coddled himself. I could see he was enjoying this game of sexual roulette.

I sighed. A moment of relief swept through my body; Prudence would never allow herself to be subjected to such a sight. It would be one thing to send me off to be manhandled by Virgil, but to watch me being fucked by another man—even Prudence in her current state of spitefulness could not accept those terms.

"Well, that is something I had not expected." She looked at me through squinted eyes and then back at Virgil, who stood ready and waiting. "Well, if that is what it must be, then yes, you have a deal." She smiled and held out her hand. Virgil accepted her hand as he raised his eyebrows to me and smiled.

"Prudence, please. Do not do this. Your plan is preposterous."

"Reece, my dear, the deal is done. Besides, I may like what I see."

"How can you say that? Men fucking men is an abomination, a sin against God."

"Oh come, dear. I hear of men out there that want nothing more than to have a prick up their ass—they prefer it, in fact, to the large cavities of a woman's cunt. They get up to all sorts of mischief and have not been struck down by God. All my lady friends' husbands have taken it up the ass. Well, at least those who wanted out of this place. No, dear, you are not the first, and I doubt you shall be the last to suffer the indignation brought on by a scorned wife." She held her hand to her mouth and pretended to giggle like an innocent schoolgirl. "Shall we commence with the activities?"

"Prudence, I beg of you."

"Beg to me, Mr. Bristol." Virgil groaned as he squeezed his affairs. "I am the one fucking you."

"Somehow I feel as if I am being fucked by both of you," I replied.

"Strip," Prudence demanded as she took a seat on the small wooden stool and pulled out a bottle of gin.

"My Lord, you knew all along?" I questioned as I unbuttoned my blouse.

"I hope you did not think that I came here for no other reason than to see you." She lifted the bottle to her mouth and took a swig. She sighed with a smile as I pulled my shirt off.

"Not at all what I was expecting from you," Virgil said as he came upon me. He moaned as he ran his fingers through the thick mass of hair that covered my chest. His fingers followed the line of hair as it trailed down my belly and into my breeches. I backed away from his touch. An instinct, I suppose, of having a man touch me in such an intimate manner. He shook his head with a half smile and pulled me to him. Our bodies collided. His stale, hot breath battered my face. I felt the rise of his prick against me. My body trembled with anxiety. He leaned down toward me. I closed my eyes to his approach. He placed his lips upon mine.

I felt his mouth open up. His tongue pushed against my pursed lips. I gave in and offered him entrance. He slid his tongue into my mouth without thanks. His unshaven whiskers pricked my face as our tongues curled and licked each other's mouths. To my surprise I felt my prick begin to respond. I opened my eyes, peering across the room as our tongues continued their exploration. Prudence sat wide-eyed sipping her gin. Her nod of approval caused my prick to falter. I felt it recoil as she blew me a kiss and grinned. Her leg bounced ever so slightly over the other knee as if she were enjoying a day in Hyde Park rather than sitting in a filthy prison watching her husband engage in the most private of acts.

"I cannot do this." I broke Virgil's embrace and backed away.

"I have an agreement with your wife." Virgil pulled me to him. "And after that kiss, you cannot simply step away." He grabbed at the band of my breeches and made quick work of unlacing them. He fell to his knees and pulled my breeches down my legs. My prick fell out in front of him, soft, unresponsive, and shriveled. He cupped my furry satchel and rolled the sensitive bulbs between his fingers. My body quivered. My knees weakened. I grabbed his shoulders to keep from falling as he took my prick into the warmth and comfort of his mouth.

"My Lord." I moaned as my prick settled into the rough and aggressive mouth of another man. I heard Prudence snicker. I held my tongue, not wanting to admit that another man was giving me pleasure. I closed my eyes while Virgil's tongue drew circles beneath the layers of skin that covered the head of my prick. My prick responded. It stretched and lengthened, filling Virgil's mouth with my unexpected rise. He gagged and pulled my throbbing prick out of his mouth. My body shook as my prick slipped out of Virgil's throat. The cool air of the prison chilled my spit-drenched prick.

"Fuck," he panted. "You have a fine tool, Mr. Bristol. Now let me see about the ass your wife has sold to me." He groaned as he turned me around. "Grab your fucking ankles, bitch, and let me see what your ass is worth."

I bent forward but could not reach my ankles thanks to my more-than-ample belly. I bowed my legs and used my knees to brace my hands on. Anxiety rippled through my body as I felt Mr. Culpepper examine my buttocks, an area of my body I myself did not know. I felt my buttocks spread open. The cool, damp air of the prison caressed me, causing my sensitive hole to quiver. I looked at my swollen prick as Mr. Culpepper continued his appraisal of my ass. The clear nectar of my prick's unnatural desire gathered in great quantity in the folds of skin.

"Your husband has a fine ass, Mrs. Bristol."

"I of course would not know from personal experience, so I appreciate your saying so. How much is his ass worth?" She stood up, a bit liquored, and came to us. She bent down and peered at my ass.

"Prudence!" I shouted.

"We shall have to wait, my lady, until I get my first fuck. The tighter the ass, the more I am willing to pay."

"Well, let us get on with this, I do not have all day for your frivolous play." She took a swig from the bottle and managed to reseat herself without falling.

"Stand up," Mr. Culpepper growled and slapped my ass. I righted myself and sighed, thinking perhaps he did not find my ass worthy of abuse. As I turned to face him, our eyes met. I could see the desire sparkling through the dark-green ovals as he caressed my nakedness with his gaze.

He stood several feet from me as he unlaced his blouse and pulled it from his shoulders. His chest, covered in a tight curl of moss, glistened with perspiration. His tits were erect with desire. He pinched them and moaned before unlacing his breeches. He kicked off his shoes and stripped himself of his remaining clothes.

Mother of Mercy, I thought as my gaze fell upon Mr. Culpepper's hefty prick, which hung with great weight between his legs. A sudden gasp came from the corner where Prudence sat. I knew she had caught a glimpse of his more-than-adequate prick. He looked down at his prick and fondled it. He tugged it. It grew further in length and girth.

"Get over here, bitch." He curled his finger at me. With uneasy steps, I approached him. A crooked smile formed across his face as he noticed my apprehension. He grabbed my shoulders and threw me against the iron bars of the cell. They rattled and clanked as I fell against them.

"Please be light with your handling," I pleaded. I closed my eyes as I felt him shift behind me. He squeezed and spread my buttocks. I readied myself for the pain of his insertion. "Oh shit," I gasped as his tongue instead of his prick slipped inside me. My legs trembled. I gripped the iron bars to keep myself from losing my balance as Mr. Culpepper buried his face in my ass. I felt him slide deeper, licking the innermost parts of my body. The pleasure he brought to my body caused my prick to leak a steady flow of dew upon the floor. "Lord, give me strength." I moaned as the most pleasurable urges rushed through my body. He removed his tongue. I shuddered at his departure. He gasped for air. Prudence snickered in the corner.

"Now to fuck," Mr. Culpepper panted in my ear as he pressed against me. I could smell my ass on his breath. My head swam with emotions I could not describe. He turned my head and kissed me, filling my mouth with the flavors of my own shit and oils. I took from him what he gave as he settled his prick between my buttocks. He broke our kiss and lifted his body from mine. I pulled myself off the bars, expecting to turn around and face him. "Stay put," he growled and pushed me back against the bars.

Fearing further embarrassment of pleasure from Mr. Culpepper, I closed my eyes to the sight of Prudence sitting in the corner. I heard Mr. Culpepper spit and then felt his damp fingers run between my buttocks.

"Yeah, this is going to be a sweet fuck." He groaned as he gripped his prick and rubbed it up and down the crack of my ass.

"Mother of Mercy," I cried as I felt the large, swollen head of his prick pop the tender hole of my ass. A fire like nothing I had ever before experienced tore through my buttocks as if he had struck his tinderbox and held the flame to my ass. "Please, no farther, you shall kill me," I begged. My head became dizzy. Tears fell from my clenched eyes. My entire body broke out in a sheen of perspiration, and yet beneath the excruciating pain there was a moment of utter bliss.

"Oh yes, my new friend, you do have the finest hole." Mr. Culpepper kissed the back of my neck as he shoved his prick farther inside me.

"Fuck," I screamed. My voice echoed through the dark corridors of the prison. "Please, stop." I begged for my life, fearing I would not live through the experience.

"Yes, that is what I intend to do." Mr. Culpepper grabbed my hips and shoved the full length of his prick inside me.

"Motherfucker!" I gripped the iron bars as the pain of his insertion tore through me. I wept like a child as he wiggled and squirmed his way deeper. He leaned into me. He held me, rocking our bodies in unison. I took several deep breaths, hoping to ease the pain.

"I have found no finer hole than yours, Mr. Bristol," he whispered into my ear. "Just relax. Breathe, yes, that is it."

My body trembled as the pain began to dissipate. I felt him pull from me. The slow, steady release from my ass sent shivers of glorious relief through my body. My prick was solid, longer and firmer than it had ever been. Clear nectar oozed from my piss slit, clinging to the tip as it fell to the floor.

The pain returned as I felt him move once again deep inside me. Within the pain, there was pleasure. I winced and breathed, concentrating on the feel of his prick moving within me. Our bodies were wet with perspiration. I inhaled our odor. The deep breaths brought relief to our unnatural act. He pushed the last of his prick into me. I groaned, unsure if the sound came from pleasure or pain.

Mr. Culpepper's body trembled against mine. He moaned as he pulled himself from me. He tightened his grip upon my hips and shoved himself into me. My breath caught in my throat as he began to fuck me with quick thrusts of his hips. Our bodies rocked upon each other, wet skin against wet skin. His large, heavy satchel slapped at my inner thighs with each forward thrust.

"Oh God, you are splitting me in two," I cried as his thrusts became heavier and more forceful. I pushed my ass toward him, hoping to ease the pain as his prick swelled inside me. His breathing became heavy, his grunts more pronounced. He pulled me up and leaned me against him, pinching my erect tits, which sent uncontrollable waves of pleasure through my body. I gave in to the unfamiliar urges, took hold of my own prick, and stroked myself feverishly.

"Yes, work that prick of yours." He groaned as he bit my neck. "Oh fuck, yes, I am going to fill you with my seed."

I pulled away from his embrace and bent my body forward. A fire burst inside me; my satchel, tight and firm, ached from the impending release. I stroked my prick in unison with his thrusts. The urge to release grew until I could not hold back.

"Son of a bitch." I groaned as a thick stream of my white pearls shot from my prick. I watched as my release clung to the rusted iron bars of my prison walls. The urge to release grew stronger as he fucked several more loads out of me, each one more potent than the last.

Remnants of my release continued to spit from my prick as a sudden rush of heat exploded inside me. Mr. Culpepper's prick shuddered within me as he released what seemed like buckets of his seed into my sore and stretched ass. He continued to fuck me with violent thrusts until I could hold no more. The muscles of my ass released, spraying his seed. It ran down my legs, clinging to the sweat-dampened hair. He pulled himself from me. My ass quivered as the last of him left me. My legs gave out. I fell to the floor weak, feverish, and spent.

"Your husband is an exquisite fuck, my lady," Mr. Culpepper panted as he leaned against the wall.

"It appears he is." She stood on unsteady legs and came toward me. She squatted down and wiped my wet brow with her handkerchief. "That was not so bad, now was it?" She chuckled. "You took it like a man."

"Please, no more." I looked up and noticed her face was blushed. Perspiration dotted her forehead.

"I must admit that watching Mr. Culpepper here take you as he did brought me near to pleasure." She patted her face and neck with the handkerchief as she stood. "I hope that you enjoyed yourself, Mr. Culpepper."

"I did indeed, my lady."

"Then shall we talk business?"

"I shall give you ten shillings for this fuck and six for every fuck forward. I hope that is agreeable with you, my lady?" He stood and walked toward his clothes, which lay crumpled on the floor.

"It is." She smiled and looked down at me. "I knew your ass would be worth a pretty penny, but I had no idea it would be worth so many." She brought her hand to her mouth to contain a giggle.

"Prudence, please, you must stop this. How much more can I take?"

"As much as Mr. Culpepper is willing to pay for," she replied as she turned toward Mr. Culpepper. "Thank you." She took the shillings and deposited them into her pocket.

"I would like to ask your permission, my lady, to invite a number of my gentleman friends to partake in your husband's offerings."

"I forbid it." I pulled myself up by the iron bars and staggered over to them. Shit, sweat, and spunk ran down my legs. I reached out and grabbed Mr. Culpepper's shoulders to steady myself. "Have I not suffered enough?"

"My dear," Prudence responded in her most endearing voice, "this is not about suffering. It is about paying off your debt." She smiled at me and then turned her attention back to Mr. Culpepper. "Would they pay the same as you?"

"I am quite sure, my lady, that they would be more than agreeable to that rate for time with your husband. I do know of two gentlemen in particular who would prefer to be fucked by Mr. Reese or to use your husband's mouth as their glory hole, and I would be happy to negotiate a higher rate in those cases."

"This arrangement of ours is becoming quite profitable. Of course, I would cut you in on those deals where you negotiate a higher price."

"Do I not have a say in this?" I demanded. "Mr. Culpepper nearly fucked the life out of me. I cannot bear this mistreatment on a regular basis."

"No, I am afraid you do not, dear." She shook her head. "Besides, you are fooling no one here with your idle woes. I saw what I saw just now, and you shall never convince me that you did not enjoy being fucked. I have never before witnessed your prick so strong and firm. I should know. I have suffered many times while you try to satisfy my needs. If only you could get that excited with me then I would not have to fake my pleasure and wait until you are asleep to be fulfilled."

"Prudence!" I spat as Mr. Culpepper laughed at my wife's confession.

"This was the best fuck we have shared in our entire marriage. My private moments tonight will be quite rapturous with the thoughts of the two of you engaged in such things." She broke out laughing along with Mr. Culpepper.

"Oh, Mrs. Bristol, you are quite the lady." He took her hand, kissed it, and then patted it. He chuckled.

"I see we have another debtor trying to pay off his debts." A voice came out of the darkness. "Mr. Culpepper, I do hope you got your money's worth." The man laughed. "I must say that the sight of this beautiful woman has my mind in a bit of a flutter." He opened the gate and entered the cell.

"Mr. Dankworth," Mr. Culpepper called out. "My apologies for my undress." He bent down to retrieve his breeches.

"No need to apologize. I have seen it all before, have I not?" He turned to me and bowed. "Aaron Dankworth." He smiled at me when I did not return his introduction.

"Reece, I am appalled." She glared at me and then turned a brilliant smile toward our visitor. "Mr. Dankworth, I must apologize for my husband's lack of manners. I am Prudence Bristol." She curtsied and held her hand out for Mr. Dankworth to take.

"I am honored, my lady." He bowed and kissed her hand as his free hand made a direct line to my affairs. He cupped my satchel and pulled upon it, giving unwanted rise to my resting prick. I backed away from his advance and covered myself with my hands.

"His untouched ass was well worth every penny," Mr. Culpepper said as he pulled his arms through the sleeves of his blouse. "It appears that I have left him in a bit of a mess."

"The state of his ass is of no concern of mine, as I prefer the warmth and tongue action of a gentleman's mouth." He smiled and winked at me before turning his attention toward Prudence. "My lady, may I inquire if his mouth is available for sale?"

"Oh, everything about my dear husband is for sale. Shall we say eight shillings?"

"A bargain, my dear friend." Mr. Culpepper laced his breeches and then slapped me on my back and laughed.

"Prudence, please, no more of this. Have I not paid enough in embarrassment and humiliation?"

"In those terms I would agree with you, but you still have quite a long way to go before you are free of your gambling debts." She turned to Mr. Dankworth. "I do hate to ask this, but if you would not mind paying me in advance, I have some business to attend to elsewhere."

"Of course, my lady." Mr. Dankworth reached into his pocket and handed Prudence the payment for my services.

"Mr. Culpepper, if you would not mind escorting me out, we can discuss our arrangement further."

"Not at all, my lady." He bowed.

"Good day, my dear." Prudence kissed me on the cheek. "Be a good boy and do as Mr. Dankworth asks." A devilish smile crossed his face as she took Mr. Culpepper's arm and walked out of the cell and into the dark corridors.

"Shall we?" Mr. Dankworth broke the silence as he pulled the tails of his blouse out of his breeches. He looked at me with a questioning gaze and then added, "I would prefer for you to undress me." He closed the distance between us.

I held my tongue as I knew nothing of small talk during these intimate moments. I looked at him as I unlaced the ties of his blouse. His chest, unlike that of Mr. Culpepper's, was barren of hair. He moaned, smiled, and licked his lips as my fingers grazed the large, erect nubs of his tits. I did not like to think of myself giving pleasure to another man, but found the ease with which my touch excited Mr. Dankworth rather enticing. His masculine odors billowed out from underneath his blouse as I pulled it off his shoulders and let it fall to the floor behind him.

"Do not be afraid to touch me." He took my hand. "In fact, I insist that you do." He guided my hand to his chest. I drew a circle about his tit. I remembered Mr. Culpepper pinching and twisting his tits. I tried to replicate it. "Fuck, yeah." He groaned. Something inside me quivered at his pleasure. "Suck it." He took my hand in his and guided my face to his chest. I inhaled the scent of him as I wrapped my lips around his tit and sucked. His entire body trembled. "Yeah, that is it, chew on it. Oh, fuck, yeah."

I found myself exploring his body despite my initial reluctance. My fingers moved through a patch of soft hair at the edge of his breeches. Without conscious thought, I moved my hand between his legs and began to fondle his affairs. His prick lengthened in my grasp. I felt its heat seeping through the material of his breeches. It felt longer but thinner than Mr. Culpepper's. I made quick work of the ties of his breeches and slipped my hand into the depth and warmth of his private area. My fingers slipped through the long strands of hair. His prick, already damp with his excitement, pulsed within my grip.

"Down on your knees," Mr. Dankworth demanded. I obeyed, pulling his breeches down as I went.

His prick fell out of its confinement and bobbed in front of my face. The thin tip brushed across my cheek, leaving a trail of his moisture coating my skin. I gripped the trunk and squeezed it as I brought my hand forward. His foreskin was plentiful and covered his stiffness completely. I milked it with my hand, allowing the clear nectar to spill from his piss slit.

I hesitated, not wanting him to think I was anxious to take him into my mouth, yet the curiosity of what a man's prick would taste like made the wait brief. I opened my mouth and let his dew puddle upon my tongue. I tasted of him. It was warm, salty, not at all what I had expected. I widened my mouth and slipped the head of his prick between my lips. My tongue, with an instinct of its own, slipped under the folds of skin. His prick's head was silky, soft, and warm.

His length was formidable. I took him in with slow, careful ease. The veins running along the trunk of his prick were swollen and pulsed against my tongue. His body quivered with my taking of him. The heavy folds of skin dangled against the back of my throat. I stopped my progression as his prick filled my mouth. His prick spat excitement. I drank from it, letting the fluids drizzle down my throat. I began to pull back. He stopped me.

"You can do better than that." He gripped the back of my head. "I paid to fuck your mouth, and that is what I intend to do." He thrust his hips against my face, shoving the entire length of his prick deep into my mouth. I gagged upon the tip as it sank into my throat. He laughed at my awkwardness, pulled out, and slapped my face with his spit-soaked prick before slipping it back inside me. "Yeah, that's it. Take the whole of me." He groaned as he shoved himself against me.

His grip tightened about my head as he fucked my mouth with growing urgency. His hairy satchel slapped my chin with each forward thrust. I wrapped my arms about his body and held on to his firm, hairy ass to balance myself against his thrusts. My mouth filled with his early release. I drank from him as he continued to fuck me. My fingers found his tight hole. I fingered him, letting my finger slip inside his ass as he pulled himself from me.

"Oh, fuck, yes, that is nice." He moaned. "Yes, fuck my shit hole. Fuck, that feels good." He growled. I felt a sudden rise within me and knew that he would soon spend himself. He thrust into me with quick, heavy slaps. His prick pulsed. It grew in length and thickness. His body shook. He panted and groaned and with one final thrust a hot, heavy stream of his seed expelled from his prick. He shoved my face against him and held me firm as his prick shook and began to spasm, spilling more of his release down my throat. I began to choke on the quantity that ushered from him. I inhaled through my nose and took in the heavy masculine scent of his affairs.

His release came with such abundance that I could not drink it fast enough. The warm, salty fluid spilled from my lips, trailed down the trunk of his prick, and gathered in the hair of his satchel. He pulled himself from me and pushed me to the floor. He stood over me and fondled himself, spraying another load of his seed over my neck and chest. The warmth of his release covered me. He fell on top of me and licked his own seed from my body, biting and sucking my erect tits as he gathered his seed in his mouth. He lowered his body to mine. Our pricks met, and in that moment of closeness my own prick expelled a stream of my desire between us. He kissed me, rubbing our soiled bodies together and sharing with me the last of him, which had gathered in his mouth.

"One would think that you like this abuse." Mr. Dankworth chuckled as he pulled himself from me.

"I endure this out of necessity and nothing more," I lied, not wanting word to get back to Prudence of my growing fondness for such abominable acts.

"Then I may call on you again?" He pulled his breeches up his legs and then tucked the tails of his shirt inside before tightening the laces. "It has been a pleasure, Mr. Bristol." He bowed and left the cell without another word.

❖

"Good evening, Mr. Bristol." Mr. Culpepper greeted me as he entered my cell. "You have not undressed. Did you not get my message that I would be arriving?"

"I did."

"Then why have you not prepared yourself and undressed prior to my arrival as I asked of you?"

"I have not honored your request because I see no need to do so." I rose from my bed of straw and approached Mr. Culpepper.

"I have already paid your wife for my time this evening, that is reason enough."

"Mr. Culpepper, it has been almost a month since the agreement between Prudence and yourself. I have marked every fuck, every instance of intimacy on the wall." I pointed to a row of hash marks that I had etched into the stone. "As you can see, that number has risen to seventy-two counts. Knowing what my wife is charging for each act, it would stand to reason that my gambling debts have been paid in full. So I am ready to be released from this place."

"Paid in full?" Mr. Culpepper laughed. "No, I am sorry, that is not correct, Mr. Bristol. Your debt is still owing."

"That is not possible. Six shillings at the minimum rate would equate to over twenty-one pounds. My debt was only nineteen pounds. I have more than paid off my debt."

"That would be correct, except for the fact that Prudence has not paid a penny toward your debt." He smiled at me.

"How can that be? She receives the money up front. What kind of game are you playing, Mr. Culpepper?"

"I assure you, I am not playing any games, Mr. Bristol. Your wife, on the other hand, has found this to be a very lucrative scheme and is playing you for the fool that you are." He laughed.

"How long is she going to continue this?"

"I cannot say, that is between the two of you."

"But I have not seen her now for nearly twelve days."

"That is not my concern, Mr. Bristol. Now drop your breeches and bend over. I have already paid for the use of your ass."

A FEW DOLLARS MORE
DALE CHASE

Bringing a herd into Abilene sets us cowpunchers loose, and we are known to not skimp on the fun. After three months on the trail, a hot bath, new clothes, and being absent a horse start things off right. After this we see to whiskey, cards, and pleasures of the flesh. Having drawn our pay, we mean to make good use of it. Most of the time I'm with men from my outfit, going across the tracks to less respectable establishments where a man can fully indulge his carousing.

We've been here the best part of a week and tonight I am thinking on a change. After supper we leave Drovers' Cottage, the big hotel where we stay, and I tell my pards to go on without me, saying I want to explore the proper part of town on Cedar and Texas Streets. They kid me on this, but I don't care. I'm tired of women crawling all over me when it's a man I want, and I believe I'm more likely to find him when in the better saloons. I also want to get as far from the stock pens as possible, being they're full and giving off a powerful stink. I walk a good distance the other direction and it's around midnight when I pass an alley and hear a high-pitched cry, then a plea of "no, no, please don't." Thinking a woman is in distress, I step down that way, as I cannot bear a man taking advantage of the fair sex. Again comes the cry, followed by the sound of slaps and a struggle. "No," comes the plea and then the response, "Take it, you bitch."

There's just moonlight in the alley, but it's enough to see a well-dressed man beating on—wait, it's not a woman. It's a boy. I move closer as the man slaps him again, keeps calling him names. The man's pants are open and I see a soft dick. The boy's pants are down and I get that he's about to be taken against his will. The man gets an arm around the boy and humps his ass, but can't do much with his length of rope.

He rears back and slaps the boy hard, then again and again. "Bitch," he growls. "Fucking bitch, filthy fucking bitch."

The boy issues another plea. "Don't fuck me. Please, no."

Well, that's enough. I step up, grab the man around his neck, and lock my forearm so he can't take air. His words sputter to a stop, as does his attempt to fuck with nothing going. I wrestle him across the alley, then slam him against a wall where I hold him. "You all right?" I call to the boy.

"Of course I'm all right, you asshole. Let him go. It's not what you think."

Lost to his meaning, I keep hold of the man, who has stopped struggling.

"Let him go!"

I release the man, who swears at me while buttoning up. He then runs off. The boy, pants still down, says, "Thanks a lot," in a way that I get means just the opposite. "What in hell is going on?" I ask.

He pulls up his pants, but not before I get a good look at a fine prick that's half-hard. "He paid to do that," explains the boy.

"Paid?"

He shakes his head and straightens his jacket. "Yes, paid, you dunce. He paid to fuck me and he paid extra to beat me. Only way he can get it up."

I don't know what to say, as it's women who charge for entrance. Men are dime a dozen, just have to find them. The boy starts to walk away and I put a hand to his shoulder to stop him. "I don't understand," I say. He's in the streetlight now and I see he's a stunner. Hair of gold, pretty face, and the lips of a woman. He huffs a sigh of impatience. "Men pay me for sex," he says.

"But you're just a boy."

"I'm twenty-three," he counters, "but I get away with fifteen, and that's what they want. You've been on the trail too long, mister. Cities are filled with boys like me, making a good living off men who have women at home. That fellow you chased off is Ned Higbee, president of the Cattleman's Bank."

"What's he doing in an alley?"

"Well, it's like this," says the boy with a sigh. "A man can pay to fuck me in my room at the Lady Day Saloon or he can pay extra to do it elsewhere. Higbee can only get stiff if he's out in the open. Feels dirtier that way. He also has to beat on me some due to guilt over what he's doing, since he has a wife at home."

"I don't believe it," I say.

"Fair enough."

He walks out onto Cedar Street, and for a few seconds I stand in wonderment. Then I hoof it after him because I can't get hold of the idea of him selling himself. There is also the fact that he's the prettiest man I've ever seen. He walks a good many blocks up Cedar, getting back to the busy part of town, then turns in at the Lady Day Saloon and goes down to the end of the bar. The bartender sets a whiskey before him without any asking and I note he does not collect money. I stay a ways down the bar, get a whiskey to sip while I keep an eye on the boy. Never mind he's old enough to be a man, nature seems to have denied him proper aging, and I find appeal in this. He's slight of build and no more than five foot six in height. Fair of complexion, his face bears none of the weathering we outdoor men show. I note his hands are delicate, long fingered, and he turns with womanly movements, as if he knows he's pretty and trades on it. Looking at him gets my prick up.

Not ten minutes after the boy settles in at the bar, a well-dressed older man comes over and slaps him on the back like they are old friends, then leans in as if to tell a private joke. I watch while they laugh and drink, and when they go through a door that leads to the back hallway and the privy outside, I realize they're going to fuck. My prick throbs in my pants and I make this worse by thinking on putting it to the boy. I have to down several more whiskeys to quiet myself.

The man soon comes out and doesn't look at all like he's taken satisfaction. He keeps his head down as he hurries out. I watch the back, and in a couple minutes there comes the boy. I can't help but go over to him. "Another customer," I say.

He grins. "You're getting a kick out of this."

"Because I've never seen it before. Who was that fellow?"

"Norman Lerude, grocer. Well known around town, widower so he can manage to fuck without extras. He was married twenty-eight years and says he's glad his wife's dead."

"You make good money?"

"That I do. A good night I can take in a hundred dollars or more. And now, if you're not going to hire me, please move off. You're holding up the line."

"What's your name?" I ask.

"Tad Willett."

He looks at me with bright-blue eyes, and in that second I know I have to have him. And he knows it too. As I back away, one side of his mouth cricks up into a wicked smile and I think I might come at the sight. My face goes hot, my heart starts to pound, and my dick tries to crawl out of my pants. To ease things, I get a bottle and settle at a corner table where I spend the rest of the night watching Tad Willett and getting drunk. Around dawn, when he's gone down that hall with more men than I can count, I stagger to my hotel where I sleep until noon.

Another day passes before I hire Tad Willett. I spend it trying to ignore the fact of him which, of course, means that I encounter him all around town. He dresses well and is a sight to behold. Fine gray suit, yellow shirt, black tie, black hat, but within it a trim body moving like a cat with just a touch of the sashay. If I go by the way he moves, I can see his years, but if I go on looks alone, he's that boy they all crave.

On the second day, I take up a spot out front of the Lady Day Saloon so I can watch him go in and out, which he does with regularity and usually in company. Then, long about four o'clock, when I've had a good bit of this entertainment, he comes to sit beside me.

"Business looks good," I say as he lights a smoke.

"Always is. That last man, fat as a pig? The mayor."

"No."

"Yep. Mayor Ramsey Fulkerson. He's the first one fucked me when I came to town last year. Struck up a conversation right off, paid me compliments, and offered to buy me supper. I took him up on that, and after, he asked to see my hotel room. Soon as we were behind a closed door, he got out his dick. I knew all along what he was up to. He bore no guilt at doing me, saying it was his wife's fault as she won't let him fuck her up the ass. Now he has me regular, gets full naked, which is a sight as that belly expands when not belted in. Due to that gut of his, he likes me astride him."

"Why are you telling me all this?"

"Because you want to hear it."

He's right. My prick is up and my nuts are about to burst. "Tell me more," I say.

He laughs. "Best one is the reverend."

"A man of God?"

"Yep. You'd think, with him conversant on the devil's ways, that he'd be able to resist. First time he caught me on the street and began to talk on my joining his church. Put an arm around me and walked me several blocks before getting to it. 'I hear you hire out for manly purposes,' he said, and I told him I do so, he asked prices. I told him five dollars to suck, ten to fuck in my room, fifteen for doing it elsewhere, and twenty if he needs to beat me."

"Which did he want?"

Tad leans over, blows smoke into my face, and whispers, "Twenty dollars' worth, but not for beating me. He wanted me to beat him, which I did while he called out to God and pulled his dick. Was really just spanking, and when he was good and red, he fucked hell out of me. Biggest dick in town. No wonder he's full of guilt. Thing like that on a man of the cloth has to be Satan's doing."

"Don't you ever do cowpunchers?" I ask.

He chuckles. "Not much. Seems you fellows see to yourselves."

He wears tightly fitted pants and I see a good bulge when he gets up to leave. He gives it a tug, then says, "You know where to find me," before going into the saloon to resume work. I sit a good while, thinking on how I've never paid to fuck any man and don't believe I should now. Then I count my money.

It's around eight o'clock when I give way. I've had supper, played some cards, and downed two whiskeys, so I am ready for a good fuck. I stand down at Tad's end of the bar while he's engaged in the back. When a man hurries out of there, my dick stirs. Then out comes Tad. "What's your pleasure?" he asks, knowing he's got me.

"I don't need any beating. Just a fuck."

"Ten dollars."

I pay him and he takes me to the back. I'm surprised to find his room done up nice with fine linens on the bed. I comment on this as Tad strips. "You going to get naked," he asks, "or do you cowpunchers like it with your clothes on?"

I laugh. "We do a lot of that on the trail due to circumstance, but I want full naked now." I then undress.

By the time I'm bare, Tad is lounging on the bed and playing around with his dick. I'm stiff as a post, but before I join him, I take in the sight as he is pretty lying there, golden hair shining in the lamplight.

There's more of it down between his legs, though none on his chest. He truly does look fifteen. "There's cream on the nightstand," he says, destroying the notion. "Grease up."

I do as told. The stuff is sweet smelling, but I don't care. I slather it on, then join him on the bed. "How do you want me?" he asks.

"All fours," I say, and he flips over and raises his rump. I get in behind, part his buttocks, and find a hole so pink it looks untried. As I stare, it winks at me.

"Fuck me," he says, so I stick him.

He's nothing like the men I'm used to. They're mostly thick bodied, dirty, and rough from trail work, and we do it standing between horses while guarding the cattle at night. Tad, on the other hand, smells so good you'd never know he fucks for a living. His passage grips me soon as I'm in, which causes my juice to boil right off. I'm not going to last, but don't care as he's the best fuck ever. I hold those narrow hips and go at him with a fury until the rise hits and I cry out, pumping for all I'm worth as I let go one hell of a load. I ride him like I'll never stop and keep on even when I'm empty, but then nature catches me and I go soft and slip out. I fall onto my back while Tad hops right off the bed. He goes to the basin and starts to wash, the sight of which helps me fight the sleep demon who always knocks me out after a come. Tad tending his dick excites me all over again and when he washes his butt crack, I think maybe I should pay another five dollars and suck his dick. I can almost feel it on my tongue, but hold off making the deal by way of forcing myself to consider the expense.

"Get dressed," he says as he finishes up. I don't want to leave, but do as told. When I pause at the door he asks my name.

"Ray Stull," I say.

"Well, Ray, you've got a fine cock. Doing business with you is a pleasure."

I don't know what to say, so I leave. Back at the bar, I get a drink. When Tad comes out he acts like I'm not there and soon Higbee, the banker, is at his ear. I figure he's asking to finish what I interrupted before. When they go out, I'm tempted to follow and get a look at Higbee having his fuck, but keep myself back. This is not easy, as I want more of Tad Willett. Getting into him sparked something, and I don't want to put out the fire just yet. I get pretty drunk as a result and wake the next day so hungover I couldn't get it up for love nor money.

In the hotel lobby I run into a couple fellows from my outfit who are just coming back from across the tracks. They start in about the women they've fucked, and I allow their tease as they know I don't go that way. Once they've had their fun, they tell me they're heading for Dodge City tomorrow. "Come along. We'll have us a time," they say.

This is how we usually do things after a drive, cutting loose in several towns, but I don't want to leave Abilene, so I tell them I'll be along to Dodge in a few days, knowing I won't. I leave them, get a meal, and walk around town while keeping a lookout for Tad Willett, who I finally see across the street. He's dressed in black this day, with white shirt and red vest. My privates take note. He's talking to the mayor, so I know he's sealing a deal, and as I watch him nod, I want to go over and shove that fat pig out of the way because Tad deserves a real man with a good body and a dick hard as a gun barrel. And I'm that man. I start to cross to them, but they walk off, headed toward the Lady Day. I follow, thinking I'll push away the pig, but once inside the saloon, I realize stepping in might put Tad off me, so I get a drink and attempt calm.

Well, this does not work. Knowing them in Tad's room, him astride the pig or maybe the pig astride him, is more than I can handle, so I go through the back door like I'm headed to the privy, only I stop and put my ear to Tad's door. I hear the creak of his bed and the kind of grunts men make when taking their pleasure, and it's all I can do not to bust in and stop it. My prick is so stiff I'm almost in pain, so I go out to the privy and piss away the hard-on, then button up, go back inside, and listen again. The bed is still creaking.

I force myself to leave the Lady Day Saloon. I walk far from it, then go to my hotel room where I wash up, hoping water can cool me down. I go to another saloon and get into a card game that I stick with much of the day, never mind I mostly lose. It's early evening when I look up to find Tad Willett standing at the bar so the bulge in his pants is there for all to see. I try to keep to my game, but lose two more hands before I cash out. I then go over to this boy who sells himself.

"Looking for customers?" I ask as I get a drink and move in beside him.

"I think I found one."

"How much for a whole hour?"

He cocks his head like he's pleased with the notion. "Fifteen."

"You've got a deal." I hand over the money and we go out.

In his room he checks his watch. "Five fifteen," he says, "so you've got till six fifteen." He then undresses. Not wanting to waste time, I throw off everything quick as I can. He hops onto the bed and raises his legs to show me his hole and I shudder at the sight, never mind I've been in there. A willing shit hole can take a man's breath away. I grab his jar of cream, slather a gob on my dick, then get over to him and poke that sweet pucker. "Fuck me," he says. "Give me that big bull dick."

He keeps talking like this and I drive my prick into him so hard he grunts. When I start to go at him, he moans and carries on like I'm driving him crazy. His own cock comes up, but he doesn't tend it. Soon it's dribbling, the knob going shiny, and I know I'm rousing him like no one ever has. "Forget those married fellows," I tell him as I shove in and out. "A real man is what you need."

"Fuck me, Ray. I need it bad, need you to fill me with come."

The bed is complaining at what I'm doing, such is the force of my dick. Then the rise beckons and I tell Tad he's going to take a good load. "Give it to me," he says. "Give it to me."

I let out a roar when I hit the peak as everything in me turns loose, dick firing like a repeating rifle and just as hard, mouth spewing animal noises I can't control, whole body in a shudder of pleasure right down to my toes. I pound and pound as I spurt, and even when I'm empty I keep on because I know that sleep demon will hit me soon as I stop.

Tad's eyes blaze as I keep at him, his mouth open, tongue wagging. I can see how caught up in me he's gotten, like he's never been fucked proper. His moans are easing off, but his look stays wild and I know it's because of my dick inside him. We go on for a few seconds more, then I lose my heft and slip out. When I fall back onto my haunches, I'm breathing like I've ridden a hundred miles full gallop, but for once find I've outrun sleep. Instead of wanting rest, I want more of Tad.

He puts down his legs so he lies flat, his dick shiny wet now. He squirms and I get what he needs, so after I draw some good breaths, I lean over and start to suck him. Holy God, it's a good suck. His cock is a fine mouthful, and after I lick his knob clean, I take in the whole of him and start to work my tongue, licking and sucking, playing around until he bucks up and fills my throat with spunk. As I swallow, I glance up as I want to see his rapture as he unloads. Once I've swallowed all he has, I stretch out beside him. "You're beautiful," I say. "Best fuck ever."

"You're not bad yourself, cowboy." Here he gets onto his side and runs his fingers into the pelt on my chest. "Man tits," he says as he finds a nub in the fur. He then leans over and commences to suck on one, and I let out a groan because nobody has ever done this. Men on the trail don't bare enough to get at some parts, and drovers in hotel rooms only fuck and suck dick.

Tad nips the tit, which sends a jolt down to my privates. He then changes over to the other and nips and plays there too. "You have a fine chest," he says when he eases back, "and I especially like a furry man." He runs a hand down onto my stomach where the hair continues, then down into the patch around my cock. Here he plays and I get to squirming, as I've never had such attention. "Big fat dick," he says as he takes my softy in hand. "Thickest one I've ever had, and you know, Ray, I'm going to need it again. My hole is aquiver at the idea, so we're going to have to get you stiff." He pulls on me some, then leaves off and crawls back up to get up close. "You are fine-looking, Ray. A manly man." He then puts his lips to mine. Another jolt goes down to my dick.

Drovers don't kiss, be it on the trail or in a room. I know men kiss women, so I'm at a loss to what Tad is doing and yet find myself eager. His lips are soft against mine and when his tongue pokes at me, I open to let it in. Holy God, I think as the tongue meets mine. I don't know what to do more than welcome it, and soon the two are mingling and my prick stirs below.

When Tad pulls off the kiss, he smiles, his eyes upon mine. His are the brightest blue I've ever seen and they all but sparkle, which I see as joy in what we are doing. "I want all of you," he says. "Dick isn't enough." Here he kisses me again and we go on that way awhile before he leaves off my lips and starts kissing other parts, neck, tits, stomach, prick. When he gets down to my nuts, I spread my legs to admit him. He takes one into his mouth, rolls it around on his tongue, and sucks some, at which I let out a cry as this is beyond pleasure. He nut-sucks a good while before kissing his way back up to my mouth.

My cock comes up again, which is a record for me as I usually need some time to recover, and that's after a sleep. But Tad is a master, and when he climbs over me and drops down to spear himself with my dick, I can't believe it. He then starts bouncing on me and I lie fucking without doing a thing but providing the rod. I pull a pillow under me so I can watch myself go up him, and the sight of that starts me boiling. There can't be a drop left in me, but arousal is a separate thing and soon my arms are flailing and I'm carrying on something awful because he's pulling the spunk out of me. I buck like a wild bronc, but Tad is not unseated. Instead he rides me to a standstill, then hops off. As I lie gasping for breath and fighting sleep, he checks his watch. "Six fifteen," he says and he starts washing up.

How in hell he knew the time is beyond me, but I don't dwell on this. I work at staying awake until Tad says, "Time's up. Get dressed."

This is like having cold water thrown on me. A man in my state as should not be turned out into the street. I want to say this, but hold back because Tad isn't looking at me now. I sit up, blow out a breath, and find my underdrawers. Soon I'm dressed.

"A pleasure," says Tad, who seems eager to wrap things up.

"It was all mine," I say. I reach out to him, but he backs up to avoid the touch. He opens the door and follows me out.

The night becomes a long one as I see no more of Tad. I hang around the Lady Day, but once he's gone out he doesn't come back. This leads me to think on him fucking Higbee in an alley or maybe doing the reverend on a church pew. I finally go around town, even go into the church, but I can't believe anybody would fuck in God's house. Back outside, I tell myself to stop chasing after the boy and I go to a saloon that is not the Lady Day and get into a card game, which occupies me until I fall to bed.

Next day after breakfast I get myself a bath and shave, put on fresh clothes, then sit out front of the Lady Day. I think to count my money, but don't. Tad comes out around noon, looking fine in a navy suit. He doesn't sit beside me, but stands leaning against a post, enjoying a smoke. When his free hand strays down to adjust his privates, I know he's teasing me. Finally I get up and go over to him. "Didn't see you last night," I say.

"Well, you did me in, cowboy. Your spunk is still dripping out of me, and I think my butt hole is a size larger."

"You recovered enough for another go?"

"I'm at your service. Ten or fifteen?"

"What gets me two hours?"

"Twenty."

"What gets me a whole night?"

"Fifty."

This will nearly break me, and I need support money until I get my next job. Tad looks off down the street as he waits on my decision. I give myself all kinds of reasons not to spend that much, but all the while I'm arguing with myself, I'm not listening. "Okay," I say and I count out fifty, which leaves me way too thin.

"How about we get a bottle?" he suggests.

"Good idea." I go into a nearby saloon and hand over my next to last dollar. We take the whiskey to his room.

"I want to do it all," I say as I pour us drinks. "First off, you get naked."

Knowing we have all night, he makes a show of stripping by turning, swaying, and wagging his dick at me. Once he's bare we clink glasses and throw back the liquor. "Now you," he says. He pulls off my jacket, then unbuttons my shirt and slips it off. I raise my arms so he can remove the undershirt, and he pauses in the stripping to pet my fur. Then the pants are undone, boots and socks come off, and I am already breathing hard as him undressing me has great appeal. When I'm down to underdrawers, my prick tenting the front, he runs a hand down inside. "What have we here?" he sings as he takes hold.

"Easy," I say. "I don't want to come yet and I sure as hell don't want it by hand."

He grins and yanks down the drawers so out springs my dick. Once I'm bare, he backs me to a wooden chair. "What in hell?" I say as I fall onto it.

"Let me sit on you," he says and before I can protest, he's greasing me, then climbing on. When my cock goes up him, I don't much care we're not in bed as the position puts his top part up close.

He sits still a few seconds, squeezing his muscle, at which I let out a laugh because this is truly wicked.

"You think that's good?" he asks with a chuckle. "Just the beginning." He then kisses me and, as I get hungry up top, he starts to grind on my prick, then raise up just a bit and drop back down, then grind some more. I think I've gone to heaven, or maybe hell, I really don't care. His tongue is after mine and we play that way while he starts to ride me with an easy stroke. I can't help but push up at him and we get a good thing going, fucking in a chair, which I'd once have laughed at. Now I've got my dick in a beautiful boy who wants my kisses.

He moves his lips down onto my neck, licking and nipping, then to my ear, which he pokes his tongue into. "That fat cock of yours owns me, Ray," he coos. "Big prick filling me, driving me crazy. You keep on, you'll drive the spunk out of me."

His dick stands stiff between us, but he doesn't tend it. He's caught up in tasting me, licking and kissing. He manages to keep to the fuck while bending enough to lick my tit and I let out a squeal, piglike, because this is beyond what any man expects.

"I need you to come in me, Ray," says Tad when he stops tit-sucking. He bounces more now and talks more. "Give me a load, Ray. I know your balls are bursting and I want it more than you can know. You come like no man I've ever had. Your stuff was running out of me for hours and I want more, need more. Do it, Ray, fill me, fuck me."

He's got me going now and I take him at the waist and drive up into him as the come he has summoned arrives. The chair squeaks so loud I think we might break it, but I don't care. I'll pay for that too, pay for anything because this is better than a gold strike. His hands are on my shoulders as he works to stay astride his bucking bronc and I go some good seconds pumping my load up into him. Then I'm done and slip out, but, as we are upright in a chair, there is no rolling over. Instead Tad starts to kiss me, little kisses as we're both breathing heavy. He does this till we're settled, then kisses me longer and sweeter. Finally, he pulls back and gets off. I see he's gone soft, but don't care on that just now. I also realize the sleep demon can't get hold of me when I'm sitting in a hard chair.

When Tad stands up, he stretches and blows out a big sigh. "Just fucked is the best feeling, short only of having your cock in me. My butt hole is atingle with all that spunk up inside. You are some good fuck, Ray Stull."

He pours us drinks and we sit on the bed, bottle in his hand. I down the liquor in one gulp, so he pours me another, which I take slower. I run a hand onto his thigh and squeeze, which causes him to squirm. I can't resist sliding my fingers onto his prick. "You didn't come," I say and he chuckles. "Plenty of time for that," he sings.

"No clock on us tonight."

"You got that. And you got me."

I get off the bed, get down between his legs, and start to suck his soft cock, enjoying both the feel of him on my tongue and the idea I need not rush. He is finally mine. I feed a good while and when he's hard, I step up the pace, which gets me some good spurts into my throat. Once he's done, I pull off as I want to see him in his satisfaction and he's a beauty, shiny with sweat, happy at getting sucked off, yet still giving me that wicked crimped-up smile. Never mind I've just fucked him. I need him all over again.

I set aside the bottle, push him back onto the bed, crawl on top, and start to kiss because I'm too riled up to lay off, and that is how the night goes. I tend his whole body, even his crack, where I lick the filthy and wonderful hole. I don't care what comes out of it. It's a treasure and I want to fuck it again, fuck and fuck and fuck but it's too soon after the first and I know that. "Get me stiff again," I tell Tad after a while.

He eases me back, climbs off the bed, and takes up the bottle. He enjoys a good swig, then starts handling the long neck like it's a dick, and I lie on my side to watch the show. He rubs the bottle over his tits and his stomach and his hairy patch, then puts it between his legs so the neck sticks out under his balls, like an extra dick. He works the neck like he can make it come and this is some sight. I can't help but enjoy a wicked laugh at the show, wondering what else he will get up to. It's not long before I find out. He turns, spreads his legs, and shoves the bottle neck up his hole and proceeds to fuck himself and I have to grab my dick because I can't believe what he's doing. He squats and grinds on the thing, shoves it in and out, then pulls it out and takes a drink before shoving it back in. I watch this for a few minutes, pulling my prick, which can't help but stir.

Soon I'm off the bed, but when I pull out the bottle, Tad says, "Take a drink," and pushes it at me. I'm so worked up I don't care where it's been and I suck down the last of the whiskey before he turns and says, "Fuck me." I ram the bottle in and start to go at him, one hand doing that, the other on my cock, as I need to get in there more than any goddamn bottle. He's riding the thing when I finally have enough heft to fuck, so I pull out the bottle, toss it aside, get my dick in, and do him standing like we do on the trail, only now I'm naked and in a room, putting it to a beautiful boy who can't get enough. I don't care I haven't got but a drop in me. Desire says otherwise and I keep at him even when my legs beg me to stop. Can't listen to any muscles but the one in my dick because that's where I live now, fucking as necessary as breathing, maybe more.

Tad starts to call out. I know he's working his prick and soon he says, "You're driving it out of me. Fuck me, Ray, fuck the come out of me, give me that fat dick." On and on he goes and I fuck so hard I think I'll collapse before I hit the rise. He's coming and carrying on and I'm pumping for all I'm worth, then finally I hit the peak and give him what he wants. As I finish and slide out, I wrap my arms around him, reach down to his spent cock, and give it a tug. Between drawing long breaths, I manage to bite his neck and kiss his ear. He pushes back against me. "Wonderful," he says and he turns and looks me straight on. "Best ever," he says and I don't argue.

We fall onto the bed after this. Night has come on but I don't care to get up and light the lamp. I fight the sleep demon as Tad curls up against me, hand in my pelt, rubbing a tit, and that's the last thing I remember until daylight intrudes. My eyes are closed, but it's too bright in there to sleep so I open up to see Tad standing at the mirror. He's fully dressed.

I throw back the covers as my dick is hard. "How about you get over here and finish up," I say. "You can see I'm ready."

"Ten dollars."

"What? No, I bought you the whole night."

"And it's morning, a new day. Ten dollars."

Here he turns to me, golden in the morning light, and truly a sight to behold. I reach down to pull my dick, but he's not impressed anymore and I get right then, in one awful moment, that I'm a fool. All Tad did, all he said, was purchased. He probably does those married fellows same as he did me, says the same things, turns and dances, maybe even bottle-fucks himself, all for nothing but money. Breath goes out of me at this point and does not come right back while my heart sinks, if that organ can do such a thing. My dick goes soft by way of being shot down and I lie more crushed than if I'd been trampled by the herd.

"No?" Tad says, reminding me there's a deal on the table. "Then you'd best be up and dressed. I have a living to earn."

I cannot get into my clothes fast enough. Hot with humiliation, I avoid him as I pull on shirt, pants, and boots. At the door I look back and he passes me that wicked smile. He's still the most beautiful thing I've ever seen. I'm the one might be fifteen.

HOLIDAY
FELICE PICANO

It was the worst New Year's Eve of my life.

Me and my ten-years-older lover had been fighting since Christmas Day, and the signs were clear that the relationship was on a slide into that pit right outside the Flaming Gates of You Know Where, a slide he was doing nothing to slow down.

I myself had reached that very delicate emotional point where I could either say "to hell with it; I always knew he was a bastard" or... well, the other alternative is pretty evident, no?

We were headed to *his friends'* New Year's Eve party, although in what he termed "the spirit of compromise," he told me we could "stop by" the apartment where *my friends* were having a party—which, by the way, had been our first invitation for the night and the one I believed we should honor alone. Okay, he said, just as long as we were out of there by 11:37, giving us fifteen minutes to get to the other flat. It was now 10:30 p.m.

He lived in the apartment above mine. So we "would gather" there.

We always gathered there. We never gathered at my place.

Once gathered upstairs, I had my entire outfit critiqued.

Not that I hadn't myself pre-critiqued it.

Obviously I'd only pre-critiqued it sufficiently for my own taste and the taste of my friends.

His friends evidently held far more stratospheric criteria, and every inch of what I was wearing was found wanting or tasteless. Especially the boots.

"Cowboy boots?" He sniffed. "With a suit jacket?" He sneered. What would his friends say to such an anachronism? Surely it would not only typify me as a mindless youth, it would signify that he had "taught me nothing."

He'd taught me plenty, little of it useful afterward.

In vain I pointed out that it was already snowing and that the snow was sticking and that the weather person had said to expect a foot or more by the morning.

He deigned to point out that we resided in Lower Manhattan, the land of superfluous taxicabs. I was to get rid of the boots and put on some adult shoes.

I fussed, I fumed, I changed into the shoes he wanted me to wear.

I was not happy.

The snow was only inches high and we could easily overstep it into the waiting taxicab he had phoned for. This was pointed out to me, pointed out to me without the use of a foot-long ruler to measure the snow, which I was told to feel lucky for.

Ten minutes later we were in an apartment off Sheridan Square, only yards from the infamous Stonewall Bar: at my friends' apartment. It was a nice party. It filled up fast. Everyone was my age, with a few older guys including Chuck Partridge, high and happy as usual, who made two, count 'em, two, overt plays for me, one of which included a rather public feeling up to accompany the swooning bent-over-backward New Year's kiss he planted on me, loudly explaining, "Since you won't be here for the moment itself."

I noted that my lover and I were the only two people there *not* wearing some kind of boots. "Stoned, ditzy, and out of it" as most my friends were, at least according to my lover, they at least had gotten the message about the foot-high snowfall to come. Even happy-go-lucky Chuck was wearing something resembling flexible-sided leather overshoes.

A minute later, I was being hustled out of the party by my lover, who had seen—who hadn't?—that Partridgean super-osculation, and who now was actually berating me for it.

We arrived down in the lobby, where people were stomping in, shaking off the already considerable wet, goopy snow that had collected upon their shoulders, hats, bare heads, and of course, they too were wearing boots. We'd only been inside for fifteen minutes or so and the snow was already a foot high. They went in as we stormed out, to the taxicab my lover had called.

Which was not there.

Which might have been there a fleeting moment, but which had doubtless been bought off for more money from someone else in a hurry, and which, therefore, was now gone.

"We'll flag one down," my only slightly perturbed lover said.

Right. On New Year's Eve. In Manhattan. That'll be a cinch!

Fifteen minutes later, the snow was two feet deep. I know, as I shook it off myself periodically.

Cabs sailed by in immense profusion without stopping or in fact without even slowing down for traffic lights: the red ones had now become ambiguously pink, covered by a two-foot-high encasement of ice and, you guessed it, snow.

Twenty-five minutes later, the snow was two and a half feet deep. Few cars, few anything sailed by. Some people, in huddled masses, did creep by, pushing snow in front of them with brooms and shovels.

And now my lover did what no sane man on earth would ever do.

He began to blame me for our plight.

That lasted five minutes.

At which point, miraculously, a taxicab pulled up. He got in. And gestured me in.

Was it only the entire awful night, or did that gesture appear to me to be the same one used to summon a wet dog inside a house?

It sure did look like that to me!

I shouted a frozen, hoarse obscenity suggesting into which endoscopic cavity he ought to place his well-barbered head, and I slammed the taxi door on him. I stalked off in the other direction of a one-way street, in what was now three feet of wet, clinging snow, wearing on my feet what another pal once charitably termed (as I was throwing them away a few days later) shiny black, silk and patent leather, ultra-thin opera slippers.

I didn't look back to see if the taxi had taken off. Of course it had taken off, uptown, to his friends' place. I didn't doubt it for a minute. The cab would arrive in just enough time for him to have put together some witticism or *mot juste* to explain my absence.

Fury warmed me the first eight blocks toward home.

Then the weather settled upon me. Was it my imagination as I turned off Eleventh Street and onto Abingdon Square, or was it all nothing more than frozen tundra? Not a single moving vehicle could be discerned even though two major avenues crossed here. Not a single human form could be descried along any of those avenues or the many radiating side streets.

The West Village can be beautiful under falling snow. The many rows of eighteenth- and nineteenth-century edifices with their *galant* Federal Era architectural details look finely frosted like so many delightful antique cakes. Even the newer, turn-of-the-twentieth-century buildings have their more solid charms when outlined in silver-white rime. The period street lamps and iron fencing, the cobblestone roads and elegant sidewalks, the many three-story-high, bare trees are all delicately laced with ice and snow. It's a pictorial paradise.

Beautiful. Icy. Frozen. Empty.

Storefronts, filled with patrons only a short while ago as we'd not so gaily cabbed away into the night, were now gated up, totally blank. I was only four streets from home. But as I dragged my soaking feet, ankles, calves, and knees out of yet another snowbank, I felt as though I might as well have been on some Chelyabinsk *taiga* a century ago in mid-December. I was completely alone, in a vast, motionless silence even more muffled by what was now about three feet of snow.

Snow I had to slog through to get home.

Three blocks away I stumbled and fell onto my gloveless hands up to my chin into the snow. I got up with difficulty.

Two blocks away, I was swearing under my breath and making promises to various deities that if my body were ever recovered... The words "Antarctica" and "extremely desperate" floated before my eyes, which were so cold that the water layer on the corneas iced up, only to be audibly shattered—ker-chick—every time I blinked.

One and a half blocks away...Was it a mirage?

A gigantic, black six-door town car pulled up along Hudson Street, whereupon I slogged on unto my certain doom. A window slid down. Inside sat a handsome fellow with blond hair and a golden mustache, wearing a tuxedo and white silk scarf and holding a flute of champagne. It looked so warrrrrrmmmm inside.

"You look like you need a ride," he said.

I unfroze my lips and unclenched my teeth long enough to chatter out: "I only live up there. I can make it."

"Nonsense!" he said. "Get in."

The door flew open and he reached out for my hand and pulled me in and onto the seat next to him.

"You look perfectly frozen. Tell the driver where he must go."

I did so.

Two minutes later, it pulled up to my building.

The driver hopped out, and I swear it, he actually shoveled a walkway through the snow up to my front door.

I turned to thank my savior. But he was pushing me out and not letting me go either.

I found my keys, frozen, of course. He managed to open first the building door, and then when we'd gotten to the end of the corridor at my apartment door, he opened that too, and sort of pushed me inside.

My tiny apartment. He scoped out the bedroom and guided me there.

"We've got to get you out of these wet things immediately," he commanded with a chuckle.

Before I could do so, he did so.

In mere seconds he had me down to my undershorts, the only item of clothing not soaking wet.

"Well, I think you need a good rubbing to warm you up."

He vanished into the tiny bathroom and appeared with towels, and with the bottle of champagne, which he insisted I drink. He'd taken off his camelhair overcoat and dropped it over a chair.

He then proceeded to rub me so well that my underpants came off, my hard-on stood up, and as I uttered something or other he began sucking on it. He seemed to have at least three hands, maybe more. He was hot, I was cold, but then I got hot too. It was fast and it was frantic. He never took off another garment in all that time.

Not five minutes later, I climaxed and then I simply collapsed onto my bed. He held me there, kissed me all over very nicely, not at all creepily, and then he tucked me in. Just before he stood up, he wrapped the white scarf around my neck.

Kissing my brow he said, "Happy New Year. And thank you, you lovely young man, for making what was looking like a so-so evening into a memorable one."

I thought I heard him exit and I tried to get up to see him out, but I was exhausted and the warmth of the bed held me. I sank into sleep.

When I woke up the next day, there was four feet of snow in the backyard. I was wearing nothing but his silk white scarf. Its label said it was "made for Dunhill, of Fifth Avenue."

I dressed in sweater and jeans and wandered into the kitchen to make coffee.

It was nine o'clock and the steam pipes were hissing out little puffs of heat.

Outside looked gorgeous.

I thought, "Now, that was exactly the kind of New Year's Eve I always wanted to have."

The man in the tuxedo had been for fifteen minutes or so exactly the older lover that I had always hoped my upstairs neighbor would turn into. I knew now he never would, and that I was done with him forever.

When I went into the bathroom I had an even bigger surprise.

Sticking out from under the bar of Ivory on the soap dish was a crisp one-hundred-dollar bill, which in 1971, just about paid my monthly rent.

It was the best New Year's Eve of my life.

PITY FUCK
LAWRENCE SCHIMEL

It was late Sunday morning, which meant that of course we were at Le Caprice for brunch: Trevor, Boris, Jeremy, and me. Sylvain, the sexy maître d', had put us in a prime spot at the front windows, which were wide open to let in the spring air, which also allowed us to both see and be seen by all and sundry, whether fellow patrons or passersby. Which also meant that we were acting up even more than usual, being in the spotlight as we were.

"Look at that utter dog over there," Jeremy said, taking a sip of his Bloody Mary and rolling his eyes at the far corner of the street.

I tried to remember if "dog" was complimentary or not this week in Jeremy-speak as I glanced discreetly at the corner in question, where three young men were sitting on the steps of a brick brownstone. I was seated next to Jeremy, so I could see the guys in question with ease just by lifting my gaze. Both Trevor and Boris had to twist around to see them, something they both shamelessly did, simultaneously, in a twist as graceful and as swift as a pair of synchronized swimmers.

"Oh, them," Boris said, turning back to his egg-white omelet with goat cheese and sun-dried tomatoes. Just like that, all three of them were dismissed as being beneath his interest. Which was saying something, since the three specimens were all quite different from one another and ran from one end of the spectrum of male beauty to its polar opposite.

From where I sat, there was the young man on the left, who I imagined was between twenty-one and twenty-three, a baseball cap covering his blond hair; he was dressed in sports sweatpants and a white tank top that revealed a section of a colorful tattoo that covered his lean, muscled torso.

In the middle was a guy who was a little younger, maybe nineteen to twenty-one, Latino or Arabic, with dark hair, dark eyes, and dark skin and a huge dose of animal magnetism. All eyes were repeatedly drawn to him, although each time it was a different detail: those plump lips, the curve of a biceps, his large hands as he gesticulated to illustrate a point to the other two, who sat at his feet like disciples, listening to him raptly. I was tempted to prostrate myself at his feet myself, which is why I was surprised Boris had dismissed the entire group so summarily and quickly.

Although when it came to the third guy...it was easy to see why. Anyone would suffer in comparison to the Adonis in the middle, but even on his own, this poor fellow was unquestionably ugly. There just wasn't any softer way to put it. He had beady eyes that weren't even hidden behind glasses, jug-handle ears, and an overbite. But more than any individual feature that made him look ugly, it was the overall effect: there was something about his features that made them not fit together right. And he was all awkward and gangly when he moved. I guessed he was between the other two, in terms of age: twenty, twenty-one. And unlike either of them, he wasn't fibrous or muscled. He wasn't fat either; if anything, that might've given him some distinguishing quality or made him attractive—even if only to chubby chasers. Instead, he had an unpleasantness about him, as if he were typecast to play an undertaker in a horror film or something, someone to give you the creeps without any possible morbid sensuality or goth sexiness. Not only was this boy not attractive, something about him provoked an active rejection the longer one stared at him.

Which explained Jeremy's comment. "Dog" meant "ugly as a dog" this week, and not "I want him to hump my leg" or "woof, he's hot!" or something like that.

Trevor was still watching the three of them with the morbid fascination of someone who couldn't look away from the scene of a car crash on the highway, even while it turned their stomach. I followed Boris's lead and turned my attention back to my food: buttermilk pancakes spread with lingonberry jam and rolled into logs which had been sliced slant-wise to create what looked like a mini fortress of spiked towers crowned with tasty, colored spirals.

"Really," continued Jeremy, never willing to let a snide comment stand when he could beat it to death with a limp response, "there isn't enough money in the world that you could pay me to make me have sex with him."

"It works the other way with those three," Boris said, not bothering to look up from his omelet, his way of signaling his utter disdain for this entire thread of conversation.

"They're hustlers?" I asked him. My voice squeaked from incredulity.

Boris did look up at me then. "You are so naïve, Eric."

"All three of them?" I asked.

"All three of them," Boris answered. "You're looking at a dying breed: the street hustler. Nowadays everything is done online, on rentboy.com or with some app that uses your GPS to locate who is available in your adjacent area. Even these three will all have profiles if you open Grindr right now. I think the blond kid was using the handle 'Blue Eye$' last time I saw him online."

I looked up again at Blue Eye$ and Latin Lover and the Ugly Hustler.

"I guess there's a market for everything," I said. "But I just can't imagine…you know, how he makes a living, I mean." There was no doubt as to which of the three I was talking about.

"Maybe he has a really big dick," Boris said.

You could tell that all of us contemplated this suggestion in silence for some time.

"Even so, not going there. Not enough money in the world," Jeremy repeated.

"I'd pay to do the one in the middle," Trevor said, still staring dreamily at the man across the street. "Not that I need to pay to have sex," he added immediately, turning his attention back to us at last. "But he looks like he'd be worth it, you know?"

I still couldn't get over the idea of that third guy being a hustler, too. I could easily see how the first two could make a living, with the guy in the middle probably being able to get rich given how in demand he would be among the sugar daddies, or maybe just the right one who'd pay to take him off the market…But who would pay that third guy for sex? I couldn't even imagine anyone being desperate enough to take money from him, as Jeremy had joked, to make it worthwhile.

"Have any of you ever paid someone for sex?" I asked.

All three of them stared at me, open-mouthed, although I wasn't sure whether they were affronted that I could even ask or that I thought they'd ever admit it if they had. Jeremy had been chewing a slice of Canadian bacon, and seeing him with his mouth open was not a pretty sight.

"Or been paid for sex?" I added, trying to save face.

One by one, my friends shook their heads.

"Someone at a bathhouse once paid me twenty bucks to let him suck me off," I confessed. "I would've let him do me anyway, but of course I took the money."

I had liked the idea of being paid for sex, even more than the actual encounter; the guy who'd paid me was not especially adept with his mouth. But being considered worth paying for really turned me on and flattered my ego.

I couldn't help wondering if that was why the third guy across the street tried to be a hustler; that rush I'd felt, even from my modest incursion into the exchange of sex for cash. Although I imagined his life must be an unending stream of frustration, watching his two buddies pull client after client while he waited, alone, on their corner, for them to come back after each job…I imagined he must have some other source of income in order to keep a roof above his head and continue to eat and all that, although his two friends were good-looking enough that they could no doubt earn enough from hustling to make a living. Especially if they were not just young but horny enough to be able to do multiple tricks a day…Of course, I imagined that while it was important for the john to come, maybe they didn't need to come with each of them, unless that was specified in the transaction and maybe paid for as an extra.

None of which was any help for the ugly hustler, though.

And while my mind was absorbed with these thoughts, my friends grew bored with this thread of conversation and took it elsewhere.

"So it takes twenty bucks to make a whore out of Eric," Jeremy said. "For me, just give me a cocktail and let me loose in the backroom at the Hole. I went there on Friday with Kenny and you would not believe how many men I sucked off…"

❖

Once I get an idea in my head, it takes root there, like a tenacious seed, and seems to grow of its own accord, flourishing and growing no matter what I try and do to the contrary. I've learned over the years that it's no use to try and change things, so eventually I had to face the harsh truth:

I had become fascinated with the Ugly Hustler.

It's not as if I did nothing but look for him, or at least think about him. I went to work every morning, went to the gym, occasionally had sex with strangers I met online, met up with friends for drinks or a film or both.

But I kept coming back to the Ugly Hustler; he was like a constant worry, like that feeling that you left the gas on even when you know you've shut it off. Or, given how unattractive he was, maybe a better metaphor might be a sore inside your mouth: your tongue keeps going back to it, time after time, even though it hurts every time your tongue makes contact, but you can't stop yourself from seeking it out again and again.

Sometimes even when I was jerking off, he would invade my fantasies; not that I fantasized about having sex with him, my thinking about him was anything but sexual, but I might suddenly get sidetracked from a fantasy, wondering what it was like for him, if he got sex in both his work life and his personal life, how he managed to make a living, things like that.

I can honestly say that I never expected to be thinking of the Ugly Hustler while holding my erect cock in my hand, yet exactly that happened more than once.

I will confess to losing my erection quite promptly on such occasions, not something that happens to me often. Although to be honest, this might have happened not just from visualizing him but also from having lost the thread of the fantasy I'd been jerking off to. I began to worry about my virility, not to mention my mental health. What was happening to me that my mind would rather think about this hideous-looking man than engage in erotic fantasies?

And every weekend, when we had brunch at Le Cerise, no matter what table we wound up at (although sweet Sylvain usually put us in the front windows whenever he could) I was sure to seat myself where I could have a clear view of their corner so I could keep an eye on them during our meal, and especially to see if the Ugly Hustler ever managed to even talk to anyone, let alone snare an actual john.

After Boris's comment, I'd obsessively logged far too many hours online until I'd hunted down all three of them and their profiles. But I never did more than just mark them as "favorites" so I could find them again.

I never IM'd any of them or sent them messages.

Once, I saw Blue Eye$ at the supermarket, but he never even glanced at me, even though I of course recognized him right away. It gave me a thrill, like seeing a movie actor or something, secretly watching them go about the mundane events of their lives, knowing things about them that they didn't know we knew…in this case, what he did for a living.

Even though I knew their online handles, I only ever used them for Blue Eye$. I'd already gotten so used to thinking of the three of them as Blue Eye$, Latin Lover, and the Ugly Hustler, it was too difficult to try and change their identities now.

The seed was already planted, and it grew and grew, too large now to weed out—no way to even try to pull it up by the roots at this point.

For all that I thought about the Ugly Hustler, it wasn't at all sexual for me.

I had certainly fantasized about Latin Lover. Even to the point of offering money in my fantasies, to do the things to me that I wanted him to do. I will admit (although never to my friends) to contemplating contacting him and offering money in real life to do those same things to me.

But I never contacted any of them.

I figured that when the time was right, I'd run into him. And that when it happened, I'd know what to do.

What I always imagined myself doing, on meeting up with the Ugly Hustler in my mind, was opening my wallet and giving him a crisp, hundred-dollar bill. And he was always so grateful. He always offered to do me, of course, but I waved him away, acting as if it were simply my will to offer largesse toward him and not any physical revulsion I felt on looking at him.

I was fantasizing about myself as the noble philanthrope, a role I'd never really envisaged myself in before.

But of course, when our paths did finally cross, the encounter went nothing like I'd imagined.

❖

Our encounter didn't take place on his corner, nor someplace innocently mundane like the supermarket where I saw Blue Eye$. We met late one evening, out on the green (four square blocks that were covered with grass and dotted with trees) when I was out cruising and he was sitting on a park bench, smoking a cigarette and waiting for someone just like me. He recognized my aimless prowling for sex right away; there was no way to hide or disguise it. He stared at me, invitingly.

And my physical reaction to him was the same as it ever was; the very idea of sex with him made my balls shrivel up, as with fear or cold.

I walked past him. My heart was racing. I didn't know what to do.

But this seemed to be the moment I'd been waiting for, these past weeks. The perfect moment to finally go through with it and thereby, hopefully, be able to move on, to forget about him.

I had some money on me, but I hurried to an ATM a few blocks over and withdrew two hundred dollars. Even as I was going through these actions, I knew that they were only partly my following through on instinct, trying to act out what I'd imagined so often these past weeks; the rest of me was procrastinating, buying myself time with the walk to the ATM and then the walk back.

He was still seated on the park bench, still smoking the same cigarette, or another one.

I felt a surge of adrenaline when I saw him; it wasn't a fear of any danger from him, that he might rob me or something, more a general fear of finally going through with something I'd only imagined until then.

He watched me, and I was aware again that he knew I'd come to the park looking for sex. Looking in that outdated way of the hunter and the hunted, fallen out of fashion with the fast-food convenience of ordering online whatever you wanted from the nearest source.

He was the one who broke the ice.

"You go stock up for tonight?" he asked, with a smile that might have been meant to be a leer but that looked anything but sexy.

Nor was it menacing. But I blurted out, "I can give you money."

"I'm not holding you up, man," he replied, holding his hands out in the classic open-palmed gesture of peace and goodwill.

"I know," I said, "I didn't say you were, I just meant, like, in case you needed some or something. If you, like, didn't have enough customers or something…"

So now it was out in the open between us, the fact that I knew he was a hustler.

"I'm not a charity case or something," he said, his dignity injured.

"No, I didn't mean that," I rambled, "it's just…"

It's just that's exactly how I'd been thinking of him. Like he were a beggar. Like he needed me, somehow.

"Look, if you don't want to fuck, that's fine, but go away, you're blocking any other customers."

I was shocked.

Not only was it bad enough that I could be seen in public, trying to make time with such an ugly guy, but even worse, I was getting blown off! I wasn't sure my reputation or my ego could survive such a blow.

"How much?" I asked, thinking I could still give him a hundred bucks or something without having to actually go through having sex with him. I couldn't look at him while I waited for his reply, but nervously scanned up and down the block, checking out whether anyone I knew (or might ever want to know) could see me.

"Two fifty an hour," he answered.

At first, I was relieved, thinking he'd meant $2.50 for an hour. So a hundred bucks would cover quite a lot.

But then I realized he meant two hundred fifty dollars.

I couldn't believe he had the nerve to ask for so much!

I thought back to the twenty bucks I'd been paid to let some guy suck me off in that bathhouse.

Suddenly, I wasn't just a whore, I was a cheap one!

"How much do your friends charge?" I asked, before I could stop myself. It was rude, to say the least, to compare them like that. Or to doubt his own quoted price. Would I ask a dentist or a surgeon how much his colleagues charge? Of course not.

And it also revealed how long I'd been circling around him, as if I'd been stalking him.

"Two fifty an hour, it's the going rate, do you want a fuck or not?"

I felt trapped. Suddenly my mission of mercy was turning out to be much more expensive than I'd planned. But it was as if I were stuck on a highway with no exits, with no choice but to keep driving and hope that eventually there'd be a turnoff somewhere. While I might've just said "no thanks," I couldn't make myself say it, couldn't be the one to reject him another time. I didn't see a way of getting out of going through with the whole shebang. With an ugly hustler who insisted on giving bang for his buck. And they say today's youth has no work ethic!

"Fine. Two fifty."

I wondered whether to assure him I had the cash on me. But then I worried that that might be an invitation to rob me or something.

Although I immediately felt ridiculous for worrying about that. Hadn't this all started because I wanted give this guy money, out of pity? And wouldn't I only feel relieved if he got the money that way, without my having to have sex with him?

He stood up.

"Your place or a hotel?" he asked.

I hadn't thought this far.

While the green was where many men came to hook up, it was too open for much to actually happen here. Usually guys did it in a car or took a car somewhere more remote and secluded.

Both of us were on foot.

I wasn't bringing him home with me. Absolutely not. Not only was there a danger that any of my neighbors might see me bringing home such an ugly trick, I didn't feel comfortable with the idea. It wasn't like I didn't bring other strangers home all the time, people I met over the Internet or at a bar, who I didn't know from Adam. But a professional hustler was different, there was an element of…unsavoriness there, of threat, that I didn't usually feel with those other pickups.

And my mission of mercy suddenly got even more expensive.

"Hotel," I answered.

Let him think what he wanted, that maybe I lived with someone. Or even let him imagine the truth, that I was too scared to bring him home, for whatever reason. Maybe he'd get a thrill out of that.

As I walked beside him, I realized that reality was nothing like I'd imagined it. For one thing, I was starting to wonder how he thought and felt. In my fantasies, I'd only been aware of how grateful he'd felt toward me, and how I'd felt, generously offering him charity.

What a condescending shit I'd been all this time!

Before we got to the next corner, he stopped and turned to me. "Which hotel are we going to?"

And I realized that he knew I had no idea where I was going, that I was in way over my head.

"Why don't you pick one," I said.

And he stared at me for a moment, no doubt asking himself what the hell was going on, if I was actually going to go through with this or not, if I was wasting his time. I forced myself to look back at him, to stare back at his ugly face.

And then he reached out, one hand cradling my head, and pulled me toward him, to kiss me, there on the street, in public.

I forced myself to hold still, to not pull away. As his face drew closer to mine I closed my eyes. I held my breath.

And suddenly his lips met mine. His tongue pushed into my mouth.

And I stopped remembering how ugly he looked. Stopped thinking of him as the recipient of my largesse, as the object of my pity.

Our breaths mingled, his tasting slightly of a cinnamon gum he must've chewed earlier, and the recent cigarette, and I realized I was kissing another human being—even if he made his living offering his body to men in exchange for cash.

Even if I'd constantly underestimated him, despising him without my realizing it, with my attitude toward him, based on his looks.

He was a very good kisser.

It was as if all his attention were focused in that one kiss, which made it one of the most exceptional kisses I'd ever had.

So often, a kiss is a prelude to something else, and both of you are already thinking of that instead of enjoying the kiss for what it is.

But the Ugly Hustler kissed me as if our kiss were the only important thing in the entire world.

Our kiss was so important that I lost track of all my worries and concerns and focused on just kissing him back.

Until he broke our kiss and pulled away.

I opened my eyes again and looked at him. His face was still ugly. The kiss had not magically changed that.

But I saw him now for what he was: a professional, offering a service I wanted, at a price I now realized I was willing to pay.

After holding my gaze for a long moment, he nodded and said, "Okay," and started walking again.

I watched him walk away for a step or two, and realized I was hard.

And I started following after him, to the hotel.

ANYTHING FOR A DOLLAR
GREG HERREN

I wish you were here," I say, watching Bobby Driscoll pouring baby oil over his chest. The oil runs down and wets his bright-yellow G-string.

"You know I hate watching you do this." Geoff's voice comes through the phone. He sounds farther away than the eight hundred miles between Dallas and New Orleans.

"We need the money." Next to me on the worn-out sofa, Sean Hawk is pouring out coke on a mirror. I watch him cutting up the rocks with the precision that comes with experience.

"Is that supposed to make me feel better?" Geoff's voice gets louder. He's getting upset. Sean spreads the powder with an ATM card. He makes several lines. He frowns with concentration. Sweat beads up on his forehead. The room's hot. Bobby is rubbing the oil into his tanned skin now, making it shine. "It's not my fault I lost my job!"

I know this. Corporate downsizing. It's the economy's fault. "I can make enough money this weekend to pay the mortgage," I say. Sean's rolling a twenty-dollar bill into a makeshift straw.

There's a knock on the door. "Five minutes, guys!" someone shouts from outside.

"Gotta go," I say. "Love you."

"I miss you. I'm sorry." Geoff's voice is quiet. "I hate this."

I hang up. Sean offers me the mirror. I take it. There's white powder around his right nostril. I put the bill up my nose and suck up one of the lines. It's good coke. Very good coke. Sean always gets the best wherever we are dancing. I stand up. My nose is going numb. I hand the mirror to Bobby and look into the full-length mirror. I look good, I decide, feeling the drip at the back of my throat. I flex biceps, then pecs, then abs. My G-string is red white and blue, like the flag. It's cut to make my cock look about ten inches long. I turn and look at my ass.

"You look fine," Sean says from the couch. Sean is twenty-two and in his last year at Southern Methodist. His ripped body comes from being a wrestler in high school. We've danced together before. Austin, Houston, Pensacola, Orlando, Nashville, and Atlanta, each city a blur of loud music, coke, and men standing around the bar staring up.

Sean's getting an accounting degree.

"Never thought I'd be doing this again," I say, frowning at my ass. I'd lain in tanning beds trying to get my ass to the same level of tan as the rest of my body.

"It's just till Geoff finds a job," Bobby says, wiping his nose. Bobby and I started dancing at the same time, a million years ago. I wouldn't call him a friend. We've known each other too long to have secrets. Bobby's been to our house for pool parties and barbecues. Always with a different date. He says he wants a long-term lover but there's always something wrong with every guy he dates. "Oil up my back."

His back is hard. His whole body looks like it's carved out of granite. I rub oil into his skin. He has a big pimple on his lower back, big and red and ugly. In the dim light of the bar no one will see it. No one wants to see it. It's too real, and we're fantasies. Fantasies don't have pimples. Fantasies don't have boyfriends. Fantasies have muscles and good tans and big dicks and hard butts. In the dark, no one will notice that Bobby's getting lines around his eyes. On the bar, we'll look young and solid and beautiful.

I hate this.

I never thought I'd be doing it again. I thought I'd left this life behind me forever. I thought I'd found the American Dream. A knight in shining armor had come along and swept me off the bar onto his horse and we'd ridden off together. I was back in school, getting a degree. We had a nice house. A pool. Three bedrooms, two and a half baths. A two-car garage. We were going to get a dog.

It was all so unlikely. I never believed it would happen to me. One night on the bar at some club in Houston I'd seen this cute guy with the biggest most beautiful eyes I'd ever seen looking up at me. I'd knelt down in front of him. "You're beautiful," he'd said to me, those beautiful great big round brown eyes shining. "You wanna get some coffee when you get off work?"

I knew I was going to sleep with him. Those eyes. I'd never seen anything like them. Blue or green or gray eyes might be rarer, but warm brown eyes are the most attractive to me. I knew he wanted to sleep with me. Everyone always wanted to sleep with the strippers. It was a fact of the bar life. I was kind of surprised when we actually went out for coffee. We talked. He asked me about my dreams. He listened. He was from Dallas, too. We laughed about the small world.

Three months later I moved in with him and hung up my G-string.

Goddamned corporate downsizing anyway.

I do one more line and make sure my boots are laced tight. The three of us walk out of the office. The bar's crowded. It's hot. We go down the stairs to the lower level. I touch the wall and it's wet. The bricks are slimy. Heat, humidity, sweat. The air's thick. Smoke clouds look blue in the black light. Loud music playing. The dance floor packed. Men with sweat running down their bodies, pressing tightly against each other as they bump and grind and move their feet. We have to cross the dance floor to get to the bar.

I hate walking across the dance floor.

The men leer and reach out and briefly touch my chest or my ass. I don't want to be touched. I've got to let them if I want to make money. You never know who's got a pocketful of ones they'll want to shove into your G.

Before Geoff I didn't used to mind. I didn't care about anything except making as much money as I could so I wouldn't have to work during the week. I didn't want to be an escort like other guys. I didn't want to make porn movies. I didn't want to take money for sex. I liked having sex with whoever I chose. Dancing on the bar I could pick and choose from anyone staring up. It was power. I liked having that kind of power over men. Now I hate it. They're going to grope and paw me. I have to smile and wink and flirt. There's no other way. Working the counter at Burger King won't pay the mortgage. I have to shake my dick and wiggle my ass.

I feel like a whore.

Finally, we're at the bar. I climb up. Eyes are watching me hungrily. I cross over to a corner. Sean and Bobby are climbing up. We're three different types. Bobby is huge, large muscles. He's the fantasy top, the one all the little bottom boys want to get fucked by. Sean is smaller, lean, and every move he makes causes the muscle cords in his body leap out. He's the fantasy bottom that all the tops want to just hold down and fuck till he screams. I'm a cross between the two. Not as big as Bobby but more defined. Bigger than Sean with less definition. I attract both types. The tops who want someone bigger than Sean. The bottoms who are afraid of a guy as big as Bobby. We work well together. Three different types of body. Three different types of fantasy. Something for everyone. The bar's crowded. We'll make lots of money tonight. They'll want to touch, kiss, lick.

Anything for a dollar.

It's hot. August in New Orleans. The only place hotter is hell. The air in the bar is thick, heavy. I feel sweat coming out of my skin as I start to move.

It doesn't require skill to dance. Just the ability to move your hips from side to side and front to back. You've got to make your dick bounce up and down. That'll make them want to tip. Almost always a dollar. Sometimes a five, maybe a ten, rarely a twenty. Bobby got three fifties from an old drunk in Houston one night. He was missing a tooth with a gut hanging over his trousers. I've never gotten a fifty. Bobby let the man stroke his dick for each bill. Sean will sometimes let someone smack his ass for a ten.

I make eye contact with someone standing at the bar. I bounce my dick for him. He goes for his wallet. Still bouncing, I bend my knees. I smile my wanna-fuck-me smile.

"Very nice," he says, stroking my ass. "I'd like to take you back to my place." His hands are soft, clammy, damp. He's not my type anyway. A little too soft. He's wearing a T-shirt and shirts. The shirt isn't tucked in. Hiding a belly. Definitely not my type. Even if I was single.

I just smile as he puts the one in my G. Someone else strokes my leg. I turn to him. Another dollar. I stand up and turn around, bending at the waist, moving my hips from side to side. A good angle for everyone to get a look at my ass. That's good for a few bucks. I work my way down the bar. A man who must weight at least four hundred pounds gives me a five for a touch of my pecs. I talk to him for a while. I can't hear him over the music. I just nod, smile, flirt. Whatever. I get another five before moving on. Bobby and I switch sides after half an hour. His G is stuffed with bills. I take mine out and put them in my boots.

This side of the bar faces the dance floor. It's packed out there. Wall to wall men. Everyone still has their shirts on. It's early yet. Later the shirts will be off. They'll be covered with sweat. The smell of poppers will linger in the air. Boys'll be cruising. Boys'll get lucky. And I'll dance above it all, an object of fantasy. The object of lust. I used to like it up here on the bar. I could have anyone out there I wanted. It used to be fun. Strangers in strange towns. Blowing in for the weekend. Make some money. Fuck a stranger or two. Be gone on Sunday. I look around the crowd. In the far corner I see a man. He is wearing a white tank top and tight black shorts. Strong legs. Muscular arms. Nice pecs. A baseball cap turned backward. He looks up. Our eyes meet. He looks away quickly. Before he does I notice his eyes. Big. Round. Brown.

Why did he look away? I get a glass of ice water from the bartender. I look back over. He's talking to some guys. Am I not hot enough? I touch my pecs, run my hands down my stomach to the top of the G-string. Just some asshole with an attitude, I guess. There's plenty of them around. Whatever bar, whatever city. New Orleans. Tampa. Orlando. Miami. Houston. Atlanta. Walking around, tight shirts, pants that hug their ass, muscles bulging, too good for other people. Gods walking on Earth. So they think.

What do I care? I have a lover. I have a man at home. I shouldn't be cruising the crowds. It's not like the old days. I used to find one in the crowd. Someone with something I liked. Eyes. Arms. Butt. Chest. Something I liked. I didn't have a type. There just had to be something there. Something that caught my eye.

That was before Geoff.

But I'm back on a bar. Dancing. The object of lust. I get a couple of ones from a pair of preppy-looking boys. One touches my dick. I should care but don't. All I care about is the coke wearing off. I need more. I look to my right. Sean is motioning for me to get down. I walk over to him.

"Break time," he shouts in my ear. We go back to the lounge. Bobby's still on the bar. We don't wait. Sean pulls the mirror out from under the couch. He taps out more coke. He makes a few sweeps with the ATM card and hands me the mirror. I do two lines quickly.

"Good night," Sean says. He's counting the bills in his G. "I've got seventy bucks already and it's only been an hour. I love New Orleans."

I nod. The coke's very good. I don't feel like counting my money. I don't feel like going back out there either. This room feels cool. I towel the sweat off my body. Sean's lining up more coke. "I'm going back to relieve Bobby. You can stay here if you want."

I do want. The door closes behind him. I do another line. Damn it, Geoff, why did you have to get fired? I want to scream at the walls. I don't want to be here. I don't want to be doing this. Geoff hates it too, but not enough to stop me from doing it. Maybe he hates it because he was one of the bar boys? One of the ones that I singled out from my perch on the bar? Maybe he thinks I'll go back to old habits.

Old habits.

I do another line.

I strip off my drenched G and put on a black one with a white stripe down the center. It makes my cock look huge. The desired effect. This one should get me more money. Bobby comes in. He pulls off his G and does his lines.

"I'm getting hard out there." He strokes his dick. "Some troll offered fifty bucks to blow me. Think I should do it?"

"Fifty bucks is fifty bucks." I shrug. Where do I draw the line? Geoff wouldn't like it if I let someone blow me for fifty bucks. He doesn't like the idea of me dancing with my ass hanging out either. But here I am. He could've stopped me. He didn't try very hard. It's okay if we need the money. I feel tired in spite of the coke. I don't want to go back out there.

Bobby is still stroking his dick. It's big. It's always semi-hard. He never has to use a cock ring. He grins. "You wanna party when we get through here tonight?"

I shrug.

"Geoff doesn't have to know."

I say nothing.

"This guy offered to pay us five hundred each."

"For what?" I say.

"He wants to watch us wrestle. Winner fucks the loser." He winks.
"Sounds fun. I always wanted to do you."

"You see his money?"

He nods. "He's got it, all right."

"I'll think about it."

Complication. How would I explain the money to Geoff? I jump
up on the bar. I'm parading my naked ass in front of all of these people.
Where do I draw the line? I'm the one bouncing his dick. I'm the one
getting pawed and touched and groped and licked. Maybe it would be
fun to get fucked by Bobby. Maybe it would be fun to fuck Bobby. Five
hundred bucks is five hundred bucks.

The guy from the corner and his friends are at the bar. I smile.
Look at me, you bastard. I reach down and tap him on the shoulder.
He looks up. I smile at him. He looks away. Uh-uh. Not again. I kneel
down. I poke his shoulder. "Hey!"

He smiles at me. His face lights up. His eyes are like Geoff's, big,
round, brown, expressive. I catch my breath. He leans in toward me.
"I'm not going to give you money," he shouts above the music. "I don't
tip strippers."

"Why not?" I shout back.

"Nothing personal." He shrugs. "I just don't. So I try not to make
eye contact with you guys. That way you won't think I'm going to."

I start to laugh. So that was it. It wasn't rejection at all. Thank
God. It couldn't have been. "That's nice."

"I'm a nice guy." He smiles again. He reaches over and touches
one of my pecs, then pulls his hand away as though burned. "You're
very hot."

"Thanks." I stand back up. I watch him and his friends go out
to the dance floor. He looks great in his white jean shorts. He has a
great body. Better than Geoff. Long, hard muscles in his legs. Broad
shoulders. The muscles in his back ripple as he starts to dance.

I want him.

I go through the motions and get more ones. I peel the G down to
show my package off for a ten. The bar is getting more crowded. The
shirts are coming off the boys on the dance floor. I can see my boy with
the cap taking his shirt off. His chest is beautiful. I shake my head. Stop
it. Don't even think it. He's beautiful. Geoff would never have to know.

And hey, I'm paying the mortgage, right? Why shouldn't I have some fun?

Why not?

Bobby walks over to me. We start dancing together, my ass against his crotch. He's still hard. "That's the guy over there, the guy who wants us to wrestle," he says before licking my ear. I look. The guy looks okay. Not a serial killer. Bobby's chewing on my lobes. I'm getting hard. One of his hands snakes around the front and starts shaking my dick. Guys below us are cheering and waving money. My legs are getting touched by everyone who can reach. I kneel down and pick up some cash. I look over on the other side of the bar. Sean's picking bills up with his ass. A skill I never had. Never wanted. He has his thumb in his mouth, sucking it. Little-boy fantasy. He has the body for it. Older men love him. He knows how to work it.

Bobby moves back to his end of the bar.

They're nameless, faceless. Just dollar bills in my G. Just hands touching my legs, pinching my nipples, touching my dick, grabbing my ass. Like tricks in the old days. Sweat pours down me. I need to change.

I get off the bar. I push through the dance floor. It's almost impossible to get through. Sweaty shirtless bodies everywhere. I smell poppers. The disco ball is rotating. Tiny points of light are twirling through the air. The music is loud. I can feel it. Tribal. Urgent. I try to get by some guys. Two arms snake around my waist and I'm pulled backward. I can feel a bare chest on my back. It's hard, solid, sweaty. I turn around.

It's him. He's smiling. "Dance with me."

I want to. "I'm working."

He pulls me in close. "Dance with me." He kisses me. His tongue goes into my mouth and back out again. He sucks on my lower lip. Oh God oh God it feels so good. He's handsome, hot. I want him. I kiss back. My hands grab his ass. The music keeps on. Someone sticks a bottle of poppers under my nose. My head starts to take off, whirling and spinning out of control. I grind my crotch into his. He's hard. Oh god oh god oh god. We go on kissing. It seems like forever. He stops. He's smiling at me.

"I've got to go change." I push away from him. I stand on the stairs, trying to catch my breath. I need more coke. My God. My dick's hard. I want him I want him I want him.

Geoff never has to know.

I hold on to the brick wall as I climb the steps. It's slimy with moisture. This whole fucking city is wet. Everything's wet. The steps are wet. The railing's wet. Damp and heat. I slip but catch myself. A couple of guys are coming down. I let them pass. They stop. One of them touches my dick. It's still hard. I push his hand away. "I'm on a break."

He pulls a wad of money out of his pocket. The money's wet. He holds a dollar bill in front of me. Like a carrot in front of a jackass. I start climbing the steps again. Just let me get to the office. Please God let me get to the office. He yells after me. I don't look back. Asshole. I get to the door and slip in, locking it behind me. I sit down on the couch and take some breaths.

The guy's beautiful. He can kiss. Geoff doesn't need to know. He'd never know. He'd never find out.

I change into a white G. It'll be like wearing nothing when it's sweat soaked. I do more coke. The office has a window that overlooks the dance floor. I light a cigarette. So much for quitting. Old habits. First night back on the bar and I'm snorting coke, smoking cigarettes, and making out with hot strangers. Fuck it all. I shouldn't be here. I should be home in Dallas. Not here. Not in a damp sweaty bar in New Orleans. I look out the window. I see him down there dancing. He's with his friends. No one's wearing a shirt. Water's pouring off everyone on the dance floor. The drugs have hit. It's party time.

I smoke the cigarette.

Damn you, Geoff.

It's his fault. He took me out of this world and promised me a new life. Some fucking new life.

It would serve him right if I picked someone up.

I pull on a pair of shorts and walk out. I head for the balcony. I need air. I stand out there. Even the balcony feels wet and slippery. The lights of the Quarter are reflecting off the clouds. There are people in the streets. The Dumpster at the end of the balcony smells rotten. Heat, damp, and garbage isn't a good combination. I feel the coke drip in my throat.

"Hey man, wanna bump?"

I turn my head. He can't be more than twenty. No shirt, and those baggy-ass pants that look ready to fall off. He's maybe five-four. Nipples pierced. Tattoo on his arm. He's cute, though. He's not wearing underwear. His pubic hair is showing at the waistband of his jeans. He's holding out a bullet. I take it from him. I inhale. I hand it back. I lean over and kiss his cheek. He pulls on one of my nipples. I take his hand away gently. I walk back inside. I go downstairs. Different staircase. I don't want to cross the dance floor again.

Back on the bar. The music pounds. Bobby's flexing for some guy kissing his biceps. Sean is bent over at the waist. Someone's face is between his cheeks. I wonder how much he's getting for that. I walk along the bar. It's an obstacle course of beer cans and drink glasses. I get a glass of water from the bartender. He's hot. He's wearing a white T-shirt and jean shorts. His teeth glow in the black light when he smiles. He's pretty. I kiss his cheek. He recoils from me.

Whatever.

I take a drink. The water feels good. Cold. I take an ice cube and run it between my chest. I look down. Someone is smiling at me. I run the cube up and down. I shiver. It feels good. I kneel down in front of him. My crotch is right in his face.

"You're beautiful." He reaches for his wallet. I smile. He pulls out a ten-dollar bill. He pinches one of my nipples. I keep smiling. He shoves the bill into my hand and shakes his head. "Jesus." He walks off through the crowd.

I'm making more money than earlier. The sweaty white G always does the trick. More hands. More bills. Touch me. Feel me. Stroke me. Wanna see my dick? Ten bucks. Wanna kiss my cheek? A dollar. Lick my navel. Stroke my legs. Grab my ass. I'm making a lot of money.

The mortgage will get paid this month.

I see the baseball cap bobbing on the dance floor.

I want him.

My reward for a job well done.

Two o'clock. The show's over. I head back to the lounge. I pull off the G and wring it out. My boots are full of money. I pull on a pair of cotton shorts and count. Six hundred and seventy-three dollars. Not bad. "I'm not gonna do it, Bobby," I say.

He shrugs. "Sean said he would if you wouldn't."

I pull on a tank top. We walk out. They head for the guy Bobby pointed out earlier. They leave together. I have a beer at the bar. The dance floor is still packed. The drugs are in control out there. Everyone's shirtless. Some are dancing in their underwear. The baseball cap is bobbing on the dance floor. I walk to the edge.

I watch. He looks at me and smiles. I smile back. He's so beautiful. I turn my head.

I finish the beer and walk outside. The heat is like a sauna.

Alone, I walk back to the place where we're staying.

ABOUT THE EDITOR

TODD GREGORY is a pseudonym of an award-winning New Orleans author and editor. As Todd Gregory, he has published three novels (*Every Fratboy Wants It, Games Fratboys Play, Need*), a novella (*Blood on the Moon*), and numerous short stories. He has edited numerous anthologies, including *Rough Trade* and *Raising Hell*, both of which were short-listed for Lambda Literary Awards. His short story collection, *Promises in Every Star and Other Stories*, was published in January 2013.

CONTRIBUTORS

DALE CHASE has written male erotica for sixteen years with over 150 stories published in various magazines and anthologies, including translation into Italian and German. Her first novel, *Wyatt: Doc Holliday's Account of an Intimate Friendship*, was published by Bold Strokes Books, as was her collection *The Company He Keeps: Victorian Gentlemen's Erotica*, which won a 2012 IPPY silver medal from the Independent Publishers Association. Bold Strokes Books published Dale's first e-book collections earlier this year: *A Private Business: Victorian Erotica* and *Crack Shot: Western Erotica*. Dale is currently researching her next western novel while continuing to write short fiction.

GREG HERREN is the award-winning author of over twenty novels and fifty short stories, under his own name and various others. He also has edited over twelve anthologies, including the award-winning *Love, Bourbon Street: Reflections on New Orleans*. His most recent YA novel, *Lake Thirteen*, was published in August 2013. He is currently writing his sixth Scotty Bradley mystery, *Baton Rouge Bingo*.

WILLIAM HOLDEN (williamholdenwrites.com) is the author of more than sixty short stories. His first book, *A Twist of Grimm*, was a finalist for a 2010 Lambda Literary Award. His collection of erotic horror stories, *Words to Die By*, was released in March 2012 and received second place in the 2012 Rainbow Book Awards. His first novel, *Secret Societies*, set in eighteenth-century London, was released in October 2012. *The Buckish Young Men of Banbury* was released in January 2013.

JEFF MANN has published four books of poetry, *Bones Washed with Wine, On the Tongue, Ash: Poems from Norse Mythology*, and *A Romantic Mann*; two collections of personal essays, *Edge: Travels of an Appalachian Leather Bear* and *Binding the God: Ursine Essays from the Mountain South*; a book of poetry and memoir, *Loving Mountains, Loving Men*; two novels, *Fog: A Novel of Desire and Reprisal* and *Purgatory: A Novel of the Civil War*; and two volumes of short fiction, *Desire and Devour: Stories of Blood and Sweat* and *A History of Barbed Wire*, which won a Lambda Literary Award.

LUKE OLIVER is a writer, editor, and pop-culture aficionado. He has written several books under several names, mostly because he can't decide on which one to stick with. His next book will be published in fall 2014. Luke has contributed to websites, blogs, and podcasts, and has spoken about writing and the business of publishing at literary conferences across the country. Though he has never paid for sex, he once shoved a dollar bill in a stripper's thong and spent the rest of the night hoping he hadn't accidentally given him a paper cut. The memory haunts him still.

FELICE PICANO is the author of more than twenty-five books of poetry, fiction, memoirs, nonfiction, and plays. His work has been translated into many languages, and several of his titles have been national and international bestsellers. He is considered a founder of modern gay literature along with the other members of the Violet Quill. Picano also began and operated the SeaHorse Press and Gay Presses of New York for fifteen years. His first novel was a finalist for the PEN/Hemingway Award. Since then he's been nominated for and/or won dozens of literary awards. Recent work includes a collection of stories, *Twelve O'Clock Tales*, a history and memoir of his early gay life in New York, *Art & Sex in Greenwich Village*, and most recently *20ᵗʰ Century Unlimited*, consisting of a short novel and a novella.

MAX REYNOLDS is the pseudonym for an East Coast academic. Reynolds's erotic stories have been widely anthologized, appearing in the Lambda Award–nominated *Men of the Mean Streets* and *Raising Hell*, as well as *Porn!*, *Men of Mystery*, *Sweat*, *View to a Thrill*, *His Underwear*, *Blood Sacraments*, *Rough Trade*, and *Blood Lust: Gay Erotic Vampire Tales*, among others. His nonfiction has appeared widely.

JEFFREY RICKER's (jeffrey-ricker.com) first novel, *Detours*, was published in 2011 by Bold Strokes Books, and his second novel, the YA fantasy *The Unwanted*, is forthcoming. His writing has appeared in the anthologies *Fool for Love: New Gay Fiction*, *Men of the Mean Streets*, *Speaking Out*, and others. A graduate of the University of Missouri School of Journalism, he is pursuing an MFA in creative writing at the University of British Columbia.

ROB ROSEN (therobrosen.com), award-winning author of the novels *Sparkle:The Queerest Book You'll Ever Love*, *Divas Las Vegas*, *Hot Lava*, *Southern Fried*, *Queerwolf*, and *Vamp* and editor of the anthology *Lust in Time: Erotic Romance through the Ages* has had short stories featured in more than 170 anthologies.

LAWRENCE SCHIMEL has published over 100 books as author or anthologist, including *Deleted Names*, *The Mammoth Book of New Gay Erotica*, and *Kosher Meat*. He has won the Lambda Literary Award twice, for *First Person Queer* (with Richard Labonté) and for *PoMoSexuals: Challenging Assumptions About Gender and Sexuality* (with Carol Queen), as well as the Spectrum Award, the Independent Publisher Book Award, etc. He lives in Madrid, Spain, where he works as a Spanish-English translator.

NATHAN SIMS's short fiction can be found in various anthologies. For a darker turn, his short story "Imperfect Pearls" is available at Amazon.com. Dyson's further adventures can be found in *Blood Sacraments* as well as *Sweat: Gay Jock Erotica*, *Queer Fish 2*, and at Amazon.com in a short story titled "When the Village Is Already Taken." Nathan blogs irregularly at NoGoodRottenFairies.com and can be contacted at nsims55@gmail.com.

From Vancouver, Canada, **JAY STARRE** has written for numerous gay men's anthologies over the past dozen years. His imaginative and stimulating stories can be found in anthologies such as *Raising Hell*, *Sweat*, and *Wings*. His short story "The Four Doors" was nominated for a 2003 Spectrum Award. Two of his erotic gay novels, *The Erotic Tales of the Knight Templars* and *The Lusty Adventures of the Knossos Prince*, have been published recently. Contact Jay Starre on Facebook.

AARON TRAVIS's first erotic story appeared in a 1979 *Drummer* magazine. Over the next fifteen years he wrote dozens of short stories, a serialized novel (*Slaves of the Empire*), and hundreds of book and video reviews for magazines including *Mach*, *First Hand*, *Manscapes*, *Hombres*, *Advocate Men*, *Mandate*, *Blueboy*, *Studflix*, and *Stroke*.

Part comedy, part commentary, part erotic chase, "Paris Euros Giles" celebrates the competitive world of international male modeling and those men who strive to make a face for themselves. "Lips and loins, faces or feces, to some it was all the same, the endless search for beauty." **DAVEM VERNE** dedicates the story to his brother Christian, who walked the runways in Paris and Milan. You made Charles Hix proud.

HALEY WALSH (SkylerFoxeMysteries.com) tried acting, but decided the actor's life was not for her. Instead, she became a successful graphic designer in Los Angeles, her hometown. After fifteen years of burning money in the 1980s and early 1990s, she retired from the graphics industry and turned her interests toward writing. She became a freelance newspaper reporter, wrote articles for quirky magazines, published award-winning short stories, and now writes an acclaimed gay mystery series, the Skyler Foxe Mysteries. She's lived all her life in Southern California, sampling wines and chomping chocolate. Yeah, it's a living.

Books Available From Bold Strokes Books

Light by 'Nathan Burgoine. Openly gay (and secretly psychokinetic) Kieran Quinn is forced into action when self-styled prophet Wyatt Jackson arrives during Pride Week and things take a violent turn. (978-1-60282-953-4)

Baton Rouge Bingo by Greg Herren. The murder of an animal rights activist involves Scotty and the boys in a decades-old mystery revolving around Huey Long's murder and a missing fortune. (978-1-60282-954-1)

Anything for a Dollar, edited by Todd Gregory. Bodies for hire, bodies for sale—enter the steaming hot world of men who make a living from their bodies—whether they star in porn, model, strip, or hustle—or all of the above. (978-1-60282-955-8)

Mind Fields by Dylan Madrid. When college student Adam Parsh accepts a tutoring position, he finds himself the object of the dangerous desires of one of the most powerful men in the world—his married employer. (978-1-60282-945-9)

Greg Honey by Russ Gregory. Detective Greg Honey is steering his way through new love, business failure, and bruises when all his cases indicate trouble brewing for his wealthy family. (978-1-60282-946-6)

Jacob's Diary by Sam Sommer. Nothing exciting ever happens to David Jacobs until the day he and his son are thrown into the most fascinating and disturbing adventure of a lifetime. (978-1-60282-947-3)

Lake Thirteen by Greg Herren. A visit to an old cemetery seems like fun to a group of five teenagers, who soon learn that sometimes it's best to leave old ghosts alone. (978-1-60282-894-0)

Deadly Cult by Joel Gomez-Dossi. One nation under MY God, or you die. (978-1-60282-895-7)

The Case of the Rising Star: A Derrick Steele Mystery by Zavo. Derrick Steele's next case involves blackmail, revenge, and a new romance as Derrick races to save a young movie star from a dangerous killer. Meanwhile, will a new threat from within destroy him, along with the entire Steele family? (978-1-60282-888-9)

Big Bad Wolf by Logan Zachary. After a wolf attack, Paavo Wolfe begins to suspect one of the victims is turning into a werewolf. Things become hairy as his ex-partner helps him find the killer. Can Paavo solve the mystery before he runs into the Big Bad Wolf? (978-1-60282-890-2)

The Plain of Bitter Honey by Alan Chin. Trapped within the bleak prospect of a society in chaos, twin brothers Aaron and Hayden Swann discover inner strength in the face of tragedy and search for atonement after betraying the one you most love. (978-1-60282-883-4)

In His Secret Life by Mel Bossa. The only man Allan wants is the one he can't have. (978-1-60282-875-9)

The Moon's Deep Circle by David Holly. Tip Trencher wants to find out what happened to his long-lost brothers, but what he finds is a sizzling circle of gay sex and pagan ritual. (978-1-60282-870-4)

Straight Boy Roommate by Kevin Troughton. Tom isn't expecting much from his first term at University, but a chance encounter with straight boy Dan catapults him into an extraordinary, wild weekend of sex and self-discovery, which turns his life upside down, and leads him into his first love affair. (978-1-60282-782-0)

Raising Hell: Demonic Gay Erotica, edited by Todd Gregory. Hot stories of gay erotica featuring demons. (978-1-60282-768-4)

Pursued by Joel Gomez-Dossi. Openly gay college student Jamie Bradford becomes romantically involved with two men at the same time, and his hell begins when one of his boyfriends becomes intent on killing him. (978-1-60282-769-1)

Timothy by Greg Herren. Timothy is a romantic suspense thriller from award-winning mystery writer Greg Herren set in the fabulous Hamptons. (978-1-60282-760-8)

In Stone by Jeremy Jordan King. A young New Yorker is rescued from a hate crime by a mysterious someone who turns out to be more of a something. (978-1-60282-761-5)

The Jesus Injection by Eric Andrews-Katz. Murderous statues, demented drag queens, political bombings, ex-gay ministries, espionage, and romance are all in a day's work for a top secret agent. But the gloves are off when Agent Buck 98 comes up against the Jesus Injection. (978-1-60282-762-2)

Combustion by Daniel W. Kelly. Bearish detective Deck Waxer comes to the city of Kremfort Cove to investigate why the hottest men in town are bursting into flames in broad daylight. (978-1-60282-763-9)

Night Shadows: Queer Horror edited by Greg Herren and J.M. Redmann. *Night Shadows* features delightfully wicked stories by some of the biggest names in queer publishing. (978-1-60282-751-6)

Wyatt: Doc Holliday's Account of an Intimate Friendship by Dale Chase. Erotica writer Dale Chase takes the remarkable friendship between Wyatt Earp, upright lawman, and Doc Holliday, Southern gentlemen turned gambler and killer, to an entirely new level: hot! (978-1-60282-755-4)

Secret Societies by William Holden. An outcast hustler, his unlikely "mother," his faithless lovers, and his religious persecutors—all in 1726. (978-1-60282-752-3)

The Jetsetters by David-Matthew Barnes. As rock band the Jetsetters skyrocket from obscurity to superstardom, Justin Holt, a lonely barista, and Diego Delgado, the band's guitarist, fight with everything they have to stay together, despite the chaos and fame. (978-1-60282-745-5)

Strange Bedfellows by Rob Byrnes. Partners in life and crime, Grant Lambert and Chase LaMarca are hired to make a politician's compromising photo disappear, but what should be an easy job quickly spins out of control. (978-1-60282-746-2)

Fontana by Joshua Martino. Fame, obsession, and vengeance collide in a novel that asks: What if America's greatest hero was gay? (978-1-60282-675-5)

The Dirty Diner: Gay Erotica on the Menu, edited by Jerry L. Wheeler. Gay erotica set in restaurants, featuring food, sex, and men—could you really ask for anything more? (978-1-60282-677-9)

Sweat: Gay Jock Erotica by Todd Gregory. Sizzling tales of smoking-hot sex with the athletic studs everyone fantasizes about. (978-1-60282-669-4)

The Marrying Kind by Ken O'Neill. Just when successful wedding planner Adam More decides to protest inequality by quitting the business and boycotting marriage entirely, his only sibling announces her engagement. (978-1-60282-670-0)